The Endless War

By:
Tiffany Easterling

To Christine
for the loving of
Artic Romance
&
Bunnies
Tiffanyeveriy

Priestess
The Endless War

By:
Tiffany Easterling

Sometimes the most valuable things in life,
are the things we take for granted.

I certainly take my sister for granted. This is for her.
She always answers the phone when I call.
She always encourages me to follow my dream
She's spent hours listening to me talk about imaginary characters.
Thanks, Julie.

1

Tokyo teemed with the sophistication and splendor of its inhabitants as they bustled about the busy streets under the late winter sun. Its population had beautifully harmonized old-world refinement with new world technology. The city's beauty, culture, and people are nothing more than a backdrop for an unseen, never-ending war between the immortal and mankind. Keely had been sent to Tokyo because that war raged out of control there, and she was the only one who could fight on its frontlines.

The casualties, human souls, had already started to call to her from the darkened recesses of the city, begging for her help, begging to be freed. Staring out the window of the quaint café where she sat, she watched people pass by unaware, focused on the complexities of their own lives and problems. She envied their blissfully ignorant lives and wondered if they would act differently if they knew there were soul-stealing monsters lurking in their midst.

"There are a lot of hot guys in Tokyo," Sutton, her constant companion and best friend, mused aloud.

Sutton's interruption was timely since it gave Keely something to focus on other than the tension pressing on her temples. Cupping the coffee in front of her, she took a sip of the delicious bittersweet fluid. Immediately, she felt more relaxed and paused a moment to take in her surroundings. The café they sat in was nicely decorated and furnished with dark, wood-exposed beams, matching furniture, and large windows to watch the city outside. Besides being clean, the café had friendly staff. The coffee and the respite were a welcome treat after their twelve-hour flight.

"I wonder how they feel about taking on an American woman as a friend with benefits?" Sutton placed her chin on her hand and again scanned the crowd in and out of the café.

Keely grinned at her then answered, "I don't know. Probably like any other guy from any other country, depends on the guy." She took another sip of her coffee. "I'm sure you won't have any lack of interested males. We've been stared at everywhere we go." Keely looked around the coffee shop, noticing the open stares of some people and sideways glances of others.

"I know, I love it." Sutton smiled and waved her fingers at a nearby pair of girls who'd been obviously scrutinizing them since they walked in. Their faces got bright red, and they turned away, which caused both Keely and Sutton to giggle. "Anyway, I can't wait to find out." She strummed her fingers on the table. "I hope this guy isn't late. We did just get off a plane like an hour ago, and the Japanese ministry better not expect us to work salaried man hours. That would be crap."

"I'm sure they don't." Keely shook her head.

"If they do, I'm telling Jasper." She sounded like a pouty child.

"Please don't call my brother." Keely rolled her eyes. "Even I'm a little afraid of him, so let's not piss him off. Besides, I think our guy is here." She nodded toward the door just as two suited men, one older and one younger, entered the café. Scanning the room, they walked through rows of tables and chairs, then cautiously came to their table.

"You are the Priestess?" the older Japanese man asked in his native tongue as he stood over Keely. His distinguished features were marred by the slight frown of disappointment pulling at the corners of his mouth. "The courier?" He changed his question, still sounding disbelieving.

"I am," Keely answered in his language. She flashed Sutton a knowing smile over the rim of her coffee cup. "Please," she motioned to the open seats across from her, "have a seat." They'd agreed to meet their newly assigned client, share a cup of coffee, and see if he was someone they could help.

"Many apologies," the man apologized and bowed his head slightly. "I expected... I was told the courier was a Priestess."

"She is," Sutton confirmed, screwing her mouth sideways in annoyance.

The man still seemed like he wanted to question them, but his face softened to resignation. "You may go," he said to his stiff-suited companion before taking a seat across from them.

The man's reaction to Keely's appearance wasn't uncommon. No matter what country or city she was in, people judged by appearances. Keely felt the people who knew who she was assumed she'd show up in flowing robes with an ethereal demeanor. They certainly didn't anticipate her unique style. It was directly opposite the somber appearance expected of a Priestess. Ignoring his still obvious skepticism, Keely asked, "Who has put you in need of a Priestess?"

"I've come to ask for your assistance." He bowed his head and clasped his hands together.

"Mr. Oshiro," Keely interrupted. "While I appreciate your courtesy, please dispense with the formalities."

He lifted his head then bowed again before looking at her with tears formed in his eyes. "My daughter Ayano, we found her...her body. She's alive..." He stopped and took a deep breath. "The doctors say there is nothing physically wrong with her, but—"

"Ayano is a body with no soul. She's just a shell," Keely finished for him. "The ministry has informed me. I know. I didn't know she was your daughter. My apologies." She'd encountered hundreds, if not thousands, of human shells in her lifetime. They were a sad casualty of the war she fought. "How long has she been that way?"

"Two days," he answered.

"How many days was she missing before that?" Sutton asked, producing a notepad from her purse then scribbling down notes.

"One," he answered solemnly.

Keely hid a frown. She only had seven days to return a soul to its body. Their time had almost been cut in half.

"I think I can help you. You were informed of what I require. Did you bring the vessel?" Keely asked.

Mr. Oshiro nodded and reached into his leather satchel. "I have a necklace I gave her when she finished primary school." He offered her a long, blue, velvet box.

Keely stared at the box, searching for the touch of a soul, an imprint of the warmth or happiness from a thing that was loved. Her impression was that the box and its contents were cold and impersonal; it was merely something discarded. She frowned at the box and set her cup down hard on the table. Her tiredness was causing irritation. She didn't want to take the time to re-explain what should have already been thoroughly explained. "Was the ministry not clear about my requirements? Your daughter doesn't have a lot of time left, and you bring useless trinkets."

7

Sutton cleared her throat, reminding Keely not to lose her temper with Mr. Oshiro. "Our Priestess can sense when a soul has cared for an inanimate object."

The tears that had formed in Mr. Oshiro's eyes started to spill down his cheeks. "I apologize." He breathed in heavily through his nose. "I love my daughter. She is everything to me."

"I know you do." Keely softened her voice. She could not only see but sense he did love his daughter very much. "I apologize for being impatient with you, but I require a tangible item she loved. Whatever is in that box doesn't bare the touch of something loved by a human."

Sutton, reached across the table, took the box from him and opened it, revealing an expensive diamond neckless. "Are you sure? I mean I could fall in love with this?" she asked in English

Keely snorted then replied in the same language, "No, Sutton." She stared at the man, noticing a flash of a grimace before he looked down at his folded hands. "That's not enough, but I think he has something else to offer," she said in Japanese for Mr. Oshiro's benefit.

"I wasn't sure," Mr. Oshiro said as he dug in the bag again and produced a paint-smeared cherry wood box. "My daughter wants to be an artist." He handed her the box. "The last time we talked, we fought about it."

Keely stretched out her fingers and tenderly took the box from him. The essence of warm wind bursting with earthy fragrances filled her senses. The box did hold some of Ayano's soul, some of her happiness. It was something only Keely could feel. "This will be enough." She carefully stowed the box in her bag, making sure it was secure in a padded pocket.

"Do you have the addresses and details we asked for?" Sutton asked Mr. Oshiro.

"Yes." Mr. Oshiro produced an envelope and handed it to her.

"Also," Sutton took the envelope, "the fee is three million yen plus expenses," she informed him. Sutton wasn't one to play politics or politeness when it came to what they earned. She expected them to be paid well for risking their lives. If the victim couldn't pay, she made sure the ministry did. Religious organizations were some of the wealthiest corporations in the world.

The man wiped at his tears, reached inside his coat pocket, and handed her another envelope, only this one was thick. "Six million should cover all of your expenses and your time, but if it is not enough, let me know."

"It will be enough." Sutton smiled, took the second envelope, and stowed it in her purse.

Keely reached across the table and took the man's hands. He was surprised by her actions, and he stiffened. "I will do everything in my power to bring your daughter back to you." She squeezed his hands. For a moment he was pensive, then he simply looked lost. His fingers softened and wrapped around hers before he bowed his head, took a deep breath, and pulled his hands away. "I'll contact you in twenty-four hours. Go home and comfort your family. Let them be with Ayano's body. And do not tell anyone beyond who is necessary about what has transpired here today."

"Yes." He pressed his hands together and bowed before standing. "Thank you, Priestess." He bowed again, only this time it was a formal bow that emanated from his waist. With a worried frown, he turned away from her and quietly left the café.

Keely watched him through the window of the coffee shop as he got into a dark sedan. "Four days isn't long," she said to Sutton in English.

"No, it isn't," she agreed in the same language. "But then, seven days isn't a whole hell of a lot of time to start with."

∞ ∞ ∞ ∞ ∞

Chance stepped through the door of the café with one of his best friends, the lead singer of their band, Tau, walking next to him. He'd come in search of two things: a place to sit and a good cup of coffee. Band practice had been arduous. Not that he liked to complain, he was living his dream, but it had been a tedious rehearsal with a lot of mechanical and electrical issues. He needed coffee and a break before their performance that night.

"That was a cool bike," Tau said, wistfully talking about the black and gold motorcycle they'd passed on the sidewalk outside the coffee shop. "I'm torn between buying a sports car or a motorcycle. I think I want a motorcycle."

Chance was only half listening since Tau changed his mind about the vehicle he was going to buy, depending on the day and what they passed on the street. "It was a cool motorcycle," he agreed half-heartedly as he looked around the café for a place to sit. His eyes were immediately drawn to something obscure. Across the room, a pair of foreign women sat at a table quietly drinking coffee and talking to an elderly man with gray hair, wearing an expensive looking suit. Foreigners weren't an uncommon sight in Tokyo; he'd encountered a lot of them, but these two women definitely drew more attention than most. He and Tau weren't the only ones staring.

One of the women was very eye-catching. Her dark brown hair was piled on top of her head and cascaded brown, red, and blonde curls down her back and over her shoulders. She had a rounded face that reminded him of American movie idols from the past, especially with her black choker enhancing the length of her neck. Her porcelain skin looked like flawless ivory, making her lipstick seem redder. Sunglasses covered her eyes, so he couldn't see their color, but he was curious.

Next to her sat another woman who seemed younger and had very pronounced features. Her caramel colored skin and purple streaked, sandy-blonde hair made her stand out. Both women drew attention because of their attire. The younger woman wore a checkered halter top that showed a lot of skin, and the brunette wore a form-fitting, white blouse with a deep v, offering a view of her ample cleavage. Japanese women were more conservative. They didn't wear figure-enhancing clothes or show a lot skin above their waist.

"Wow, I don't think they're Russian," Tau said from beside him. "American, Canadian, or English?" he asked.

"It's hard to tell." Chance answered. "But I agree, definitely not Russian."

"Let's find out," Tau smirked mischievously and walked over to the empty table next to the two women. If he was trying to be coy, it didn't work. All the eyes in the room followed him. His hair was a vibrant shade of blue, which was an uncommon color for hair in Japan. Chance smirked at his friend and moved to join him at the table.

As he walked across the café, the dark-haired woman looked

10

up and moved her head as if looking around the room, glancing over him and Tau in the process. If she noticed either of them, she didn't show any outward sign. He sat down at the table across from Tau with his back to the women at the table next to them. The arrangement was probably better. His position enabled him to hear their conversation, if it was something he could understand.

Chance settled into his seat, feeling slightly awkward. Intentionally eavesdropping was rude and something he didn't normally do, but then he forgot all about his discomfort when he heard, "Our fee is three million yen, plus expenses." He was momentarily shocked. The price quoted was exorbitant, and he hadn't expected either of the woman to speak Japanese nearly flawlessly.

"What did they say?" Tau inquired anxiously in a low voice, probably in response to Chance's stunned expression. Chance put a finger to his lips, silencing his friend a second before his mouth fell open with shock. The old man they were sitting with gave them double what they asked for.

"What are they saying?" Tau asked in a slightly louder voice. "That older man is wearing an expensive suit, he looks well off. What are they talking about? Are they prostitutes? I don't know why such unusual foreign women would talk to him unless they were prostitutes."

"Shh, you're too noisy." Chance leaned in and shushed Tau. "They can speak Japanese. They'll understand you if they hear." He leaned back to listen again, but he'd already missed most of the rest of their conversation. The older man thanked them, called one of them Priestess, then left. He was utterly confused and absolutely intrigued by what he'd heard. Tau opened his mouth to talk again, but Chance put a finger back to his lips, signaling him to be quiet. Unfortunately, that was all of the conversation he was going to get, because the two changed languages. He immediately recognized it as English but didn't know enough of the language to know what they said. "I think they could be American," he told his friend in a quiet voice.

"You know, American women are wild in bed," Tau whispered with a grin. "I'd like to have one, one day."

"Not me," Chance replied, waving his hand at a waitress. "Excuse me," he said. A young woman with a welcoming smile came to their table. The two of them placed their order, and the woman hurriedly scurried off. "They aren't my type."

"Do you have a type?" Tau asked with a knowing smirk. Tau wouldn't say it out loud, but Chance was popular with women and had a fair amount of experience. Although, he'd never entered into a relationship with any of those women. Tau would say Chance wasn't the relationship type. Chance would say he'd never had the inclination to have a relationship.

"Yes and no," Chance answered. "I know what I don't want," he admitted honestly. He'd never bedded an American woman. Eternity's End had a few foreign fangirls. Some of them were American, pretty, and very sexually intriguing. None of them had made offers, and he wasn't sure what would happen if they did.

"Really? You're not even curious?" Tao leaned forward and whispered, "The dark haired one has really big tits." He moved his head to look around Chance. "I can't tell her age, but I honestly wouldn't care."

Just then one of the two women behind him let out a loud sigh. Chance glanced over his shoulder to see if they were listening to his conversation, after all, he did listen to theirs, but they were focused on some papers laid out on the table in front of them. Chance couldn't see them well, but at a distance, they looked like maps. It was very possible they were looking at train line maps.

"Hello," a younger woman with short, dark hair and glasses said from beside their table. If Chance had to guess, he'd say she hadn't yet graduated from middle school. "Tau and Chance." She bowed. "Could I get your autograph?" she asked, with red spreading across her cheeks.

"Sure," they both answered in unison. The girl smiled excitedly and held out one of their band's pictures.

Chance took the picture from her. "Do you have a pen?" he asked, looking from her face to her empty hands.

"No," she said. Her face went pale, and she bowed her head, but then she moved to the table behind him and asked in Japanese. "Excuse me? Can I borrow one of your pens?"

"Sure, pink, purple or orange?" the dark-haired woman directly behind Chance answered. For a moment, the girl looked dumbstruck, probably because a foreigner spoke so eloquently. He found it comical, considering the girl did ask in Japanese. "Here, how about

12

pink?" She gave the girl her pen, and still, the girl looked shocked.

"Thank you," Chance offered to the woman since the girl hadn't. She turned around, reached up, lowered her sunglasses, and looked at him. Violet. Her eyes were violet. He'd never seen such brilliant eyes. He was so caught off guard by the depth and beauty of their color; he didn't react when her lips turned up slightly, and she winked at him. He regained his senses the same moment she turned to her friend and said something in English he didn't understand. She looked at him over her shoulder one last time, offering a brilliant smile as she pushed the sunglasses back up on her face, covering her captivating eyes. He couldn't help but smile in return before he turned back to the girl.

"Pen?" Chance asked the girl. Pink flushed across her cheeks, and she bowed deeply then offered it to him. Taking the pen, he signed the picture and slid it across the table to Tau. Tau did the same and then handed the pen back to him and gave the picture to the girl.

"Thank you," the girl said excitedly, bowed several times, then skipped away.

Chance smiled at her enthusiasm before turning back to the woman behind him, gently tapping her on the shoulder and offering her pen. She looked over her shoulder. "If you're so popular, you may want to keep it. Here." She turned around in her seat and held out her hand. He was confused by her conflicting words and gesture and didn't move. "Let me see." She reached over her chair and grabbed his hand then snatched the pen from it. Dexterously she scrawled something on the back of his knuckles, and he didn't think of pulling away. Her fingers were soft, and her skin was almost electrifying to touch. Smiling at him, she pulled her hand away and offered him the pen again. "A gift."

He hesitantly took the pen and said, "Thank you." Nodding slightly, he turned back to his table, staring at the bright pink pen.

Tau grinned and leaned forward. "Did she give you her phone number?" he whispered.

Chance looked down at his hand, almost expecting to see numbers scrawled across it. Instead, there was something written in English with a pair of pink lips drawn next to it. "No," he answered, both mystified and curious.

"You want it though?" Tau said, laughing.

He turned around in time to see the two women stand. The brunette was tall, especially in her heeled boots. He stared at her lengthy, black-clad legs as she donned a long, black jacket and packed her belongings into a pink bag covered in skulls. She lowered her sunglasses, smiled, and winked one last time before she turned around and walked out of the café with her friend in tow.

He turned back to Tau. "No," he answered, but then he wondered if he just lied to his friend because mixed with his curiosity, he felt disappointment.

2

"Oh my god, did you see his smile?" Keely asked as she unlocked the security lock on her black and gold BMW motorcycle. Shipping it from France in less than twenty-four hours had been a logistical and expensive nightmare, but she was glad she had it. Getting around on the train or using a taxi could have proven tiresome, and she was usually running from or to something. A motorcycle could dexterously navigate traffic and narrow alleyways most cars couldn't get through. She picked up her red helmet and added, "Smiles like his turn me into puddles of mushy, giggling, girl-ness."

"They really do," Sutton agreed, taking her purple helmet. "You definitely have a type." She stopped and looked thoughtful for a moment. "When he walked in, I knew you'd be drooling all over yourself, but you do know he's short? Definitely shorter than you, even without heels."

"I don't care. His smile could stop wars." Keely sighed, thinking of the man's inviting smile and his warm brown eyes. She hadn't noticed him when he'd walked in, but then her senses had been attuned to the neverborn, not humans.

"What did you write on his hand?"

Keely laughed and shrugged. "If he's curious, he'll figure out. Although, he probably won't understand, and I doubt he will care much, so let's call it me flirting badly."

"I'm sure it was cute whatever it was. Did you see his friend?" Sutton asked in return.

"You and blonds, or in this case, guys with light blue hair," Keely chided.

"You and skinny, dark-haired guys with great smiles," she countered.

"It wasn't just his smile. I mean his lips, they looked…like they'd taste like a rare sweet fruit. His smile was the chocolate coating."

"You've given that way too much thought." Sutton put on her helmet and lifted the visor.

"He was cute though," Keely sighed again. "Oh well, by the looks of things, he's some sort of celebrity and probably knows he's cute. I'm sure the fangirl in the café was one of many."

"Yeah. So, don't feel bad. Obviously, we aren't the first ones to fall for their charm."

"I really need to quit crushing on younger guys and find someone my age to settle down with." Keely put on her helmet, pulled her motorcycle to an upright position, and kicked the kickstand back into its nest.

"No," Sutton disagreed. "You need to find a younger guy that crushes back on you, likes to have wild sex, and doesn't treat you like shit. I think that guy could totally do it. I have confidence in him and if not him, then some other short hotty with dark hair and a great smile."

"Not that it matters." Keely straddled her bike. "Guys like him are born with hot girlfriends waiting on them. Anyway, we have to get to work. Ayano is waiting."

"Yeah, she is." Sutton straddled the bike behind Keely. "Are we finally going home now?"

"Yes, but not to sleep. So, don't get too excited." Keely informed. "We have work to do."

"You want me to drive?"

Keely was about to kick start the motorcycle, but abruptly stopped and turned around. "Hell no, I want to get there before Wednesday."

"That's not nice. I don't get lost all of the time." Sutton crossed her arms over her chest.

"Do you really want to have this conversation? If so, I'm going to bring up Austria."

"Fine." Sutton gave in in a loud voice.

Keely was about to turn around but stopped again. "I think after this we should take a day off. Maybe go to Osaka? I've never done the tourist thing, and France was a little exhausting." She thought about the six months they'd spent in France. They'd traveled all over the country but didn't really get to see any of it. The French ministry had made sure she worked or fought every minute of her time spent there. Keely had been used as a fighting tool, instead of being treated like a human being. In part because of their treatment,

16

she'd started acting like a fighting tool and was losing her humanity.

Sutton's face brightened. "We are in a city famous for host clubs." She raised an eyebrow at Keely. "You know, a place where we can pay hot guys to serve us drinks and fawn all over us."

"You think they have hot, short guys with sensual lips."

Sutton leaned in close. "On the menu." Keely nodded, turned around, and kicked the bike engine to life.

"Squee," Sutton yelled over the engine. "Hot guys fawning all over us."

∞ ∞ ∞ ∞ ∞

Sutton walked into Keely's apartment and stopped. "Wow, we live here, in this building, in Tokyo," she said, looking out the floor-to-ceiling windows replacing two walls of the apartment. The expanse of Tokyo City spread out beyond the glass. "I could totally shoot the lights out of Tokyo Tower from my apartment window." She walked past boxes and took a seat next to Keely at a counter that separated the kitchen from the living/dining room. Setting her laptop down on the tan marble counter, she spun around in her stool, looking around at the pristine apartment. "It's a shame we don't have time to settle in and unpack before we have to go to work. My bathtub and bed are calling out to me so they can lavish me in hot water and sleep."

"We've four days," Keely said as she marked an 'X' on a map sprawled out in front of her. The neverborn won't go within twenty kilometers of the body," she marked another 'X' on the map, "and that was the last of the addresses Mr. Oshiro says Ayano frequents." She threw down her pen, and it rolled across the counter. Sutton could see tears of frustration glistening in Keely's eyes. They'd been researching everything about Ayano for hours, had few leads, and they were iffy ones at best.

Sutton had known of the neverborn all her life. She descended from a long line of craft-practicing, Italian gypsies, and the neverborn was the boogie man of all the children. It wasn't until Sutton had been chosen as Keely's monk that she realized they were much more terrifying than anything she'd imagined as a child.

Neverborn were aptly named. They were never born, would never grow old, never die, and couldn't be killed. They were creatures that existed beyond the ravages of time but were also tormented by it all at once. To mend their time savaged souls, they stole the souls of humans.

Sutton had been fighting them alongside Keely for years, but she hadn't seen a neverborn in its natural form. Normally, she saw dark shadows that seemed to block out the light in patterns resembling a human. Occasionally she'd catch a glimpse of cracked grey skin or a half of a torso but nothing really definite to describe. Somehow that made them all the more terrifying. She did know they had hands twice the size of a human's hand, and generally only had three fingers and one thumb. The only reason she knew was because she'd had the misfortune of nearly losing her life to a neverborn. It had grabbed her by her leg and drug her through the streets of Budapest. When she'd put enough arrows in it to force it to let her go, it had left a black, three-fingered bruise spanning her leg.

"Well, we've got one thing going for us," Keely said as she stood and went to the refrigerator. "The neverborn has had enough time to take on Ayano's face and personality. All we need to do is figure out where she would go."

For the neverborn, taking human souls came with an advantage. They took on the personality of the soul, including all the desires, passions, and hatreds. They also adapted to the physical form of the person, or at least, the physical form of how the person saw themselves. Depending on the confidence level of the soul, the actual appearance from the human could differ but almost always resembled some version of the stolen soul. Still, the neverborn wore stolen skins and were easy to spot, if you knew what you were looking for.

"And bonus, its strength will be limited by the confines of the soul. Hopefully, that means less ass-kickary for you," Sutton said. From Keely's experience fighting them, she'd learned the neverborn were impossibly fast and strong whenever they were in their natural form. When they took on the shell of a human form, their strength and speed were limited by the soul they were mimicking.

"Probably won't make our lives easier though." Keely opened the refrigerator and smiled. "I had some groceries delivered. I think I'm going to like the convenience of Japanese innovation." She

18

reached in and pulled out a bottle of pear juice, popped the top, and took a long drink.

"Which reminds me, I thought we were going to Beijing next. You know, China, the country with the highest population per capita in the world?"

"Unfortunately, it was decided differently. Japan has a culture of conformism. It's not a bad way to live, but a lot of people repress their feelings and those feelings attract neverborn. They've been a prime hunting ground for neverborn for decades."

"So, what you're saying is, they pulled some political maneuver to get us here. They want something, so that's the sales pitch they gave." Sutton frowned. "And you have no idea what that something is?"

"Yep," Keely replied.

Sutton frowned at Keely. She didn't like that their lives, especially Keely's, were set or disrupted on the whims of the ministry. Keely wouldn't ever complain or object; she never had. Some unexplained force drove her to fight the neverborn, but her life would always be a life of fighting. There would never be an end to the war with the neverborn.

For a moment, Sutton studied Keely. She was worried about her health. Her make-up was starting to wear off, and Sutton could see exactly how tired she was. Her red eyes looked sunken in, and there was light purple puffing around their edges. Her skin was drawn and pasty, and her shoulders were a little more hunched than usual. France had taken a heavy toll on her, and now they'd stepped off the plane, and the Japanese ministry had immediately put her to work. Keely wouldn't have said no to Mr. Oshiro anyway, even if she was drop dead exhausted. Once Keely found out a neverborn was involved, for her, there was no choice. She had to hunt, fight, and save Ayano's soul.

Sutton frowned, thinking she needed to call Keely's brother or even her parents. It wasn't that Keely was tired, she was changing. She didn't smile or laugh as often as she used to. She often avoided activities once loved. Keely hadn't been to a salon in more than eight months. She hadn't spent any time shopping, listening to her annoying music, or practicing her ballet. Her apartment in France was never unpacked. Sutton would have said she was depressed, but it was more

19

than that. Keely was changing into someone hard and jaded. Sutton didn't like the woman Keely was becoming. She'd been with her eight years, and in the last year, she'd seen something in Keely dramatically fade.

After they finished their assignment in Japan, Sutton was going to make damn sure Keely got a month-long break. In the meantime, she had every intention of engaging her friend in human activities. Sutton opened her laptop and smiled at the image that lit up as the computer came to life. At the very least, she could encourage a distraction for Keely, a distraction that would remind her that there was more to life than fighting neverborn.

"I did find something that might help us," she said, smiling at Keely over the monitor of her computer.

"Something is better than the nothing I have." Keely started to walk to her. Sutton quickly snapped the lid of the computer closed. "Okay?" She stood on the other side of the counter, looking confused.

"Before I tell you what I found. You and I need to talk," Sutton said as Keely's face turned sour. "I sent the report on France to Jasper and…" Sutton tapped her fingernails against the counter. She hated fighting with Keely and had a feeling she was about to. "I've asked him to take France off the rotation."

"What?" Keely straightened up as if she was startled. "Why?"

"We were there for six months—six months of hunting and releasing or reclaiming. That's one hundred-eighty days we walked past some of the most beautiful places and best gourmet food in the world because the French ministry chose to play master instead of host. They wore your ass ragged and put their ministry's comfort and safety above yours. I found out after we left, while you were in Limoges getting your head smashed into a wall, their clergymen were on holiday in Nice."

Keely frowned, and the crease between her eyebrows appeared. She opened her mouth, and Sutton knew she wanted to complain. Keely wouldn't complain or utter one word of objection for some unknown reason Sutton wasn't privy too. That didn't stop Sutton from making her own complaints known. She'd told Jasper precisely what had happened, how hard they'd worked, and how badly they'd been treated, especially Keely.

"I know." Sutton sighed. "You didn't want him involved, but I

20

had to. We've been together for eight years and… You don't ask for breaks." She stopped for a moment. Keely really didn't ever ask for time off. Normally, she didn't have to. The ministry of whatever country she'd been assigned gave her whatever she needed and made sure she had rest between reclaiming souls and releasing them. Keely was usually allowed to set her own timeline unless they had to rescue a soul, but the French ministry had almost used her up with their never-ending list of urgent issues. So, Keely voicing she wanted a break was indicative of how exhausted she really was. "Keely, you don't just look tired; you look worn out and abused, and… I'm worried."

"I know. I am tired. But I feel like you've tattled on me," Keely said.

"I didn't tattle on you. I tattled on them. The ministry's job, first and foremost, is to protect the Priestess. And my job as the monk, the superior fighter, warrior, protector assigned to you, is to make sure what happened in France doesn't happen again."

"Why are you lecturing me?" Keely asked with a deep sigh, then finished her bottle of juice.

"Because you put me in a position to, and I hate that shit. But Japan will not be a repeat of France. After you retrieve Ayano's soul, we get five days off. And that's after you completely recover from the fight."

"Fine," Keely agreed, and Sutton saw her relax. It was almost as if she was relieved that she was being told she needed a break and was getting one. She looked around the kitchen. "Where's the trash?"

"Japan has crazy strict recycling laws. Set it on the counter, and we'll figure it out later."

"Fair enough." She set the bottle on the counter and came back to the table. "Okay. Now, what did you find?"

"Good news and really good news." Sutton smiled at her friend and opened her laptop again. "I think I know where the never-born will be."

"Really? That fast?" She came around the bar and sat on the stool next to Sutton.

"Ayano goes on and on about her favorite band Eternity's End. They play a subgenre of music called visual kei otherwise known as V-kei. Think eighties glam-punk meets rock-revival," Sutton snorted, "lots of guy-liner. Totally up your alley. Anyway, apparently,

Eternity's End makes the music that speaks to Ayano's soul, and she has tickets for one of their concerts. And it's like...in two hours."

"That's good news." Keely genuinely smiled, and it took away some of the tiredness from her features.

"Oh, it gets better." Sutton turned the monitor to Keely. "Here's what the members of Eternity's End look like. And just in case you miss it," she tapped on the screen, "take a good look at the bassist, stage name Chance. As in, take a chance on me," she sang out, then folded her arms, sat back in her chair, and waited for Keely's reaction.

Keely looked at the computer monitor, and her mouth fell open. "You're making this up." She snatched the computer off the table and pulled it closer to her then inspected the picture again.

"How would that even work?" Sutton huffed.

"Oh my god." Keely's face started to flush red as she stared at the picture again. "Oh my god," she repeated.

"So how awkward are we talking? Scale of one to ten. One being you ran into a door, and nobody saw, ten being you were in front of a room giving a speech and farted really loudly."

"Twelve. Like when you walk out of the bathroom, and toilet paper is dragging out of the back of your pants," Keely replied with a serious face as she slowly set Sutton's computer back down on the counter.

Sutton laughed. "Oh god, what did you write on his hand."

"You see," she cleared her throat, "I thought the chances of me seeing him again were like slim, to none, to non-existent. There are thirteen million people in Tokyo."

"What did you write?"

"Really bad eighties indie-pop lyrics," Keely answered, staring at the floor. "I drew a pair of lips and wrote 'lips like sugar'."

Sutton was stunned for a moment, then the hilarity of the situation struck her, and she laughed so hard at Keely, she started uncontrollably snorting. After a few minutes, she wiped away tears. "And you wrote it in what language?"

Keely cleared her throat. "English," she said quietly. "I thought I was being clever. You know his perfect and sensuous lips." She flashed a grin. "Anyway, there is a chance he won't ever know what it means. And even less of a chance he'll recognize the reference."

"You should have just given him your phone number," Sutton advised her, still giggling.

"Well, I figure a lot of women do that...and I wanted to be different. Plus, you know, counting on never seeing him again."

Sutton started laughing all over again. "Trust me, you are different."

Keely blew out a breath between puffed cheeks. "Flirting is not my thing. I mean...do we have to go? And if we do, do we have to go inside?"

"You know we do."

"Fabulous. I'm going to feel like a total awkward creeper now."

Sutton laughed and patted her on her head. "There-there, little ostrich." Sutton used her pet name for her friend. "But aren't you a little bit excited you'll get to see him again."

"Sure." Keely scowled and scooted the computer back to her. "But what are the stalking laws in Japan?" She was quiet for a moment, and her eyes went to the paint-smeared, wooden box sitting on the corner of the counter, then she got serious. "Not that we will have much time for stalking. If we find the neverborn, we're going to have our hands full, especially in a crowd."

3

"Sold out show," Sutton informed Keely. "Are we sure she's here?"

"We won't know it's her until we get closer, but there's definitely a neverborn in there," Keely confirmed. When a neverborn was nearby, there was a strange sort of negative emotional pull. It was like being around a cluster of angry or upset people, only more concentrated. As she got closer, she'd be able to sense more individuality from the souls it carried, even feel their individual sorrows and desperation. Usually, she had to be less than twenty feet away to get a good sense of those souls and how many resided in the neverborn. At that moment, all she knew was that a neverborn was in their vicinity and not much else.

"Great." Sutton looked around. "This isn't going to be easy in this crowd. Who knew? Our first day in Japan and we meet pseudo-celebrities. I guess they're not just pretty faces."

"Well, we're going to find out," Keely said as she folded the mirror she'd used to check her freshly applied make-up and stowed it back in her bag.

"Any bright ideas how we're going to get in? Posing as prostitutes?"

"What is it with you and the sex trade? That wouldn't work here anyway." Keely scowled at her friend then turned her attention to the problem at hand. Assessing the entrance, she noticed some of the people entered the music hall by giving tickets to a wiry doorman with a ponytail. She watched for a long time so she could get a good idea as to what the tickets they held looked like. "There's always plan B." She hiked her bag up on her shoulder and straightened the tight-fitting, black jacket she wore. "Stay right behind me, follow my movements and un-focus your mind, or you'll break the illusion."

Sutton breathed in and out heavily. "What about Bellearmos?" she asked, motioning toward the crossbow strapped across her back with a leather strap.

"That's why I need you to clear your mind; otherwise the illusion will project your thoughts. I don't have a detailed picture of the tickets, so this may not work." Keely looked around at them, keeping a firm hold on her concentration. One illusion, such as hiding the presence of Sutton's crossbow from one onlooker, was easy. A mass illusion, such as keeping it hidden from a crowd, was harder, but pulling off a mass mirage and an additional illusion—very difficult. Especially when the minor illusion had to have sensations like touch. If the man at the door over scrutinized the illusion of the tickets, all the illusions would likely be broken. There was a fifty-fifty chance her plan would work. "C'mon and smile pretty."

Keely walked up to the doorman and handed him two tickets. The thin man tore off the tabs and handed them back without so much as a glance her way. She walked past him without much fanfare. Sutton elicited a smile and a nod, which wasn't uncommon for her.

Sutton was stunning with her delicately defined features, large green eyes, and blemish-free, caramel skin. She was also very petite at her five-foot-three inches but still managed to be subtly voluptuous. Keely was almost Sutton's opposite. She was tall, over six foot when she wore four-inch heels, and overly curvaceous, even if her body was toned and well defined from years of fighting neverborn. The one distinguishing feature that got her a lot of attention was one she wasn't born with. Most of the time, she wasn't sure how she felt about her unique eye color. Though she'd lived with them since she was a teenager. At times, seeing light violet eyes stare back from the mirror still surprised her.

The inside the club looked like any other club in any other country. There was a stage almost overloaded with lights and electronics, a large area for an audience, a bar with bartenders making sure no glass stayed empty, and room to sit along the wall around the main floor.

"This is going to be difficult," Keely commented, looking around. The only way to identify a neverborn once they'd taken on the persona of a soul, besides comparing physical similarities, was to look directly at their eyes. Neverborn in human shells had light grey pupils. Not that they were hard to spot once you knew what you were looking for, but most people didn't really pay attention to small details.

"This is the most insanely organized concert I've ever seen."

Sutton commented on the almost lethargic way the people in the club were acting. There were no seats or numbers on the floor, but the concertgoers had lined themselves up neatly and patiently waited for the band to play. It was strangely quiet for a club. "I read a little about how this works. We're not going to get anywhere near the stage or the bar. Those spots are reserved for the best ticket holders, A.K.A. the most dedicated fans."

"How dedicated do you think Ayano is?"

"I'd say if she's not in the first row, then she's in the second." Sutton frowned and looked around at the people packed in around them. "There has to be nearly a thousand people here. Even if we find the neverborn, an outright fight would be a bad idea. People would get hurt."

"It's probably not safe for the band either. If Ayano is obsessed with them, the neverborn could try and take one or all of their souls."

"Damn, I hadn't thought of that. Protect the crowd, protect the band, and save the girl. And do it so no one knows what's going on. This job..." Sutton sighed and adjusted Bellearmos. "Why can't we protect a bed? You know by sleeping on it?" She covered her mouth as she let out a long yawn. "I guess splitzies is a bad idea?"

"It'd be too easy to lose each other and the neverborn," Keely replied. She scanned the crowd in front of her. "Well, at least I'm taller than pretty much, well, everyone. It might make it easier for us to spot her."

"Bonus to the tall, hot chick, but what's the plan? Wanna make the rounds and flirt with some guys. The bartender is hot." Sutton looked over her shoulder then turned to Keely, smiling.

Keely rolled her eyes. "Yeah, that would be great, but the neverborn is wearing a female skin. As far as I can tell, Ayano has all the heterosexual female desires to go with it. And aren't you the one constantly giving me lectures about bartenders?"

"I'm not built like you. I'd only like him for a little while. He'd annoy me eventually. Probably sooner than later. You know, like say something stupid or act like a douche, and then I'd break his heart. That's how I work." Sutton scanned the crowd again. "This is going to be so much fun. And by 'fun' I mean the opposite of." Sutton sighed, "I want my bed."

"Soon," Keely promised. "In the mean-time, I have an idea."

Keely saw a sign indicating the woman's restroom and stepped into the crowd. Sutton followed. "If the neverborn has taken on a female form, eventually she will probably end up going to the bathroom," Keely said quietly over her shoulder in Gaelic, in case anyone thought to eavesdrop and could speak English. Sutton and Keely had learned and forgotten several languages, with the help of Jasper. Since English was so common, they used Gaelic to communicate with each other when they were in public and wanted to talk privately.

"Good call. But can we find a spot that lets us watch the band too? You shouldn't miss out on your hot bassist," Sutton replied in the same language.

"Sure, why not? I wanted to add stalker to my many titles." Keely smiled as she moved through throngs of people. The flow of the overcrowded club forced them to travel around half the circumference of the room. All the while, Keely and Sutton searched the faces of all the females they encountered. It wasn't surprising they didn't find Ayano. When they made it to the restrooms the two of them took up post, leaning against the wall next to a long hallway. They had a good vantage point, could see the faces of all the women coming and going to the bathroom, and there was an exit nearby. Unfortunately, only one half of the stage could be seen because of a large pillar, but then, they weren't there to actually see Eternity's End.

Twenty minutes later Keely had looked at a lot of faces, including the men, in case what she felt wasn't Ayano's neverborn, but all of them were human. She was starting to feel impatient and frustrated when the lights dimmed. The crowd clapped softly as a man in a neat suit came out. After a short introduction, the lights went out, music started playing, and everyone began to clap in unison as they chanted "Eternity's End." Strobe lights flashed, and the stage exploded with light from the spotlights. One at a time, the members of Eternity's End walked onto the stage, smiling and waving at the crowd as they took up their instruments. Keely's eyes were immediately drawn to the dark-haired bassist she'd met earlier that day. She couldn't look away.

He was dressed in dark red pants, light blue t-shirt, and a long, black jacket ornamented with studs and chains. His hair had been spiked up, and his eyes were highlighted by dark eyeliner. The make-up didn't change his features as much as it enhanced them. Though

Keely couldn't see the sultry brown of his eyes, the make-up made them very captivating, and she hoped he wasn't wearing light blue contacts like the lead singer. He smiled and waved at the crowd as he settled his bass on his shoulder. Her heart pounded against her ribs as she wondered what it would be like to spend hours kissing his voluptuous lips. Suddenly, an overwhelming attraction she'd never succumbed to before flooded all of her senses. It distracted and held her captive until she heard Sutton's voice in her ear.

"Please pick your panties up off the floor and focus on the task at hand."

Keely felt blood flood into her face, and it got hot. "Sorry." She forced her attention away from the stage and back to the crowd.

Sutton laughed. "Don't be sorry. He's a rocker-guy. Panty dropping is in the job description, even in Japan."

"I shouldn't let it distract me." The line of people streaming into the bathroom had thinned, so Keely scanned the crowd.

"Get distracted. It's natural." Sutton smiled at her. "Besides being panty-droppers, rocker-guys are designed to be crushed on. Crush away."

Keely glanced at the stage. "But, remember he's a rocker-guy."

"Now you're getting it."

Almost an hour later, they had assessed over half of the crowd, some of them twice. Still, the neverborn wasn't among them. Occasionally, Keely would steal a glance at the stage and watch Eternity's End, specifically the bassist. The more she watched, the more she found him not just distracting, but intriguing. He danced, jumped, or bobbed his head to the music as he played his bass. Occasionally, he mouthed the words along with the singer or encouraged the audience to sing along. She also found herself staring at his hands and forearms. A man's forearms had never seemed attractive to her before, and she thought it strange to suddenly discover they were. In fact, she'd never been so distractingly attracted to a man in general. She'd had boyfriends in the past and had feelings of attraction for them, but the pull she felt for the bassist was something on a whole new level. She wasn't sure how she felt about the new feelings, except she didn't like that they were distracting.

Sutton was right, the fans in the audience were subdued. They banged their heads or raised their hands in time with the music, but mostly, they simply stood watching the band. Keely had never been to a concert so tame. The punk-rock shows of her youth had a lot of mosh pits and stage diving. If she hadn't lived a life that made her numb to culture shock, she would have been stunned by how a subdued the audience was.

Despite the audience's polite, muted enthusiasm, the bassist had plenty. He performed like someone who truly loved creating and playing music for the masses. It was very easy to get caught up in his exuberance. As she watched him, she realized he had a stage presence that couldn't be faked or taught, and it held her, and probably many other women, captive. By the end of their performance and encore, Keely had decided to invest in their CDs despite the unwanted new feelings she was experiencing.

After their set finished, the lead singer of the band thanked the audience, bowed, and quietly exited the stage.

"Well." Sutton leaned in as they watched the crowd split, gathering around the stage or heading toward the door. "I'm starting to think Ayano is more of an obsessive fan than we gave her credit for."

"I'm getting the same instinct. The neverborn is still here, just not close enough for me to get a good feel of it. I'd say, very close to the band."

"And that means we get close to the band," Sutton stated the obvious.

Keely took in a deep breath and blew it out through puffed cheeks. "Let's hope we find it before it decides to steal one of their souls." Keely looked at the floor then back to Sutton. "You do realize this means I'm going to get labeled something derogatory, like rude foreigner or creepy stalker, for doing my job."

"Yeah, and since when did that bother you?" Sutton looked at her sideways.

"Since when do I awkwardly flirt with a total stranger in a café?" she countered.

"Are you forgetting you're a hot badass?" Sutton smiled up at her. "Look on the bright side, you get to get closer to your bassist."

"Yeah," Keely frowned. "Like I said, derogatory label."

4

Chance loaded his bass into a van packed with instruments, electronics, and amplifiers. The van would be a tight fit with them and their instruments, but Eternity's End was mediocre in its popularity. Their production budget only allowed for one extended passenger van and two roadies until the band played larger venues and earned more revenue.

"Looks like we have a nice selection waiting on us tonight. Want to go talk to them?" Tau suddenly appeared next to Chance, offering him a bottle of water.

Chance looked over his shoulder to where a group of six women stood some thirty feet away, politely waiting to be noticed. They all had different styles, but they all looked the same. They wore too much make-up and clothing more revealing than was the standard for Tokyo nightlife.

Fans who waited after a show generally only wanted one thing: sex. Worst case scenario, they'd push for more, which almost always ended up in Mitsu. Mitsu was the paid relationship between fans, mostly obsessed ones, and their favorite band members. This relationship could include personal emails, phone calls, or dates. Depending on the fan, the band member, and the money exchanged, Mitsu could also include intimacy.

Mitsu was a frowned upon, hushed practice, but many bands, especially those struggling with money, enjoyed its fruits. Eternity's End had had their share fan sex and Mitsu relationships, even Chance. Although Chance kept in contact with a minimally few fans, he'd quit Mitsu altogether. Mitsu was a difficult relationship to keep up with and one that could quickly turn toxic. That was why Chance had limited experience with it. Other than the money, it offered no real value. So, Chance had taken to bedding fans with the understanding there would never be any strings attached. Even those relationships got tiring because there were still expectations. While the sex could be worthwhile, it was still just sex. He could never truly be himself and always had to be guarded. Not that he minded, he liked sex, but to him, those relationships were superficial and lacking in meaning.

Many other band members tried forming relationships with fans, and very few succeeded. Chance wasn't looking for a relationship. Nonetheless, he knew a deep connection couldn't be formed from an overzealous fan or Mitsu. Occasionally he met women who had no idea he was a musician and fell outside of the category of a fan, but he'd yet to find a woman compelling enough fall in love with. Chance had never been in love, so he'd never felt the inclination to be in a monogamous relationship. However, even if he wasn't sure what he wanted in a woman, Chance was certain about what he wanted in a serious relationship. He wanted it to be genuine, he wanted her to like him as himself, not as the marketable musician. The woman, whomever she was, had to be secure enough to trust him and his feelings, despite his lifestyle. And yes, he would want that relationship to be monogamous.

"I'm tired tonight." Chance stepped away from the van, opened the bottle of water, and took a long drink. The band's two roadies made sure the contents of the van were secure and closed the doors.

"Yeah, I guess I am too." Tau yawned and stretched, but then he froze, and his face got serious. "But I didn't expect something new to present itself." He stared past Chance to the crowd of women. Chance turned to see what had gotten his attention. He was somewhere between pleased and shocked to discover the two foreign women he and Tau had met at the café earlier that day, walking down the side street leading to the back of the club.

"Wow." Their manager Itsuki, who also acted as one of their roadies, joined them along with the rest of Eternity's End. "I don't think you've ever gotten foreign fans waiting on you after a gig before."

"Those are the women I told you about," Tau excitedly informed the group as they all stared at the newcomers who were walking toward the small group of women.

The two women had changed since the last time Chance and Tau had seen them. The petite one now wore form-fitting jeans, a leather jacket, and platform boots so tall he wondered how she could walk in them. She was eye-catching, especially with her dark blue lipstick, but Chance's eyes were drawn to her taller companion. Her new outfit was both revealing and conservative all at once. Knee-high boots covered most of her legs, but then he could see a tantalizing glimpse of creamy thigh below the hem of her shorts. The black, crop jacket exposed a flat and defined stomach and accentuated the fullness of her breasts but still hid a lot of her figure, especially with its length in the back. Her long, brown, red, and blonde, tiered tresses hung free in waves to her midriff, partially covering the ivory skin of her stomach. As he stared, his eyes moved up to her rounded face and delicate features. She intrigued him, especially her dark, painted lips. He'd never kissed someone with such full lips, and he found himself wondering what it'd be like. Then she glanced at him. He felt as if he'd been caught in a spell and forgot everything he was thinking about. Her violet eyes had been set ablaze by dark make-up. When she looked away, he found himself wondering what he could do to get her attention so she'd look at him again.

"When Tau told us what happened in the café, he didn't describe how attractive they were," Ren, their lead guitarist, said, breaking the spell.

"I kind of pictured something different myself," Simeon, their drummer, agreed.

Tau had told Simeon and Ren what had happened at the coffee shop. Chance had endured the retelling only because Simeon had a firm grasp of English, and he wanted his friend to translate what she'd written. When Simeon announced it read 'lips like sugar', there was no end to the teasing he'd endured. Chance had a feeling 'sugar-lips' was a nickname that was going to stick.

Later in the day, Itsuki gave him more clarification about what was written on his hand. He'd pulled him aside and shown him a video from a band popular before Chance was born. The song's title matched the words on his hand. Chance had been both flattered and impressed that a pretty woman had used a musical reference to compliment him. Although, he was mostly embarrassed. Still, he hadn't washed off what she'd written.

"I like our new fans," Tau grinned. "I would definitely spend the night with either of them, and if they wanted Mitsu, all the better."

Chance felt both exhilarated and disappointed. If the violet-eyed woman was a fan, then she was practically there for the taking. However, if she was a fan looking to sleep with one of her favorite band-men, then there'd never be anything but a superficial relation-ship with her, even if it did include sex.

"Shall we go introduce ourselves to our newest fans?" he asked no one in particular.

"I knew you'd change your mind." Tau winked at him before walking toward the crowd of women.

"I know I should go home. I don't want to give the fans ideas," Simeon said. He was one of the very few band-men with a successful marriage, but then, he married his wife before joining Eternity's End. "I have a feeling Tau isn't going to get either of those women into bed, and I want to see how it plays out."

Chance watched the taller foreign women try and engage the others in conversation. They politely nodded at her, but he knew something the pretty women didn't. Fans, especially fans in their sub-culture, were very jealous and possessive. They wouldn't have much to say to her. In fact, they'd probably hate her for her unique eye color, as it made her stand out. While he watched, one of the women in the group moved away.

"I'm betting he doesn't get either of them into bed either," Ren agreed. "But I'm curious to see what they have to say to you." He nudged Chance, forcing him to step forward.

Chance walked to the group of women with Simeon and Ren following him. He offered them a bow and a polite, "Hello." All of them responded in kind, smiling sweetly at them. All of them except the newcomers. Their attention seemed to be focused elsewhere.

"Did you all enjoy your evening with us?" Tau asked.

Almost all the women smiled and nodded at him answering, "Yes."

"What about you?" Ren spoke to the foreign women directly.

For a moment, the two of them seemed to not have heard him, then the shorter one looked at him and smiled prettily. "Oh us? Yes, you're decent."

Chance had no idea what she meant by 'decent'. It wasn't a word Japanese people used to describe something, but before he could ask for clarification, a young woman stepped forward and held out a paper gift bag for him. She was slightly smaller than average, but she had a pretty face framed by short, dark hair.

"Chance." She bowed her head. "I made you this gift. I hope

you will accept it as a gift from my heart."

Chance smiled at her and carefully took the bag from her out-stretched hands. "Thank you." He bowed his thanks.

"Ayano," the dark-haired woman spoke up as she came to stand next to the woman. "We've been looking for you all night."

"We really have." The petite foreigner joined her friend on the other side of the girl. "I think we should take you home now."

"Aw, you should stay, maybe hang out with us," Tau offered with a smile. "You did come to see us, and not many fans get this kind of offer."

"How generous of you," the petite foreigner said with a fake smile. "But we weren't here to see you. We only came to take our friend home."

"I don't want to go home," the woman called Ayano said and stepped away from the two foreigners and toward Chance. "Chance, I'd like to go for a drink with you." She stared at him with large pleading eyes, but there was something off about their color. Maybe the subdued light was affecting them, but her irises weren't black, but a dull gray.

"I think it's a little late for a drink." The brunette stepped forward. "You've had your fun for the night. It's time to go home."

"I think Chance should decide." Ayano stepped closer to Chance. She lifted her hand as if she meant to touch him, maybe his chest. Such a gesture was out of the ordinary but not uncommon for obsessed fans. Her actions alarmed him. He didn't know why, but he felt something very odd coming from Ayano.

Before she could actually touch him, the dark-haired woman stepped forward and slapped Ayano's hand away with a loud pop. "You shouldn't touch people without their permission."

Ayano held her hand to her chest and her face contorted into something ugly, then she turned on the dark-haired woman. "I…" she started.

"Come out with us," Tau persisted, oblivious to the discom-fort Ayano was causing. "It would be a lot of fun."

"It's a generous offer," the blonde said. "And any other time we might consider it, but we're here to make sure Ayano gets home safely."

"Ayano," the brunette said softly, "I can see why you like

Eternity's End; they aren't bad."

"Not bad to look at either," the blonde spoke up. "But we have to go now."

"Say goodbye to the gentlemen," the brunette instructed Ayano before she bowed and spoke to them. "Goodbye and thank you for a nice evening."

"Yeah, thanks." The blonde bowed as well.

Ayano looked stricken with disappointment for a moment, then she lifted her hand again. A weird uneasiness overcame Chance, and he leaned away from the girl's touch. He didn't need to worry because the brunette intervened. Again, she slapped Ayano's hand away with another resounding smack.

"Many apologies," she said, staring directly at Chance. "Our friend is shy, so she can be awkward sometimes. We're going to take her home now." The two women wove their arms though Ayano's, almost forcing her to turn around. The three marched down the street and away from them as Ayano stared at him over her shoulder. Tears were welling up in her eyes, and Chance felt sorry for her, despite their awkward encounter.

Suddenly, Ayano broke away and started running toward Chance. A strange intuitive fear gripped him. He couldn't say where it came from. He only knew his body stiffened as if preparing for a fight. The two women got to Ayano before she could get to Chance. Both the brunette and the blonde had Ayano in a bear hug of a hold.

"Sorry," the brunette apologized again as Ayano struggled against her hold. Seconds later, she broke free and shoved the brunette away from her with more strength than Chance thought possible for such a petite woman. For a shocking moment, he thought the brunette would fall, but she skidded across the concrete with a cat's grace and kept herself upright. Ayano broke free from the blonde woman's hold, ran down the tiny alley, and around the corner faster than any human he'd ever seen run before.

"Fuck," the blonde woman swore, saying one of the few English words Chance understood before both she and the brunette ran after Ayano.

There were a few seconds of stunned silence before Simeon broke it. "I have no idea what just happened. Are we supposed to do something?"

"Me neither," Ren agreed. "I'd say call the police, but I think it's a little late for that."

"The girl, Ayano, seemed odd." Chance involuntarily shivered. Something was off about her. "I'm pretty sure the foreigners have, whatever it is, under control, and they don't appear to want to hurt her." Chance replied, opening the bag Ayano had given him. He reached in and pulled out a painting. Holding it up, he stared at it, unsure what to think other than it made him uneasy. It was a painting of Ayano, almost a perfect likeness, and she was smiling. That part of the picture was normal, but the monster encroaching on her, almost capturing her, wasn't. It had long spindly arms, three-fingered claws, and no face, except for eyes. He had no idea what the painting meant.

"I'd say she's a good artist, but I'm not sure about the content?" Tau commented over his shoulder. "Maybe she's writing a horror manga."

"Yeah," Chance agreed, putting the picture back in the bag and folding it closed. He looked at the remaining women and smiled his best smile. "Well, it's been an exciting night, hasn't it?" Their worried and confused looks melted into smiles of expectation. Chance was suddenly not just tired, but exhausted, and didn't want to deal with them. "I'm sorry," he bowed politely, "I have to go home early tonight due to work responsibilities, but my friend will make sure you receive a special gift from the band."

He turned away from the women and stopped long enough to give Itsuki a nod before he headed to the van. Itsuki would provide the girls with special photos of the band usually kept for promotional offers. Offering a small token such as picture was easier than spending ten minutes politely engaging them in conversation. Plus, it could prove prudent, as the girls would more than likely become more obsessive fans and buy more of their merchandise. It was a crass way of thinking, but then, good business practices were usually crass and manipulative.

Ten minutes later, Chance sat in the van with his eyes closed, trying not to doze off, when the front door of the van opened. Tau got in, made himself comfortable, and fastened his seatbelt before offloading several bags. "Some of these are for you Ren, and Chance you have one."

Chance took the bag Tau offered and was happy it was only

chocolate inside. He closed the bag and set it next to him. "Can we go now?"

"Yeah," Tau answered, handing Ren three bags. As Itsuki turned the key and revved the van into life, Tau looked around the seat with a deep frown marring his face. "You did hear what they said?" Chance shook his head and shrugged in confusion. "The foreigners, they said they weren't here to see us." Tau turned away, folded his arms over his chest, and huffed loudly.

Chance smiled at his friend's behavior, then turned to look out the window. He watched the building the club was in ease by as the van inched forward. For some strange reason, he was glad the two women weren't their fans, even gladder they'd gotten rid of one fan making him apprehensive.

The van pulled out into the street. Unexpectedly, Chance was pitched forward and slammed into Tau's seat, with a loud squeal echoing in his ears. He pushed back against the cushioned upholstery and righted himself, looking through the windshield for the cause of their sudden stop. A blinding headlight lit the van, making his eyes water slightly. They focused in time for him to see two American woman speed past on a gold and black motorcycle. The brunette was driving, the blonde was sitting backward on the back of the bike, holding something he couldn't quite make out. The loud engine of the bike filled the van as it passed, and everyone in it moved forward so they could watch the red taillight disappear down the street.

Tau was the first to speak up. "I know it's farfetched, but I still say prostitutes. High priced American prostitutes."

"What is it about those two women that makes you think prostitute?" Itsuki asked incredulously.

Tau held up a finger, took a deep breath, then paused. "They said they weren't fans."

Ren grimaced and shook his head. "You want them to be prostitutes, otherwise you wouldn't have a chance of getting either of them into bed."

Chance stared at the empty alleyway, thinking about his encounters with the brunette foreigner from the café that day. He had to admit he'd never been more intrigued by a woman in his life. The fact she wasn't a fan gave her appeal. "I hope Ayano's friends made sure she gets home," he mused aloud, not really caring, considering the girl gave him a bad vibe. Still, his curiosity about the brunette was far from satisfied. "I'd really like to know what that was all about," he stated, thinking of the brunette with intense violet eyes as he stared at the writing on his hand.

Simeon stared at him for a moment before leaning in closer. He turned his head to stare down the now empty street. "For some strange reason, I hope you get to see her again to find out," he said low enough for Chance alone to hear.

5

"I don't see it," Sutton shouted from behind Keely. The motorcycle swayed as she shifted from left to right. "Do you sense anything?"

"No," Keely shouted, splitting her concentration between driving and keeping Ayano's soul earthbound. A human soul was heavy, sometimes more substantial than the body it occupied, because they were laden with memories, emotions, and desires, in short, a person's essence. Souls were not an easy thing to carry, and it was exhausting. She weaved her motorcycle in and out of traffic until she reached open road. Pulling back on the throttle, she zoomed past the cars as if they were standing still. Five minutes later, they came to a screeching, sliding halt in front of a large, gated house.

"Four minutes," Keely said between pants, laying her motorcycle on the ground as she dismounted from it. She'd be upset about mistreating it later, but her main concern was the soul she carried in the paint-stained box inside her backpack. It was getting heavier by the second. She was starting to find it hard to walk under its weight. Just as she and Sutton approached the black iron gate surrounding the house, a uniformed woman opened it and bowed as they ran through.

Keely's legs got too heavy for her to lift when they reached the steps. "Sutton," she said between wheezing breaths and reached for her friend.

"Come on, lazy ass." Sutton ducked her head under Keely's arm and pulled her up the stairs.

"To the left," Keely directed, following the pull of Ayano's body. The two of them stumbled into a sparsely furnished room with a wide picture window looking out onto a lit garden. The walls were painted with branches that bloomed muted pink flowers. A woman lay on a futon in the center of the room covered with a blue quilt, Mr. Oshiro sitting next to her. Keely stumbled into the room and fell to her knees next to the woman. Immediately, she recognized Ayano. She looked different from the image she'd projected onto the neverborn, but somehow, still the same. Ayano had shining, dark hair and delicate features and was much prettier than she saw herself.

"Hello, Ayano," Keely said softly as she fished in her back-pack for the paint-stained box. The box weighed so much her hands shook, and she could barely lift it out of the bag. Straddling Ayano, she took a quick assessment of the room and its occupants. Besides Mr. Oshiro, there was a middle-aged woman dressed in a housekeep-er's uniform. Their souls stretched out to Ayano's with worry and love. Looking to Sutton, she nodded, giving her the okay to leave, then turned her attention back to Ayano.

Sutton, or anyone that did not genuinely care for a soul, could not be present for the reformation. To a pure soul, emotions were tan-gible, both good and bad. People who didn't genuinely love the per-son Keely was trying to restore could be projecting any number of negative feelings. If a soul sensed negativity, they would reject mor-tality for the joyousness of heaven. Surrounding them with people they loved reminded them of who they were as a mortal. Often, when a soul sensed how loved they were, and remembered how much they loved in return, it slowed or stopped the soul's ascension.

Focusing her mind, Keely concentrated on Ayano's soul. She could feel all of her emotions as if they were her own. At that moment, the most prevalent was fear, but that was normal for a soul stolen from its body. Still, Keely could feel her love: love for her art, love for a world she always found beautiful, and most of all, love for her father. A chant began to form in Keely's mind. Besides saving the soul from the neverborn, the chant was a crucial part of the restoration process. The chant itself was more like a song, a song sung in the lan-guage of the divine. The song needed to be full of welcome, calm, and love, and it had to be unique to the soul Keely was trying to return. Once she opened the box holding Ayano's soul, it would start to ascend. Keely's job was in part to entice and in part to force a soul back into its vessel or body. If that soul was touched by heaven before Keely could entice/force it back into place, then it would slip through her fingers. There would be nothing she could do. The soul would go to heaven, and the body would die.

Keely stared at Ayano's sleeping face and spoke softly. "There are many things in this world but none so rare as eyes constantly see-ing the beauty in it. Eyes that take what they see and put it onto a can-vas and share it so beauty can be seen by all. Beauty and art are your gifts, Ayano Oshiro, and this world needs what you have to offer. There are people who love you and a lifetime of wondrous marvels for you to discover. Beauty is waiting for you to find it. Do not turn away from a life to be lived as an artist." Keely chanted in a language she'd never been taught but spoke fluently. Carefully, she opened the box, dipped her hand inside, and scooped out Ayano's soul. "I call forth your soul and bind it to your body so it can never be stolen again."

She unfolded her fingers. A warm prismatic light exploded from them, filling the room and everyone in it with its brilliance. Keely carefully held it with her hands and her will. Her muscles burned; her chest felt like she couldn't breathe in air, and her heart beat loudly and painfully against her ribs, but the soul didn't move toward heaven. Instead, the warm essence of Ayano settled into Keely's hands. She no longer just felt Ayano's emotions but absorbed them. All her sorrow, struggles, pain, laughter, joy, happiness, and love momentarily filled Keely, and she felt tears well up. Ayano was beautiful and pure. With a soft smile on her face and tears flowing from her eyes, Keely pressed the light into the center of the woman's chest and watched it sink in. A pulse of glowing color radiated outward, and the soul merged into its body.

In the heavy silence that followed, Keely moved from atop the woman. She knew what was coming next, and it wouldn't be easy for the girl. Ten seconds later, Ayano sat up, opened her mouth, and let lose a gut-wrenching, pain-filled scream.

"The morphine," Keely shouted over Ayano's ear-piercing shrieks. She held out a hand, and a syringe was slapped into it. Keely had to move quickly, or Ayano would become violent, and it would be harder to calm her even with drugs. Hurriedly, she found a vein and slid the needle beneath Ayano's skin, depressing the plunger. Her reward was a hard smack on the side of her face from one of Ayano's knees. Keely dodged the next blow; she pulled the needle out of the girl's arm and scurried across the floor. Ayano screamed and flailed for another forty-five seconds before her breath seemed to catch mid-shriek, and she fell back onto the mattress. Moments later, she closed her eyes and fell asleep.

Keely let the syringe she held fall from her fingers, sat back on her haunches, then plopped to the floor, tired and hungry. Her overpowering exhaustion made the worlds spin, and her strength was waning.

Sutton was suddenly next to her, picking up the discarded syringe before sitting down next to her. "Remember, you said host club," she said in Gaelic.

"I can't wait," Keely responded in English. The muscles in her arms turned to rubber then gave out, and she collapsed onto the floor unable to keep her mind focused or her eyes open.

Sometime later, Keely couldn't tell how long, she felt a cold, wet cloth carefully press against her forehand and cheeks. A far-off deep voice asked, "What should we do with the Priestess?" She vaguely recognized the voice belonged to Mr. Oshiro.

"Give her some time," Sutton answered. "It takes a few minutes for her to recover."

"I understand." Mr. Oshiro's voice came from next to Keely. That was when she realized he was the one dabbing at her face with the cool cloth. "So young and pretty, to have such a heavy purpose in life." Keely slowly rolled open her eyes and looked at him. "Priestess." He offered her a relieved smile that took away some of the worry lines from his face.

Keely rolled to her side, and despite her shaking arms, pushed herself up off the floor. "Thank you for tending me." She managed to keep herself from swaying and falling back to the floor.

"We are honored by your presence and blessed by your assistance." Mr. Oshiro dropped the towel and bowed so deeply in front of her his head touched the floor. "There are no words to express my gratitude."

Embarrassed by his formality, heat rushed to her face, making her head swim. "There is no need, Mr. Oshiro. Please do not be so formal with me. Besides," Keely smiled at his bowed head, "I did wear shoes inside your great house. I apologize for the offense."

Mr. Oshiro lifted his face and stared at her with a surprised look. "I assure you the matter of your shoes is trifling."

Keely smiled at him. "Then shall we call ourselves friends?"

She held out a hand to him. He took it in both of his and nodded curtly. "We shall." He smiled. "And my daughter has been returned?"

"Yes." Keely nodded. "But the next couple of days will be

hard. It will seem like she can't walk or talk. Remember her soul has to readapt to her body, and it will be painful for her."

"I understand," he said and closed his eyes. A tear slid from beneath his grey lashes. "But my daughter can overcome it."

"I'm sure she can. She has the support of people who genuinely love her, and that's the best medicine for a returned soul. Remember, she's an artist. No one should ever try to change or take away her gift."

"I won't." The old man bowed deeply.

"Good." Keely felt she was finally able to not only sit up but stand. Pulling her feet in close, she tried to push herself off the floor but only made it halfway before she fell back down. Her legs simply wouldn't hold her. Suddenly, Sutton and a man she'd never met before were next to her lifting her up. They held her until she was able to steady herself. "I'm sorry, please understand I must take my leave." She bowed slightly.

"Of course." Mr. Oshiro bowed again.

She turned and left him, carefully walking to the door, wanting nothing more than her bed. Slowly, she made her way out of the house. Sutton walked beside her each painful step of the way. "A car is waiting downstairs. I've made arrangements to have your BMW dropped off at the apartment."

"Okay." Keely had made it to the front entrance and could see the shiny, black sedan waiting with an open door. If she hadn't had Sutton to lean on, she'd have fallen down the front steps of the house. Keely wasn't sure how she got to the car but did manage to fall into its back seat. As she settled against the soft leather, she closed her eyes. "I promise to try to not sleep for forty-eight hours."

"I can't say the same," Sutton said from beside her, yawning. "France, the move, and this all has taken a lot out of me. I may sleep for a week."

"Yeah," Keely agreed.

"Keely?" Sutton asked, leaning her head on Keely's shoulder.

"Mm?"

"I was totally serious about going to a host club."

"Mm-hm." Keely smiled. "I was serious when I said we'd go." As she fell into sleep, she had the passing thought that no host club host could be as good looking as the bassist of Eternity's End.

6

"Oh my god. The blond guy was so hot," Sutton said with a slight slur as she lifted her arm out to keep from swaying. Sutton and Keely strolled arm in arm down a brightly lit sidewalk in search of food. They'd enjoyed the unusually warm March night, taking advantage of as much Tokyo nightlife as they could.

"Yeah, they were yummy and very good for my self-esteem." Keely smiled to herself.

Sutton giggled. "Not that you suffer from self-esteem issues. But I love being doted on by hot guys." She stopped talking and looked pensive. "Do people still say doted?"

"I think they do when they're talking about host clubs." Keely giggled as well. She was only slightly tipsy, tipsy in a good way. Her alcohol intake had been just enough to make her feel warm, not flushed, and in a relaxed, good mood.

"Well, of course, they doted on us." Sutton swayed again as she walked. She had reached the point of intoxication, hence the need for food. "I mean, did you even look in the mirror before you left?"

"I did." Keely smiled and looked down at the long, dark red dress she wore. She smoothed her hand over the soft velvet. It was a simple halter dress with detached sleeves and long, flowing skirt. Still, the deep cut of the bodice, high split of the skirt, and the perfect fit made the dress look like it had been made specifically for her. Her gold, strappy shoes matched the gold choker on her neck. With one of her hands she swished the long folds of her dress back and forth. "I...we look pretty. I've decided I love getting dressed up and drinking with pretty host boys."

"I know, right? Tonight was a lot of fun. We needed fun...and alcohol." Sutton swayed and then wrapped both of her arms around one of Keely's to steady herself. "I'm hungry though. Are we at food yet?"

Keely consulted her phone. "Not much further."

They'd decided to walk from Shinjuku's 'red-light' district since they weren't in a hurry. There was something mysterious and wonderful about a city at night. Keely liked walking through Tokyo, underneath its canopy of tall buildings, staring at the many shops, bright lights, and people. Sometimes she'd listen to tidbits of a pleasant conversation or hum along with the music of the shops they passed. Add the wonderful smell of Asian, spiced food, interspersed with the crisp, night air, and she was sure Tokyo held some kind of exotic magic. It was one of the few times she felt connected to humanity as a human, not as its only protector. Sutton didn't mind Keely's penchant for urban discovery, so they decided against the overcrowded, last trains in their search for a late-night meal. After that, they'd get a taxi.

"Do you think our hosts actually liked us?" Sutton asked.

"I'm sure they did. You know, you're a hot piece of ass. So yeah, they liked you." Keely looked over at her friend. She'd chosen to wear a strapless, lavender mini-dress that flounced with her movements. "And if they didn't like us, they sure as hell liked our two hundred thousand yen we dropped on them."

Sutton stopped mid-stride with a shocked expression on her face. Money was a serious matter to her, especially in large sums. "We just blew seventeen hundred dollars?"

Keely stopped and started giggling uncontrollably. "Yes, we did. Or did you forget the four bottles of very expensive champagne?"

"Oh yeah, well that explains so much right now."

Keely had another fit of giggles. "Totally worth it."

"How worth it?" Sutton asked, starting to casually stroll down the sidewalk again. "Did any of our pretty boys replace hot rocker-guy in your affections?" When Keely didn't say anything, Sutton stopped again and stepped closer to her. "Oh my god, you're still stuck on rocker-guy. You only talked to him for five seconds."

"No." Keely momentarily looked away from Sutton's scrutinizing stare. "It'd be stupid to be stuck on a guy after talking to him for five seconds. And hot rocker-guy equals ego—equals pussy marauder—remember you told me that. And for the record, I'm not really stuck on him. I'm just really curious," she admitted honestly then frowned.

"Wow. You must have really liked him."

"I can't say that. I can say, he was hotter than any of our hosts. But don't worry. I'll get over it quickly. I'm not so naïve to think a pretty face and irresistible lips are the end all to be all in men. Idiots and assholes can have the initial panty dropping effect if they're good looking, but that changes if they open their mouths and you find out they *are* an idiot or asshole."

"Amen sister. Don't I know it. Totally kills a lady boner," Sutton giggled. "Actors, rocker-guys, and bartenders." Sutton sighed, "Pretty jerks."

"Yeah, so it doesn't matter how curious I am if he's an asshole that falls into column B. And I'm sure the rocker-guy probably has the ego to go along with it."

"Yeah," Sutton agreed. "I think it's kind of ironic really. We travel the world and meet all these crazy ass cultures with all these crazy-ass rules. Ya know? There are still those constants in human nature. The bad boy will always be a bad boy. But," she lifted a finger, "I give you permission to crush on him all you want."

"Like I said, not a crush so much as he's hot and I'm curious. Anyway." Keely smiled and took two steps backward. "Since we only have one day left of our vacation, let's go to a spa, an expensive one, that will pamper us into putty."

"Oh, that sounds fun," Sutton skipped to her, "but…" She stopped and suddenly looked sad. "Are we going home now?"

"What? No! Tokyo is perfect tonight. I didn't say anything about going home yet." She smiled. "First, we find food, then, we find a bar and put your Italian alcohol tolerance to the test." Keely turned around and started to walk again, only, at that same moment, several drunken men came at her, shouldering past, making her stumble toward the street. She tried to catch herself, but the heel of her shoe got caught on a crack in the sidewalk and pitched her in the opposite direction she wanted to go. Flailing her arms, she tried to keep herself from falling into oncoming traffic, but her momentum was unstoppable. She watched headlights speed toward her, wondering if getting hit by a car would hurt more or less than getting thrown into a brick wall by a neverborn.

"Careful," a male voice said in Japanese as an arm wrapped around her waist, and she was snatched away from the car and the street.

She exhaled sharply, and the world spun, making her feel more drunk. Involuntarily, she clung to her steadfast rescuer her until she could catch her balance. After a moment, she twisted around in the arms holding her and found herself staring into warm brown eyes. "Excuse me, but are you alright?" The bassist she'd met in the café several days earlier flashed her a heart-stopping smile.

"Y… Yeah," she managed to stutter as she disentangled herself from his hold and stepped back to Sutton. Heart pounding in her ears and butterflies fluttering in the stomach, she cleared her throat. She couldn't look away from his warm brown eyes, and it made her wonder at the power of rocker-guys. Were they all that seductive?

Sutton wound her arm through Keely's, leaned closer to her, and whispered loudly. "Is there supposed to be four of them, or am I seeing double?" Her voice broke the spell Chance had cast. Keely looked at the four men in front of them. The dark-haired bassist stood next to the blue-haired man who had been with him at the café. Beside him, was a tall man with long, black hair swept back into a ponytail at the nape of his neck. On the far left stood a slightly shorter man with red and blond striped hair. "And why are they so happy to see us?" Sutton commented on the smiles they all wore. "Did we give them seventeen hundred dollars too?"

"No." Keely smiled, fighting off a new bout of giggles. She'd been caught coming from a host club on the verge of being overly tipsy. Her eyes went back to Chance's face, where she found herself both breathless and flustered by him. By way of justification, all she could think of to say was, "We look pretty."

∞ ∞ ∞ ∞ ∞

Chance couldn't help but smile at the brunette. She did look pretty. Actually, she looked stunning in her low-cut, long, red dress, which enhanced every one of her curves. Her long hair had been pulled up in glittering pins with wayward curls spilling out of them. Its tresses seemed to be caressing her ivory shoulders in such a way it made him wonder about the softness of her skin. His eyes were drawn to her cleavage because the dress was scandalously deep cut. He had to own he appreciated the view.

"Yes, you look very nice," he agreed then smiled more broadly when he saw her cheeks tint with pink.

"You look pretty too," she complimented and offered him a slight shrug.

He looked down at his unremarkable camouflage pants, grey t-shirt, and patch-decorated, denim jacket. Then he remembered, they'd just come from a gig. "We had a concert tonight," he explained. "I probably didn't get all of my make up off." He rubbed at his eyes, examined his fingers, then wiped black smudge on his pants.

"Oh, now I remember you." The women with blonde hair slurred as she swayed and pointed. "We saw you play. You're not bad." She turned to the taller woman and whispered loudly. "Why are all the men tonight so pretty? How much are we paying them?" The brunette's skin from her chest to the top of her forehead turned bright red. She bent closer to her friend and whispered something he couldn't quite hear. He wouldn't have understood it anyway since what he did hear didn't sound like English or Japanese.

Finally, the shorter woman looked up at them and explained in Japanese, "Apparently, I need coffee or food because I've had too much champagne." She turned to the brunette and said something else he didn't understand before asking them in Japanese. "Do you want to come?"

Chance considered declining. It had been a long and exhausting week, full of interviews, rehearsals, and finally a gig. Until he'd spotted the two women walking down the street, he'd wanted to do nothing more than go home, play a few video games then fall into his bed. Suddenly, he'd changed his mind. Food and beer had a whole new appeal.

"You know you want to come with us." The shorter woman smiled up at him. She wasn't wrong.

The two women had been the topic of many conversations between the four of them, and their curiosity about the events they'd witnessed was almost obsessive. If their van hadn't broken down and if they hadn't been rushing to catch the train, they might have missed the unique opportunity presenting itself. He'd be a fool not to take advantage of that opportunity.

"Sure," he replied with a smile.

"I think tonight is going to be very interesting," the shorter woman observed, looking pointedly at him. "Will all of you be joining us?" Her eyes scanned over Tau, Simeon, and Ren.

Chance looked at his friends and knew by the collective smiles and nods they'd all be going to 'coffee or food' with the two women. Tau slightly shifted his head sideways, raised his eyebrows, and nodded before he turned to the woman. "I think this will turn out to be an interesting evening."

The shorter woman disentangled herself from her friend again. "I'm Sutton." She offered Chance her hand in greeting.

"I'm Chance." He took the hand and bowed his head slightly, not feeling the slightest bit awkward about the American greeting. "This is Tau." Tau bowed then saluted the two women. "Ren." Ren also bowed then offered them a peace sign. "And Simeon." Simeon simply bowed and offered them a smile.

"Sutton," Sutton introduced herself to them again and shook each of their hands. Then with a flourishing gesture, she motioned to her friend. "This illustrious creature is Keely," she slurred then hiccupped.

He thought Keely would be embarrassed and feel awkward around them after her friend's antics, but instead, laughter that sounded like the soft tones of pretty bells filled the air. She bowed to them. "Not illustrious. It's nice to meet all of you."

"Anyway," Sutton continued, looking around the street, "we were in search of a ramen shop or a café or something open this late. Our directions say…" She stopped and looked at Keely.

Keely pulled a phone from a fringed purse and pointed behind Chance. "Five blocks that way... I think."

"I think I know the place," Ren offered with a smile.

"Oh good." Sutton stepped forward, weaving her arms through Ren's and Tau's. She started walking, dragging them both forward.

It was almost comical to Chance when they both turned around and looked at him with shocked expressions. Ren's shock appeared to turn to worry as he let Sutton drag him down the street. Tau's seeming shock didn't last long either. It was replaced with a broad 'I told you so' smile that split his face, and he nearly skipped down the street as they walked away.

Simeon raised an eyebrow at him as if to say, 'I can't wait to see what happens', then followed behind them.

"Well, she's made up her mind. I better go with her, especially if there's going to be more drinking. Your friends might find her behavior egregious if she's left alone with them." Keely flashed him another smile and started walking after the others, but there was a loud snap. She stumbled and pitched forward.

Chance moved quickly and caught her. "Careful," he warned for the second time that evening, keeping her in a firm hold until she found her footing. All the while, he could feel the length of her body and its curves. Even though she was taller, she melded to him perfectly. He had the passing thought that all he had to do was dip his head and he would be touching his lips to her breast. He found the idea tempting. Then, his eyes locked wither her pretty violet ones, and he didn't have any coherent thoughts. It wasn't just the color he found mesmerizing; it was the way she looked at him. He couldn't describe it except to say, whatever her thoughts about him, they were intense and sincere.

"I'm sorry," Keely apologized, turning her gaze downward and ending the spell. She tried to step away from him, faltered, and put a hand on his shoulder to steady herself. "I think my shoe broke." She reached down pulled off the shoe and inspected it. One of the ankle straps had been torn from the bottom of the shoe. "Well, not unwearable, just slightly more difficult to walk in," she sighed. "And these were one of my favorite pair." She frowned before bending over and putting it back on. Releasing his arm, she stepped away from him, smoothing her hands over her dress, then combed stray strands of hair from her face. She offered him a small bow and said, "Thank you for keeping me from falling on my face." She held up two fingers, smiled, and added, "Twice. In America that would mean I should buy you a late dinner or a drink at the very least." She started to walk away with a slight limp, probably because of the broken shoe. After a few steps, she stopped and looked over her shoulder. "And don't worry, we're not as scary as first impressions would lead you to believe."

He watched her walk after the others, thinking he was slightly embarrassed and felt a tiny bit awkward around her, but he wasn't scared. He wondered if he should have been.

∞ ∞ ∞ ∞ ∞

Keely sat next to Chance, trying not to be distracted by his smile as she described what it was like to hike through the late winter frozen waterfalls in Germany. "It was freezing cold, but so pretty. The sun would hit the ice, and it was like hitting crystals. There were rainbows everywhere. In some places, the ice wasn't frozen all the way through, and water still flowed on the inside of the ice sheets. I don't think I want to do it again, but I'm glad I got to see it because it was so pretty."

"What she's not telling you is," Sutton leaned around Keely, "it was also super slippery, and she fell on her ass so much that when we got back to the hotel, she couldn't actually sit down for three days." She held up four fingers and laughed, swaying in her seat.

"Ouch," Chance said with a smile.

"Thanks for that," Keel mumbled. "I wasn't actually going to tell him my more humiliating moments," she added, and Chance laughed outright. It was a rich infectious laugh that made her smile despite the heat in her cheeks.

The part of the story Sutton didn't tell; she had a sprained ankle from a fight with a neverborn. At the time, Sutton had not mastered the chant of healing, and they'd no choice but to pass through the frozen mountains on foot. Slippery ice was not kind to someone with a sprained ankle.

"Sutton didn't fall, once, ever," Keely said, proud of her friend.

"The advantages of being short." Sutton hiccuped and turned her attention to Tau who sat on the other side of her.

Chance, Keely, Sutton, Tau, and Ren were crowded around a little table in a small ramen shop. Initially, Simeon had joined them, but he'd politely left them, citing family responsibility. The ramen shop was one of the few places in Tokyo left open, but it seemed they catered to late- night drinkers and people who'd missed the last train. It was a quaint restaurant with clean wood furnishing and paper lantern lights. It had been more than an hour since their empty bowls of ramen had been cleared away. The group of them sat drinking beer. Sutton drank two huge beers, while Keely nursed the single one she'd been given, maintaining her pleasant buzz.

Although, she did talk a lot due to being slightly inebriated. If talking too much ever made Chance feel awkward, he didn't show it. Initially Chance was shy, but it didn't take long for him to ease into conversation with Keely. They'd talked about a broad range of subjects, some American, some Japanese. He was intelligent, charming, and shared the same sense of humor, which Keely appreciated. When he smiled, his sultry lips and warm inviting eyes made her heart pound hard in her chest.

"Anyway," Keely smiled at Chance, "Germany was pretty even from the vantage point I had on the ground."

Chance laughed again. "I'm sure it was. I'd like to tour in Germany."

Eternity's End was one of the few subjects they didn't explore too deeply. Keely didn't get the impression Chance didn't want to talk about his music, but it wasn't a subject they'd explored.

"I think you'd be successful. A lot of post-punk bands do well there."

"So, you travel a lot for work?" he asked.

"Yes." She nodded.

"What kind of work do you do?"

Keely's experience had taught her that she could never answer this question honestly. She skirted the truth because no one would believe her unless they'd encountered the neverborn or knew what they were. In her opinion, it was a good thing she wasn't well known. Anyone who had faced the neverborn or knew what they were was sure to experience the fear or tragedy the neverborn wrought. "It's hard to explain. I'm sort of a retrieval consultant." She gave him the same answer she gave to everyone who wouldn't understand.

"How long have you been working at your company?"

"Well." Partial truths were distasteful to her especially when she was lying to someone she liked. She'd started to genuinely like Chance, so the partial truth felt like a lie. "I started training for my job when I was thirteen. I kind of have a talent for what I do."

"I imagine you'd be good at anything you attempted." He smiled at her again, only this smile seemed more intimate like it was something for her alone.

She looked away from him, downed the remaining half glass

of beer, and tried to quell the pounding of her heart. The beer didn't help the loud thrumb in her ears or the fluttering in her stomach. A flush of warmth radiated from her chest, and she almost giggled at the sensation. Leaning closer to him she quietly confessed, "I imagine you're good at kissing."

Even before she finished her statement, the tops of his cheeks dusted with red. She immediately regretted being so blunt. He cleared his throat and shifted in his seat. Staring at the entrance, he took a sip of his beer as an awkward silence fell between them.

"I'm sorry." Keely looked at her hands feeling warmth spread across her cheeks. "That was too blunt, even for me. I'm sorry," she repeated. "I'm used to speaking my mind." She tried to control the rush of blood making her neck turn hot. "Ignore what I said or pretend I didn't say it."

Luckily, before she could say anything else and make the situation more awkward, Sutton leaned back over to her. "We're going to go to a manga café. Apparently, you can stay up all night reading manga, watch movies, or play video games. You down?"

"I think I should go home," Keely replied in Gaelic. "I..."

Before she could explain, Sutton replied in the same language. "I didn't know you had it in you to move so quick. It's about time you did something impetuous. Life's not about fighting neverborn."

"I..." Keely tried again, but Sutton interrupted a second time.

"Chance," Sutton said in Japanese, looking around Keely. "Could you be a gentleman and make sure my best friend gets home safely?" Keely was trying to shake her head no, hoping Sutton would see the look of abject horror on her face, but her best friend ignored her.

Keely fought monsters and had been in several potentially lethal situations, but she'd never considered using her power of illusion to make herself disappear until that moment. "It's not what..." she tried one last time in English, but Sutton remained oblivious to Keely's pleas.

"I'd owe you." Sutton smiled and winked at Chance.

Keely looked sideways at Chance, catching the last traces of a frown before he bowed his head. "Yes."

"Now that that's settled." Sutton smiled and stood up. "We have a vicious game of street fighter to play." The others stood up

54

with her. Sutton bent close to Keely and whispered in Gaelic in her ear. "I already paid the bill." She kissed Keely on her forehead. "You can thank me tomorrow. Remember to use a condom, and don't fall for the rocker-guy." Keely was too embarrassed to make much more than a small squeaking noise as she watched her friend walk out the door with Tau and Ren following.

Without looking to Chance, Keely grabbed her purse from the back of her chair and quickly stood. "I can find my own way home." She bowed, without looking at him, turned and walked toward the door as fast as her broken shoe would allow. She made it outside the ramen shop and stopped to take a deep breath of the fresh, night air, hoping it would soothe the humiliation she felt.

"Where do you live?" a deep voice asked from beside her, and she jumped. She took a step away, looking at Chance.

"No really." She bowed. "I'm fine. I'm really good with direction I can get home on my own."

"I agreed to escort you home."

"I didn't... I mean." She took a deep breath, trying to overcome her embarrassment and attraction to him. "I'm certain you're tired. Being a rockstar sounds fun, but it's probably demanding." She bowed one last time. "So, thank you for sharing my evening and goodnight." Turning, she headed in the direction of the nearest street, hoping to find a taxi.

Despite her quick pace, even with her broken shoe, she heard footsteps behind her. Looking over her shoulder, she found Chance following. "Shoo." She motioned with her hand, picked up her pace and turned onto a brightly lit street in her efforts to get away. So, did he. After twenty steps, she came to an abrupt stop. "This is ridiculous," she said to herself in English and turned to face him. "I will pay you," she opened her purse and pulled out several bills, "three thousand yen to turn around and forget tonight happened."

He looked incredulous then he gave her a wry smile. "Forget tonight happened, for three thousand yen?"

"Yes," she waved the bills at him. "I think it's a fair amount for you to pretend I didn't humiliate myself."

He stepped closer. "Keely." It was the first time he'd said her name. He said it so quietly it reminded her of a soft breeze blowing through her hair. "I'm not going to forget tonight or pretend it didn't happen." He reached out, covered her hand with his, and pushed it away. The electrifying warmth of his touch made the butterflies in her stomach flutter wildly. "And, I don't go back on my word. I agreed to get you home safely."

She looked down at the hand still covering hers then looked back to him. "Chance," she said softly. "It'd be better if I find my own way home. If you go with me, it's going to be awkward for you, because I won't be able to keep it a secret that I really do want to know what it's like to kiss you."

Chance's eyes slightly widened, and he looked taken aback by her candor. She thought he'd give in and leave her alone, but then he scrunched his mouth up like he was deep in thought before he smiled at her. Stepping in closer to her, he said, "You're not the only one who's curious." He stepped away from her and walked down the street, smiling at her over his shoulder.

Keely was overwhelmed with chaotic emotions she hadn't felt in a long time, and they'd never been as strong as she was feeling right then. Swallowing, she opened her purse and put her money back into it, then took a look around to get her bearings. Her mouth almost fell open, and she couldn't decide if she was embarrassed at or thankful for the irony of her own luck. They were in the middle of the love hotel district of Shibuya. She considered a million different scenarios on how the evening could play out. Almost all of them ended up with Chance rejecting her in some polite way that would probably make her feel very awkward, but it didn't stop her from coming to the inevitable realization. Kissing him wasn't the only thing she was curious about.

She watched him walk a couple more steps then stop, turn around and ask, "Are you coming?"

Keely took several slow, shy steps to him. "What if I told you I had other curiosities about you, beyond kissing?" She made a point of looking around. She knew she was awkwardly offering herself, but flirting wasn't something she was practiced at. Inviting a man to spend the night with her in a hotel, a love hotel, was something she never dreamed she'd do.

Again, she'd shocked him. She could tell by the way his mouth practically fell open before he corrected his facial features. He frowned and she had an intense moment of anxiety. "I'd wonder." He paused and offered her a slight grin. "If that was an invitation?" All she could do was nod. After a moment he smiled, making her breath catch at how stunning it was. "Then, I'd suggest," he pointed to a building decorated with pretty ornamented lights and a stone façade, "that one. It's the cleanest and has large beds."

7

Keely stepped into the genkan, or entranceway, of the hotel room and slid off her shoes. She decided against the slippers supplied. Her feet were big, and the courtesy shoes offered looked child-sized. They were obviously way too small, and she wanted to feel less awkward. She'd never had a one-night-stand before much less, booked a hotel room specifically designed for that purpose. Without a constant intake of alcohol, she was sobering and starting to doubt the decision-making process bringing her there.

Walking into the hotel room, she looked at the dark, paneled walls, fluffy bed, and nearly half-wall sized television. "Posh," she commented, staring up at the crystal chandelier hanging above the bed.

"What is posh?" Chance asked from beside her.

"It means luxurious," she replied absently. Her eyes fell to a machine with clear doors housing a myriad of vibrators, lubricants, and condoms. "Well, luxurious with your standard sex-toy vending machine." She grinned at her own joke then turned her attention to the ceiling to floor glass-front wardrobe that covered an entire wall. "And," she went on, walking over to one of the cabinets. Opening it, she took out a microphone. "Karaoke in case you feel like doing it naked." She smiled at him hoping he didn't notice her nervousness. "Oh." She dropped the microphone back into the cabinet and picked up a video game controller. "Naked Call of Duty?" She turned and smiled at him again.

He moved closer to her. Without her heeled shoes, she was only a couple inches taller than him, which almost put her at his eye level. She very much liked staring into the warm depths of his eyes, and for a moment she was caught in their spell.

"How about some music?" He asked with a smile before walking over to the bed and touching a button on a lit panel placed on a wall behind it. Strategically hidden speakers came on, playing techno dance music. He pressed another button, and the music changed to a song Keely vaguely recognized before the music changed again.

"Hey," Keely pointed up at the ceiling, "that was you, wasn't it? Wow, I had no idea your band was so popular." He looked at her with a quizzical expression as if he doubted what she'd said. "Don't worry; I won't hold being a rocker-guy against you." She offered him her most brilliant smile. For a moment, he looked at her and seemed even more confused before he smiled brilliantly in return. "I can see why you're so popular."

He changed the music again, this time settling on soft and orchestral. "Why do you think I'm so popular?" he asked, stepping across the room. Taking the controller from her hand, he set it back in its cabinet.

"It's just," she started and stopped.

She took a moment to think about how she should respond. She wondered if she should be honest or if it would make him feel uneasy. She wouldn't necessarily call Chance shy, but he was definitely reserved. Her nature was passionate and exactly opposite to his. At that moment, it was making her feel self-conscious. She wasn't ashamed of who she was or her nature, but she'd felt she needed to tame it lest she make him uncomfortable. Suddenly, after thinking about the circumstances leading her to where she was, she realized he was in a hotel room with her. He wanted the same thing she wanted, so there was no reason she should be self-conscious or hide her nature. For the one night she had him, she wanted him without pretense or awkwardness. She wanted to enjoy him with every ounce of passion she had in her.

"It's just," she said again, "your lips sometimes make me forget I have the capability to form coherent thoughts."

She closed the gap between them. Lightly pressing herself against him, she rested her hands on his hips, and lowered her mouth to his. At first, his response was minimal, until she caressed his lips with her own. His lips got suppler, and the kiss between them turned tender. Her heart started pounding against her ribs, and the fluttering butterflies returned. She slightly parted her lips yearning to taste him, but he didn't accept her invitation

Frustrated, she found herself wrapping her arms around his middle before she let her tongue taste his bottom lip. His hot tongue suddenly entwined with hers as an arm circled her waist, and his other hand came up to caress the side of her face. His tongue delved deep into her mouth in sensual, aggressive discovery.

He crushed her to himself, and she could feel the length of his body. It surprised and delighted her how well they fit. The heady sweet and spicy taste of his velvet tongue almost made her moan as she explored every aspect of his mouth. She'd never been so engrossed by a kiss or the feel of someone's body, but she was completely enthralled by the sparks of electricity passing between them. Everything faded away, the sounds of the city outside, the music overhead, and even the heavy pounding of her heart. All she was, was the sensation he was igniting and flaming inside of her.

After a very heated exploration on both their parts, kissing him wasn't enough. Keely's body started to want for more. He must have sensed her need or maybe felt his own because he backed toward the bed, taking her with him. She felt impatient to feel all of him, not just his mouth. As she continued kissing him, she unhooked her arms from around his waist, reached up and pushed the jacket he wore off his shoulders. Grabbing handfuls of t-shirt, she pulled it up, letting out a low whine of disappointment when he drew his lips away from hers so he could help her peel off his shirt. His mouth returned to hers, and if at all possible, their kissing got fiercer, so much so, occasionally their teeth scraped together.

She wanted more, needed more.

Before she could act on her need, the two of them toppled over onto the bed behind him. Their heads knocked together with a loud, painful thump. Keely rolled off the top of him, rubbing at her forehead and blinking back the tears suddenly filling her eyes. A warm hand replaced hers, and when she could focus her eyes again, she found herself staring up at Chance's broadly smiling face. "Are you alright?" he asked.

She smiled back at him. "Are you?"

"Yes."

"Are you sure?" She reached up and wrapped her arms around his neck. "Because you stopped kissing me."

He bent his head down and slowly rediscovered her mouth then pulled away. Crawling on top of her, he hovered there as he reached for a panel behind the bed. She had the most glorious view of bare chest and stomach. Keely couldn't resist kissing then licking at his soft skin. He stiffened, his stomach muscles hardened, and she

60

rewarded him with another soft kiss to the top of his hip. The lights dimmed, and he was on top of her, kissing her again. He ended the kiss before it got as heated as she wanted. "Stay like you are and don't move," he ordered in a low whisper then rolled off of her and the bed.

"Okay," Keely replied breathlessly, instantly missing the heat of his body. She lifted herself up on her elbows so she could watch him as he walked across the room.

For a musician, he was surprisingly toned and broad-shouldered. She longed to run her hands along the slight ridges and curves of his stomach and chest so that she could feel what her lips had tasted. He reached out and opened one of the clear doors of the vending machine and pulled out some condoms. Keely found his hands and forearms fascinating. They were slightly larger than what someone his frame and build should be, but his fingers were still graceful. The muscles of his forearms swelled and relaxed with strength as he moved. That was when she noticed the dark red and green serpentine dragon tattoo that was coiled around the entirety of his upper arm. Nearly realistic red and green scales ended in a massive head with horns and giant teeth that were clamped down on its own tale. Tattoos weren't something she usually found attractive but the Ouroboros, the serpent dragon symbol for eternity, suited him.

Mesmerized, she continued to stare at him wondering what his lovely hands could do to her. The pressure of want made her body ache for them to touch her especially the now pulsing area between her legs. She wondered what it would be like to have him pushing inside of her, and she suddenly got impatient with wanton lust.

"I like the way you look at me." Chance smiled at her as he came back across the room and crawled up on the bed on top of her.

"I like looking at you." Keely leaned up and kissed the side of his jaw and moved her lips down to his ear, before gently biting and sucking at the sensitive skin of his neck. She felt a warm hand run down her leg then slid inside the slit of her dress before rubbing up her thigh. She shivered. His lips were on hers again, and she relaxed into the bed. Warm fingers slipped under the edge of her lace panties before they slid down her legs and off her feet. Then he was pressing his full weight on top of her.

Lifting her legs, she wrapped them around his waist and

pressed her pelvis to him. Even through the thick jeans she could feel his hardened length rub against her. He moved, and her need to have him inside her became almost painful. She reached down and unbuttoned then unzipped his pants. The folds of his jeans and the soft cotton of his underwear parted and freed his hardened flesh. Their kissing had gotten so ferocious she wasn't sure how she was breathing. She was only aware of two things; his mouth and her need to be intimately joined with him.

She moved her hand up and down, and he moaned into her mouth. "Keely," he whispered against her lips then lifted away from her. He kneeled between her legs, pulling his pants and underwear down past his hips, removing the remaining barriers between them. The smoldering depths of his dark brown eyes held her captivated, making her want to be devoured by them. She had an awareness of his hands moving between them before his weight was back on top of her. His lips covered hers, and his tongue committed glorious assault on her mouth.

Something hard moved against her, rubbing the spot that seemed to be the focal point for every nerve ending in her body. She shuddered, whimpered, and wrapped her arms around him feeling as if he was the lifeline to her erotic salvation. Rocking her hips, she pushed herself against him so he slid inside her when he moved again. At first, the plastic of the condom seemed cold and foreign, but then his body heat started to radiate through it at the same time as he slowly slid in and out of her again. She shuddered and moaned as his hands splayed across her outer thighs and held her in place on the bed underneath him.

Her small moan was accompanied by his low grunt as he glided in and out of her again. She met his next thrust, pushing against him so he could go deeper. Suddenly, they both seemed to lose patience for taking things slow. He was thrusting inside of her harder, deeper and faster while she spread her legs apart and lifted herself to meet each one of his thrusts. A wonderful intensity was building inside, promising blissful release, and her pleas of 'don't stop' came out in heady low screams. Abruptly, deep, loud moans escaped him, overpowering the sounds of her screams. With a few more thrusts, he went limp on top of her, panting heavily in her ear.

She managed to suppress a soft cry of frustration as the amplified intensity dissipated into tingling sensations that radiated to her fingers and toes. Before she could decide what to do about her still-pulsing need, begging to be satisfied, his lips were on hers again. The kiss was slow and soft and stole her breath away. The pressure from inside of her was pulled away, and she let out a small whimper, but Chance was still kissing her as if to make up for the sudden loss. The bed shifted as he partially lifted from atop her. She opened her eyes to find him resting his weight on his arms, staring into her eyes.

"Um." Keely felt blood rush to her face as she gazed up at his sweat moistened face. "That was fun," she said in English.

"What?" he asked in Japanese, rolled to the side of her and brushed some strands of hair out of her eyes.

"It was a compliment," she replied in the same language. Suddenly she felt uncomfortable around him. She'd gotten exactly what she wanted from him, even if it wasn't all of what she wanted. Unfortunately, Keely didn't know what happened next. An uncomfortable silence stretched on between them before she cleared her throat, rolled away from his penetrating gaze, and sat up. "I... uh..." She pointed toward a smoked glass door and the large bathtub beyond. "I'm going to take a bath."

Sliding off the bed, she walked to the bathroom, resisting the urge to run into it, lest Chance see the mix of emotions very likely written on her face. Quietly, she closed the door and let out the breath she'd been holding. She sank down onto the edge of the bathtub, giving her shaking legs a break. What was she supposed to do next?

The situation and politics booty calls were new. After a few minutes of staring at the smoked glass door, she decided it was almost terrifying that she didn't know what he was thinking or thought of her. Then she realized she wasn't supposed to care. Their moment together was supposed to be nothing more than a quick lay. Surely, he'd be like every other male on the planet after having sex with a girl they'd just met; he'd be scrambling to get dressed and out the door.

So she didn't have to face him before that happened, she decided to take advantage of amenities in the bathroom while she waited for him to leave. After that, she planned on taking advantage of television, video games, and large bed. Considering she'd yet to unpack, the hotel had a homey feel her apartment didn't have. A long, hot bath and a night in a semi-luxurious room watching movies was exactly what she needed to recover from her first ever one-night-stand.

Standing, she stripped off her dress, turned on the bath water, making sure it was near to scalding, then walked over to the shower stall and turned on the cold. The cool water sprayed over her still heated skin, calming it. As she washed, she was unhappy to find she was still swollen and wanting. God help her; she wanted him again, and there was nothing she could do about it. She couldn't blame him for not being more obliging, considering she'd been in as big of a hurry as he had; maybe she was even responsible for his quick climax. Considering how short their encounter was, she wondered if it meant she was good or bad in bed. Smiling to herself, she decided good. If she were bad, then there would have been a lack of his obvious enjoyment.

After she washed her body, she stepped into the hot bath, sunk down into the water, and turned off the tap with her toe. She relaxed and thought about her evening; more than that, she thought about laying underneath Chance with him inside her. It would be a long time before the memory wasn't a vivid one. She would enjoy reliving it for a while even if she didn't have completion. To him, she was probably another fan-girl conquest. To her he was the one night, perhaps in her life, she'd enjoyed a man's body without restraint.

Twenty minutes later, she emerged from the bath, relaxed and a little less horny. She dried herself and dressed in the soft light blue robe hanging from the bathroom door. The robe was way too small; barely covering her butt and containing her breasts. She smiled at her reflection as she removed the pins from her hair, thinking she looked like someone wanting to have sex, not someone who just had it. No one would see her, which made it more comical. After pulling out the many pins that held up her hair and vigorously brushing it, she opened the bathroom door and stopped. The smile on her face faded.

Chance lounged on the bed, wearing only his pants, holding out a game controller for her, and offering her a stunning smile. "Naked call of Duty?"

Keely had a moment of intense confusion. She looked at her feet to hide her expression, unsure what she should do or say, Why Chance was still there? She glanced up and instantly forgot all of her bewilderment. His warm smile and soft brown eyes welcomed her back into the bed she'd vacated. That was when she made the firm decision she wouldn't allow herself to feel awkward around him since they'd only ever have one night. Keely wanted to take full advantage of it if she could.

"Sure, naked Call of Duty sounds fun. I should warn you," she said as she stepped across the floor and bounced onto the bed. "When I play with Sutton, I'm the meat shield."

"Meat shield?" he questioned as he handed her the controller, but his eyes shifted from her face to nearly exposed breasts more than once.

She took the controller and offered him a slight smile in return. "It's someone that acts as a human shield." Settling on her stomach on the bed next to him she added, "basically I'm going to die a lot."

"At least you've played before." He scooted closer to the upper half of her body and settled himself next to her. Even though there were several inches between them, the heat radiating from his body warmed her.

"Yeah," she added clearing her throat. "I like killing zombies. I just suck at it." She looked over her shoulder and winked at him. He smiled in return.

It didn't take long for Chance to figure out exactly how bad she was at playing video games or that her greatest skill was putting her avatar between him and whatever was trying to kill them. Still, their conversation turned light with banter and laughter.

"Are you running in circles?" Chance asked from beside her.

"I'm the decoy," she answered, "and my gun is broken." She shook the controller at him.

He leaned over so he was laying on top of her, wrapped an arm around her, and quickly pushed a button on her controller. "You need to reload."

That close, the heat of his body penetrated through the thin robe she wore and reawakened her body's desire. She wanted to kiss him, touch him, and feel him inside of her again. He made no moves to extricate himself from on top of her, and her want turned into need. Turning her head, she moved closer and nuzzled the side of his neck then pressed her lips to the corner of his jaw just underneath his ear. The arm around her tightened, he turned his head, and his lips reclaimed hers. The kiss was gentle and sensual but still managed to feed her lust. Dropping her controller, she turned into him and wrapped both her arms around his neck. His tongue slipped inside her mouth and started to slowly tempt and taste hers.

"Chance," she whispered and pulled away, wanting more from him and wondering if he wanted the same.

"Your eyes are very unusual." He reached up and ran a finger along her eyebrow, sweeping strands of hair away from her eyes.

Keely took his words as a compliment and smiled. "I get a lot of compliments on my eye color," she confessed in a soft voice.

He bent down and kissed her. "Your eyes are beautiful, but it isn't just the color. It's the way you look at me. It's honest." His statement confused her, but when he licked at the sensitive spot on her neck before he rediscovered her mouth again, she forgot all about her confusion. He tasted like coffee and sweet spice, a personalized aphrodisiac for her alone.

She moved closer to him, making sure she didn't miss one second of his sweet mouth. Wrapping her leg around his, she shifted her weight, rolled him on his back, and was delighted to find herself straddled across him. The hardness of his arousal pressed to her center, and she growled in frustration because his jeans were still a barrier between them.

Chance abruptly pulled his mouth away from hers, and she was momentarily dumbfounded by the loss. That was when she realized she might have been too aggressive and maybe, despite his obvious arousal, he didn't want what she wanted. "I'm sorry," she said softly between quiet pants and made moves to get off of him.

His hands shout out and grabbed ahold of her hips, his fingers slightly digging into her flesh. He slowly sat up; all the while his intense gaze seemed to be trying to stare into her soul. "Don't deny your inclinations." He leaned in and kissed the center of her chest, releasing his hold on her hips so he could tug at the loosely tied fabric of her robe. "I like how uninhibited you are." The soft cotton fell away, freeing her breasts. He pressed his face between them. His soft hair tickled her skin, and she giggled. Her giggles were soon lost to moans when he took one of her erect peaks into his mouth. She began to pant heavily, and she started moving against him, wishing the jeans separating them would melt away.

66

Lifting her hands and running her fingernails through his hair, she managed to breathe, "Chance." It was her way of begging for release because the pressure at her core was almost painful for need of fulfillment.

His hands slid from around her back, over her ribs and reached up to gently squeeze her breasts as his mouth switched to the other neglected nipple. Heavily callused fingers slid down her stomach, pausing long enough to tug away the fallen robe ties before they continued their gentle exploration. Carefully, his hand slid between her legs, and she felt those same fingers smooth over the sensitive skin between her legs. Caressing her swollen folds, he parted them and started massaging her. She spread her legs, opening herself to his exploration His fingers found the sensitive nub throbbing for his attention and made circular motions. Her body tightened, she threw her head back, and let out a near scream. The pressure between her legs changed to a pleasurable one that was slowly building in intensity with his careful fondling.

"Look at me," Chance said in a tight whisper. Keely opened her eyes, looked down, and found him staring at her with powerful desire sparking in the warm brown of his irises. A soft smirk pulled at the corner of his lips, and the fingers controlling her pleasure quickened their pace. The delicious pressure made every muscle in her body tense. When he plunged his fingers inside of her, that tension exploded in a storm of incredible thundering waves that shook her whole being and stole her breath. She was only aware of two things: the intensity of the pulses delighting her body and Chance's powerfully lust-filled gaze.

When the spasms subsided, she was barely able to catch her breath because Chance's persistent fingers kept alternating from pumping inside of her to rubbing at the convergence of every nerve in her body. The exquisite pressure started to build again, but before it could be released, she was tilted back, and Chance's body was pressing her into the bed, his lips tantalizing hers into uninhibited discovery. She couldn't get enough of him. She wanted more than the feel of his skin next to hers, more than their frantic kissing. Winding her legs around his waist, she pulled him to herself and let out a disappointed whimper. The thick layer of his jeans still separated them.

Pushing against her legs, he extricated himself from her hold.

"Don't move," he said breathlessly, standing and reaching for the front of his jeans. She couldn't move even if she wanted to. She was transfixed by watching his muscular hands unfasten the snap and pull the flaps of his pants apart. The raspy sound of the zipper sent chills down her spine as she watched him push his pants and briefs over his hips and down to the floor. Picking up another condom, he tore it open with his teeth before his dexterous fingers rolled it into place. Unabashed, she wantonly stared at the hardened, thick flesh standing out from a matt of dark hair that promised of erotic fulfillment. She found his nakedness breathtakingly beautiful with all the planes, curves, and lines of his toned body.

Impatient to feel his body again, she sat up, shrugged out of the robe, and crawled across the bed toward him. With a sly smile, he walked on his knees onto the bed, sat back on his haunches, and waited for her. When she got to him, he bent to down and pressed his lips to hers, grabbed her hand, and pulled her into himself. Her breasts brushed over the warm, silken skin of his stomach and chest, making her shiver as she settled herself in his embrace. She licked at his lips, frantically needing to taste its spicy warmth. Their kissing quickly turned intense and ferocious as their tongues and mouths melded together. Wrapping her arms around his neck, she pulled him closer to her. He responded by folding her in a crushing embrace, enveloping her in the heat of his body. As he sank down onto the bed, he lifted her up onto his lap and in the next instant exquisitely heated, swollen latex slid inside of her. Unexpectedly, pulses of bliss overtook her, and she would have thrown her head back and let out a loud moan, but Chance's hand was suddenly cradling the side of her face.

"Look at me. Let me see how good it feels."

She was rocked back, and his weight covered her as he pushed deeper inside of her and slowly moved in and out. His eyes never left hers. It seemed like he was trying to see all she was and discover every one of her secrets, or maybe just the secrets of her body. His thrusted faster, and she moved with him because the tension promising release had returned, escalating in its intensity. When the crescendo of euphoria crashed over her again, she couldn't stop the cries of wonderment that went with it.

She lost her mind and body to the pleasure of their joining and a few moments later, so did Chance. His face tensed then relaxed as one final loud moan escaped him. She felt him swell inside of her as his body tightened with his climax then he went limp.

Neither of them had a chance to calm down before Chance's lips fell to hers. He took her breath, in return, giving his as his mouth took a long slow sensual drink from hers. Taking her bottom lip between his teeth, he gently sucked on it as he slowly slid out of her. She sucked in air, hissing at the pleasurable sensation in response. He kissed her one last time before lifting his weight and rolling off of her. For a long moment, he stared down at her with an expression she couldn't read then he stood up and walked toward the bathroom. She watched his butt ripple with his steps as she tried to control her panting. He disappeared behind the bathroom door, and she smiled as she ran her fingers through her sweat-dampened hair.

After several more minutes, her pounding heart and heavy breathing settled. Soon after, she got cold. She contemplated getting up, getting dressed, and heading to her apartment, but then she remembered she'd already decided to stay in the hotel until morning. Besides, the bed was soft and comfortable, and her apartment didn't hold any appeal. Rolling over, she lifted the folds of the bedding and crawled underneath it.

Chance would probably leave after he had a shower and got dressed. She stifled the voice that would have liked him to stay and ignored the small part of her that cared. Settling into the bed, she pulled the blanket up to her chin and closed her eyes. It didn't take long for sleep to start to invade, and she was on the verge of dozing when the bed shifted. Rolling back her heavy eyelids, she turned toward the cause of bed's disturbance and found Chance getting underneath the blankets next to her.

"What are you doing?" she asked softly.

"Going to sleep?" he replied, lifting an eyebrow at her.

"Okay." She smiled and scooted nearer to him. Snuggling her body closer to his, she turned so her butt was pressed against his hip, her back next to his chest, and her head resting on the pillow next to his. At first, he was stiff, and she thought he'd push her away, but then he softened, nuzzled her hair, and nestled into her. As she was sinking into the pillow, he wrapped an arm around her waist and pulled her into himself. The length of his body warmed hers, making her sigh sleepily. The oddness of their actions, especially when their unspoken intention was a one-night-stand, was lost to blissful sleep.

8

"Coffee with your walk of shame," Sutton said, holding out a cup of coffee. Unsurprisingly, she was waiting for Keely outside the hotel's entrance with a broad-smiled look of pride.

"Tsk. Who's ashamed? I had sex. No shame there." Keely took the cup of coffee offered, and she made her ascent up the small hill leading to where Sutton had parked her silver dune buggy.

Sutton walked beside her with her hands folded behind her back, looking at Keely expectantly. "Well?" They made it to the car and stopped "Did he..."

"Chance doesn't have anything to be ashamed of either." Keely smiled genuinely and took a sip of her coffee.

"Holy shit, you had a one-night-stand with orgasm?" Sutton jumped up and down clapping. "Lucky."

"Like he wasn't." Keely giggled as she opened the car door and sat down into it. "Okay, yes, I got lucky," Keely admitted. "That man is too sexy for my good."

Sutton walked around the car and slid in behind the driver's seat. "Does this mean you'll be seeing him again?"

"I want to. He's so sexy, damn. But he's probably younger than me; he's shorter, and I hunt monsters. So, no." Keely shook her head. "And believe it or not, I paid attention to all your lectures about bartenders and rocker-guys."

"To be fair, I was using those tropes for example."

"Tropey or not, he is a rocker-guy, and I have no intention of succumbing to his charms," Keely stated. "Well, completely succumbing, anyway."

Earlier, she'd come to wakefulness with a pleasant warmth radiating through her chest. It was only after she'd opened her eyes she realized she was curled against Chance's broad back with her hand draped over him and her fingers laced through his. For a few minutes, she lay staring at his mussed hair as the morning light reflected blacks, blues, and reds in its dark color. Then she caught and mentally shook herself. One-night-stands were not supposed to be as intimate as she had felt at that moment. Plus, she considered herself intelligent and heeded Sutton's warning not to fall for the rocker-guy. Casting an illusion of absolute silence over Chance, she got out of the bed and quickly got dressed. When she left the hotel room, she made sure to pay for an extra night so Chance would have the luxury of the room for as long as he wanted. She left him sleeping peacefully, without saying goodbye or leaving a note, but still silently thanking him.

"So, what do you want to do today. We've still got another day of vacation. Maybe even longer actually, the ministry has not scheduled your ceremonial introduction until next week." She sat back in her seat and looked at Keely.

"Well." Keely thought about it. "I need a bath and some panties."

"Seriously?" Sutton asked. "You're that woman?"

"I'm afraid I am," Keely admitted. "Get some food, unpack, go shopping, maybe do the sight-seeing thing. Definitely check out an onsen. I hear Japanese hot springs are the best."

"I want to tell you, it's good to see you smile. I like it." Sutton paused and smiled at Keely. "And that's all totally accomplishable." Sutton put the key in the ignition, twisted it, and gassed the engine to life. "But I was informed your welcoming ceremony included a day at a spa."

"Oh god." Keely rolled her eyes. "You mean a day pampering and preparing the Priestess to be presented to her ministry." She let out a heavy sigh. "How about we go to an onsen with good food and rent a with a private spa and a good view."

"Sounds like a plan." Sutton turned the wheel and pulled out into the street. "After you unpack. You've been living out of boxes since Cuba, and I'm sick of looking at it."

"Okay," Keely agreed, taking a sip of her coffee. "But..."

"No arguing." Sutton gave her a stern look.

Keely laughed at her friend. "Our apartments are," she pointed behind them, "that way."

∞ ∞ ∞ ∞ ∞

72

"So, when are you going to tell me what happened with Keely?" Tau asked casually from beside Chance as they walked down a busy street in Ochanomizu district of Tokyo. It was the university region and also housed a lot of music and instrument stores. He needed some new bass strings and a couple other pieces for some of his guitars. Usually he'd get them from the record company or have them delivered, but he liked going to the instrument shops. He liked holding and playing the guitars or stringed instruments on display. If he happened to find something new and different, it was an exciting day. Tau accompanied Chance, partially out of boredom and partly because he sought inspiration for songwriting out in the world.

"Well," Tau prompted. "It's been over a week, and you haven't said a word. Did you sleep with her or not?

"I don't want to talk about it," Chance replied, trying to be nonchalant but unable to keep the grin from touching the corners of his mouth.

Tau didn't miss it. "Oh, oh." He pointed at Chance's face. "What's that?"

"Nothing." Chance looked away from his friend.

"You did sleep with her." Tau stepped in front of Chance, walking backward down the street, dividing his attention between watching where he was going and scrutinizing Chance. "Did you hear from her? Did you call her? Are you going to see her again?"

Chance felt uncomfortable. He wasn't one for kissing and telling. Tau, on the other hand, bragged about his conquests, past, present, and future. Chance thought it was one of Tau's more annoying qualities. In the interest of ending Tau's line of questioning, he answered honestly, "No. No. And, no."

After their night together, Chance had woken up alone in the bed. He was surprised since he genuinely expected to see Keely next to him. She'd left, and he didn't so much as stir. He suffered from insomnia and was a light sleeper, so it was unusual her departure didn't wake him. After he assured himself he was alone, he'd taken a moment to look for a note, maybe something with her phone number, but there was nothing. The only thing she'd left behind was a pair of dark blue, lacy panties he'd found underneath the edge of the bed. When he'd gotten dressed, he'd shoved the panties in his pocket because he thought it would be rude to leave them behind. However, when he'd gotten home, he hadn't thrown them away. Instead, he'd tossed them in the laundry with his dirty clothes, and Keely's panties currently resided in the back of his sock bin. He didn't know why he'd kept them; he just couldn't manage to throw them away.

Nor could he manage to get the memory of his one night with Keely out of his head. He found himself continually sucking on his lower lip when he remembered the feel and taste of her mouth. The vision of her crawling across the bed, eyes ablaze with lust, preoccupied his thoughts. Distractingly often, he relived what it felt like to have her exquisitely curvy body entwined with his. In the late-night hours, he was haunted by the vision of how her face relaxed into a soft smile as her eyes glazed over when her body was shaking with pleasure. More than once, he found sleep impossible unless he masturbated.

He'd had his share of women. In the music industry, sex appeal was as marketable as music. He was a rock-star, and there was no end to fangirls wanting him. Some had even paid to have him, but they had one thing in common. Almost all of them were obsessed with an image. They memorized all of his interviews, continually showered him with gifts of his published favorite things and acted like they know all about him from the snippets of himself he shared. None of them bothered to try and understand who he really was beyond being the bassist for Eternity's End. They fell in love with a marketed image. Often, he was a conquest, nothing more. Those women wanted their fantasy as much as he wanted a quick lay. Carnal pleasure was all those women could offer. Any emotions they had were based on façade. The women who'd shared his bed knew little to nothing about him. They didn't want to know.

Not that Keely knew him, she didn't. She was different because she didn't pretend to know him, didn't care what he did for a living, was far from star-struck, and wasn't obsessed with the marketable persona. She only wanted the pleasure of his body while offering him the pleasure of her own. They shared one night of uninhibited passion that didn't have the complications of demands. Chance knew, for certain, if he had the opportunity, he'd do it again.

Without warning, Tau grabbed him by his arm and pulled him out of sidewalk traffic. "Did you at least use a condom? I mean she is a prostitute. And how much did she charge you? Was it worth it?"

Chance shook his head and frowned disapprovingly at Tau. "She didn't charge me because she's not a prostitute." Deciding to brag, he smiled and added, "And I used several condoms."

Tau's features were frozen in momentary shock before he smiled. "Of course, you did." He slapped Chance on the shoulder. "Sutton was not nearly as accommodating, but then we didn't get to talk price either."

Chance shook his head again. "They're not prostitutes." He shouldered past Tau and rejoined the stream of walkers, only to be yanked aside again. "I'm done with this conversation," he stated, turning to Tau.

"So you say, but I don't think so," Tau said with a face-splitting smile and nodded toward the window they stood next to. Chance looked through the glass of a coffee shop and was stunned to find Keely and Sutton standing at the counter.

"And I'm sure you're probably wondering the same things I am," Tau added over his shoulder, opening the door to the shop and waiting for Chance.

Chance's feet moved on their own, and he walked into through the door, staring at the two women. They both stood out as they were beautiful foreigners standing in a coffee shop wearing Kimono. Keely more so, because she was so captivating. The sky-blue, silk dress had been painted with pretty pink flowers, and cinched in with a dark purple obi, seemed to suit her tall curvy figure. Her waist-length hair hung free but was kept out of her face by an ornamented flower pin. Chance had no idea why she was dressed the way she was, but he was tempted to take out his phone and snap a picture.

"You're buying my coffee, right?" Tau asked as they joined the line of patrons.

"Sure," Chance answered absently, staring hard at Keely. The women behind the counter gave her a cup of coffee, and she smiled and bowed in return, offering her thanks. She turned toward him, and he thought for sure she'd notice and stop. She didn't. She walked toward the door followed by Sutton and six suited men. He hadn't realized the men were there with her until that moment, and he wondered who they were.

He wanted to call out to but hesitated. Tau didn't. "Priestess?" he said softly. One of the six suited men stopped and turned toward them. If the man hadn't been openly scrutinizing them, Chance would have elbowed Tau in the stomach.

The suited man, a younger one with neatly combed hair and kind face, stepped forward and asked, "Are you in need of our Priestess?"

"Not me," Tau answered and turned to Chance.

"Are you in need of our Priestess?" he asked Chance.

"No. I don't need a Priestess," Chance answered. Frowning and feeling uncomfortable, he put his hands in his pockets. Three more of the suit-clad men joined the man, and his discomfort grew.

The man's expression hardened. "How do you know our Priestess?"

"That is not how we operate," Sutton said sharply from behind the man.

The younger man bowed his head. "Many apologies."

At that moment, Keely stepped forward. The air filled with citrus and vanilla, reminding him of how she tasted. "Thank you for your attentiveness." She waited until the four men stepped away from Tau and Chance before turning her attention to him. The gentle smile she gave him softened her expression and made her violet eyes glow. For a fraction of a second, he was mesmerized. "Hello, Chance." She bowed her head slightly.

"What are the odds you'd see each other again? Especially in a city as big as Tokyo." Sutton looked at him then Keely. Chance had the impression she was trying to convey something to Keely, but he had no idea what.

Keely answered, "Maybe Tokyo isn't so big after all. How are you, Chance?"

"I'm doing well." Chance bowed his head. "How are you?"

Sutton sighed heavily and rolled her eyes, and Keely gave her a pointed look. "Right, Priestess." She saluted Keely and stepped away.

"I'm sorry," Keely apologized. "I can't talk long, but I'm glad we've met again."

She was so formal with her words and posture Chance couldn't tell if she meant what she said. The Keely he remembered was relaxed and outgoing. Still, he was glad fate had somehow thrown them together again. He was about to dig in his wallet for a card to give her his phone number when one of the black-suited men approached Keely.

"Priestess, many apologies, but—" He bent closer to her ear, and Chance couldn't hear all of what was said, but he did distinctly hear the words 'Yushima Seido' which was the name of a nearby shrine. When he was done speaking, he bowed and stepped away.

"I'm sorry. I have to go, but maybe we'll meet each other another time." Keely bowed and turned away from him before he had the opportunity to stop her. He watched her leave the coffee shop, surrounded by four of the men, his mind filling with questions.

Sutton muttered something under her breath Chance didn't understand before she stepped to him and Tau stood. "That was awkward to watch," she said bluntly, and Tau sniggered from beside Chance. Motioning to one of the remaining suited men standing at a distance, she snapped her fingers at him and ordered, "Give me a pen and something to write on." The man opened his jacket and pulled out what she requested from his breast pocket. "Go away." She waved him off then turned her attention to Chance. "I'm sure you'll meet another time because you're going to call her." She wrote on the back of a card and held it out for him. He took the card with both hands and bowed. "Tonight," she instructed sternly. Offering them a curt bow, she turned and left the coffee shop, taking the remaining suited men with her.

As Tau and Chance watched the group disappear out of the frame of the window, Tau asked, "Are you going to call her?" Chance didn't answer, and he went on. "She's definitely into something kinky. No one walks around Tokyo with six bodyguards dressed in an expensive formal Kimono. Some rich pervert is probably paying her to be his live-in escort."

Chance frowned and looked at the card in his hand. It was a plain green card with concentric circles embossed on it in heavy gold in a strange symbol he didn't recognize. On the back was a very neatly scrawled phone number. "She's not a prostitute," he repeated.

"If you say so." Tau shrugged. "You do know you could have any one of hundreds of fan-girls, more than one at a time if you wanted. They'd even pay you for the privilege."

Chance pulled out his wallet and slipped the card inside. He smiled, feeling like he'd gotten exactly what he wanted as he put it into his back pocket. "Yeah, I know, but I want a Priestess, not a fangirl."

9

Keely sat on a thick pillow with her legs folded underneath her in front of several men and women dressed formally in Kimono or perfectly pressed suits. She hated the formal ceremonies she had to endure in every country she was assigned. It was a host of new introductions and rituals that were often tedious. By the time they were done, she was exhausted from maintaining a reserved persona and uncomfortable from whatever formal attire thrust upon her. As much as she'd hoped otherwise, Japan was no exception to the rule. In fact, the ministers and clergy there seemed to be trying to set the standard. Everything she'd done that day had been orchestrated under rigid rules, and the Kimono, though pretty and exquisite in quality, felt stifling. Free movement was difficult, and though the obi made her posture perfect, it was also making her back stiff.

Normally, she didn't find the host country's formal welcoming so annoying. The shrine maiden's dances were pretty, and the clergymen's display of skill with their bows and swords was impressive. However, she'd been preoccupied the entire day. She'd never expected to see Chance again, certainly not in some random coffee shop, her dressed in a formal kimono. From his facial expression, he was as stunned as she was, even though he'd quickly masked his feelings behind bland features. When Sutton had told Keely, she'd given Chance her phone number and told him to call, she'd felt a strange nervousness. She'd spent several hours resisting the temptation to repeatedly check her phone. After actually discretely checking it several times, she'd given the device to Sutton with explicit orders not to let her have it until they got home. After that, she was able to concentrate on the day's proceedings, despite the knot that'd taken up residence in the pit of her stomach.

Her day had started before dawn with a sanctification from the Japanese Cassock. Cassocks were the highest level of the clergy, having been consecrated. When a human soul was invited into heaven, saw all of its blessings, and was sent back to earth, they were marked. Their eye color lightened or changed. Keely bore that mark, but she was the extreme because she'd been tasked with a purpose and given the gift of illusion. Cassocks were rare and could have gifts such as heightened intuition, but only one other had been blessed with abilities as powerful as Keely's. Jasper, was also a Cassock. However, he was called the Sunderer instead because people feared his power. The Japanese Cassock's eye color wasn't extreme, but the light amber was out of place for his nationality.

He was also a kind man, with the beginnings of deep wrinkles and lines of gray in his dark hair, who smiled easily. Keely liked him and felt they'd work well together, but she sensed he wanted something beyond the reasonable request. So, Keely had born the day's long ceremonies, wondering what his ulterior motives were, feeling anxious to know if Chance had called or texted.

Finally, after a large feast and whirlwind introductions, the Cassock got up from his place next to Keely and stood in front of the room with his hands folded behind his back. When the room didn't quiet, he cleared his throat, and a hush spread throughout it. "Thank you all for joining us and welcoming the Priestess to Japan." He turned and bowed to her. "Welcome, Keely Sheppard. As you know, I am Shoma Kagawa, your humble servant. It is my distinguished honor to attend to any needs you may have."

"I'm honored to be a guest in your country, Cassock Kagawa. I appreciate everything you've done today." She turned her attention to the small audience sitting around long tables in front of them and placed her hands on the floor in front of others, bowing deeply. "Thank you for the glorious display of beauty and strength. Japan's ministry is powerful." She sat up and nodded to the Cassock.

"At this time, I'd like to review what we have achieved in our fight with the neverborn." He motioned to a man in his mid-thirties wearing glasses, sitting at the first table across from them. "We have accomplished much."

Keely was out of patience, and she didn't need a history lesson. "I'm sorry, Cassock Kagawa, I must interrupt. It seems you've forgotten Japan was one of the countries where I was trained, and I'm quite familiar with your ministry's accomplishments in the fight against the neverborn." She bowed slightly again. "If I may be informal, I'd like to ask you to dispense with the remaining formalities and tell me why you requested my presence in Japan. Please, tell me, what

80

you require of me."

There was a stifled gasp from the audience. The Cassock lifted a hand in silent reassurance that Keely's boldness wasn't considered rude. "I had indeed forgotten you did train in Japan for some time." Shoma gave her a considerate look before settling back onto the thick pillow he'd abandoned. "Then I will indulge the both of us and speak informally from now on." He smiled brilliantly at her and Keely couldn't help but smile in return.

"You're are correct. We did some political posturing to get you here." Shoma pursed his lips together momentarily before going on. "But, our need of you is great. So great, we feel thousands of souls and lives are at risk." Keely didn't respond, and he went on. "Are you familiar with Aokigahara?"

"Yes. It is known to me as the suicide forest of Japan."

"A crass name to be sure," the man with glasses said, stepping forward and handing Shoma a thick brown folder. "The name attracts more attention, more death."

"Thank you, Henry." Shoma took the folder, setting it on a table that had been brought out and placed in front of Keely. "I can't say I disagree." He said as he opened the folder, pulled out a map, and laid it out. "Aokigahara is a dense forest at the base of Fuji mountain." He pointed to an area highlighted on the map. "It's approximately twenty-five kilometers."

Sutton pulled out her cell phone and began furiously tapping on it, her face was set in a tight frown of deep thought. "It's estimated more than a hundred people kill themselves in Aokigahara every year. Some statistics say more." She set her phone on her lap and looked at Shoma then Henry. "Japan has one of the highest suicide rates in the world. That's not something Keely can affect."

"Let them explain." Keely said softly to her friend and received a look that said, 'I don't like this' in return.

"To our shame, yes, all of what you say is true. But the number of deaths is much greater than what is published. The government has decided to keep those statistics hidden, lest it lead to more instances of suicide." Shoma pulled several more pieces of paper from the folder. "I will say we are an honorable culture, and suicide has always been a part of that honor. However, the death toll in Aokigahara has tripled each year over in a few short years. At one time, it was roughly twenty a year. At present moment, we can safely and easily estimate that total at more than six hundred."

Keely looked at the papers in front of her; they included sickening proof. "That's too high." Keely picked up a paper and read through the reports on bodies found in Aokigahara. It turned her stomach. As she read through the information, she said absently, "Something is drawing people there."

"We have evidence several neverborn have taken up residence in Aokigahara," Shoma said in a low voice edged with sadness and anger.

He produced a map of the forest, and several areas were highlighted in different colors. Keely stared at the map for a moment. "My god, you think there's a hoard there?" She was silent as she wrapped her mind around what the implications of a neverborn hoard could mean. "There could be thousands of souls trapped in Aokigahara. That much misery could be sensed by any living creature. A human could easily be drawn in by it, especially if they were already anxious or depressed." She looked up to find everyone in the room intently staring at her. She turned to Shoma and stated, "You want me to cleanse the Aokigahara."

He bowed so deeply his head rested on the floor. "Yes." The rest of the room followed his lead, with Sutton as the exception.

"Keely," Sutton warned softly, shaking her head.

Henry was the first to lift his head and look at her. "We know how dangerous this is, but—"

"Henry, you speak out of turn." Shoma lifted his head from the floor and looked at Keely pleadingly. "Today's exhibit wasn't just a ceremony. It was a show of our strength; we are all prepared to fight alongside you."

"That's not how it works," Sutton interjected angrily. "The moment Keely freed the souls from the first neverborn, you'd all be instant targets. Protecting you would get her killed."

"Sutton," Keely gave her a sideways warning look, "how many neverborn do you suspect?"

"Thirteen," Henry answered in a cracked voice, his eyes darting from Keely to Sutton.

Keely picked up the map and examined it, her tactical mind quickly thinking up all the problems of clearing such a small area of so many neverborn. "They'd have to be expelled all at once, within twenty-four hours would be okay, but twelve would be better."

"No," Sutton stood, "this—"

"I'll do it," Keely interrupted her, staring absently at the map in her hand, thinking of all the lives wasted and the souls trapped.

"Absolutely not," Sutton said sharply, getting the full attention of everyone in the room. "You can't do this alone, not even with a dozen monks healing you and a magical elixir giving you stamina. You wouldn't be able to fight off that many neverborn once you released those souls. They'd frenzy and hunt relentlessly for new ones. You're going to need Jasper," she spoke the last sentences in Gaelic.

"No," Keely said over her shoulder then turned her attention back to the elder. "There is no question of asking me. I will go into Aokigahara and release those souls." Hushed whispers of gratitude suddenly filled the room, and its occupants were bowing again.

Shoma bowed his head, and she could see his shoulders visibly relax. "Please forgive me, child, but I've already arranged for every clergy and minister in Japan to participate in this battle. We've begun to prepare with the hope you would agree to assist us in this desperate matter. With your agreement, we will continue our preparations. We've also researched and readied some of our most sacred rituals and seals to help and protect you. We are well aware of how danger-ous this task is, and we do not ask you to do this alone. We are willing to lay down our lives to remove the cursed from Japan's suicide for-est. Aokigahara."

"This is not something easily done," Keely admitted honestly as she thought about the battle she'd agreed to fight. "I may not be Priestess enough to do it. However, a word of warning. Do not call in my brother for assistance."

Shoma shook his head. "No, we shall not call forth The Sunderer."

"If you don't, you're sending Keely on a suicide mission," Sutton argued loudly.

"Sutton," Keely warned without looking at her companion, "it's not for you to decide," she reminded her friend in Gaelic. Jasper was strong, but his ability was not kind to souls. He also paid a hard price when he overextended himself. The misconception was that mind/soul reading was easy for the reader. It would have to be something extreme before she'd ask for Jasper's help. Thirteen neverborn wasn't an extreme enough emergency for the torment it would cause him. "No." She shook her head. "This is not something Jasper needs to be made aware of."

"I think it's a bad Idea," Sutton stated but gave in.

"And," Keely continued looking pointedly at Sutton over her shoulder, "I go alone."

"Fuck no," Sutton said in English, picking up her cell phone. "You're not pulling any shit like that. I'm calling Jasper."

Keely concentrated and cast a dark shadow illusion, obscuring them from all the room's inhabitants. All they would see was darkness where Keely and Sutton once were. Reaching up, she put her hand on Sutton's phone. "If you call Jasper, I will dismiss your assignment and call in another monk."

"Keely," Sutton whispered, looking at the floor and dropping her hands to her sides. "It's my job to protect you."

"Consider what Jasper is capable of and how easily he loses control. Think about what it does to him afterward. Think about what it does to all the souls within his vicinity. Think about what you're saying before you say it."

"I get it." Sutton stared at her feet, shaking her head. "But," she took a deep breath, looked up at Keely, and her expression hardened, "even if you dismiss me, you're not going into Aokigahara alone. I get that you're special and all, but… Why are you in such a hurry to put yourself in harm's way? You don't always have to be the hero."

"Sutton, thank you for being my best friend, but I have to go. Those souls are separated from their bodies and heaven. It's a torture that can't ever be described. They need to be released." Keely stood up and took one of Sutton's hands in both of hers. "And I can't risk losing your soul amongst the hundreds if not thousands already there," she said softly. "This isn't going to be a retrieval. This is going to be a release. I will not be able to keep any souls earthbound with so many trapped."

"I'm still going."

"Of course, you are, but you won't set one foot inside the forest," Keely ordered. She smiled at her friend. "Are we done arguing?"

"If you're done agreeing to shit that could get you killed."

"For today I am," Keely reassured her with a smile. Then she frowned and grabbed a fistful of the Kimono she wore along with the panties underneath. "But my more immediate problem, my panties keep going up my butt, and my god, could they go on any longer before they got to the point?" She righted the offending clothing.

"Yeah, they took a while even for culture as rich as theirs." Sutton smiled at her. "I took my panties off earlier. Makes wearing a kimono way more comfortable."

Keely adjusted her obi and looked at her friend. "Who are you trying to fool? You don't normally wear panties."

"I know, and today is justification as to why I don't."

Keely shifted her breasts so they weren't so smashed by the obi then pulled the dress from its bottom so it was neat again. "Okay, I'm done. Are you ready?"

"Yes."

"Remember, you've been rude in front of our hosts, so you better make your contrition look good. I'm tired of sacraments. This has been a very long and embarrassing day for me."

Sutton rolled her eyes. "Lots of apologetic ass-kissing coming right up." She fell to her knees, bowed, and touched her head to the floor. At that moment, Keely released the illusion keeping them hidden from sight. There was collective gasp, and then everyone around her was bowing and touching their heads to the floor.

"This is unnecessary." She walked around the table and between the two longer ones set up perpendicular to hers. "Please. I serve you in as much as you serve me, and I am grateful to all of you." They ignored her and remained as they were. Annoyed, she turned her attention back to the front of the room. "Cassock Kagawa, you have yet to show me the gardens." She prompted, hoping she could speak to him without a room full of onlookers.

He nodded, seemingly catching her meaning. "Of course." He stood and walked to her. "This way, Priestess." He motioned with an arm, smiling and bowing slightly.

"Thank you." She walked out of the crowded room, through some pillars, and found herself in a stone-paved courtyard.

Night had fallen, and the shrine glowed from the strategically placed lights around it. The sky looked like black velvet dusted with sparkling stars. The air was crisply cold, and when she breathed out, mists escaped her and ascended upward.

"It is a cold night," Shoma commented from beside her. "Do you need a jacket?"

"No, thank you." Keely smiled at him, appreciating his consideration. "It feels very refreshing."

"Indeed." He nodded. "The stars warn winter will stretch far into spring," he added, looking up at the sky.

"Yeah, I can sense it," Keely agreed.

"The garden isn't as well-lit at night, but I think you will find it enjoyable." Shoma again motioned, and Keely followed his direction. She heard footsteps behind her and didn't have to turn around to know Sutton had was behind them.

They walked down some steps to a path cutting through a manicured lawn speckled with shrubs and plants. There were also some wide-trunked trees with sprawling roots she couldn't name. They were beautiful with their thick, expansive branches budding with small leaves. It was too dark to see them, but she imagined they'd be a myriad of spring greens. "It's pretty here, and peaceful."

"Yes." He smiled and bowed his head. "What is it that needs to be said between us in private? Or is it that you tire, as do I, of today's ceremonies?"

Keely was taken aback by Shoma's bluntness, but then she smiled. "If I was rude, I apologize. Admittedly, I was impressed with your show of strength."

"It was an unnecessary, prideful display. I have faith in our country's clergy, but there are rumors about discontentment with France's ministry. Our clergy wanted to prove they were willing to fight with you." He folded his hands behind his back and stared at the stars. "I will confess that ten hours of ceremony can be taxing on an old man such as myself."

"Can you keep a secret?" she asked, and he nodded in return. "The rituals of the Vatican City are much more taxing, and they last two days."

He smiled a second time, and Keely found herself genuinely liking the older man. "Child, you are as refreshing as a blooming spring after a long winter."

"And you're as comforting as a warm fire on a cold night."

He laughed, and rich deep tones filled the air. "Thank you for not comparing me to an old blanket. I much prefer warm fire."

Keely laughed in return. They had reached a sizeable, solemn statue of Confucius. He stood, watching over the garden, wearing long decorated robes, with a knowing look on his face. Sighing, she asked, "When do you think I should invade Aokigahara?"

"Our seals will be most powerful during a dark night. I believe it is called the night of the new moon."

Keely shuddered involuntarily when an old fear tickled at the back of her mind. "And how many days away is the new moon?"

"Seventeen, but we will not be prepared. Our clergy will be ready by the following new moon, forty-six days hence, or if you need more time to prepare, seventy-five days."

"Forty-six days should be sufficient if you can prepare your seals." She looked from the statue to Shoma. "I know the souls trapped in Aokigahara will not be going anywhere, but to them, it's a matter of urgency."

"Then we shall be ready in forty-six days. You should rest and prepare—"

"I will prepare, but I will not disregard my duties. If I am needed, you're to call. There's no need for me to rest."

He opened his mouth as if to object then closed it. Several seconds passed, and he just stood silently, staring at her. A frown touched his lips, and he asked, "Child, you're so young. Do you not want more from your life than to eternally fight against that which we cannot win?"

His question and his scrutiny made Keely feel uncomfortable. She wasn't sure how to answer, so she decided to tell him the truth. "How could I want more than what heaven has tasked me with? And our fight with the neverborn may be never-ending, but every soul I return or set free is a victory. That is where my hope lies."

"Child," he repeated, looking down at her as a father would a daughter. "You're truly a magnificent Priestess, and I will pray the battle in Aokigahara is kind to you. I will also pray you are blessed with more than a life of continual fighting."

"Thank you," Keely said genuinely, suddenly finding herself deep in thought. He wasn't wrong. Her life was one battle after another, and because the neverborn were immortal and could never die, there would always be fighting. If she was honest with herself, she did feel like she was missing out on things other people took for granted. Most days she felt defeated. And deep down, she knew she'd always be painfully alone. Even if it was in her nature to want to lavish someone with passion and love, how could she invite anyone into her life? It was tumultuous, violent, and dangerous.

"Forgive my informality. I do sometimes take advantage of the fact I am an old man. It seems I've upset you." Shoma produced a handkerchief and wiped away an errant tear rolling down her cheek. "That was not my intention," he added softly. "Remember child, heaven may have tasked you with a heavy purpose, but you are still human."

"I'm not upset, just…thoughtful," she admitted. "Heaven didn't task me to do this without a choice," she said softly.

"No, it couldn't. Which is why you are so rare. And unfortunately, the truly good are burdened beyond measure." He folded the handkerchief. "Sometimes what seems impossible is exactly what is needed. Happiness is not easy. It has to be relentlessly pursued."

Keely looked at him, wondering if he could read her thoughts. Even in the dark, she could clearly see his light amber eyes, and they had a knowing to them that made her wonder. "I've never met a monk or Cassock like you," she confessed honestly.

He threw his head back and laughed. "I will take it as a compliment."

"I meant it as one," Keely said blushing, wondering if she insulted him.

"Come, child." He motioned back toward the shrine. "I think both you and I are ready to end the day's ceremonies and retire."

Keely smiled at him again. She looked over her shoulder to Sutton. Sutton pointed toward Shoma and quickly gave Keely a 'thumbs up' gesture. Sutton liked him too.

Their walk to the shrine was a comfortable, quiet one. As the three of them approached the steps. Keely asked, "Maybe next time we can meet and talk less formally?"

"I'm available for you at your request." They'd reached the shrine, and he bowed. "For now, I've taken the liberty of having a car prepared." He looked past her to the shrine's entrance.

Keely turned to see a small, white, compact car parked on the street. "Thank you," she said gratefully.

"No child, thank you for all you do to protect the lost." Shoma took her hand in both of his and bowed over it. "What I said holds true. I'm at your disposal." He didn't wait for her to respond before he turned away from them and walked back into the shrine.

"There's something about that man. He knows too much. It's a little creepy," Sutton said from beside Keely as the two of them watched him ascend some steps and walk back inside. "I like him, but he's definitely creepy."

"I like him too," Keely agreed. "Home then?" She started walking to the street. "I'm so tired." She yawned and stretched.

"Sure, but you know it's only ten o'clock," Sutton informed her. They made it to the street, and she opened the door to the car.

Keely slid inside it anxious to get home and out of the Kimono. "Is it? It feels later." She stifled a second yawn. "Besides, what is it you want to do?"

"It's not what I want to do, it's who you want to do?" Sutton pulled Keely's cell phone from the inside of her obi. "You've got a missed call."

10

Keely sat crossed legged on her bed staring at the phone that lay in front of her, hesitating and wondering if calling Chance back was a good idea. His message had been simple, just a hello, tell her he was looking forward to her call, and give his phone number. It had made her happy he'd called, and she thought because of that small elation, it might be a bad idea to return his call. He was the rocker-guy, and there was more than a slight possibility she liked him too much already. Indeed, she liked being naked with him. She tapped a finger on her chin, deciding the fact she wanted to be naked with him was precisely why she should call.

Picking up the phone, she hit the call button and cleared her throat as she waited for it to connect. After three rings, it went to his voicemail. For a moment, Keely listened to his voice, but then she hung up, dropped her phone, and flopped back on the bed. Chance had rejected her call.

Once she got over the small pang in her stomach, she decided it was a good thing. She'd was tired and probably needed to sleep. She and Sutton had a day of home supply shopping planned the following day, and the ministry could call her at any time. Letting out a deep breath, she closed her eyes for a moment before she got up and walked to her dresser. Picking up her hairbrush, she started combing out the tangles from her freshly washed hair.

"Did you call him?" Sutton came into her room and flopped down on her bed. "Also," she lifted a can and shook it at her, "I took your last can of pear juice."

"I'll put it on the list. And yes, I called." She finished with her hair before adding, "Sent to voicemail."

"Ouch. Sorry."

"Don't fall for the rocker-guy, right?" Keely smiled half-heartedly at her friend's reflection in the mirror. "I think I'm bad at this whole one-night-stand thing. I want to do it again."

Sutton laughed as she resettled herself in a crossed legged position in the middle of the bed. "No, it means you're a normal woman with a healthy sex drive. But to be honest, one-night-stands usually suck and lack fulfillment. So you got lucky. It's probably a good thing he didn't answer. You might be disappointed the second go around. So..." She stopped at the sound of a soft hum, picked up Keely's phone, and tapped on the screen. "Or, he was busy and couldn't answer the phone and wants to meet you in an hour."

Keely marched over to the bed and took the phone from her. Sure enough, there was a text from Chance. He apologized for missing her call and asked her if she wanted to meet at the same hotel in an hour. "So, maybe I suck at one-night-stands because I'm good in bed?" She smiled at Sutton.

Sutton laughed before adding, "Or, you're really good at sucking."

"I didn't suck anything...yet." Keely said, sending back a text agreeing to meet Chance.

"Wow." Sutton looked shocked. "That is impressive. A guy wants to spend a second night with you, and you didn't suck him off. Usually, blow jobs are standard. Oh, wait." She bounced over to the bed's edge, stood up, and ran out of the room. "I got you a present," she shouted from Keely's living room before the door opened and closed.

Two minutes later she heard the banging of the door again, just before Sutton marched back into the room. She handed Keely a pretty, white paper bag. Keely took it and looked inside. She reached in and pulled out a pair of pretty lavender and pink panties, and matching bra. Keely gave Sutton a questioning look. "I wasn't planning on wearing panties."

"Boy shorts lend more to the imagination," Sutton explained. "So, put on your shortest dress, highest heels, and go fuck his brains out." She smiled coyly before adding, "and don't lose your panties this time."

Keely smiled in return. "Hopefully I won't be wearing them long. I'm not sure if that means there'll be more or less chance I'll lose them."

∞ ∞ ∞ ∞ ∞

Keely stood in the elevator staring at the blurry reflection of herself in the polished mirrored doors. Underneath a cropped, black, vinyl jacket, she wore a simple but extremely short, dark red, body-contouring dress. It was one she hadn't worn before, but she was impressed with how well it fit her curves. Plus, it showed a lot of leg especially with her tan patent-leather heals. She didn't bother with much make-up, putting on enough to enhance her features. Her hair hung free and fell in long waves to her waist. As she ran her fingers through it, she considered cutting it, but she liked her hair, even though managing was time-consuming.

The bell on the elevator rang, and the doors slid open, giving her pause. Keely had a moment where she doubted if meeting Chance again was a good decision. She had many reasons for questioning her own judgment. She knew herself well enough to wonder if she could keep her emotions out of what was obviously just sex. What if Sutton was right? What if the first night was a fluke and having sex again would spoil that night?

The doors of the elevator started to slide closed, forcing her to decide. She quickly stepped through them, huffing at herself and her own cowardice. She wanted hot sex with Chance, and he apparently wanted the same. All she had to do was go and get it.

Fluffing her hair, she blotted her lips together to freshen her lipstick and felt renewed confidence. She strutted down the hallway, looking for the room number Chance had texted her earlier. Stopping in front of a tastefully ornamented door, she quietly knocked. It wasn't even ten seconds before the door opened and Chance stood in front of her, looking devastating in his dark-colored jeans, and t-shirt, with his dark brown hair falling into his sultry brown eyes. His plump lips curled into a strange sort of half smile as his eyes roamed over her. Then he bowed, stood back, and welcomed her into the room.

She stepped into the entryway, smiling at him. "I'm sorry I'm late," she apologized.

He closed the door behind her then looked up at her and paused. "I haven't been waiting long."

"This room looks a little like the last one, but I think it's prettier." She shrugged out of her coat and hung it in a nearby closet. It wasn't much different from the first room they'd shared together.

92

"You're a lot taller than me today."

"I know." Turning to him, she stretched out her arms and rested them on his shoulders. Her four-inch heels did extend their height difference, but it wasn't something that bothered Keely. She still found herself overwhelmingly attracted to Chance, so much so, her skin heated all over from the simple act of resting her arms on his shoulders. "Does it bother you?" she asked, looking down at him.

"I'm not sure," he answered, his face blank and unreadable. "It does feel like I'm a little disadvantaged."

Keely smiled. "I think you're not considering the advantages of a tall woman." Keely moved closer to him. With her heels on, his face was right at her breasts. For a moment, he stared at her exaggerated cleavage—thanks to Sutton's gift. He looked up at her face and purposefully licked his bottom lip. She lifted a leg and slowly rubbed it up the side of his. The rough jeans and the hard muscle underneath rubbed against her inner thigh, teasing her as much as she tried to tease him. Leaning into his body, she propped herself against the wall behind him with her knee. It half rested on his hip, half on the wall. He lifted his hand and ran his heavily callused fingers over her leg, causing her skin to react. "Besides," she said lowly. "Is it a disadvantage when my legs are wrapped around you?"

"No," he said, lifting his face up to hers, seeking her lips. She bent her head to his and almost immediately found herself lost in the heated spice of his mouth. He wrapped an arm around her waist, firmly holding her against him as his velvety tongue made a careful exploration of her mouth. The hand pressed into her back slid down over her butt and cupped it. He pulled his mouth away. "I've decided. I definitely like you in heels." He tilted his head down, and she felt his teeth scrape against the fabric over her nipple, making her shiver. She raked her fingers through his hair, and he turned his attention to her other breast, this time gently pulling it into his mouth despite the barriers of her bra and dress.

"Chance," she sighed out, and his lips were on hers again, his tongue tangling and tempting hers to frenzy.

He suddenly pulled away. "I think I've developed a fetish for taller women," he confessed huskily.

"By the end of the night, I'll make sure you have." She smiled down at him as she pulled away, stepped out of her heels, and walked into the room. Grabbing the hem of her dress, she drew it up her body before pulling it over her head and tossing it onto a nearby chair. She ran her fingers through her tousled hair and turned to find Chance staring at her as if she was something to be devoured. Mesmerized by the slight smile that touched the corners of his lips and the lust that darkened his eyes and face, she reached behind herself, unfastened her bra, and let the straps fall down her shoulders. "Tall women have lots of advantages," she said, slowly pulling the bra down over her breasts and sliding it off her arms before tossing it onto the chair with her dress.

"I believe you." Chance marched across the room and yanked her to himself. His mouth found hers again as one of his hands traveled up her stomach and gently caressed one of her breasts. Both his hand and his mouth were deliciously hot, and she yearned to feel more of his skin. Reaching for the t-shirt, she grabbed handfuls of it and pulled it over his head. She had no idea where it fell because in the next instant, Chance grasped her waist and roughly pulled her back to himself. The warm, silky skin of his chest pressed to hers. She was set on fire with arousal, and she let out a small moan of pleasure as his mouth continued its wonderful onslaught against hers.

He let out a low sound that vibrated against her lips. She had the thought she liked making him react and wanted to do more of it. The idea of making him lose control and moan out loud excited her nearly as much as his lips and hands. She pulled her mouth away and slowly kissed down his jaw, and over his neck, stopping to gently suckle at his earlobe. She flattened her tongue, licking at his neck and eliciting an encouraging sigh from him. After exploring his neck and collarbone with her lips, she lightly pinch and scrape at his skin with her teeth, causing him to tremble. She sank to her knees, dragging her mouth down his chest, pausing for a moment to lick and bite at one of his nipples, enjoying the heavy pants she elicited before she found her mouth at his stomach. His skin was soft smooth and tasted lightly of salt and smelled of fresh soap. His jeans rode low on his waist, and she nuzzled her face into the beautiful divot above his hip, kissing and suckling the soft flesh there. Keely thought Chance was sexy, and she wanted him to know it.

She ran her fingers then her tongue down the indent of his hip and slowly licked and savored every inch of his skin. His heavy

94

breathing was the reward for her diligence. Loosening his belt, she quickly unsnapped the button and slid down the zipper. Its raspy sound seemed small compared to his loud breathing. Keely liked the effect she was producing and looked up into his face as she sat back on her legs and pulled down both his pants and his briefs. "And, when I'm on my knees, there's almost no effort involved for either of us."

He smiled down at her. "I've definitely got a fetish for tall woman," he said in a cracked voice. Glancing at his thickly swollen member standing out against a mat of soft dark hair, she took it into her hands and gently kissed its tip. Her eyes went back to his face because she was anxious to watch his reactions. She was satisfied to see the parting of his lips and the hiccup of his breath. Purposefully she ran her lips down the side of his shaft before she allowed her tongue to rub back up it and circle its tip. He let out a low groan that excited her, and again she licked at the tip, circled her tongue around its rim then took him into her mouth.

He snapped his head back, letting out a louder moan, and his hand came up to rest on her head. Exhilarated, she started moving her head so he glided in and out of her mouth, slowly at first, but gradually picking up speed. She moved in time with his moans, and the deeper she let him go into the back of her throat the louder they got. So, she took him in as far as she could, sucking and licking his shaft with her tongue at the same time.

Unexpectedly, he pulled away and pushed her off of himself. Momentarily, she was confused and could do nothing more than stare at his steadily rising and falling chest. Her confusion was soon followed by painful embarrassment. Maybe she'd misread his signals and hadn't pleased him at all. Carefully, she came up off her knees, sat on the bed and looked away from him, wondering what she did wrong and ashamed of her lack of prowess.

"Keely," he finally managed to say softly, but she still couldn't look at him.

Her face felt like it was burning. Would Chance know how inexperienced she was? Would he know most of her sexual teachings came from her own curiosity and adult websites? She was uncertain and still felt awkward. "I just liked…giving you a blow job," she admitted then cleared her throat. "I think I'm more enthusiastic than proficient."

"Keely," he repeated, breathing out heavily, and she felt her hair being brushed away from her face. She was still trying to figure out what she should say or do when he said, "I want more than a blow job from you." Two long fingers pressed beneath her chin, lifting her head and turning her face. She had no choice but to look at him and face her embarrassment. She lifted her eyes to his face. He stared down at her with an expression somewhere between lustful and fascinated. "I want to take advantage of the fact that you like giving me a blow job." He smiled and pushed his pants and briefs down over his legs and to the floor. "I really like both your enthusiasm and proficiency, but I want to explore my developing fetish for taller women more."

Her emotions immediately untwisted themselves at his reassurance, and she couldn't stop the smile wanting to make itself known. She tried to think of something confident and funny to say but found herself at a loss for words. Her brain wouldn't move beyond the fact that he stood in front of her naked with his swollen lips inviting her and his erect manhood promising enjoyment. He stepped closer to her and then his mouth was on hers again. Using his weight, he crushed her into the bed, and she wound her arms around him.

After several long minutes of frenzied kissing, he pulled his mouth away from hers. Keely would have voiced a moan in protest, but then he started teasing her skin with his lips. He kissed her neck, her collarbone, and then his mouth was alternating between her breasts, licking, suckling and gently biting at each nipple equally. His fingernails lightly scraped against her skin as he dug his fingers underneath the edge of her panties and slid them down her legs then off. He was back on top of her, kissing her again, and wrapping her in the velvety heat of his hot body. His mouth gave and took all hers had to offer.

Suddenly, she was impatient for fulfillment. "Chance," she moaned. "I don't like being teased." She pushed him off and rolled sideways, not to get away from him, but to reach for one of the condoms sitting in a basket at the top of the bed. As she reached out, he fell onto the bed behind her, pulled her body to his, making sure she felt every heated, electrifying inch of it. One of his hands fished underneath and wrapped around her. The other rubbed over her breast, down her side, and along her leg. He curled his fingers into the flesh of her thigh, pulling it up and slightly twisting it so it rested on his leg. Then his other hand was between her legs, and she forgot all about the condom in her hand, dropping it on the bed. His fingers started manipulating her sensitive nub and were soon joined by his other hand as he carefully slid in and out of her. The tension inside her immediately got unbearable and begged for release.

"Please don't stop," she whispered, unsure what language she was begging in as she reached up and fisted a handful of his dark hair. His fingers quickened their circular motion and started to plunge in and out of her faster. In what felt like seconds, the painful tension had built in its intensity and started to release itself in powerful surges. She lost her breath to his lips as the storm of erotic release played havoc on her body.

When the pleasure of her release subsided, she was only aware of one thing. She needed to have him inside her. She reached out, feeling for and finding the dropped condom. Ripping it open with her teeth she reached behind herself and found his thick shaft with her fingers. She wasn't sure how she got the condom on him so quickly but was thankful for her luck when he finally adjusted so the tip of his length replaced his fingers and then he was sliding inside her.

Turning to him, she sought his lips. His mouth was on hers again while his hand both spread her apart and continued its ministrations to her most sensitive spot. It wasn't enough. She wanted to be uninhibited and wild. Growling her out her frustration, she rolled on to her stomach. His body moved with hers, maintaining their intimate connection. She moved to a crouching position. It not only allowed her to spread her legs so he could penetrate more deeply, but it also allowed her to move against him. She rocked back and forth, testing to see of the motion would be as exquisite as she suspected. When he pumped in and out of her, she let out a moan of delight and pushed against his pelvis, so he thrust hard inside of her. It was so exquisite it was almost painful. They started moving and moaning in unison. Shifting, she lowered her chest to the bed thus allowing his strokes to go deeper. Erotic pressure built and released seemingly endless waves of pleasure. She was on the verge of another release when she felt him swell inside her and the fingers on her hips gripped even harder as their bodies slammed together in one final frenzy of want. The last wave of pleasure made her breath come out in heady screams, and then Chance stilled, except for the small convulsions of his body that signaled his climax.

After their moans subsided, he purposefully slid in and out of her several more times before he pulled out and fell onto the bed next to her. She rolled onto her side facing him, wiping sweat moistened hair from her forehead as she stared at him. Even though she was sated and spent, she wanted to drown in the warmth of his eyes, be devoured by his succulent lips, and forever let his hands run over her skin. Chance was dangerous for Keely, since she felt sure she'd forever crave his body.

Sometime later, after her breathing had settled, she felt soft fingertips brush hair away from the side of her neck only to be replaced by lips. She lifted her hand and ran it through his silken tresses.

"See," she pointed out, "there are advantages to being with a tall woman."

"There are," he agreed. "I've definitely got a fetish." His lips were on hers again, only this kiss was soft and slow and full of sensual rediscovery. He ended the kiss by lightly brushing his tongue over her lower lip. "I'll be right back. Don't move." The bed shifted when his weight was lifted off of it.

"Okay," she agreed. Her eyes started to close. If she'd been tired before she was pleasantly exhausted after what Chance's body had done to hers. The thought occurred to her that she'd have to get dressed and go home, but at that moment she wanted to give in to the happy exhaustion.

"Keely," a soft voice whispered in her ear.

"Hm," she managed to mumble wanting nothing more than to settle into sleep.

She felt movement beside her along with the whisper of fabric moving. "We could stay the night?"

She opened her eyes to find Chance leaning on an elbow under the quilt. "It is cool in here. The bed has a soft mattress and thick blankets."

Lifting herself up, she slid up the bed then crawled beneath the heavy comforter. Chance was right; the room was cool, and the blankets were nice and thick. When he curled next to her and added his body heat to her comfort, she fought against sleep long enough to curl into him then relax into a sated slumber.

∞ ∞ ∞ ∞ ∞

Soft musical tones drifted into Chance's dreamless sleep, pulling him from it. He blinked his eyes into focus and found himself staring at a ceiling he didn't recognize, lit by blue and red from the display of his sounding alarm. For half a second, he was confused as to why his surroundings were so unfamiliar, but then he remembered where he was: in a hotel room where he'd fallen asleep with Keely wrapped around him. Only in waking, something was missing. The voluptuous woman who stole his body heat most of the night.

Reaching out a hand, he searched for the warmth and found it nearby. He turned to find Keely curled up on the other side of the bed with the blanket tucked under her chin and a mass of hair falling across her face. He'd spent several nights over the last few weeks with her, despite having an overly full schedule, but he couldn't help himself. At the end of the day, he wanted to relieve his stress with her body and slept more soundly after their exhaustingly amorous activities. He wondered if he was oversexed because he'd spent so much time with Keely, or undersexed because he'd spend even more time with her if he could. He concluded both.

Tenderly, he reached out and brushed a mass of wavy hair away from her face so he could stare at it. Her features were relaxed into a soft smile, and her lips were slightly parted as she breathed in and out deeply. He wondered why he was fascinated to distraction by her. Mostly it was just sex between them, great sex, but still just sex and light-hearted conversation. Although, he'd never spent entire nights with a woman before, and he was sure that meant something.

Chance wasn't sure if he should wake Keely and tell her he was about to go on a short tour that would take him out of town for more than a week. Deciding against rousing her, he lightly brushed a finger over her soft cheek. He couldn't say why he made the decision, only that it seemed legitimate not to disturb her peace to tell her goodbye. Or maybe he didn't want Keely to tell him goodbye. Either way, he didn't want to say goodbye or have in-depth talks about expectations. Not at five in the morning, and not when he wasn't really sure what he wanted other than to spend the day in bed with her.

Carefully, he got out of the bed and turned off the alarm. Getting dressed, he packed the small bag he'd brought by the dimmed city lights filtering in through the cracked curtains. When he'd washed his face, and brushed his teeth, he quietly made his way back to the bed and sat on its edge before leaning over Keely and gently kissing her temple. He'd never been so sentimental before, despite his long history of bedding women, and wondered at his need to do so. Before he left the room, he paid an extra fee, so Keely could sleep as late as she wanted without being disturbed by staff demanding she leave. By the time he slipped into the backseat of the cab and gave the driver instructions, he regretted his decision to not wake Keely to say good-bye.

11

Keely sat on her bed, brushing her hair, satisfied with her accomplishments. Starting the day early, she unpacked and decorated her apartment. It had been more than a year since she'd done little more than unpack the necessities. She'd forgotten she owned so much stuff, so it was like unwrapping presents for most of the morning. Looking around her bedroom, she appreciated the familiarity that came with her possessions put where they belong and not in a box. After she'd finished decorating her apartment, she and Sutton went out to get food and do some shopping. Luckily for her, they'd stumbled onto a fantastic stylist while they were out. So, she also managed to get a cut, dye, and blow-out. Her hair had also gone neglected, and it felt good having it styled again.

Getting her apartment in order and spoiling herself had been a good distraction from the disappointment annoying her. She hadn't heard from Chance in four days. The morning after they'd spent their last night together, she had awakened alone. Finding herself in an empty hotel room was exactly what she'd expected. She really didn't anticipate hearing from Chance after. Nevertheless, she missed him a little and wanted to see him again.

She'd spent the first day after she'd last seen him constantly checking her phone and irritated at herself for doing so. The second day she'd sent him a text asking him if he wanted to meet that evening. At the end of day three, there was no response, so she decided he'd lost interest. On day four, she'd given it thought and concluded it was good he didn't call or text. She'd developed feelings for Chance, even if they couldn't be defined. It was best to cut it off before her feelings went any deeper. Because of who she was, she'd inevitably have to leave Japan and him.

At least she had the memory of him, even if she was saddened; he'd left her in the quiet hours of the morning their last night together. Still, she couldn't be mad, considering she'd done the same thing their first night together. Sighing to herself, she stood, slid her bathrobe off, and pulled on a pair of pajama shorts covered in pink bunnies and matching camisole. Picking up the remote to her television, she turned on her streaming service. Sutton had recommended an eighties-genre, thriller horror that held the promise of drowning out her continued thoughts of Chance.

The show was still loading when her phone started sounding and vibrating. She paused its progress with an audible huff. It was nearly midnight, she really wanted to watch a movie and not think about anything, so of course, the ministry would be calling. When she picked up her phone and saw Chance's number, she almost dropped it. Fumbling with the phone, she finally managed to slide the answer indicator across the screen and say, "Hello."

"Did I wake you?" Chance asked.

She answered, "No," through a smile.

"I would have called sooner. I've been on tour, it has been busy, and I haven't been alone until now. Sending a text to explain seemed...lacking," he clarified.

"I understand," she said honestly. "It sounds like things have been hectic."

"Yeah," he agreed. "We're on a short tour, and long or short tours are hectic. I would have explained, but I didn't want to wake you the morning I left. You looked very peaceful."

"Yeah, I guess I was tired. Thank you. You were right though; the bed was soft and warm."

"Did you miss me?" he asked.

"Well, it did get a little cold after you left," she teased.

He laughed rich musical tones that tickled her ear and made her smile. "What have you been doing?"

"Well, I got my apartment unpacked and decorated, went shopping for some appliances and dishes, and normal, boring, girl pampering," she said, staring at her freshly painted fingernails. "What about you?"

He let out a sigh. "Well, our tour van broke down the first day, and it feels like we've been behind since." He went on to talk about how frantic his trip had been and how they were continually behind schedule. Keely could easily imagine how an agenda of meet and greets, interviews, and then performances could be overwhelming. Not that Chance complained, he didn't, he just felt the last couple of days had been rife with chaotic rushing. When he talked about per-

102

forming and their audience's reactions, she was almost jealous. Keely could see he loved making music, playing, and affecting people with it. In her opinion Chance wasn't just a musician who wanted a rock and roll lifestyle full of attention, money, and women. He was a musician who loved his chosen craft.

"Despite that, I really think our fans had fun," he said in conclusion.

"I'm sure. I've seen Eternity's End play. You all have very powerful stage presence; you play well, and you're exciting to watch."

"So, I have a new fan?" he asked.

"I don't know yet. I've only seen you play once, but I will make sure to go and buy some of your CD's next time I go shopping and let you know."

"You could ask me for them. I'd give them to you," Chance pointed out.

"Well…" Keely paused. "See the thing is, what I should have said is, I went shopping and bought all of Eternity's Ends' CD's and planned on listening to them later. It just seemed kind of awkward and stalkery to admit."

"I did think you were a stalker," he confessed in a voice tinged with laughter. "I thought it was weird when I first saw you in the café, then at our gig that night." He paused. "But you weren't there to see Eternity's End or even me, were you?"

"Well." Keely swallowed. "You put on a good show, and that was definitely a bonus, but no, I wasn't there to see Eternity's End, or even you."

"So, you were there because of your job?"

Keely frowned; he was asking about her obnoxious behavior when she went to his show and manhandled and chased a neverborn wearing a stolen skin. Eventually, she knew this question would come up. "Chance?" she asked softly. "What if I told you my job is very complicated and I couldn't talk about it except to say, I retrieve missing people." It wasn't a lie; it wasn't the whole truth either.

"So, the girl at the concert?"

"Went missing several days before, and her father wanted her safely returned home."

There was a short silence. "Which was why you and Sutton were in the café?"

"Yes," she admitted.

There was another short silence. "So, if you didn't help people, we wouldn't have met?"

She smiled into her phone at his acceptance her partial truth. "Well, who knows I could have become some rabid, fangirl stalker after listening to your music. I could have gone to all of your shows, bought all of your merchandise, and expressed my undying love through fanfiction."

More rich tones of laughter came over the phone's speaker. "I don't think you're the fangirl type."

"Really?" she laughed herself. "What type am I?"

"I'll let you know when I figure it out," he said softly. "What are you doing?"

"Right now, talking to you, but before you called, I was about to watch a scary movie. Is this where you ask me what I'm wearing?"

"No," he sighed audibly. "Phone sex with you would be very frustrating, and then I'd be tempted to come back to Tokyo."

"Well, I'm wearing white, lacy panties under bunny pajamas."

"Cute. Maybe you'll wear them for me when I get back?"

"The panties or the bunny pajama's?"

"Both… What scary movie are you watching?" he prompted.

The two of them fell into easy conversation. They discussed any manner of subjects, and Keely learned how similar they were despite their cultural differences. She found out how varied his interests were. Besides being a talented musician, he spent his spare time, when he had any, building small robots. She confessed about how she obsessively decorated with butterflies and occasionally danced around her apartment when she was alone. They talked about their families, and she told him of Jasper, her brother, and his wife. He told her about his six-year-old twin brothers whom his parents had late in life. When he talked about their misadventures, she could tell he loved them even if she caught underlying tones of exasperation. Still, she could tell that the two children had him wrapped around their fingers, and she found it endearing.

Eventually, their conversation returned to television or more movies. Chance asked, "You like scary movies?"

"In general, yes. But my tastes are unusual. The one I was going to watch tonight, is a thirty-year-old movie about a man turning into a fly. And I have to watch scary movies alone."

"Sounds like something I'd like, and why do you have to watch them alone?"

"Well, I'm jumpy, and I'm a squealer. So every time something scary happens in the movie, I jump, scream, and cover my head. It annoys anyone watching with me. I do like scary movies; it's better if I'm alone. And sometimes that's not the best time to watch them."

"We can watch them alone together."

"Sounds like fun," she confessed. "But there might be lots of screaming involved."

"Don't worry I will protect you," he promised, then added, "I didn't realize it was five the morning."

"No, it's not." She stopped and looked at her phone. "It is. I would apologize for keeping you up and stopping you from getting sleep, but I'm not really sorry."

"I'm not either," he agreed, and she could hear the smile in his voice. "But I should go. I will call you when I can while I'm away and for sure when I get back."

"And I'll answer," she promised before saying her goodbyes and disconnecting the call. She dropped the phone onto the bed and flopped back, smiling up at the butterflies hanging from the ceiling over her bed. She was excited about Chance's next call and couldn't wait to see him again. Before she could wonder at what it all meant her phone was sounding again.

She sat up, readying a quip for Chance since he'd called her back so soon, but froze in place when she looked at the number on her cellphone's screen. Quickly, she answered it and offered a solemn, "Hello."

"Priestess," a soft-spoken man replied on the other end of the line. "I'm sorry to disturb you so early in the morning, but we believe your assistance is required."

12

Keely and Sutton stood in front of large, ornate, Japanese gate. The Gods of Wind and Thunder sat underneath a mansard style roof decorated to their status. The two stone warriors stared down at them from behind menacing masks, their bulky bodies poised to attack if offended.

"I hate six o'clock in the morning," Sutton complained.

"Same," Keely agreed.

"So, this is Senso-Ji. I wanted to come here one day, preferably when it was actually open. You know, as a tourist," Sutton said as two of them walked through the ornate pillars of the gate and underneath a gargantuan red lantern. "It wouldn't have been before sunrise unless I'd pulled a drunken all-nighter and ended up here."

"Well, think of it this way. We get the super special Priestess tour." Keely smiled at Sutton. They walked down a stone sidewalk lined with quaint, old-world shops decorated with colorful banners. All the shops were closed, but their paper-style lanterns and lights still shone brilliantly, lighting their way. Metal doors concealed the wares inside, but Keely imagined them just as colorful and beautiful as the outside.

"You're in an unusually good mood." Sutton squinted her eyes and cocked her head sideways. "I'm kind of afraid right now."

"Don't worry, I will be bitching about being tired in an hour," Keely responded under her breath as they neared the end of the shops and approached a second ornamented gate. Four men, wearing traditional shrine Yukata, waited. They varied in age from seemingly young, to middle-aged. Though each of the men had distinct features, to Keely, they all looked the same, since they all had disapproving frowns. Mentally, she rolled her eyes. She knew why they were frowning. They probably thought the Priestess shouldn't be wearing the skin-tight, black jeans, knee-high boots, and hooded, white jacket. Formal kimono was probably what they preferred and expected. She hid her frustration at their obvious disdain with a gracious smile and said, "Good morning."

"Good morning, Priestess," one of the men, a middle-aged one, said, and they all bowed in unison. "I apologize for calling on you at this time and so informally."

"The nature of what I do doesn't always allow for such courtesies," Keely bowed in return. "What's happened?" She vaguely remembered meeting them at the welcoming ceremony but could not recall their names. She would not ask, lest it embarrassed them she forgot.

"A body was brought to us, and we have some concerns. If you follow us, we will take you to what may be a human shell. Again, we apologize for calling you on such a simple matter, but the body is such that we cannot tell if her soul has been taken or not."

Clergy usually had ways to determine if the body was soulless. It seemed unusual to Keely they wouldn't be able to tell. She looked to Sutton, who frowned and shrugged in answer to her unspoken question.

"Certainly, I can assist," Keely said, wondering if they had an ulterior motive.

"This way." The man motioned to the gate in front of them. The gate had three large hanging lanterns instead of one. Behind it was an artfully decorated, single story pagoda, with a second multi-story pagoda towering behind it. Elaborate, ambient lighting lit the platform roofs and gables, projecting the serenity of Buddhism. The middle-aged clergyman motioned toward the taller pagoda before he turned away from them and walked through the gate.

During the day and even late at night, the temple was a hot tourist spot for foreigners and natives alike. At six o'clock in the morning, it really was a somber temple. The clergymen led Keely and Sutton into a large, stone courtyard, past a group of women who looked like they'd come from a night club. They stood together huddled in a small group, looking nervous.

"Who are they?" Sutton asked the clergy who walked in front of them.

One of the clergymen to the rear slowed his step, cleared his throat, and said softly, "They are hostesses."

That explained what they did for a living, but not why they were standing outside the temple. Keely was suddenly concerned, but before she could pursue the matter Sutton asked, "Did you hire them?"

A tall clergyman who looked to be in his mid-twenties turned and bowed. He could have been good looking, except for the tight-lipped frown that gave him a sour face. "No, Priestess, they came with the body of a woman believed to be a shell."

Keely stopped walking and scowled at the man. "You left them in the cold?" She couldn't keep the aggravation from her voice. "How long have they been here?"

"Only a couple of hours," another clergyman answered; this one appeared to be in his thirties.

"So," Keely ground out between her teeth, looking from one clergy to the other. "These women come to you for help in the middle of the night with a lifeless body, and you leave them to stand out in the cold?"

"They are—" the tall younger clergy started to answer.

"That was a rhetorical question," Keely interrupted him much to his confusion. "My question wasn't meant to be answered. It was meant to make you consider what you've done wrong." She didn't give them a chance to respond. Instead, she turned her back to them and walked over to the crowd of women. There were eight of them in total, and the general dress code amongst them was tiny mini dresses or hi-cut shorts and low-cut tops. They shifted from one foot to the other, rubbed at their arms, or simply stood shivering.

"Hello," she greeted them with a smile and a deep bow. "I'm Keely Sheppard. I apologize you have been left out in the cold, especially when you were seeking help."

A shorter, pretty girl with a round face and bob-cut hairstyle to match stepped forward and bowed. "You're a Priestess?"

Keely was taken aback and blinked at her before she answered, "Yes." Her existence wasn't common knowledge beyond the ministry, and she was sure the clergy of Japan had not informed the women of who she was. "Do you know of me?" she asked, wondering if the woman did, and how she and the others knew to bring a corpse-like body to the shrine.

"Forgive me." The girl fell to the ground despite her bared knees. "My grandfather was a clergyman at a different shrine, and he told me of the chronicles of the Priestesses and Priests of the past. He was very excited to learn a new Priestess had been discovered but did-

108

n't live long enough to meet you."

Keely got down on her knees in front of the girl and unzipped the jacket she wore. "I'm sorry for your loss. I know what it's like to lose beloved family."

She started to shoulder out of the jacket, and the girl held up a hand. "I don't want anything from you but to save our sister. She is my...our family."

Keely would have argued with the girl and forced her jacket on her, but she could see self-assured pride in her expression. She also saw intense worry. If the girl knew the chronicles of the past, she'd know of the neverborn and how dangerous they were. "I will do all I can to help her, if it is within my capability to do so." She put the jacket back on and offered a hand instead. "Let's go inside. I'll look at your sister; that way we will know for certain if I'm needed." The girl took her hand, and the two of them stood up. "In the mean-time, you can tell me about her."

The girl wiped tears from her eyes. "But we are..."

"You're a human, with a kind soul, who has unjustly been left out in the cold when you were trying to save someone you love." She turned to find Sutton standing behind her with a beaming smile on her face, surrounded by the four clergymen who bowed their heads in contrition. "I assume you have some food and tea prepared?" she asked them.

"Yes Priestess," one of them answered.

"Then we will be sharing it with my guests," she added pointedly then turned back to the woman. "Will you walk with me, and tell me what brought you here in the middle of the night?"

"Yes, Priestess." The girl bowed again.

"And," Keely added. "Call me Keely as proof that from now on you and I are friends."

The girl's mouth fell open, and her eyes nearly bulged. "But you are the currier and the illusionist and the..."

"Call me Keely," Keely insisted.

The girl looked at her with a questioning expression then smiled. "I am Aoi. The woman, our sister, is Hannah. I'm sorry for the lack of honorifics, but we don't use last names."

"I understand," Keely responded. The two of them started walking toward a towering pagoda with everyone else falling in step behind them.

Aoi offered a weak smile to Keely, then a sad frown pulled at her features. "Hannah is like our boss, but she is also our big sister. She protects us and makes sure we are paid well. She keeps the abusers and the thugs out of our club, and she's made it one of the most successful in Japan. Japan may not condemn us, but they don't condone us in good houses either. We carry stigma. A lot of people will tell you differently, but we sleep with who we want, not our clients. We aren't jaded or cynical about who we are though." Aoi paused and then added in nearly un-accented English, "We are well paid, well educated, and some of us even own property. But our lives wouldn't be what they are without our sister, Hannah."

"How did you meet Hannah?" Keely asked, switching to English as well.

"The usual way." Aoi made a small dismissing gesture with her hand. "A grandfather who died when I was barely sixteen. I had nowhere to go, no one to help me, and enormous medical debt and no money to pay it."

"Didn't you say your grandfather worked for the ministry?" Keely asked.

"Many, many years ago. Before he was crippled," Aoi explained. Keely wanted to ask the girl why the ministry hadn't taken care of her grandfather's expenses and given him an allowance, because that was standard practice as far as she knew, but she didn't. If Aoi wanted to share any information she would.

"Anyway," Aoi went on. "I was so desperate for a job I went looking for one in unsavory places, but before I could get pulled into a life where I would have to sell my body, Hannah found me." Aoi stopped walking and turned to Keely. "We are not ashamed of who we are, even if we are left standing out in the cold. I make my own money and choices."

"I don't think you should be ashamed," Keely agreed. "Now tell me why you think Hannah's soul was taken by a neverborn."

Aoi opened her mouth to answer, but before she could say anything, a loud male voice yelled out, "Where is Hannah?" in Japanese.

They all turned to see a young man come marching through the gate behind them. His hair was mussed, but he wore well-fitting

110

and expensive looking clothes underneath his long, dark green coat. "I'm only going to ask once," he threatened, emanating violence with his hard-set face and puffed chest.

The women who had accompanied Aoi came together and stood between him and Keely, with Aoi moving to lead them.

"Fun. It's going to be that kind of night," Sutton said lowly with a smile as she walked through the crowd, placing herself in front of everyone.

As he got closer, Keely could see wet streaks trailing down the man's cheeks, and the stale smell of alcohol tainted the air. "Where is she?" he demanded as his eyes glanced over them.

"And you are?" Sutton asked politely, too politely. It was the tone she used when she was hoping there would be a fight. For some reason, she'd decided she didn't like the man, or it could be that he was there, and she wanted to work out her frustration on him. Either way, Keely knew her friend well enough to know if he pushed her, it would be painful for him.

"That's none of your business." He reached out a hand, and it looked as if he had the intention of shoving Sutton out of his way.

Sutton had other ideas. Keely didn't intervene even as she watched her friend grab his hand, twist his wrist, and kick his legs from underneath him. When he landed sprawled on the ground, she put a booted foot on the back of his neck and twisted the arm up, painfully assuring he'd stay there. "You're right. It's none of my business, but then you've inserted yourself into something that's none of your business." Sutton twisted the arm harder, making the man yell out. "Although, there is the slim possibility I could be wrong, but I doubt it."

Keely stepped through the crowd of women and over to the man. Squatting down next to him, she asked, "What is your name?"

"Minori Hattori," he answered between hissing teeth.

"Of the Hatorri family?" Sutton asked, sounding somewhat astounded but didn't let go of him.

"Yes," Minori replied and rested his head on the ground, looking somewhat defeated.

"If you promise to be a well-mannered-gentlemen, my friend will let you go," Keely said, smirking up at Sutton.

"Fine. Okay." Minori said more calmly. Sutton removed her

foot from his head and let him go. Slowly, and with a lot of swaying, he got to his feet, dusted his clothes, and calmly asked, "Where's Hannah?"

"I'll answer after you tell me who you are to her." Keely motioned for him to walk with her and started walking toward the large Pagoda again. It wasn't that she didn't care what he had to say or was trying to be rude, but the clock was ticking on Hannah's life and soul if she actually was the victim of a neverborn.

Minori quickly stepped forward and matched his pace to Keely's. Sutton followed closely behind him, probably to make sure he behaved.

"I'm the second son born to the current head of the Hattori family." He bowed then looked away from her as if he was ashamed, and Keely looked back at Sutton for better understanding.

"Think Japanese mafia," Sutton explained in Gaelic. She'd refrained from saying 'yakuza' because there would be no end to the complications it would add. It was part of Sutton's job to know such things, but it always amazed Keely at how adept she was at it.

"So, your family is…" Keely tried to think of a polite way to put it.

"Street rulers," he supplied for her.

"And strangely enough, given what they are and do, Hannah isn't good enough. It doesn't matter that she's smart and beautiful. They'll never see beyond the fact that she's a hostess. Hannah will not lower herself to be your mistress while you marry another woman," Aoi said from behind them. "Stop asking," she added angrily.

Minori stopped walking and turned to face the women behind them. "You've spoken out of turn," he nearly shouted.

Keely stepped between him and the woman, lifting a hand to silence the woman behind her. "Like you, they are concerned about Hannah. But why don't you tell me about your relationship with her?"

Minori took several deep breaths and unclenched his fists. "I'm the second son, not the first, and even though my family is rich, my inheritance will never be as prestigious as my brothers. I will have to very nearly start from scratch to build a business." He stopped and stared at his feet as if he was deciding what to tell her before he looked at her again. "I asked Hannah to be my wife, and she refused."

"She had every right," Aoi stated, and an argument between

the women and Minori exploded around Keely. The clergy from the temple silently stood by, shaking their heads in dismay. While Sutton smiled openly, entertained by the drama.

Keely didn't let the arguing continue for more than a minute. "That's enough!" She made a point of looking at everyone. "I have a good understanding of who Hannah is now. If you want to help her, then stop your bickering and judgment." She looked at the clergy last.

"That was entertaining, but I was wondering how long you were going to let it go on," Sutton said in Gaelic, still smiling.

Keely rolled her eyes. "Can you deal? I think the quickest way to straighten out whether I should be involved or not is to see Hannah, and at this point, I think it's best I do it alone," she explained to Sutton in the same language.

"You," Sutton barked to the younger clergymen. He startled to attention. "Take the Priestess to the human, and you," she pointed to the middle-aged one who seemed to be their elder, "I'm sure you have a warm room capable of receiving the Priestess' guests."

The clergyman whom Sutton had assigned to Keely stepped forward. "Priestess." He bowed. "I will be honored to assist you." He bowed again and walked toward the pagoda. Glancing over his shoulder, he paused until she started following him.

The man led her to the building through an inconspicuous door and down some steps before they ascended another flight of stairs. They paused at a genkan, or threshold, long enough to remove their shoes, then it was up a second flight of stairs and through a sliding door. She was led down a narrow hallway with highly polished wood floors and matching exposed beams on its ceiling. Near the end of the hall, another set of sliding doors was opened, but Keely knew what lay beyond the doors before she stepped through them. Hannah's body was an empty shell.

Keely could sense souls. To her, every individual soul had a distinct feeling, sound, and sensation. Each seemed to play its own orchestra, but the music could be felt and seen, not heard. All humans emanated this sensation, but the souls ripped from their bodies were louder and had a stronger effect on her sense. That was why it was easy for her to track the neverborn. The side effect of being able to sense souls was, she occasionally got sensations of pure emotion, unfiltered by thought. Those could be very overwhelming. A soulless body was exactly the opposite. The feeling was just as strong, but when she was near a shell, it felt like an unnatural emptiness.

Keely walked into the room, intent on making a closer inspection. The clergy should have been able to tell whether the body was soulless or not. At the very least, they could have called a monk or the Cassock for assistance.

Hannah had been laid out on a futon and covered with heavy blankets. Shells tended to have a cooler body temperature, so it was common practice to wrap them in thick blankets to conserve the heat the body did generate. She was stunning with her heart-shaped face, perfect doll-like features, and long, dark hair. Keely stared at her relaxed expression. Behind her eyelids, her eyes moved back and forth; her hands twitched, and her breathing was occasionally sporadic. Shells did little more than breathe. The subtle movements would've confused the clergy, and for a moment they confused Keely, but then she felt it. A tiny ember of energy. A new soul gathering life force and starting its own song. Luckily, the child was so new to life it didn't have enough feelings or emotions to attract the attention of the neverborn.

"Dammit," she cursed, turning and storming out of the room. "Take me to Aoi and the others," she demanded of the clergyman who stood outside the door with a bowed head.

He quickly righted himself and led her through a maze of hallways and stairs. She didn't pay much attention because she was both frustrated and concerned. The clergyman led her to a large room with bench tables and a large, open fireplace. Tension had settled on the group, and they all sat quietly with worried looks on their faces as two of the shrine's clergy served them tea.

"How long has Hannah been like that?" Keely asked to no one specifically as she walked into the room.

"I found her in her room that way early last evening," Aoi answered, standing up.

"How long had it been since you had seen her acting as herself before that?"

"Um, maybe a day," another woman with long, braided hair answered.

Keely didn't have the patience for them to guess. She slapped her hands down on a nearby table, leaning down and scowling at the

114

women. "I need specifics. How many hours? Down to the minute."

The woman looked taken aback, but she answered, "No more than four hours before that."

Keely pulled out her phone. "Aoi, what time did you find her?"

"About eight o'clock," Aoi answered certainly.

"It's six now." Keely turned to Sutton and gave her a pointed look. "That's eighteen hours. At best, we've got forty-two left."

"Shit, you really like challenges, don't you?" Sutton asked, standing and grabbing a handful of what looked like biscuits from a tray a clergyman held. "Bring me a bag of those," she told him, and he scurried away.

"I'm sorry, Priestess, I don't understand," the older clergyman asked from beside her. "I thought you could return a soul up to the evening on the seventh day."

"Under normal circumstances, I could." Keely stomped through the room and stopped in front of Minori who sat at the wooden table with his head bowed. "But an unborn child doesn't just rely on its mother for sustenance and growth. Their souls are intrinsically linked." Keely hunched over the table, staring hard at the top of Minori's head. "Did you know?"

"That she is pregnant with my child?" He looked up at her with glistening eyes. "Yes."

Keely leveled a hard stare at him. "Then you better hope you can help me find her quickly, or I will lose the soul of the child, and the mother's will be sure to follow—if I even get it back."

13

Sutton was hunched against a wall next to Keely underneath a large awning as rain pelted down around them. "You need to get some sleep. I'm sure we can find a café or somewhere for you to sleep, and I can keep watch for an hour or two."

Keely pulled out her phone, looked at the time, and returned it to her back pocket. "We have less than eight hours," she responded. Adjusting her stance so she could rest her elbows on her knees, she let her head fall into her hands. "And I feel like we're looking in the wrong place."

They were still in what was considered the red-light district of Tokyo. That was where Hannah's club was. Albeit, it was the nicest club on the strip, but it was still housed on the street with other host and hostess clubs. In their research, they found Hannah had strong attachments to her club, the girls working there, and not much else. Since the woman who worked at the club refused to leave the body, and the neverborn wouldn't go anywhere near Hannah's shell, that left only one place to search for the neverborn, Hannah's club.

"I don't know, Keely. It feels wrong to me too. I think there's something we're missing."

Before Keely could answer, her cellphone started ringing. She pulled it out, silenced it and put it back in her pocket. Folding her fingers into a steeple, she asked, "Why did Hannah refuse Minori's marriage proposal?"

"No one seemed to know." Sutton changed the subject. "Was that Chance?" She already knew it was Chance calling Keely. His call would be the only number she'd reject, and Sutton wondered why.

"Yeah," Keely confirmed absently. "When the neverborn took Hannah, she was pregnant, and she'd rejected a proposal from the father."

"Which is weird. Whether he's a Yakuza or not, a woman in love doesn't reject the father of her unborn child without reason," Sutton mused aloud. "I mean you just rejected the guy you like."

"Different set of circumstances," Keely said, then added, "I'm not answering because I like him."

Sutton gave her a pointed look. "I think he's good for you. He makes you laugh and smile and remember what it's like to be a human being, not a Priestess. So don't ruin it by ignoring him."

"Fine." Keely pulled out her phone and started tapping on the screen. "I sent him a text telling him I'd call him later. Happy?"

"I don't understand what your reasoning is."

Keely sighed. "If I answer the phone, it puts him in the middle of this."

Sutton nodded her understanding. Sutton could tell Keely liked him more than she was willing to admit, so she wanted to protect Chance, maybe even protect herself. If she acknowledged it, then she would have to think about all the complications and implications of liking someone. Instead of pursuing an in-depth conversation of Keely's feelings, she asked, "Are you planning on answering eventually or actually calling him?"

"Yes. Just not when I'm…when I'm a Priestess."

"Fair enough."

They fell into silence. A half hour passed; the rain stopped. People had started to flood the streets of Kabukicho, the active red-light district in Shinjuku, and it was starting to become lively. Sutton liked the flashy lights, the themed clubs and bars, and the party atmosphere. It was like an amusement park for adults, an expensive and flashy amusement park. They were still watching the faces on the street when a Japanese man, looking like a pop star, came running toward them.

"I like this part of the job. Hostess boys to boss around." Sutton stood as he approached and bowed.

"We've looked up and down the streets in a fifteen-kilometer radius and have not found the woman you seek." He lifted perfectly lined, dark brown eyes to Sutton's and frowned through mussed strands of dyed blond hair. "I'm sorry."

"You did good." Sutton smiled at him. She really did like the availability of the pretty boys for hire in Japan. She wondered how hard it would be to make that particular one a boy toy. After they were done with their current assignment, she intended to find out. "Thank you for your hard work."

The man looked down at the ground then said, "The Hattori

family isn't one we can disappoint. There will be consequences if we don't find your friend."

"What's your name?" Sutton asked.

"Shige Ino," he answered with a slight bow.

"Shige." Sutton took his hand. He stiffened and looked taken aback, but relaxed when she smiled. "I will make sure the Hattori family knows you worked very hard and were indispensable to us."

He looked down at her with a charming and genuine smile. He let go of her hand then reached into his jacket pocket and pulled out a card. Holding it with both of his hands, he offered it to her with a bow. "If you are ever in need of anything, you can always call me."

"I absolutely will," she replied and took the card.

Keely suddenly stood and addressed the man. "Would there be consequences if the second heir to the family married a hostess?"

Shige frowned and looked as if he contemplated whether he should answer her question or not. "It is not common for high-ranking families to marry hostesses. Marriages of those families, even second sons, are political maneuvers."

Suddenly, Sutton caught on to Keely's way of thinking. "Crap. Why are love and marriage so convoluted? She'd go to the head Hattori family herself." She pulled her own cellphone from her pocket and started tapping on its screen as the two of them quickly walked to Keely's motorcycle. With minimal effort, she had the information she needed. "I have the address."

Ten terrifying minutes later, because Keely had driven so fast through traffic it looked like the cars were standing still, her motorcycle roared to a stop in front of a large, fenced-in house. "There's a neverborn here," Keely said, staring up at the three-story home with large windows. Aesthetically pleasing lights made the beige house glow behind the shrub-decorated, metal gate. It was the picture of serenity.

Keely grimaced, walked over to the white iron gate, and pressed a button on a decorated box. A stiff voice ordered her to identify herself. She caustically asked, "Is there any answer I could give that would make you open the gate?"

"Mr. Hattori is not accepting visitors."

"That's what I thought you'd say. You should open this gate before the Hattori house becomes one of tragedy," Keely warned.

When it came to rescuing souls from a neverborn, she didn't have much patience, and the voice on the other end of the speaker had already used that up. Keely didn't negotiate, and she wasn't compassionate to those that unwittingly stood in her way. "Open this gate, or I will leave this house in ashes."

Sutton dismounted from the bike, adjusting her crossbow so she could more easily access it and its bolts. "Okay, we're doing this." The threat was real for the neverborn, but Keely couldn't be sure what skin it wore until they actually saw it.

"Are you threatening the house of Hattori?" the speaker boomed.

"No. I promise death if you don't open the gate." Keely's body elongated and grew taller by two feet, wings coated in a black membrane sprang from her back, and spiraling horns grew from her temples. The clothes she wore caught fire and scattered into ash on the wind as her skin turned into something glistening and scaly, but sickly, as black veins spread across it. She turned her skeletal face to Sutton and winked one of her flaming eyes before red, molten fire dripped from a mouth overcrowded with pointed, grey teeth.

"We're doing the demon thing," Sutton said under her breath, taking position behind one of the concrete pillars. Keely's demon illusion scared her so badly, the first time she saw it she'd frozen in place, even forgetting to breathe, and passed out from her own fear. Since then, when Keely used the demon, she had to force her body not to shake and to swallow away the knot in her stomach. As bad as the demon scared her, it scared the neverborn more. While they were busy trying to cope with their fear, Keely easily freed their stolen souls.

"I hate the demon thing," Sutton said aloud, suppressing a cringe.

Keely lifted a bony white hand with dark orange flames igniting in its palm. The flame hovered in her palm for a moment before it launched over the fence and flew toward the house. A second later there was a loud explosion, and debris rained down on them. Sutton knew it wasn't real and tried to tell her body that even as she lifted her arms to protect herself from the falling pieces of stone and wood. The illusion was so complete she could also feel the heat from the fire now consuming the house.

Keely's demonic form crawled up the fence like a spider

crawling across a wall before she jumped over it. Sutton ran after her, dexterously climbing up the gate behind her and vaulting over its top. When she landed on the other side the two of them were faced with four terrified looking guards aiming guns at them. Keely lifted her hands, and streams of orange fire shot from her, igniting the men before they could shoot. They screamed and clawed at their skin as they rolled across the ground, completely believing in the illusion cast on them. Sutton almost vomited at the smell of the sulfur and burning flesh. She momentarily scrunched her eyes closed, wishing her mind was stronger so she didn't fall victim to Keely's illusions.

"God, why can't you be a unicorn?" she asked, covering her nose and mouth, trying to fend off the illusion. "Everybody loves unicorns. And how sick are you for coming up with this shit? Burning flesh, really?"

"Shut up," Keely hissed over her shoulder and walked toward the house, leaving burning footprints behind her. When she got to the front door, she was met with more armed men, but after seeing their comrades burning in heaps on the ground behind Keely, they turned and ran back into the house, stupidly leaving the front door open.

Keely stepped up to it. The door and the frame blew apart, sending burning wood, stone, and plaster flying onto the yard. The two women filed into the house, and Sutton followed Keely through the house down several hallways until they reached its rear exit. There, they encountered two more guards, protecting a cowering, white-haired man who stood clutching the arm of Hannah's terrified looking doppelganger.

"Kill it," the elderly man ordered.

The two guards lifted shaking guns and aimed them at Keely as she spat flames at them, catching them on fire. The small hallway filled with smoke, the smell of burning flesh, and sulfur. Sutton wanted to cover her nose and mouth against the stench, but she had to keep her crossbow trained on the neverborn, in case it overcame its fear and attacked. Still, the shrieks of the men made her almost feel sorry for them as they tore at their clothes in an effort to douse the flames.

"Master Hattori," Keely said in an other-worldly voice and slowly stepped forward. "You've invited a demon into your house. I've come to take it back to hell." Her illusion, though it was affecting him, wasn't for Mr. Hattori's benefit. It was for the neverborn, and by

120

the look of it, Hannah's doppelganger was as terrified as everyone else. She sunk to the ground, hiding behind Mr. Hattori's leg.

Sutton's and Keely's attentions were so focused on Hannah that the sound of a reverberated report was a surprise to both of them. Mr. Hattori was holding a gun, staring hard at Keely. To Sutton's horror a blood spot appeared on Keely's low back. It was quickly swallowed by her illusion, but she was wounded, and judging by the size of the hole, it was bad. Sutton aimed and pulled the trigger on her crossbow, it's bolt piercing through the gun hand of Mr. Hattori.

"What do you want?" Mr. Hattori screamed, dropping the gun. His face contorted to madness caused by his fear and pain.

"To protect a mother." Forced to act, Keely closed the gap between herself and the neverborn. The illusion of her demon and all that went with it melted into the floor and disappeared. No one moved or said anything except Keely. Speaking in a language sounding like a song, her pure, powerful voice commanded everyone to listen.

Keely reached out and lifted her hand to hover over the neverborn's throat. Hannah opened her mouth, and a small, sparkling spec trickled out of it and fell into Keely's waiting fingers. Keely took a step back from the neverborn and the confused looking Mr. Hattori. She pulled a glittering comb from her front pocket. It was a gift from Minori and was to act as Hannah's vessel. Holding the comb underneath her other hand, she carefully loosened her fingers. A tiny light slipped out of her hand and alighted into the comb.

Keely's voice filled the air a second time, only the beautiful words sounded sorrowful, like regret, before her tone changed, and her words turned hopeful and beautiful. It was so beautiful Sutton's eyes began to water with tears as the notes of divinity echoed around the hallway. More tiny lights started to trickle out of the neverborn's mouth, hovering in front of its chest between it and Keely. The tone of her words changed again, and as the last tiny souls trickled out of Hannah's mouth, they started to glow brightly, reflecting their beauty and brilliance. Keely's voice and power allowed anyone nearby to see souls. All of them watched, mesmerized, as one by one, they ascended and disappeared into the unseen heavens.

An eerie quiet enveloped the hallway. No sound was heard. No movements were made until the neverborn reached out a shaking hand, grabbing for Keely. Since it no longer had a soul to maintain its human form, its skin tore with its movements, slowing it enough so she could get beyond its reach.

It was Sutton's turn to act, and she did, firing one crossbow bolt after another into the neverborn. Most of them bounced off, only damaging the human skin it wore, leaving it grotesque looking, with its gray stone-skin showing underneath. She needed to focus her thoughts so her arrows would penetrate its hard flesh, but she was distracted, knowing Keely had been wounded. Biting down on her lip, she caused a sharp pain to center her mind. The next barrage of bolts pierced the neverborn's thick hide. Lifting a hand to defend itself from Sutton's relentless onslaught of arrows, it let out a scream. At first, the piercing shriek sounded human, but it quickly faded to a deep monstrous roar.

"I can't kill you, but I can make damn sure it's painful as fuck for you to stay here," Sutton promised as she took a step forward, reloading and firing the crossbow so fast that six bolts pierced its skin before she finished her sentence. She kept firing. Fifty-seven arrows were protruding from its torn apart body when it screamed again, a terrifying guttural sound, before it tore an exit through a wall.

With shaking legs, Sutton followed it through the hole and into a kitchen, steadily firing her crossbow at its back. It crashed through a window on the other side of the room and disappeared out into the night. Breathing hard, she kept the sights of the crossbow trained on the window. She didn't want to be caught off guard if the neverborn decided to come back and claim a different soul. She counted to thirty before she turned her attention away from the window and went back to the hallway.

"Keely?" Sutton shouted as she ran down the hallway and found her friend laying on the ground with the hairpin clutched to a wet red spot in the middle of her abdomen. She lay staring at the ceiling, her beautiful violet eyes shimmering with tears.

"I don't think I can hold the soul." Keely hiccuped and coughed. "Hanna's baby..."

"Did you forget you have a badass witch with you? And you're a badass Priestess who's been through worse, so I know you can hold on to Hannah's soul."

Something cold and hard was pressed against her temple. Sutton didn't have to look to know what it was. She was very familiar with guns. Slowly, she lifted her hands, glancing sideways and assessing the threat. One of Mr. Hattori's men stood, holding a gun to her head, sneering down at her. She found him so comical with his man-bun and foul breath she nearly laughed. He was the opposite of intimidating.

"You dare come into this great house." He tried to sound menacing.

With reflexes like lightning, Sutton grabbed the gun hand and yanked, pulling him off balance. She drove her fingers into the man's throat and jerked the gun from his hand. After Sutton dropped the clip and unloaded it, the gun went crashing through a nearby window. "A fucking thank you will do," she said, annoyed he kept her from helping Keely. "Did you see the thing you were protecting?" She purposefully startled at him, and he jumped back a step and retreated, child-like in his fear of her, as he clutched his throat. "I didn't hit you that hard, pussy."

Sutton turned her attention back to Keely who was now putting so much effort into breathing her body was convulsing from it. "I know it hurts," she soothed and pulled the jacket and shirt away from Keely's stomach, exposing an inch-wide hole. She already knew the bullet had passed straight through. "The good news is, I don't have to dig out the bullet. The bad news, it's still going to hurt like hell."

She put her hand over the hole and carefully started chanting a spell she'd spent many months memorizing. Calling upon the power bestowed on her coven then given to her, she recited each passage, not stopping even for Keely's screams because the spell was so long and so difficult to perform that mispronouncing even one syllable would render it ineffective. Sixty long seconds later she ended the passage, pulled her hand away, and was happy to find Keely's unblemished, pale skin underneath.

"You still with me?" Sutton asked, scooping a hand underneath Keely's back and lifting her off the floor.

Keely took several deep breaths then leaned over and vomited up blood and bile. After she finished, the color came back into her face, and she wiped her bloody mouth on the sleeve of her jacket. "I really liked this jacket. I should punch that asshole in the face for ruining it."

Sutton smiled. Keely was covered in her own blood and

looked like she couldn't stand, but she still had spirit. "At least you have your priorities."

Sutton helped Keely to her feet, through the house, and down to the waiting, open gate, ignoring the hard stares from Mr. Hattori and his men. By the time the two of them climbed onto Keely's bike she was no longer shaking. Hannah's soul would be restored, then Keely would allow herself to feel her evident exhaustion. Sutton predicted she'd sleep twelve hours after they got home, justifiably so.

Keely kick-started the bike into roaring life. "Dude, that ass-hat shot me."

"Well," Sutton settled herself behind her, "you were doing the demon thing again. People don't normally shoot unicorns."

14

Chance stood in a darkened corner, resting an arm on a high table, and politely smiling and conversing with anyone who talked to him. His record label was having an event, and his attendance was mandatory. Industry parties were major networking opportunities, but not very exciting, despite the abundance of free food and drink. As Eternity's End's leader, it was his job, along with their manager, to handle most of the business and promotional dealings. The logistics of the music industry were boring, but he loved what he did, so tedium didn't bother him, as it was a means to an end.

It was early in the morning. He'd made all the rounds, negotiated interviews and live events, and spoken to all the necessary people. He'd even found time to email a few fan club presidents and hinted at new music, and more tour dates. The night wasn't entirely wasted, but he was ready to go home. He wouldn't be able to leave for several more hours, despite being exhausted and irritated. Although, his irritation wasn't because of the party. He was annoyed because he hadn't heard from Keely, except to say she'd text him when she wasn't working. That had been more than a week prior, and all of his texts since then had gone unanswered.

"Hello, Chance," a soft voice said from next to his ear, and he turned to find himself facing a scantily clad, pretty woman staring back at him with a bright smile on her lips.

"Hello, Shiori," he said with a half-hearted smile and bowed his head.

"How are you?" she asked, bowing in return before taking a seat on the stool next to her and setting her drink on the table in front of them.

Shiori was a frequent guest at industry parties because she was intelligent and politely sophisticated. She was also traffic-stopping beautiful, especially when she was dressed up. The record label paid money for her, and other models like her, to be there and entertain their guests. Shiori was exceptional at her job and very popular, especially with the male guests. Most of them clamored around her trying to earn a dimpled smile or a soft touch of her elegant hand. A very few lucky ones got to share her bed. Chance had had the privilege more than once.

"I'm," he paused. "I'm doing well," he answered formally. Realizing that even though the two of them had shared intimate moments, they were still bound by the rules of politeness.

"Eternity's End has gotten very popular. I thought you would do well the first time we met. I'm impressed." She smiled and folded her hands together in her lap. "A lot of people are talking about you lately. Some say you have a fan-following reaching the U.S."

"We do have a small fan-following in the U.S. and other countries. Hopefully, it will grow," he said, staring at her violet dress and thinking of Keely's violet eyes. Absentmindedly, he checked his phone to see if Keely had called or texted.

"You seem distracted," Shiori said with a smile.

"I'm sorry." He quickly put his phone away. Before either of them could say anything else, one of the record label executives showed up at the table and escorted Shiori away.

Tau came to his table after that, looking pleased with himself. "Did you hear? We're going to be interviewed next week, syndicated nationally."

"Yeah, I know," Chance answered. "It was confirmed over an hour ago. You don't tend to notice these things."

"I did notice. Just not right away." Tau smiled at his friend. "This is why you're our leader. You're very driven. It's why we are as successful as we are."

"I'm surprised you don't give yourself the credit. You're a very charismatic singer."

"Oh, I do give you a good product to sell," Tau joked, nudging his friend and the two of them laughed.

Shiori walked back to their table, scooting onto the seat she'd abandoned, and crossing her legs in such a graceful way that both Chance and Tau stared at them. She really was alluring just not as alluring as she used to be. With a graceful dip of her head, she smiled and said, "I hope you don't mind my sharing your table," she asked.

"Absolutely not," Tau answered, smiling at her.

The three of them fell into conversation, mostly talking about Eternity's End, their prospects, and the upcoming interview with a major radio station. Shiori would occasionally be escorted away by one executive or another but would return and continue whatever conversation they had. Soon the party was breaking up, and people were either going home or trying to entice some of the models to go home with them.

"Well, until next time." Tau bowed at Shiori before turning to Chance with a bright smile. "I'll see you later," he stopped and looked at his watch. "Today." He winked and left, leaving Chance alone with Shiori.

"I've had a good time with you, as always," she smiled.

"Me too," he smiled in return.

She stepped closer to him and wrapped an arm through his. "We don't have to end our morning here."

Chance considered her offer. Shiori was beautiful and good in bed. He had enjoyed the nights he'd spent with her, but their encounters were lacking. Now that he'd been with Keely, he knew what was lacking between them. He and Shiori didn't share the uninhibited passion and honesty. Even though he hadn't heard from Keely for more than a week, and had no idea where he stood with her, he knew he didn't want Shiori.

"I'm sorry." He covered her cold hand with his before he pulled it off his arm. "I'm going to have to decline."

"I thought you'd say no." She smiled graciously, and her pretty dimples made an appearance. "You've been preoccupied most of the night."

"I'm sorry," he repeated. "I do have rehearsal and a gig tomorrow."

"I've been working for this industry long enough to know that's not why you're declining my offer." She stepped closer to him, reached out and straightened the collar on his jacket. "I'm actually glad for the person who's preoccupied your thoughts." Bowing slightly, she stepped away from him and walked away.

Chance watched her glide across the room, smiling at the other partygoers as she went, and wondered how often she was told no. Pulling his phone out, he frowned at the lack of blinking indicator. He considered sending Keely anther text but changed his mind and put his phone back in his pocket. Hopefully, she'd contact him in her own time. If not, hopefully, one day, his craving for her would subside.

∞ ∞ ∞ ∞ ∞

Keely opened her eyes, suddenly wide awake and very hungry. The smell of cooking, spicy meat and sweet bread filled the air. Her stomach growled, craving what she was smelling. Smiling at her good fortune, she sat up and stretched, testing her muscles and checking for pain before jumping out of bed. She ran to the bathroom as she always did when she'd slept for more than a day. Twenty minutes later she emerged dressed in a bathrobe. She skipped through her apartment to the kitchen. Sutton stood with a pair of tongs in one hand a plate of fried chicken in the other. Behind her, on the counter, was a plate with a large stack of waffles.

"Oh my god! You made waffles and fried chicken," Keely said excitedly. "I adore you right now." She grabbed a piece of chicken from the plate and bit into it.

"Hot," Sutton warned.

"Hot," Keely huffed and breathed through her open lips, trying to cool the burning food in her mouth. "I love your fried chicken." She chewed the spicy, salty meat and swallowed the juices.

Sutton smiled at her. "I thought your favorite food might get your ass out of bed. And next time, wait until it cools a tad." She went back to a frying pan and loaded two more pieces of chicken onto the plate and set it on the counter. "Here." She picked up a waffle, slapped it onto its own plate, and slathered it in butter before smothering it in syrup. "If you'd have stayed in bed any longer, I'd have been forced to call Jasper. She set the plate on the counter and added chicken. "Eat."

"You don't have to tell me twice." Keely sat down on a stool, taking another bite of the piece of chicken she held. "Mm," she mumbled and rolled her eyes with delight. "How long have I been asleep?"

"Twenty-one hours."

"Well. Falling twenty feet did hurt." Keeling pointed out, grabbing the fork and knife
Sutton offered.

"You weren't paying attention." Sutton put her hands on her hips, looking like a frustrated mother.

Keely sawed off a large piece of waffle and put it in her mouth. "Remember, I got shot this week too," she said between

128

chews.

"Again." Sutton threw her hands up in the air. "The demon thing is fucking scary."

"Hey." Keely pointed the piece of chicken at her, waving it around. "It took me years to perfect and include the smell of sulfur, burning human flesh and hair. And it actually works with the never-born. They're scared shitless of my demon thing."

"It also scares the shit out of people. Hence the shooting." Sutton's mouth twisted into a frown. "Keely, you've fought two neverborn inside a week. You haven't taken more than twelve hours to recover in a long time. I'm not sure you've completely recovered from France. Remember, fractured skull, concussion, three broken ribs, a punctured lung, and the list goes on. I can help you heal, but your body still suffers from the trauma of it. You need some downtime to truly recoup. And now you've agreed to this suicide forest crap."

Keely put down her chicken, dusted her hands and stared at her plate. "I don't know what to say to make you feel better." She looked up at Sutton, noting the moistening of her green eyes. "Priestesses have never been immortal, and I'm not going to stop fighting for the souls the neverborn take. Unfortunately, that means I'm going to get hurt. There's a chance I could die. You're going to have to find a way to deal with it."

"Dammit, Keely, it's not what you do that has me worried." She picked up a bowl with batter remnants in it and slammed it into the sink. "I'm trying to make the conditions optimal so you don't get hurt or killed. Fighting them when you're exhausted or overused is asking them to take your life." She went to a cabinet, pulled out a plastic container, and started slamming waffles into it. "And to be clear, I'm not worried because you're the Priestess. You're my friend, so I am allowed to worry."

Keely took a deep breath and tried to give Sutton a reassuring smile. "Okay, how about this. We tell the Japanese ministry if they want me to go into the suicide forest, I need time to prepare."

"You do need time to prepare."

"Let me finish. Any stolen souls between now and then, they have to do the leg work. Meaning, finding both the human and the neverborn wearing the human shell. And I will only hunt the never-born we come across on our pseudo-vacation." Keely picked up her

129

fork and stabbed it into another piece of waffle.

"Deal," Sutton agreed without a second thought. "And since you've agreed to go into said suicide forest, you start training for dexterity, stamina, and splitting your focus so you can cast an illusion and dodge at the same time. You need to improve your reflexes."

Keely dropped her fork, crossed her arms over her chest, and glared at Sutton. "So the chicken and waffles were because you had to tell me I was going to train? Not as a nice thing to do?"

"That and I figured the smell would get your ass out of bed."

Keely frowned for half a second then picked up her fork again. "If I weren't so hungry, I'd throw this plate at you in protest."

"If you don't want it." Sutton reached for the plate, and Keely slapped her hand with the back of the fork.

"How about that? My reflexes are just fine," Keely taunted.

"Bitch." Sutton smiled at her, rubbing at the new red spot on her hand.

"Rude-ass twat," Keely countered and went back to eating.

"Whatever." Sutton rolled her eyes. "Anyway, when I told the ministry here you needed a place to train, they found a gym and offered some volunteers. We start tomorrow afternoon."

"Yeah, sounds like something you'd do." Keely rolled her eyes. "Uch, training… Do I have to?"

"Yes. We both have to. But I will make a deal with you. Do it the rest of the week, and I will find a nice ryokan for us to go to this weekend." Sutton stopped and smirked. "That's if you don't send for or get a booty call from Chance." She reached behind herself and retrieved Keely's cell phone from her back pocket. "He did call three times."

Keely jumped out of the chair, sprinted the three paces across the kitchen, and grabbed for the cell phone. "I'd say something about boundaries—"

"Please. You'd have told me about it anyway." Sutton snorted and let Keely take the phone from her.

"At least give me the chance to live my life so I can tell you about it."

Sutton shrugged. "I got curious."

"Not a good excuse." Keely unlocked the phone, and sure enough, there were three missed calls and four texts from Chance. The texts pretty much read the same thing: 'Call me when you're not working?' or 'Is now a good time to talk?'. The most recent call had been four days ago at midnight. Her stomach knotted slightly, and she wondered if he'd take her call. She wondered if she had the right to call him. Her life as a Priestess didn't allow the luxury of relationships, even if they were just about sex. The last week had proven that.

After she'd returned Hannah's soul, she'd gotten a desperate call from the ministry about an elderly science teacher. While his soul was not difficult to retrieve and return, it wasn't easy, especially after facing off against another neverborn. She wanted to call Chance, but she felt if she did, she'd be exposing him to the darker parts of her life and somehow get him pulled into it. Protecting Chance was more important than being with him. She looked from her phone to Sutton and then back to her phone, wondering what to do.

"You look confused." Sutton turned Keely around and pushed her out of the kitchen. "Let me help you out. Go call him before your brain talks you out of it."

15

Chance sat in Eternity End's van watching the small ember on the end of his cigarette go in and out of focus as he fought against sleep. They'd stopped for gas so their manager could drop them all off at their prospective homes, and unfortunately, Chance's apartment was the last on the list, after Simeon. That meant it would be an hour before he got home to his bed. After staying up all night at an industry party, rehearsals, then playing at a three-man, or a three-band show, he was beyond exhausted.

Musical tones emanated from his front pocket where he kept his cellphone. He was momentarily stupefied since he couldn't think of anyone who would be calling him at eleven-thirty at night. Perplexed, he pulled out his cell phone and was surprised to see Keely's number flashing across it. Almost a week had passed since he'd heard from her, and he assumed that was her way of ending things between them. For reasons he didn't understand, he was annoyed. Hesitating, he took a long drag from his cigarette then slid his thumb across the answer key.

"Hello," he said impatiently, blowing out a puff of smoke.

"Okay, bad mood. I get it. I'll call back," Keely's accented voice said gently, then the phone disconnected.

He pulled the phone away from his ear and stared at the blank screen in disbelief. Before he could consider what had happened, his phone went off, and Keely's number flashed across it again. Frowning in confusion, he slid his thumb across the answer key.

"Hello."

"That's a tiny bit better, but you still sound like you're in a bad mood. I'll call back later." The phone went dead again.

Chance stabbed his cigarette out in the van's ashtray, feeling more than a little exasperated. He was about to call her back when the phone started ringing a third time. Tau, Ren, and Simeon grumbled at the noise since they were trying to sleep. Quickly, he answered the phone, but waited a full three seconds before he said in English, "Hello, Keely."

132

"Hello, Chance." Her soft accented voice answered in Japanese. "I feel like you're getting a lot of calls today. Am I interrupting something?"

He couldn't help but smile at her antics. "I feel like you're making a lot of calls today; are you sure I'm not interrupting you?" he asked, returning to his native language.

"No, but I can always call back later."

He laughed out loud. Strangely enough, the tension from his exhaustion eased from his shoulders. "I can talk," he said quietly, looking around at his sleeping friends. "How've you been?"

"Busy, tired, and sorry."

"Work that difficult?"

"No. More of the same. Being busy makes me tired," Keely explained then got quiet. "I'm sorry," she apologized softly. "I didn't call, but work was... I can't call you when I'm working.... Even if I want to call you, I can't. All I can do is try and find a good way to apologize after... I mean...when I don't call you."

He could hear sincerity in her voice, and the part of him that was angry and slightly hurt by her lack of communication immediately forgave her. "It sounds like you've had a hard time."

"Yes and no, more the usual kind of thing for what I do."

She'd told him she retrieved people, and he hadn't asked any questions, because it didn't seem like she was willing to share, but now his head was spinning with lots of them. He chose the most important one. "Are you okay?"

"I am," she assured. "How did the tour go?"

"I think our fans enjoyed it." He didn't want to talk about his Eternity's End, his music, or the tour, beyond what he'd already told her.

"I'm sure they did," she said casually as if it was fact. "Oh, so today I got a package from my sister, Addison," she said, changing the subject, and he wondered if she could sense his reluctance to talk about his music. "I haven't opened it yet, but I'm sure it's clothes. She's a clothing designer, so she sends me lots of amazing things. And she puts in gourmet chocolate. I love getting mystery packages from her."

"I would too," he admitted. They fell into easy conversation about nothing really, but somehow, he still found her engaging and enjoyable to talk to. Talking to her made the day seem less strenuous. A couple of minutes later, his manager opened the door of the van and got in, signaling they were gassed up and ready to go.

"So, what are you doing now?" he asked.

"What would you like me to do?" she asked with a huskiness in her voice that made his pulse quicken as his imagination ran amuck.

"So many answers to your question." He smiled into his phone. "But I can't answer it now."

"You should come over and tell me in person then," she invited softly. "I mean, wow, that came out sounding pretty awkward." She huffed into the phone. "Chance, would you like to come to my apartment? Maybe watch a scary movie? Maybe eat some fried chicken and waffles?" An invitation to her apartment was something he didn't realize he wanted until she offered, but before he could answer she added, "or we can do it another time if you're tired."

"A scary movie and some fried chicken and waffles sound good," he replied, wondering if she could hear the exhaustion in his voice.

"Okay."

"Okay," he agreed. "Send me your address."

"Are you sure you don't want me to call you back and give it to you then?" she joked.

He smiled into the phone. "No, but I will call you when I get there."

"I'll answer when you get here," she replied. "See you soon, Chance."

"And I'll answer your question then." He ended the call, and a second later he got a message with her address. Smiling broadly at his manager, he informed him of his change of plans, happy he'd get to a bed before anyone else in the van, even if not to sleep.

Fifteen minutes later, Chance stood outside a glass-front, luxury apartment in the Roppongi district of Tokyo. When his manager stopped outside the building, he questioned then verified the address. Even then, he wasn't assured he was in the right place after he climbed out of the van until the doorman bowed and opened the door for him. "Miss Sheppard is expecting you." He said politely and waited on Chance.

134

It never occurred to him Keely might be an upper-class woman. Her style of dress didn't convey she was high status, and she certainly didn't let on she was a woman of means. Retrieving people must be more lucrative than he'd thought for her to be able to afford such a lifestyle.

"Miss Sheppard is on the twenty-seventh floor," the doorman informed Chance before he let the door close.

Chance walked past a pretty woman dressed in a plain uniform, standing behind a modernly decorated marble concierge desk. She gave him a slight bow as he passed through an expensively furnished lobby to the highly polished, mirrored doors of the elevator. When he pressed the 'up' button, they immediately opened. He stepped through the doors and jabbed the twenty-seven button, feeling more awkward and out of place than he ever had in his life. The feeling was unusual for him, and he wondered why he had such a nervous knot in his stomach. The elevator stopped, and the doors opened to a wood-paneled hallway with marble floors. Dragging his feet, he made his way to the apartment number Keely had texted.

Lifting his hand to the doorbell, he hesitated. He was the son of a middle-class couple and played in a band for a living. He wasn't poor, but he didn't live comfortably either. He'd gone into debt with unsavory people to pursue his art. Music didn't just take hard work, it took money. For Eternity's End to be noticed by a record company, money had to be invested. He didn't regret his decision, and he was meeting his obligation, but he still had debt and not much more to offer. He wondered if he was even at Keely's status. A whirlwind of what ifs and should bes made his head swim. After a few confusing seconds of fighting self-doubt, he found his confidence again and knocked on the door.

The door swung open and Keely stood in its frame, smiling at him. "I was about to call you." She held up her phone.

He smiled back, letting his hungry eyes drink in the sight of her. She looked stunning in her red, lace-trimmed shorts and her blue, off the shoulder top, especially with her hair freed and swaying with her movements.

"And I was about to..." His voice trailed off as he pulled out his phone and quickly took her picture. "You should definitely call more often."

She smiled mischievously at him, snatched the phone out of his hand, and turned away from him. He watched as she adjusted her clothes and tossed her hair behind her shoulder. Holding the phone up, she took a selfie with it then smiled at him over her shoulder. Tones from his phone echoed into the hallway before she turned and handed it back to him. He lifted the phone to look at the picture, but she grabbed his hand and pulled him into her apartment. "No cheating. You can't see it until I call." She closed the door, and he slipped off his shoes and followed her inside.

"Are you hungry?" she asked.

He was hungry but forgot all about his growling stomach when he walked into her apartment. The entranceway opened into a room larger than his entire apartment and partially surrounded by floor to ceiling windows. It was a pretty, panoramic view of Tokyo, which was virtually unobstructed. The lights of the city sprawled across the earth like a twinkling sea and each building was a mighty wave washing over the world. Small apartments with views like the one Keely had cost a small fortune; he couldn't imagine what a large one cost.

In the center of the living room was a muted blue, wingback couch with two matching chairs sitting on either side. A large television sat on a short chest of drawers intricately carved with flowers and butterflies. It was exactly as she'd told him; her entire apartment was decorated with butterflies. A small, glass cabinet the size of an end table held a number of colorfully painted or crystal butterflies. Mobiles of them hung from the ceiling. She even had butterfly shaped lamps. As luxurious as Keely's apartment was, it seemed to suit her.

Keely grabbed his arm and pulled him into the dining room and up to a bar-height-table. "Are you okay," she asked, dragging out a stool for him to sit at. "I know it's rude to say, but you look tired."

He tried to smile at her, but only managed a grin. "I think I'm just hungry."

"Oh, well." She smiled softly. "I have a solution for that." Walking into the adjoining kitchen, she picked up some plates from the counter and walked back to the table. "Sutton made fried chicken and waffles for me, so I can share them with you." She set two plates on the table in front of him. One was piled with chicken, the other piled with waffles. She went back to the kitchen and returned with

136

some plates, chopsticks, and two bottles of water. "I already ate some, but I could eat again."

He looked from her to the view outside then back to her, swallowing the lump he had in his throat. Keely wasn't like any woman he'd ever met before. She was smart, beautiful, and honest, and she was strong. With her looks and her money, she could have any man she wanted, and not just any man in Japan.

"Hey," she said softly. "If you're afraid of heights or something we can go somewhere else."

"I'm not afraid of heights." He picked up the bottle of water she set in front of him and took a ong drink, trying to soothe the knots in his throat and stomach.

"Okay." She looked at him then the set table. "How about a tour?" Before he could answer, she took his hand, weaving her fingers through his, and drew him off the stool. "Since you're already acquainted with the dining room and what I do there, you know, eating, we'll start in the living room." She motioned around the room. "This is where I do my TV watching, sometimes work, and occasionally fall asleep while I'm bingeing a show."

"Bingeing a show?" he questioned.

"Well, sometimes I watch shows in entire seasons." A slight blush dusted over her cheeks. "Yeah, I don't have much of a life outside of work sometimes." She led him out of the room down a short hallway and opened a door. "Guest bathroom." She switched on and off a light, showing him a toilet and a sink. "Which is conveniently located next to the guest shower." She knocked on an adjoining door. "Not much to see there, I kind of don't use it." She pulled him around a corner and opened a second door. "My study." She clicked on a light, revealing a wood-paneled room lined with bookshelves. In its center sat a desk with a laptop resting on top. The shelves were full of books. Their titles were in English, so he had no idea what they were about. "Yeah, not much happens in here. I store my books and occasionally work." Turning off the light, she directed him out of the room and down the opened a door directly across from it. "Spare room with nothing in it." She closed the door, and they walked back toward the front of the apartment.

"My room," she opened the door and pulled him into it. One of the walls was floor to ceiling window, revealing another stunning view of Tokyo; its lights filled the room. A large bed covered in a quilt embroidered with more butterflies sat in the center. Above it was another mobile of hanging butterflies, and there was more ornate furniture with butterflies carved into it. "I have my own bathroom so I can bathe here, get dressed here, and mostly sleep here." She stepped closer to him and pressed her lips to his cheek. "And notice all of it is solidly built."

"Doesn't Sutton live here?" he asked looking around. "It seems big...Lonesome."

"She's has a key, and she's here all the time, but no she doesn't live here. Sutton lives next door." She lifted his hand to her mouth and press her lips to the top of his knuckles. The gesture was both reassuring and pulse quickening. He looked into her violet eyes and the knot in his stomach all but disappeared. Suddenly he knew the reason for his self-doubt and awkwardness. This woman was so much more than he ever thought he'd find in any woman. The realization that he didn't want any other woman was almost calming. Understanding he didn't want to share her either set his nerves on edge, and he wasn't sure what to do about it.

"Why don't we eat?" She led him back to the dining room and let go of his hand as she took a seat. He sat down across from her, and she put a piece of chicken on his plate. "I forgot syrup," she hopped out of her seat, retrieved a dark bottle of syrup from the kitchen, and set it in front of him. "I know it seems odd, but trust me, it's good."

"Thank you," he said, giving her a slight bow.

Picking up the chicken and taking a bite, he chewed lightly. It was deliciously spicy and crunchy, which was in direct opposite of the sweet waffle, but flavors were tasty together. The two of them ate in silence, and he noticed Keely was starting to feel his awkwardness. Maybe she had sensed it all along and interpreted it as a fear of heights. She didn't really look at him and barely ate any of her chicken, just picked at it. After a few bites, she stopped eating altogether. Instead, she sat, leaning her chin in her hand and staring out of the window.

He ate quietly, wondering how to solve the dilemma and wondering what his feelings meant. After he finished the delicious food, he said, "It was good. Thank you for the food."

"No problem." She stood and cleared away the dishes on the

138

table. "What do you want to do now?" she asked from the kitchen. "I mean, we don't have to do anything. You didn't have to come all this way if you're tired." She frowned and looked at the floor. "It suddenly feels weird between us."

Her honesty caught him off guard, but then it usually did. He liked that she said exactly what she was thinking, even if at times it was awkward. Keely was never boring, and the more he thought about it, the more he wanted her to himself. He'd gotten to know Keely well enough to know If he wanted her to himself, he'd have to tell her how he felt no matter how uncomfortable it made him. Chance decided to do something he never thought he'd do—be honest about his feelings. He got up from the table and walked to her. "I think we should talk."

"I thought you might say that." Her frown deepened.

Lifting his hand, he brushed a mass of silky hair away from her face. "I don't know how to say what I have to say," he admitted honestly. "But you should know I'm… I'm experienced." She didn't say anything, and he went on. "Last night I attended an industry party, and a woman I know was there." He stopped and considered his words. "A woman I've slept with."

"You don't have to tell me this." She stepped away from him and went into her living room. He followed. The two of them stopped next to the window, her staring out at the city, him staring at the back of her head. "You know, I know that you're a rockstar and have plenty of women throwing themselves at you, so I shouldn't be jealous. We didn't really have..." Her voice trailed off. "You didn't have to come all the way here to tell me you're seeing other people. I assumed you were. I don't need a detailed explanation about the other women you see. And you didn't have to come here to tell me you want to end things. I know you're polite, but yeah, you could have called, texted, or just not have answered when I called." She stopped and stepped away from him. "You don't have to explain," she repeated.

Part of him was elated she'd all but admitted she was jealous. Mostly he was unsettled since his confession had hurt her feelings. He stepped closer to her, reaching out and again used his fingers to comb hair away from her face. "I'm explaining so you'll know what's in my past."

"I don't think you need to explain. Like I said, I know what the rock and roll lifestyle is like."

"I'm sure you do, but I'm explaining my past because I want you to know that last night, I declined her offer. Shiori, the woman I slept with before." She didn't respond, only kept staring out the window, and he went on. "I'm explaining badly, but the reason I'm explaining is because I want to tell you I don't want to be with other women."

Slowly, she turned and finally looked at him, but she was still frowning and now looked confused. "Okay."

"I only want to be with you," he clarified. "And I know it's selfish, but I don't want to share you either."

Slightly tilting her head, she looked at him sideways. She was quiet for a moment. Then she lifted her thumb to her mouth, bit at its tip and smiled. "So, there's a thing between us?"

"Thing between us?" he questioned, thinking her gesture genuinely cute.

"Monogamy is usually a kind of start to a relationship," she clarified, still smiling.

"I suppose it is," he agreed. "I guess there is a thing between us."

"And we're deciding to be monogamous?" she asked, and the smile changed to a grin that wasn't shy at all. In fact, there was a sparkle in her eyes making him wonder where her thoughts had turned.

"That depends on how you feel about it?"

"I… I like the idea." Her smile was so stunning, he felt like it was a gift for him alone. "And if you change your mind, you will be honest and tell me?"

Smiling, he nodded, feeling like he'd won a rare prize. "I assume you'll do the same."

"I promise; if something changes either way, I'll tell you." He was confused by her statement, but quickly forgot his confusion when she leaned in close. He met her lips for a long kiss that took only moments to turn hungry and passionate. Only Keely could elicit such heady desire, a desire she seemed to share. Her mouth was hot, velvety, and again, reminded him of citrus and vanilla. It didn't take long for his body to react to her passion, and he was crushing her to himself, appreciating the feel of her supple breasts and soft curves.

Suddenly she pulled away, breathing hard through her nose. "I

140

wasn't lying when I said you looked tired." She combed her fingers through his hair and brought her hand down to let it drape across his shoulder. "I'm glad you came over but…"

"Yes, I am tired." He finally admitted, finding comfort in being able to talk to her so freely. "But that isn't going to stop me from enjoying you." He tilted his head up and kissed her. "And I don't have anything to do until tomorrow afternoon."

"Oh, so I get to spend the night with you? How fun." She ran her hand down his arm and wove her fingers through his. For a moment, she stared at him, and he found himself lost in the warm depths of her beautiful violet eyes. "Naked call of duty?"

"Naked anything," he countered.

With a smile he'd come to recognize as mischievous, she let go of his hand, crossed her arms over her chest and peeled off her shirt. It floated to the floor next to them. Her bra, shorts, and panties soon landed on top of it. "Okay." She sashayed across the room and sat on the couch. "I like being naked with you." She smiled as she crossed her legs, leaned back on her hands and stared at him with a soft, inviting smile.

He was stunned by her brashness, but then he smiled, liking her impetuousness. Unbuttoning the thick shirt he wore over his t-shirt, he slid it off and dropped it onto the pile of Keely's clothes. Slowly he moved toward Keely, savoring the image of her sitting on the couch with her hair framing her lovely, curvy body, porcelain skin, and plump breasts. The smile on her face may have been inviting, but there was something more in her violet eyes. It was an alluring summons he couldn't say no to.

When he got to the couch, he lifted his knee to its edge, and crawled on top of Keely pushing her into it. As he settled his weight on her, she wound her arms around him and pressed her lips to his. He explored her sweet, warm, velvety mouth as if he'd never kissed her before, and soon he was consumed by their shared, potent lust. It made him impatient to be inside her. She must have sensed his urgency or even shared it because she lifted her legs and wrapped them around his waist. The body heat emanating from the valley between her legs warmed him through his jeans and underwear, and it aggravated him that he was still dressed. He soon forgot his frustration when she ran her hands down his back and tucked them underneath the waistband of both his jeans and briefs and dug her fingers into his butt. He let out a small moan and moved against her, and she responded with her own soft moan.

The harsh, loud tone of a phone ringing startled Keely. She stiffened and pulled her lips from his, leaving him almost desperate from rising frustration, but then he looked down at her, noticing her suddenly serious expression.

"Is something wrong?" he asked over the sound of the still-ringing phone.

"I'm sorry," she apologized and disentangled herself, sliding out from underneath him and sitting up. "I..." She frowned and looked away from him. "I have to take this call."

"Work?" He sat up and placed a soft kiss on her shoulder.

"Yeah, and it's important." She looked at him with very evident worry. Reaching behind herself, she picked up her cellphone from a nearby table. "Hello," she answered, and he could see her physically tense at the sound of the voice on the other end. After a moment, she said, "Sutton makes those arrangements. One moment and I will get her, then we will discuss the protocols you should follow," she added in a stiff voice.

Pulling the phone away from her ear, she stared at its screen for a minute before she muted it and turned to him. "Chance, I'm sorry. I wouldn't..." She stopped and seemed to be searching for words. "I have to take this call, but I don't want you to leave. I know I'm being rude and very inconsiderate right now..."

There was such a painful contradiction written on her face that he interrupted her apology. "Go do what you have to." He reached out and smoothed away the crease that suddenly appeared between her eyebrows.

"It's not that my work is more important than you," she explained. "It's just more important than me."

He had no idea what she meant, but he had a feeling pursuing the matter might upset her. Instead, he leaned in and pressed his lips to her temple. "I'll wait."

She smiled, and he was caught off guard by how stunning she was, especially when she smiled at him.

"Come on," she held out her hand, and he took it. Standing, she pulled him behind herself and led him back to the short hallway

142

leading to her bedroom. For a moment, he was distracted by her creamy nakedness, but then she turned and kissed him lightly on the corner of his mouth. "If you want to take a shower, everything you need is in the bathroom. I should be back by the time you get done."

"Okay." A shower sounded good, and her bed looked comfortable.

She went back to the living room, stopping at the pile of discarded clothes, she put on her shorts. "Can I borrow this," she asked, picking up his discarded shirt.

"Can I take it off of you later?"

"You won't have to." She picked up the shirt and headed to the front door of the apartment, sliding her arms into it as she went. He smiled as he watched her try to adjust the slightly too small shirt so it covered her plump breasts. After she fumbled then managed to fasten some of the buttons, she looked at him and whispered, "Thank you." Disappearing around the corner into her study, she spoke in such a low tone he couldn't hear any more of the conversation.

He blew out a loud breath, trying to relieve some of his sexual frustration. It didn't work, and adding to his frustration were the million questions he had about what Keely's job was and why she'd acted the way she did. Strangely, Tau's voice made its way into his head. "I bet she's a high-class prostitute." Immediately he dismissed the idea as ridiculous, but he did wonder where the voice had come from.

∞ ∞ ∞ ∞ ∞

The bed moved underneath Chance, and he opened his eyes to see what had awakened him. He turned to find Keely sitting on the bed's edge, removing his shirt. "How long was I asleep?" he asked, reaching out a hand and smoothing it over her bare back. Her skin was cool silk, and it rippled slightly under his fingers. He liked that something as simple as touching her caused such an effect.

"An hour and a half," she said softly. Turning and taking his hand in hers, she wove their fingers together. "I'm sorry. I…" Her voice trailed off. "It's my job, it's unpredictable."

"You don't have to explain." He said, staring up at her face.

143

The lights of Tokyo danced across her skin and made her violet eyes sparkle. There was something hidden there, and he wanted to discover what it was, but he instinctively knew she wouldn't tell him until she was ready. "Just come here." He tugged at her hand and pulled her on top of him, maneuvering her so she straddled him.

He intended to pull her close to comfort her, but his intention was soon lost in the sudden desire that sparked between them. She must have felt it too because she smiled and settled on top of him. The softness and warmth between her legs heated his quickly hardening manhood despite the layers of clothes between them. He regretted not taking a shower and going to bed naked, but when he'd tested the softness of her bed, he'd immediately fallen asleep.

"Maybe I should have gotten undressed first," he commented, openly staring at her magnificent breasts.

"It's a little more fun this way." Her smile changed to mischievous as she lifted his hand to her mouth, pressed her lips to his knuckles then took the top of his index finger between her teeth and swirled her tongue around its tip.

He never thought such a small thing would be so erotic, but the way her luscious tongue swirled around the pad of his finger made all of his skin feel like it had been electrified. It mystified and excited him that the two of them could cause such immediate, overpowering reactions in one another. He was experienced, but everything they did together felt new, even the things he'd done before. It wasn't that it was new, it was that he was opening himself up and less guarded with his own ideations of sex. He hadn't realized how inhibited he'd been, but with Keely, he was free to explore her body with his own, without hidden intentions, just passion.

With one last gentle scrape of her teeth, she pulled his finger from her mouth then turned his hand and kissed its palm. She cradled his hand against her cheek before she pulled it down over her neck and collarbone. The soft velvet of her skin flowed underneath his callused fingers. When she pushed his hand down over her breast and used it to caress the soft flesh there, she let out a quiet sigh he almost mimicked her.

"Chance," she said throatily, squeezing the hand still holding her soft breast. She pushed his hand down over her stomach, across her hip, and down her leg then back up her thigh. No silk could ever

144

be as soft as her skin. Seeking his other hand, she grabbed it and used it to massage over her breasts, stomach, and thigh. The skin of his palms warmed against her, and his body tingled with want. She let go of him, reached down between her legs, unbuttoning his jeans and pulling down his zipper. Her fingers wrapped around his hardened member and gently stroked up and down it, stimulating the tingling lust he was already experiencing.

His breath hitched, and his body tightened. He was torn between letting Keely have her way as he watched or kissing every inch of her. He chose the former, considering he could still ravish her if he lost all his patience. Watching her was giving him a different kind of pleasure, and he was curious to see what she'd do next.

She lifted away from him, tugging at his pants and briefs then slid his clothes down to his hips, removing the barrier separating them. Again, she settled on top of him and the folds of her soft, moist skin nestled around his exposed flesh. She was hot, wet, and welcoming. Arching against her heat, he sighed loudly. She tilted her head back and let out a low moan. He sat up in search of her lips and quickly found them. Their kiss was immediately fierce, and their tongues twisted and entwined together as she slowly started to move against him. A moan escaped him as heated skin softer than silk slid back and forth over his shaft.

He wrapped his arms around her and laid back down on the bed, taking her with him. Their new position allowed him to slide inside of her, and he did so slowly, enjoying the high-pitched moan she breathed against his lips as the hot, tight chasm between her legs accepted his erotic invasion. Their joining was so overwhelming with sensation that he stilled. A shudder passed between them, and he couldn't tell if it was her or himself shaking.

She pulled away from him and sat up, and he slid deeper inside of her. Her fingers scratched down his stomach, her nails scraping over his t-shirt. "I want to take this slow," she explained breathlessly, looking down at him. He wasn't sure he had the patience for slow, but his curiosity had him willing to try.

Bracing her hands against his lower stomach, she slowly moved up and down and his breath caught in his throat. His reaction seemed to please her because she smiled slightly and did it again. He ran his hands up her inner thighs, slightly digging his fingers into her skin. Then her hands were covering his, prompting more thigh caressing and encouraging him to explore and discover her intimately. Curving her fingers around his, she pushed them into the soft folds of wet heat between her legs. He felt her swell when she moved his fingers back and forth against her swollen flesh. A throaty sound came through her parted lips, and she started to slowly move up and down on top of him. Taking the initiative away from her, he started circling and massaging her swollen heat. Moaning softly, she reached down and covered the hand that still gripped at her thigh with hers, making his nails dig into the soft flesh. Her moans got louder. She moved back and forth, intensifying the sensation and making him shudder.

Between the salacious stroking and the way her breasts heaved with each movement, Chance was overwhelmed. It was erotically fascinating, watching her roll her hips back and forth with a look of bliss on her pretty face, at the same time benefiting from her stimulation. Soon her moans got louder. Her movements changed to a serpentine dance that stroked and caressed his shaft, making his whole body tense with delight. He could feel climax building, but before his release came, she stopped moving, moaning; she even stopped breathing as her body started to tremble. He felt her tighten in pulses, and it made him groan with want, but the pressure in his groin never got its release. Not that he minded, as he'd liked watching her ride him and enjoyed his body's response.

When her breathing returned to normal, she was staring down at him with a dazed look that seemed astonished. "Keely," he said huskily, drawing her gaze back to his face.

"Chance." She smiled. There were flames of lust burning in her violet eyes, and she started moving again, but Chance didn't have any self-control left. He wanted to come. Sitting up again, Chance wrapped his arms around waist her, pulling her close to him, burying his face between her breasts. Rolling her back onto the bed, he thrust deep inside her. Her moans joined his as he started moving faster and pushing harder. Again, he felt her tighten around him, and it set off his own climax. He lost his breath as his body tightened then shook with pulses of pleasure.

He was kissing her before he had a chance to catch his breath, but he wanted to capture her pleasure with his lips. Their kiss started out fierce but settled into something tender. Her tongue carefully

146

wove together with his, relaying a sensual message words could never express. After his heart rate and breathing had slowed, he allowed her to end the kiss, but couldn't resist gently sucking on her lower lip one last time before licking the sweetness off them.

Keely looked up at him and smiled sheepishly. "I think I may have gotten over enthusiastic."

"I like your over-enthusiasm." He smiled back at her and again pressed his lips to hers.

"I guess it's too late to have the condom talk?" she sighed.

A douse of cold water couldn't have been more sobering to his lust. He pulled out and rolled off of her, unsure what to say. Potential consequences had him feeling overwhelmed. "Yeah, it is."

She rolled on her side to face him. "I'm sorry. I've ruined the mood." She sighed and flopped back down on the bed. "There are things I feel like I should do and say, but then I forget because..." Her voice trailed off. "Well, it's not a baby issue. I mean that's taken care of. And I'm healthy." She got quiet again. "Okay, I'm shutting up now because I'm bad at this."

"Yes, you are," he agreed, almost shocking himself with his own honesty. He wasn't sure why they were having such an uncomfortable conversation after having such good sex. He was forced to wonder where Keely's thoughts had gone. "You're on birth control?"

"Not that I do this often, but yes." She cleared her throat, rolled away from him, and sat up. "Although, sex is definitely messier without condoms. Anyway...I'm going to take a shower."

He was starting to learn Keely's moods, and he knew she was retreating from the sudden awkwardness between them. Usually, he'd stay quiet, but Keely's honesty was something he treasured. That meant he'd have to listen and receive whatever she had to say. Quickly, he rolled across the bed, reached out, and grabbed her wrist stopping her. "You started this conversation. Whether it's bad timing or not, we should finish it."

"I'm not sure if I want to," she admitted. "I'm not experienced, just impetuous, and you are..."

"Healthy," he finished for her. "I can't change my past. I've had other women, but if you're asking, I'm healthy."

"I know you've had other women." She looked down at him with her lips turned down slightly. "It's not that I'm jealous of the other women. It's none of my business. Okay, I am, but I'm intimidated too. My experience is very limited. And you are..." She stopped and let out a deep breath. "I was only trying to say, I really don't want us to use condoms. I like sex with you a lot better without them. And I'm embarrassed because I should have had this conversation before I...we...I forced the issue." Her frown deepened. "I have cum dripping down the inside of my leg."

He blinked at her, astounded, then he started to laugh. Her candor and her confession had caught him off guard. It was a humor only Keely could bring to his life. When he finished laughing, he got onto his knees, uncaring that his pants were still around his hips. Carefully, he cupped her face in his hands. It amazed him she could look so confused and vulnerable while still remaining so alluring.

"Keely," he bent and pressed his lips to hers. She immediately kissed him back without any hesitation or shyness. "You have cum dripping down your leg because I didn't want to use a condom either." He kissed her again. "If you're offering the choice, I wouldn't ever use a condom again."

She seemed to consider his words for a moment then smiled. "Good. But I still need a shower. You should join me." She wound her fingers through his. He let her pull him off the bed and lead him to her bathroom. "You did cause the cum dripping issue, after all."

Again, her candor caught him off guard, and he laughed. "I have a feeling it's going to happen a lot between us."

She paused to look over her shoulder at him. "I genuinely hope so, or I'll be very disappointed."

16

Keely stood in the small living room, looking down at the face of a dark-haired boy with bright, brown eyes. His name was Yuuto; he was six years old, and she'd learned a lot about him over the past forty-eight hours. She knew he was a smart, funny, and kind boy. He proudly talked of his father and lovingly told stories about his mother. He worked hard and succeeded at school. Animals liked him, and he wanted to be a veterinarian one day. Unfortunately, Keely knew something about him he didn't know himself yet.

His mother's soul had ascended, and her body had died. Keely had been too late to save her.

Yuuto's father, Iesada, must have read what she had to say by her expression, because he scooted around closer to Yuuto and scooped the boy into his lap. "Yuuto," he said gently, hugging the boy.

Keely blinked back tears. It wasn't her right to cry. She didn't even have the right to be there, but she wouldn't let anyone else tell Yuuto and Iesada she'd failed to save their family. Looking over her shoulder, she frowned at Sutton, giving her a silent message.

"Give them a minute," Sutton said to the two clergymen who had come with them. The three of them left, leaving Keely alone with the orphaned boy and widowed father.

Biting back a hiss and ignoring the sharp stab of pain in her side, Keely sank to the floor across from them. It was difficult to find a comfortable position on the floor since her body protested even the tiniest movements. The neverborn had been strong and fast, and its strikes had been precise.

A heavy silence settled in the room, and Keely was at a loss for words. All she could think was that she'd been seven hours too late. Keely had known she was too late even before she pulled Yuuto's mother Kaori's soul from the neverborn. Still, she'd tried to keep her soul earthbound because the boy needed his mother, but heaven's will had become too strong for Kaori to resist. She couldn't remember the loves that held her to earth after being tormented inside of the neverborn for nearly eight days. Though Keely tried her hardest, spoke her sweetest invitation, Kaori slipped through her fingers.

"I wanted to thank you for letting me use this," Keely finally said. She reached into her bag and pulled out a book Yuuto had let her borrow. When he'd given it to her to use, he'd practically recited the entire fairytale before he explained that reading it had become a nighttime ritual for him and his mother. She carefully set the book on the tatami-covered floor between them.

"What about my mom?" the boy asked, looking from her to his father. Iesada simply shook his head and hugged him tighter.

Keely cleared her throat, swallowing back tears. "Yuuto," she said softly. "I... Your mother loves you very much."

"He knows." Iesada declared, tears running down his cheeks. "Where is she? Kaori should tell him how much she loves him." Both Keely and Iesada knew the impossibility of his words, but he was clearly saying them in a desperate hope she would agree and tell him the opposite of what she had to say. He sucked in a loud breath. "The monks at the temple said you could help. That you could bring her back." He buried his face in one of his hands and started quietly weeping. "A boy needs his mother."

"I know. I was just too late." Keely didn't want to leave them in the misery of their loss, but there was little she could do to help them even with all of her abilities. "I can't offer any consolation, but I can tell you your mother..." She stopped and looked at Yuuto's father. "Kaori, she was welcomed into heaven and will forever be loved there. She will forever love you from there."

"How...how do you know this?" Iesada stuttered.

"Because." She swallowed. "I'm called Priestess."

Silence blanketed the room for a long time while Keely searched for a way to offer them some consolation. "Yuuto, I can't give you your mother, but I want to give you a small gift that I hope brings you some comfort." She took a deep breath, concentrated, and put all of her will power into calling forth the resonance of Kaori's soul. When Keely had touched that soul in heaven's presence, a minute portion of its resonance stayed with her. She could give that tiny resonance to Yuuto.

When she spoke again, she spoke in divine tongues. "I bind all the resonance of Kaori's soul to what was meant to be her vessel so Yuuto will always remember his mother's love." Tiny particles of the

150

soul's essence gathered into her fingertips. She reached out and touched the book on the floor in front of her. "This is all I can give you." She picked the book up, held it out for Yuuto, and waited for him to take it.

His small, shaking hands reached out and wrapped around the book. He looked surprised, and then he started weeping loudly along with his father. "Mom," he called out as tears spilled out of his eyes and poured down his chubby cheeks. Keely couldn't do anything to comfort them. She couldn't even share in their tears. It wasn't her right. After a long time, the boy's wails subsided, and he turned his sorrow-dulled eyes to her. "You se...sent my mamma to heaven, and she's no longer sick?"

"She's no longer sick." Keely scooted closer to him and spoke softly. Reaching out, she gently wiped away the tears on one of his cheeks. "But I have to tell you, I didn't send your mom to heaven. Heaven invited her because she was good, kind, and full of love. I simply escorted her on her journey." She reached out and smoothed down his dark hair. "And one day you will see her again." She lifted her eyes to Iesada. "Both of you."

The two of them stared at her. All their hurt and sorrow was written on their faces before they turned and sought comfort in one another. There was nothing left for her to do but leave them to their grief. Slowly, and fighting against the pain of her injuries, she stood up and walked to the door. "I'm sorry," she whispered as she opened it and stepped through, losing the battle against her tears.

"Keely." Sutton was suddenly in front of her. "I need to heal your injuries."

"Okay." She swayed and was caught by two pairs of strong hands belonging to the suited clergymen who had accompanied them. They lowered her to the floor in the hallway outside the apartment, and she was silently grateful for the help. Her body had started to ache so badly she couldn't actually tell where the pain came from anymore. Or maybe it was her unrelenting sadness because even her tears felt like they caused her pain.

"Seven hours," she said. "I was seven hours too late."

"Keely, there was never going to be enough time to save Kaori." Sutton tried to reason. "It's not your fault. And I'm sorry, but right now I have to make sure you don't follow her."

151

She lay a hand on Keely's forehead and on her chest over her heart and started reciting a chant Keely knew all too well. Soon, her ribs began to burn, then throb, before sharp pains webbed back and forth from her chest to her abdomen. Her head did the same, and she thought for a fraction of a second it would split in two, but seconds later, all the pain dispersed. Her hip started to throb, and she heard, more than felt, the bone pop back into place. Tears of pain watered down her cheeks, but she managed to remain silent. Then it was over, and she was left wishing there was a healing spell that would take away her sorrow and regret.

Sutton pulled her hands away and grabbed one of Keely's arms. She and the clergy helped Keely off the floor, not letting go until they were sure she could stand. "You need to eat," Sutton said.

"So do you." Keely leaned against the wall and waited until her legs didn't feel like rubber then stepped away from Sutton's hold. "Thank you." She bowed her head to the men who had accompanied them. "Go home and get some rest..."

"Keely, you're the one needing rest. We're not the ones that took the beating tonight." Sutton countered in English.

"It's how it works," Keely said, wiping at her tears. Their streams had lessened, but they still moistened her cheeks. "Go home, eat, and get some rest." She looked at one of the men who had been assigned by the Kobe City's ministry. His face was kind even though he frowned with worry. "Please see that my companion makes it back to Tokyo safely," she ordered in Japanese then turned away from them and walked down the hallway to the elevator, feeling more than defeated. She felt as if there was nothing in the world but sorrow.

The street outside Yuuto's apartment was teeming with life as people came and went, warmed by the bright afternoon sun. It seemed odd that the world would still go on despite the tragedy of Kaori's family. She wanted to believe the continuation of life as time went on was good, but at that moment she couldn't find any solace in it. She did find solace in the fact that the ministry had brought her motorcycle from Tokyo. Even though she knew she wouldn't, she wanted to try to outrun her feelings of sorrow and failure.

The soft vibrating of her phone against her bottom reminded her that she'd also disappointed someone else. When she pulled the phone from her pocket, she could have wept at seeing Chance's num-

152

ber flash across the screen. Even though she'd seen him the previous morning, it felt like years not days.

They'd spent several days together shopping, going out with perspective friends, or simply being together. They had been days full of laughter and happiness. At night they'd fallen asleep entangled in one another, only to wake up that way the next morning. It didn't just feel like another time; being with Chance felt like being in another world, a world where neverborn didn't exist.

She felt she shouldn't answer, considering her mood, but for unexplainable reasons, she needed to hear his voice. Sliding her thumb across the screen, she put the phone to her ear and said, "Hello."

"Keely," she could hear the smile in his voice. It made her smile, even as tears started to slide down her cheeks again. "Are you working?"

"Not anymore."

"What are your plans?"

"I don't really have any plans," she answered softly, wiping at the new tears.

"Are you alright?"

"Yeah." She managed to stifle a sniffle then continue in a nearly normal voice. "Work was..." Her voice trailed off. What could she say? "It's going to be a bit before I get back to Tokyo. I'm in Kobe right now?"

"Are you driving back to Tokyo?"

She cleared her throat and ran a finger over the handlebar of her motorcycle. "That was the plan. After that a shower." She realized she not only wanted to see him, but part of her needed to because she needed the comfort of his presence. "I can meet you after if you're free."

"Why don't you save forty-five minutes and come right to my apartment?" She didn't answer right away, and he added, "I will make curry."

"It's tempting, but there are two flaws in your plan. I don't know where you live, and I don't have any clothes there."

"Both easily remedied," he assured. "I can send you my address, and I think I can manage to find you something to wear. Or?"

"Or?" she prompted, smiling, surprising herself she could.

"You don't really need clothes?"

She laughed, unable to think of anything witty to say in reply. "Okay, naked dinner at your place then?"

"I like this trend we have," he replied. "I'll send you my address and see you at about five."

"Okay," she repeated. Another wave of guilt and sadness made her chest hurt. Suddenly, she changed her mind. She didn't have the right to be near him when she was feeling the way she was feeling. She didn't have the right to expose him to her world, the one she lived in as a Priestess. "Chance," she started.

"Keely," he interrupted. "Be careful and get here safely." The phone disconnected before she could say anything else.

Almost five hours later she found herself standing in front of Chance's apartment door, shivering and trying to wring out her rain-soaked clothes. Even though she wore a thick, leather, riding jacket and helmet, she was drenched and dripping. As she twisted pieces of the velvet, tunic-style shirt she wore, water dropped to the ground, and she again questioned whether she had a right to be there. She wanted to be near Chance, but that seemed selfish to her and unfair to him. Changing her mind, she turned away from his door, and almost ran into a red-headed Tau.

"Looks like the rain has sent the ostriches running for shelter." He smiled at her. "Although, in your case, you look like the rain tried to drown you." Before she could reply or wonder how he knew Sutton's pet name for her, he reached around her and pressed the buzzer next to the door. "Are you coming to see Chance?"

Keely cleared her throat and brushed wet strands of hair away from her face. "I was trying to get out of the rain." The door next to her opened. She turned to see Chance standing in its threshold, looking at her through a pair of glasses and holding a towel. He was dressed casually in a pair of jeans and plain tee-shirt, but her heart started to race.

"I thought you might have hit the storm." Chance stepped forward, holding open the towel, but stopped when he noticed Tau standing next to her.

Tau looked from Chance to Keely, nodding and smiling. "Your mom called and told me she brought you some of her curry." He explained his presence.

154

"I wish she'd quit doing that." Chance frowned.

"She thinks I'm starving, and she likes me." Tau shrugged. "And I've had an idea for a song. I already have a basic chorus."

"You told me on the phone." Chance shook out the towel and handed it to Keely then stepped away from the door. "Remember the conversation where I told you I had plans."

"I ignored you." Tau shouldered around Chance into the apartment, slipped off his shoes and walked inside.

"I can come back another time," Keely said, wanting to stay but thinking she didn't have the right, not in her current condition. She lifted the towel and tried to hand it back to him. "I need a shower anyway."

"You're already here, and I have a shower," Chance pointed out. "And my mom does make good curry."

"It's, um, well…" Her voice trailed off, and she looked at her feet. "I'm a little tired from work."

Chance's soft fingers caressed the side of her face, then lifted her chin, so she had to look at him. "I know. You sounded tired when I talked to you. Which is why I asked my mom to make curry."

Suddenly, her sorrow lightened. She didn't have to wonder why. Just being near Chance had comforted her, especially since he'd been so considerate. She thought herself a fool to contemplate leaving him for her empty apartment. "I guess I can't say no."

"No. You can't," Chance agreed.

"You coming?" Tau asked from behind Chance before disappearing into the apartment again.

"I'm sorry," Chance apologized. "When Tau wants to write music, he doesn't give anyone else a choice in the matter."

"Just point me to the shower." She smiled at him. "But I'm going to need clothes." She looked past him into his apartment. "Naked dinner might be a bad idea with Tau here."

Chance smirked, stepped closer to her, and whispered. "I'll still be imagining you naked." He stepped aside and held the door open for her.

"Same," she said, smiling at him as she stepped into his apartment. She stopped at the genkan and slipped off her boots but didn't go any further since she was dripping wet and didn't want to track water everywhere.

He closed the door behind her. "I'll get you some clothes." He walked down a narrow hallway and around a corner.

After setting her bag on the top of a nearby shoe cabinet, Keely stood, toweling the water out of her hair. She examined what she could see of Chance's apartment. A tiny, clean kitchen to her right had a small stovetop, toaster oven, and open shelves bursting with dishes, utensils, and food. Across the kitchen was a half-open pocket door she assumed led to the bathroom. Beyond the hallway, she could see an open room with a small window. From her vantage point, all she could see was the corner of a bed and the end of a brown couch sitting next to one another. She leaned over to peer through the see-through shelf/wall into the living room because she was curious, but Chance came around the corner holding a bundle of clothes.

"I think these will work." He held out the pile to her.

Keely reached for them and stopped. On top of the pile was a pair of panties she recognized as her own. Looking at Chance, she smiled and lifted an eyebrow in question as she took the clothes.

"I'm not that kind of pervert," he said quietly with a blush. "You left them on the floor of the hotel the first night we spent together."

"I wondered what happened to these." She used her fingers to lift the blue, lacy panties. "And you washed them?" Thinking about him washing her panties made her blush, and she couldn't say why.

"I'm not that kind of pervert," he repeated. "I don't wear women's panties."

"So, you are some kind of pervert?" she asked.

"Yes," he admitted, looking up at her almost challengingly.

She stepped closer to him, making sure Tau couldn't see before she pressed her lips to his. "As long as you like me better than my panties, I'm okay with whatever kind of pervert you want to be."

He smiled at her and opened his mouth to say something, but then suddenly, his face hardened. He reached up and brushed his fingers through the hair at her temple. "Are you bleeding?" he asked, stepping closer and inspecting her temple. "Keely, you're bleeding."

She touched her hand to her hair, and it came away with flakes of dried blood. "Oh that," she said softly.

"Come here," he ordered, grabbing her arm and pulling her down the short hallway into a tiny bathroom. The tub and sink were

156

strategically crammed into a room half the size of Keely's closet. The two of them barely fit.

"Sit down." Chance ushered her to the tub, pushed her down on its edge, and turned to a cabinet. Opening the doors, he started going through small bins inside it.

"Chance, it's okay," she tried to explain softly. "Someone has already looked at it." He shoved things around and slammed bins back into place. "It's okay." Her assurance seemed to fall on deaf ears. "I didn't know you wore glasses." She tried to change the subject, hoping to diffuse his anger.

"Apparently, there's a lot we don't know about each other." He slammed another bin back into its place. "Are you going to tell me what happened?"

"If you're going to listen."

"I'm listening," he said quietly.

She took in a shaky breath and clutched the clothes he'd given her to her chest, fighting back the tears. "There was a big fight. I more or less lost, and a family was irrevocably torn apart."

He turned around and looked at her. "That's not the whole truth?"

She shook her head. "That's as much as I can tell you."

"No," he disagreed, reaching out and wiping away a stray tear. "That's what you think you should tell me. And what I think you should tell me is whatever it is making you cry."

Though Keely hated being called out, she adored Chance all the more for his bluntness. She couldn't tell him what really happened. She wouldn't be able to tell him how badly she'd wanted to return Yuuto's mother to him, and how shattered his family now was. More tears spilled down her cheeks. She felt like she was going to drown in her sadness all over again.

"There was a boy," she sniffed, "and his father. They've lost a wife and mother today." She couldn't really explain without explaining. "Their lives have been shattered. They'll never be the same, and the world keeps going on like it's nothing."

He squatted down in front of her, cupped her face, and wiped away her tears. "You know, and now I know."

"Nothing can be done. I can't make it better for them."

"Keely." His face softened. "Did you do all you could?"

157

Short of reversing time, she had. "Yes," she whispered.

He leaned in and rested his forehead against hers. "I still don't understand all of it, but you tried to protect these people, and you still carry them inside of you. The world may not need to know because you know, and now I know," he repeated. "And though neither of us can do anything, we both share their grief."

He wasn't wrong. The world may not be sympathetic to Yuuto's and Ieseda's grief, but she did know, and so did Chance. Knowing he cared lifted some of her sorrow. After a long moment, he kissed her forehead and dropped his hands. "But, Keely... I have to ask. Is your job dangerous?"

She could see the muscles in his face and neck tense. "Yes," she confirmed, unable to lie.

He pursed his lips together and frowned. "Tau thinks you're a prostitute."

For a moment, she wasn't sure if she'd heard him correctly, then the words actually registered. Laughter bubbled up inside her chest, and the next moment, she was hunched over her knees, unable to control the fit that followed. "What?" she finally managed to ask through giggles. "Where did that come from?"

He didn't see the humor in his statement, and his expression got tight with worry, which made her serious. "Keely, tell me what to do. Now that I know your job is dangerous, I want to protect you."

She lifted her fingers to his hair and ran them through the soft, dark strands. "I don't need you to protect me." Her heart swelled. "I need you to understand until I can tell you all of the truth and believe me when I tell you I'm fine."

"Physically or mentally?"

"Physically, I was fine before I left Kobe. Mentally, I was better once I got here, and I'm even better now," she admitted honestly.

He was quiet for a moment, scowling with deep thought. Then he leaned in and pressed his lips to hers for a quick kiss. "I'm glad I could do that much for you then. Shower, have a hot bath, and get warm. Then we'll eat."

"You know, if Tau wasn't here you could bathe me," she suggested in a soft voice.

"If he wasn't here that's exactly what I'd be doing." He smirked and stood up. "Stop teasing. It's mean," he added, leaving her alone in

158

the bathroom.

Forty-five minutes later Keely hung her wet clothes up to dry and quietly opened the bathroom door. She could hear soft tones of guitars and didn't want to interrupt Chance and Tau. She emerged relaxed, warm, and dressed in one of Chance's jinbei, a man's yukata set, only with shorts instead of pants. The top fit her reasonably well even if it accentuated her breasts, but the shorts didn't fit. They were too tight and dug into her waist. They were uncomfortable, but she had no choice but to wear them since Tau was there.

She slowly walked down the hallway and looked around the corner into the main room of the loft apartment. Chance and Tau sat on a loveseat with guitars in their laps. Tau strummed a tune, and Chance copied the fingering on his guitar. His face was intent as he listened to the notes, nodding his head to an unheard rhythm. His dark hair fell into his warm brown eyes, slightly swaying with his movements. His fingers moved with expertise up and down frets of the guitar, and there was a slight upturn of his lips. It was more proof he wasn't just a musician. He was an artist, and she found herself staring. Chance must have felt her eyes because he lifted his head and smiled at her. It was a devastating smile that made her forget she could think coherently.

She swallowed and looked away from him, embarrassed she got caught staring. Instead, she examined his loft apartment. It wasn't overly small, but it was cluttered, especially with a large harp sitting in the corner, surrounded by a myriad of guitars. In the opposite corner was a bed; it wasn't as small as a twin-size bed, and it wasn't a double. In Keely's exhausted state, his bed looked extremely cozy. Sleeping where he slept had a comforting appeal. Besides the small couch where Chance and Tau sat, there was a coffee table. At that moment, it was cluttered with music sheets, a laptop, and a small keyboard. Behind the couch, there was a small, smoked glass window that let light filter in. The windowsill was cluttered with tiny figurines of all varieties. Caddy-cornered from the sofa and across the table was a wooden chair piled with guitar straps and cases.

While his apartment was full of his music, it also reflected his other interests. An inset wall shelf was nearly overloaded with more figurines, only these looked like robots or cyborgs. There was also a shelf dedicated to video games and another shelf filled with books,

159

some on music theory and some on mechanical and electrical engineering. The walls in his apartment were mostly bare, except for single poster advertising a long past play date for Eternity's End. Keely had a feeling the poster had more sentimental than decorative value. His apartment had a homey, lived-in atmosphere. She liked it.

"Make yourself comfortable," Chance invited, interrupting her study of his apartment. He kicked Tau in the shin. "You can sit here."

"Fine." Tau rolled his eyes and stood up, taking his guitar with him. "I'm the lead singer. Why do I have to move?" he huffed and sat down again.

"You're also an uninvited guest," Chance reminded him.

"If I'm keeping you from working..." Keely started.

"You're not," both men said in unison.

"We have some things that need to be worked through." Chance smiled at her. "Come on, sit." He patted the couch next to him. "I'll get us something to eat." He set the guitar in his lap on the floor next to him, leaning it against the couch. Standing, he stepped closer to her and lightly caressed her arm. "Please, relax." He motioned to the couch.

"Okay." She smiled at him, unable to express her feelings verbally.

"If you two want to kiss, it won't bother me at all," Tau announced.

Keely stifled laughter with a snort and turned to smile at Tau. "Aw, so you're a voyeur."

"Pervert," Chance added.

"Yeah, I'm not going to deny either of those statements." Tau smiled and started strumming his guitar. "But this time it's not about me being a pervert. The two of you should feel comfortable around me and do whatever you like."

"Right now, I'd like food." Keely stepped around Chance and sat down.

"That's something I can resolve." Chance went into the kitchen, and she heard the clicking and ignition of his gas stove. "Do something useful," he demanded to Tau.

"I guess it's the least I can do since your mom cooked," Tau said, setting his guitar next to Chance's, and started clearing the coffee table.

160

Fifteen minutes later, Chance set a bowl of steaming rice covered in meat, vegetables, and curry sauce on the table in front of her. He handed her spoon and some chopsticks. "It's good, I promise."

"I don't doubt it. Thank you for the food." She smiled at him and took the utensils. Impatient, due to her growling stomach, she scooped a large helping of the rice and sauce into her mouth. The meat was soft, the vegetables fresh, and the sauce had the right amount of earthy spiciness. "Oh my god." She covered her mouth with her hand since it was full. "This is good," she said to Chance and Tau's smiling faces. They looked at one another and shrugged. They already knew how delicious the food was.

She ate her fill, nearly moaning out loud with every bite. Though, she was a bit sad because she'd eaten all she'd been given and there wouldn't be any leftovers. "That was delicious. Your mom is an amazing cook." Standing, she started clearing away plates and bowls.

"I know." Chance put a hand on her arm to stop her. "Tau will get that. Just sit and be my guest."

"I'm your guest too," Tau complained.

"Uninvited guest," Chance reminded.

"Whatever." Tau stood up and started stacking up dishes.

When Tau disappeared into the kitchen Chance leaned toward Keely and carefully took her hand. "I'm sorry, but I'm going to be busy for a while"

"It's okay. I'm tired anyway so I should get going soon."

He stared at her hand and absently traced her fingers over her knuckles. The warmth of his hands and the feel of his callused fingers tracing over her soft skin made her shiver. "I think you should stay." He looked up at her with an expression she couldn't interpret, but his voice was soft and inviting.

"I do want to stay, but I don't want to interfere. I like Eternity's End." She smiled. "If I didn't know you, I'd be joining the ranks of your fangirls."

"What's your favorite song?" Tau asked as he walked into the living room and picked up more dishes.

"Well, it wasn't one that was popular." She removed her hand from Chance's, not that public displays of affection bothered her, but she was very aware Japan had its own rules and culture. Public displays of affection were very taboo.

"Which one?" Chance asked, taking her hand back in his and weaving their fingers together.

"Lunar Horizon," she answered. "It's kind of bittersweet, full of regret and still hopeful."

"Of course, you'd like that song." Tau rolled his eyes and carried away more dishes.

Keely looked at Chance, wondering at Tau's reaction.

"I wrote it," he explained, almost beaming with pride.

"I didn't know, but It's definitely my favorite." She stared into the deep warmth of his brown eyes and felt something pass between them. At that moment, all of the day's failure, sorrow, and her pain was lost to something wonderful.

"Time to get back to work. We don't want to waste our studio time next week." Tau came back into the living room, sat down in the chair and picked up his guitar.

Chance didn't let go of her hand. Instead, he covered it with his other hand and asked, "So, you're staying?"

"Yes," she nodded.

He smiled brilliantly in return, and her heart started beating harder. "Good," he said, pulling her down to the couch next to him. Letting go of her hand, he reached for his guitar.

She settled back on the couch and made herself comfortable. Chance and Tau went to work immediately, debating melody and musical composition. It didn't take long for the soft strumming of their guitars to lull her. She leaned her head back and fell into a light sleep filled with Chance's music. After a time, she started to feel cold. Seeking warmth from the couch, she adjusted her positions closer to its cushions.

"Her work must be tiring," Tau said as if from a distance.

"It is," Chance agreed as something soft, filled with his scent and warmth, covered her.

"Thank you," Keely mumbled, snuggling against the blanket. The soft strumming started again. She felt sheltered from the world where neverborn existed. She was warm and felt tranquil and fell into a deep sleep.

A shrill tone cut through her sleep, shattering her serenity. She was standing up and searching for her phone before she could process

162

a cognitive thought. It was an automatic response from years of answering the call of the ministry, no matter what she was doing. She found her phone inside her slightly damp backpack, sitting in the entryway. Sliding her thumb over the answer key, she said, "Hello."

"Keely, I'm sorry, but I'm here, brought you a change of clothes. You need to come." Sutton's voice was soft and regretful.

"What's happened?" she asked in Gaelic, aware of the two pairs of eyes on her back.

"A neverborn has stolen the soul of a monk. They've got it cornered, but that's all they can do without you."

Keely let out a small sigh and raked her fingers through her hair. "Bring me the clothes. I'll send you the address."

"Yeah about that, I guess you didn't hear me. I'm sitting outside of what I presume is Chance's apartment."

"Give me a second." Keely frowned and hung up the phone. Without turning around and facing the eyes she knew were still staring at her, she stepped to the front door, opened it, and took the bag that Sutton quietly offered. She turned back around and jumped. Chance stood right in front of her, and she hadn't heard him approach.

"You're leaving?" His voice cracked, and he looked at her with an intensity she couldn't translate.

"I have to." She stepped around him. "I'm sorry. I need to use your bathroom again."

She maneuvered around him and slipped inside the bathroom. She quickly changed into the black pants, fitted, burgundy shirt, and hooded coat. Boots in hand, she opened the door to the bathroom, only to find Chance waiting outside of it.

Strong fingers wrapped around her arm and Chance hissed in her ear, "We need to talk." He directed her back into the bathroom and followed. Taking a deep breath, he leaned against the sink and folded his arms over his chest. "You know I have a thousand questions. I keep telling myself you will tell me when you're ready, but I'm not sure how much patience I have left."

"I can't answer your questions. I'm sorry," Keely apologized.

"You came to me in a terrible state, and you were bleeding. And now I'm supposed to let you leave?"

Keely was suddenly angry. She wasn't sure if it was at his words or the fact that she had to leave him and go fight a neverborn.

She chose the former. "You don't have the power to let me do any-thing."

His eyes went to hers. There was a moment of unspoken chal-lenge between the two of them. Either tiredness or stubbornness made her unyielding. Regardless, Keely wasn't going to back down.

Chance must have sensed it, because he looked away, frown-ing. "I didn't mean it like that. I meant how am I supposed to watch you walk out my door and not be concerned?"

"Chance," she sighed heavily. "I don't have the time to have this conversation. Someone is counting on me, and I have to go." She stopped and cleared her throat, trying to swallow down the sudden pain in her chest. "If you can't accept that you're going to have to not only trust me but believe in me...I don't know how we—"

He came up off the counter and covered her mouth with his hand. "Keely, think carefully before you issue the 'trust me, or we can't see each other anymore' ultimatum." A heavy silence stretched on between them, and again they were at an impasse. His face seemed to tighten and then relax as if he'd decided for them both. He pulled his hand away and rubbed his thumb over her bottom lip making it quiver. "I'll be waiting for you to get back."

Tumultuous emotions made her chest and stomach tighten. She knew she hadn't won in their battle of wills. She only bought herself some time. Mental exhaustion had already taken a heavy toll on her, and the thought of having a lengthy conversation about who she really was made her want to cry. She wondered how differently Chance would treat her once she told him the truth. He probably wouldn't believe her and think her insane. The truth could put him in danger and most certainly would change things between them.

Looking at his face, she read expectation, patience, and worry there. "Chance, our relationship is very new."

"I know. What are you trying to say?"

She opened her mouth, closed it, then shook her head. "I'll call you in a couple of days."

"I already said, I'll be waiting for you," he reassured.

She took another deep breath and blew it out of her nose. "You may not be ready to see me at my worst."

Her confession had him shaking his head before he cupped her face between his hands and lightly pressed his lips to hers. "That's

164

something we're going to find out together. I find myself wanting to know more about you, all of you, even the worst parts."

17

Keely and Sutton walked down a narrow alley toward a big warehouse with a crowd of people standing outside. Amongst them was another monk, several clergy, the body of the monk who had their soul stolen, and the Cassock. A monk with a stolen soul was serious. It was possible the entirety of the Tokyo ministry was present.

Monks were rare. There were less than one hundred of them in the world. Clergy could see and sometimes use spells against neverborn. Whereas, monks could not only see, but their will was as such that they could hurt them. Japan didn't have any of their own monks. They did have one on loan from Korea and another from India. Strangely, India had the most monks of any country and felt it an honor when other countries asked for their assistance. Unfortunately, it was India's monk who had lost a battle to the neverborn. Until Keely had been tasked as the Priestess, the ministry would be forced to watch their monks die when they lost their souls, but Keely had changed the war with the neverborn for them.

As they neared the crowd, Shoma approached them and bowed. "Priestess, excuse the lack of formality and the time of night…"

"Shoma," Keely interrupted him. "I thought we were friends. In my country, formalities, especially in situations that could be tragic, are unnecessary."

"Thank you, Keely," he said softly, and she sensed his tension lesson. "I will say, I'm worried though." The two walked to a body that lay on a gurney. "Monk Ramya Prasad's body has serious injuries, and there is nothing we can do."

"I know." They'd reached the gurney and the woman who lay on it. She was attractive, probably in her thirties, with dark hair and sun-kissed skin. Unfortunately, that skin was marred with cuts and bruises. Several clergy stood around her, softly chanting healing casts, but they would do little more than keep Ramya from dying.

"I don't understand why she is not healing," a familiar tall monk said from the other side of the gurney, looking to Keely with pleading eyes.

"A body cannot heal without its soul, even when a crafter casts a healing spell," Shoma explained.

"I still don't understand," he admitted.

"Clergy Eli Hada is training under monk Prasad," Shoma explained under his breath, sparing Keely the embarrassment of asking the monks name. "After meeting you the night you saved Hannah's life, he began to push himself to become a monk."

Keely looked from the man to Shoma. Monks didn't become monks just by choice, but Keely didn't want to pursue the matter because she had work to do. Instead, she simply explained, "A body does not have the will to live; that comes from the soul." He seemed satisfied with her answer, and she turned her attention back to Ramya. "Let's get her closer to the neverborn," she ordered to the crowd surrounding the body, and they all walked toward the door of the warehouse.

"You're going to take the body inside with you to face the neverborn?" Eli asked, helping to push Ramya's gurney. Keely had a feeling he already knew what her answer would be.

"Yes."

"I would like to join you," he stated, his face hardening with determination.

Keely wasn't going to deny his request, but she did warn, "The closer the body gets to the neverborn, the more agitated and dangerous it will get. It will not be selective when it strikes out. You could get hurt."

"So could you," he countered.

"Fair enough." They had come to the entrance of the warehouse. Two steel doors separated her from the hollowness and sorrow she felt coming from the neverborn. "I assume this is the trap?"

Sutton appeared next to her, carrying her crossbow. "I've been told this is a fortified cell specifically designed for neverborn," she explained.

"No prison ever built has ever held a neverborn more than five days. What were they planning on doing with one once they caught it?" Keely asked in Gaelic. They came to a stop, staring at the darkened doors.

"I don't know, but I feel like they didn't think it through,"

Sutton replied in the same language.

"Once we get in there, the neverborn will get more aggressive because it will sense Ramya's body, and her soul will start to revolt," Keely warned. "You keep Ramya and Eli safe first."

"No can do. My orders come from the one person I won't ever argue with." Sutton shifted her bow to the ready, sighting it on the door. "We doing this?"

"Yeah." Keely turned toward her best friend. "Sutton, I don't want to escort any more souls to heaven today."

"I know." Sutton reached out and put a hand on Keely's shoulder. "But my priority is to make sure Chance's piece of ass gets out of this alive. As for the others," she looked over at Eli and Ramya's body, "this neverborn would have to be some kind of asshole to make me chose between you and them."

Keely smiled at her friend's reassurance. She was right, the neverborn would have to be extremely fast and powerful. Fortunately for them, that didn't happen often. "Okay, let's get this done."

"Hells yeah." Sutton smiled in return and signaled the clergy around them. The doors to the warehouse opened. The three of them slowly walked in with Keely in the lead, Sutton close behind. Eli brought up the rear, pushing Ramya.

Keely didn't know what to expect, but to find the neverborn standing in the middle of the floor waiting on her wasn't on her list of contingencies. She stopped, mid-step, staring at it. Because of the nature of what she was, Keely was the only person on the planet who could see the neverborn in complete detail. She wished she couldn't. This one was taller than most and had extremely elongated limbs. Its deformed, three-fingered, clawed hands dangled at its knees. She wasn't fooled by their deformity. Those hands weren't useless and could strike quickly and painfully. If she wasn't careful, its strikes could be deadly.

The grey skin she could see was coated in scales resembling flacking stone, but that was what she could see. The rest was covered with skin, human skin, since it was trying to take on Ramya's face and form, although the cracked, glistening skin only tethered across the right side of its body and partially up its neck, leaving its face visible. Slight shivers went down her spine and settled at the base of her stomach. When she stared at its mouthless face, its white eyes captured her gaze. Cocking its head sideways, the neverborn seemed to be examining her, probably assessing whether her soul was worth taking or not. It took a jerky step forward, and its face stretched then split apart where its mouth would be. Black blood oozed out of the tear.

There had been a time when the sight of a neverborn paralyzed Keely with fear, and she could not fight them. That fear had not lessened any. She'd just strengthened her ability to cope. Swallowing, she took a step forward. "I think you know who I am." She stepped to its right and watched as the white eyes followed her movements. "Or at the very least, you know what I've come for." It lifted its clawed hand and struck the floor, sending pieces of concrete flying and leaving deep scratches in it. It opened its mouth again, and more black blood oozed from new tears in its skin, dripping down its chin and over its neck.

Keely's instinct was that this neverborn fell into the powerful anomaly category. Sutton must have sensed it too, because she warned, "Keely, it will know who you are and what you can do. Remember, it has Ramya's thoughts and memories. And for god's sake, don't let it hit you."

"I know, but it hasn't actually seen what I can do." Keely concentrated, forming an intricate illusion in her mind. Unfortunately, to make the illusion believable to the neverborn, she wouldn't be able to contain it to the neverborn. "Sutton."

"Crazy, scary shit about to happen, got it." She replied as a distant scratching could be heard.

The scratching sounds were joined by high pitched squeaks that were soon followed by the eye-watering smell of ammonia, feces, and rotting meat. The scratching and high-pitched chirping got louder, and they were suddenly surrounded by thousands of glowing red eyes. Shadows shifted around them and started moving across the floor.

"I don't like this. Keely, what have you done?" Sutton asked, sounding nervous.

The neverborn lifted its hand and again scratched at the floor, taking a deep chunk out of the concrete. It raised the rock in one of its long hands and threw it at Keely. She side-stepped, and the piece flew by her head only to be followed by another one. She easily ducked underneath it, but the neverborn's attention wasn't really on her anymore.

The red-eyed shadows had moved closer, and the smell coming from them got stronger. Scratching noises preceded thousands of rats as they came stampeding toward the neverborn. Sutton let out a short scream, then both she and Eli balanced on Ramya's gurney as the rats ran toward Keely. However, she wasn't their intended target. The rats ran between her legs in a stampede of grey fur, scratching claws, and gnashing teeth. They were bloodthirsty and intent on devouring flesh, the neverborn's flesh. It only took a moment for the rats to crawl across the floor and up the legs of the neverborn, engulfing it in splotches of dark grey, moving fur. The neverborn swatted at and even managed to squish a few, but the hoard of rats Keely created easily overpowered it. Squishing, eating sounds echoed around the room as the rats started to bite and tear away at the human skin the neverborn had grown. A low moan that sounded something like a hollow wind emanated from the neverborn and made Keely fight against her need to run away.

Keely wasn't done. She needed to make sure when she went to rescue all the souls it carried the fight would be minimal. She needed to make sure the neverborn believed it was caught in her lurid trap. Metallic rattling emanated from her feet as chains swirled up from the ground, circling around her then launching at the neverborn. Five separate barbed chains snaked out, four wrapping around each limb, and the fifth tethered around its neck. The chains tightened so quickly they cut apart rats, spilling their blood over the neverborn's grey skin.

"By heaven," Eli exclaimed from somewhere behind her, and he started chanting, making the neverborn even more desperate. It pulled and jerked at its illusionary chains, but they dug into its body, cutting into both flesh and hide, immobilizing it. The neverborn believed it was caught.

That was Keely's opportunity to take back what it had stolen. Despite her fear and her exhaustion, she moved faster than she thought possible. As she ran through rats and chains, she started chanting. "I call forth and to tear apart what is unnatural sewn, to free what is hidden, what has been stolen." She reached the neverborn, grabbed ahold of one of the neverborn's arms, lifted herself and wedged her foot against the other so it couldn't strike her. "I call forth Ramya Prasad's heart," she commanded in the tongues of divination.

The neverborn coughed, gagged and opened its mouth, tearing its face from ear to ear, exposing a hole leaking black blood. A tiny flicker of light appeared in the recesses of that hole, rolled forward, and trickled down into Keely's waiting hand.

"I release all the souls you've claimed, calling them forth in heaven's name. I act as the beacon so they may return home" she said, her words sounding like an inviting song.

Convulsions made the neverborn twitch and press against Keely's hold. Then it had one final spasm, its chest sunk in, and tiny lights started to fill its mouth, trickling out then upward.

"Now," she shouted, disentangling herself from the neverborn and falling to the floor. Rolling to her feet, she ran toward Ramya's body, putting all her effort and strength into transporting her soul back to it. Without a vessel, she wouldn't be able to hold onto the soul for long. Ramya's essence was already so heavy she could barely move. Her arms felt like they'd pull out of her shoulders, and her legs felt like they were on the verge of giving out with every step she took.

A storm of arrows whizzed by her, and she could hear them hit their target. It sounded like a hammer striking wood. For a moment, that was all she could hear, even over her own breathing. She made it to Ramya's body faster than she thought she could, most likely because Ramya's soul guided her there. All the while Ramya's raw feelings and emotions poured into Keely. Her wants, fears, and loves all flowed from the light that was her soul. Most of all, Keely could feel Ramya's desire to live.

Standing over the body, she took a deep breath to calm her pounding heart. Her focus so fixated on the task at hand she had to let go of her illusion binding the neverborn and trust that Sutton could drive it away. Taking in a deep breath, she spoke to the soul in her hand. "Ramya Prasad, you have fought like the warrior you are. You have remained truthful, fearless, and kind despite the battles you've had and will have. I honor your loyalty to humanity and to the ministry and to me by restoring your soul and binding it to your body so it will never be stolen again." With her final words, Keely opened her hand and pressed the tiny, brightly shining ember into the center of Ramya's chest and watched a light pulse through her body as it settled back into where it had come from.

Keely grabbed ahold of the side of the gurney to try and

steady her shaking muscles. Carrying a soul was exhausting, and it took a toll on her, especially when she was already tired. At least she didn't have to transfer Ramya's soul to a vessel, then to her body.

Trying to catch her breath and willing her legs to stop shaking, she watched Ramya twitch back to life. Without warning, Ramya sat up, stretched out a hand, and wrapped it around Keely's throat, digging her nails into the soft skin of Keely's neck. The attack was so fast and so precise she began to lose consciousness in less than a second. All she could do was stare into Ramya's blank expression as she desperately tried to pull the hand away from her throat. She was too weak, and the world started going dark. A deep voice was yelling as if from far off as her throat collapsed, and her legs gave out. Before she fell into darkness, she registered the sound of a hard smack, and the fingers that dug into her throat released their hold. Keely fell to the floor, coughing and gagging for air as she pried at her neck, trying to get air through her crushed airway.

"Apologies, Priestess." Eli appeared in front of her and yanked her shirt apart, sending buttons flying. Her lungs burned; her eyes watered, and the dizzying black rose to claim her again. Eli lifted a piece of paper with some kanji written on it, said a chant, and slapped it against her breastbone. Cold exploded from her chest and tethered outward. Immediately, she started shaking. After a second, she drew in air and was relieved to find she could breathe unobstructed. A mist came out of her mouth; her teeth started to chatter, and her body spasmed from the cold. She tried to get up but could do little more than shake. Eli scooped an arm underneath her and pulled her against his chest. Involuntarily, she clung to him desperate for his warmth.

"What the fuck?" Sutton was suddenly kneeling over her, placing a warm hand on her cheek. "Keely, are you alright?"

"Yes," Keely managed to answer between chattering teeth. "Just cold."

"I apologize." Eli bowed his head. "I did not know Ramya would...attack."

Sutton stood and looked around. "Damn, that's a hell of a punch. She'll definitely feel it." She put her fingers to her lips and let out a loud whistle. Seconds later, the room was filled with clergy.

Keely could hear Sutton barking orders but gave little to no care since she was so cold. Then someone was lifting her off of Eli, placing her on a gurney, and covering her with blankets.

"Why am I so cold?" Keely asked to no one in particular.

"Because the idiot monk transferred his essence to heal you. You're being so cold is a side effect," Sutton answered, appearing at her right.

"Is he okay?" Keely asked, feeling tears well up and pool in her eyes.

"He is well," Shoma said from the other side of her gurney, looking down at her with a kind expression. "Your job is done here. Only concern yourself with what you need. You will be warm soon. The coldness you feel is temporary." He looked to Sutton, and his expression tightened in anger. "One of our own attacked the Priestess?"

"Ramya attacked out of instinct," Sutton explained. "If I had thought about it, I'd have had her tied to the gurney." She looked at Keely. "I'm sorry."

"The neverborn?" Keely asked.

"Apparently, it didn't like getting turned into a pincushion and ran away. Who knew?" Sutton answered with a reassuring smile.

"Everyone is okay?" Keely asked, knowing they were but still needing to hear it.

"Yes," Shoma answered. "All are safe, Priestess."

Relief filled Keely, and she suddenly found herself quietly crying between bouts of shivers. It embarrassed her, making her cry harder. To hide the tears, she threw an arm up over her eyes. She wanted to be home alone where she could cry; she wanted to cry until she couldn't cry anymore, but most of all she wanted Chance.

18

Sutton watched Keely sway with the inertia of the moving car as she fought sleep. The day had taken a hard toll on her friend, and Sutton was more worried than ever. Keely didn't look just exhausted. She looked beat down, both physically and emotionally. Sutton decided her next phone call was going to be to the Cassock. He needed to know Keely required rest and preparation before her mission to the suicide forest would be a suicide mission. If he didn't listen, she'd call in the big guns; she'd call Jasper.

The car swerved slightly and came to a slow stop. "We're at the address you requested," the driver said softly.

Keely startled out of dozing, sat up straight, and looked around. "Where are we?" she asked then answered her own question. "You brought me back to Chance's." She looked at her hands, then to Sutton with a frown, deepening the weariness that showed on her face.

"It's where I got you from."

"I want to go..."

"No, you don't," Sutton interrupted her. "And even if you've convinced yourself you do, I'm not taking you home." She reached in her pocket and rattled the set of keys that resided there. "And I have your keys."

Keely again looked at her hands before turning to stare out the window. The bottom of Chance's building was full of shops. All of them but a small convenience store were closed. Its lights polluted the street with dull yellow. "I'm going to have to tell Chance."

Sutton frowned. "Yes, I know."

"He won't believe me." She stared at Sutton without really seeing her and then added, "I'm going to have to tell him I'm supposed to leave Japan in another five months."

"I know that too." Sutton couldn't think of anything to say to make Keely feel better. Chance had been good for Keely. He'd brought out Keely's fun human side, which was why Sutton had encouraged the relationship. She didn't consider that it might be more damaging in the end because Keely would fall so hard. Keely would be devastated when she had to leave Chance and Japan behind. Their war with the neverborn would continue, and Keely could possibly end up alone and in a worse state than she'd been in before she'd met Chance. Sutton genuinely hoped that wasn't what fate had in store for her. The part of her that hadn't been jaded by life, the part still believing in happy endings, wanted them to work it out. However, Keely would have to tell him the truth for their happy ending to have a chance.

At that moment, Keely's phone started ringing. She pulled it from her back pocket and stared at the screen. The sad, wistful expression on her face nearly broke Sutton's heart. "Maybe it's best if I end it."

Sutton snatched the phone out of her hand and slid her thumb over the answer key before Keely could object. "Hey, it's Sutton," she said before Chance could say anything. "Can you meet us down at the street in front of your apartment?"

"Sure," he answered, sounding confused.

"Great." She hung up the phone and turned to Keely. "If you end it, that's up to you. But tell him the truth first—all of it. Don't ghost him. And don't end it with that it's not you; it's me, bullshit." She huffed then added, "And stop lying to yourself. You like him, a lot. Tell him that too. Then if you still want to hurt his feelings and end it, at least he will know it's because you're scared and not because of anything he did." She put Keely's phone in her pocket next to her keys. "And I'm taking your phone. The ministry can live without you for forty-eight hours." Keely looked at her, blinked, opened her mouth as if she was going to say something, but then closed it. "Yeah, you don't have the corner market on bossy bitch."

Seeing Chance step out of a small doorway, she reached around Keely and opened the door. "Your escort's here. Now get out." Keely half turned toward the door, then turned back to Sutton. She raised her finger and opened her mouth as if to object, but Sutton interrupted her again. "Now."

Keely slid out of the car, and Sutton slammed the door behind her. She let out the breath she held and sighed with relief. Bossing Keely around was risky because it could lead to a fight between them. Sutton had never really won a full-on argument with Keely. If she pushed Keely too far, Keely would simply ask for another monk. There would be nothing Sutton could do to stop her. She hoped their friendship was stronger than that, but she always had an underlying fear because Keely was the only family she had left.

The car pulled out into traffic, and Sutton turned around to watch Keely and Chance out the back window. When Chance reached out and took Keely's hand, she knew she'd made the right decision forcing the issue. She settled back into the seat, smiling at her own highhandedness. Then a frown marred her pretty features. Keely was petty about things like being bossed around, and she'd find a way to return the favor to Sutton.

∞ ∞ ∞ ∞ ∞

Keely looked down at Chance's hand, marveling at the warmth it radiated into hers. She was almost too afraid to look at Chance because she felt like he'd see the day's mental battle scars written on her face. "I'm sorry," she apologized, finally turning her eyes to his.

"Why?" Chance asked, looking at her with such scrutiny she couldn't hold his gaze.

There was so much she wanted to say, but instead, she chose to answer, "It's four in the morning, and you need your sleep."

"I said I'd wait."

"You did," she agreed.

"Come on," he pulled her behind himself, and they went through the small doorway that led into his apartment building. He didn't let go of her hand until they were in his apartment. "Tau left about an hour ago," he said, pulling off her jacket and hanging it on a set of hooks next to the door.

"I hope you got what you needed to get done, done." She pulled off her boots and set them neatly in a corner. Feeling awkward, she stood in the middle of Chance's genkan unsure what to do or say.

"Yeah." Chance had already slipped off his shoes and stood, leaning against his hallway wall with his arms folded over his chest, staring at the floor. "Keely," he said softly and looked at her. "I want to be patient with you. I want to wait until you're ready to tell me

176

about your job, but I don't think I can. Not when you show up bleeding one second and looking like you do now the next."

Keely was dumbstruck by his confession. It wasn't that she didn't expect his questions or didn't feel like he wasn't entitled to know, she just took his patience for granted. "It's…" she started and stopped. "I want to tell you, but I'm not ready for the consequences of the truth."

"So, you don't find people and return them home?"

"I do." She nodded. "That's the very oversimplified version of it."

"And tonight?"

"A woman named Ramya Prasad needed my help," Keely said softly, still feeling the remnants of Ramya's emotions.

"So, you had to go find her and return her to her family?"

"Yes." She wanted to tell him more. She couldn't because she knew she wasn't ready to put him in the middle of her war. A sudden realization made her frown. She hadn't been honest with herself. Chance being in danger was only a minor part of why she kept the whole truth from him. Whether he believed or not, the truth about what she was and how she felt would also leave her vulnerable. The truth wouldn't just put him in the middle of her war with the never-born, it would put her heart at risk.

"No one else could have helped her?" he asked, looking back down at the floor.

"No." She slowly shook her head. "There is no one else."

He pushed himself off the wall and stepped close to her. She tried to look away from his intense staring, but he moved so he was in her line of sight. "Were you hurt?"

For a split second, she considered lying, but the 'no' got stuck in her throat. "Yes," she said softly. "But it's already been seen to." She tried to smile, but her mouth barely curved upward. "I'm fine."

He lifted his hand and ran his fingers over her cheek and down her jaw. "I want to believe you, but I don't." He dusted his fingers over her neck. Though their tips were hard with calluses, they gently brushed over her skin in a way that felt both reassuring and protective. His fingers made their way down the center of her chest and started pulling the buttons from their holes. His mouth was set, and his eyes intently stared at her skin. The last button came free, and he tugged the shirt from her shoulders and down her arms. "Where? Where did you get hurt?"

"You know about my head," she touched her fingers to her temple, and he did the same, rubbing his against her scalp, feeling the freshly healed skin.

After he seemed to satisfy himself she wasn't cut or bleeding, he turned his attention back to her face. "Where else?"

"My side." She lifted her arm to point at the left side of her rib cage, but he caught her hand in his, stopping her movements.

"Just tell me. I can look for myself." He ran his thumb over the top of her hand before pulling her into the living area of his apartment. Stopping in the middle of the floor, he turned on a bright lamp. He stepped back to her again and let go of her hand. Wrapping his arms around her waist, he reached up, unfastened her bra, and slid it off her shoulders. Then his hands were on her skin again, warm, and soft, yet unyielding in their assessment. His flat palm and careful fingers ran over both of her collarbones and sternum. He gently examined her breasts while making sure no blemish marred her skin. There was no spark of lust in his eyes, but there was need. He needed to reassure himself she truly was unharmed, so she allowed his intimate evaluation. She even managed to resist the urge to laugh when he felt at each one of her ribs to make sure they were intact. After that, he circled his hands over her stomach and back, slightly massaging her as he felt up and down her spine.

"Where else?"

"My right hip, I think. Maybe my leg," Keely answered, without meeting his gaze.

His nimble hands went to the front of her pants, unbuttoning them and pulling the flaps of her jeans apart, despite the loud protest of the zipper. He slipped her jeans down over her legs and let them bunch up around her ankles. "Step back," he instructed, squatting down in front of her and patting her calf. Pointing her toes, she slid her feet out of her jeans, and he scooted them across the floor then got down on his knees in front of her.

Taking her right ankle into his hand, he lifted her foot off the ground and smoothed the other over it checking first her toes, then her ankle. His flattened hand traveled up her leg, massaging her tight muscles, and she felt heat flood into her face. "I came here from

178

work," she said.

He looked up at her with a confused look on his face. "I know."

"I didn't have time to shave my legs."

He held her eyes in his, half smirked at her then shook his head, and continued his inspection as his fingers gently probed her kneecap. Holding her leg behind her knee, he brushed his hand up her thigh and over her lower part of her stomach. She shivered because of the stark contrast between the coolness of his apartment and the warmth of his hands. He felt at the prominent bone at her hip before kneading his fingers into the flesh of her joint and butt. After he was satisfied the bones were intact, he let go of her leg and sat back on his haunches. "Anywhere else?"

She considered lying but felt he'd read the lie on her face. "My neck."

He stood up. "Is that all?"

"Yes," she answered, nodding.

Reaching for her jaw, he cradled her face between his hands. His fingers stroked her cheeks and chin, then flowed down over her neck in light caresses. Seemingly mollified, he cupped the side of her face and tilted her head down to look at him. His brow was furrowed, and a frown pulled at his mouth. "That's a lot to go through in one day."

"I know." She covered his hand with hers. "But I promise, I'm okay."

He shook his head slightly. "You look tired, and your stomach is growling." She hadn't noticed the gurgling of her stomach until he mentioned it, but he was right. She was hungry. "And." He went silent then brushed the pad of his thumb over her cheek.

"And?" she prompted.

He lowered his hand, stepped away from her, and picked up the jinbei she'd worn earlier. He got close and wrapped the soft top around her. "I think some of what hurts isn't physical." Using the back of his fingers, he brushed hair away from her temple.

Keely smiled genuinely at him as she slid her arms into his shirt and pulled it closed. "It's currently being seen to." He seemed to consider her words then smiled brilliantly at her in return. "It's getting better every second. Especially," she added, feeling suddenly breathless. She closed the gap between them and draped her arms around his neck. "When you smile at me, it's marvelously distracting."

He pulled her into himself and lightly touched his lips to hers. "I like being able to distract you." He smiled again. "But your stomach is really loud."

She giggled. "Yeah, it's a little hungry."

"I have some onigiri," he offered. Kissing her lightly again, he let go of her and walked into the kitchen.

"That sounds perfect," she said, tying his shirt closed.

A short time later, the two of them sat on his couch, eating seaweed-wrapped rice balls. Keely wasn't sure what flavor Chance's was, but hers was a delicious, smoky, salty, fish, probably salmon, mixed with creamy mayonnaise. "This is so good," she said, stuffing the last bite into her mouth. After chewing and swallowing the delicious concoction, she turned to Chance. "Thank you."

"I thought you might be hungry when you got back, so I went to the convenience store," he said, finishing his own rice ball.

"Not just for the curry and the onigiri." She stopped. Brushing her hands down her bare legs, she straightened her arms and pushed against her knees. "Just, thank you."

He reached over and brushed her hair back from her shoulder. "It's almost five in the morning. We should both get some sleep."

"Okay," she agreed with a nod and helped him clean up the coffee table. Rubbing her eyes and yawning, she padded her way to his bed. After stripping off his jinbei, she lifted the comforter and slid underneath. Chance's scent, coffee and musk, filled her nostrils, and she thought she'd sleep quite soundly. By the time she settled into the mattress, Chance had turned off all the lights, except for a small lamp that sat on the kitchen counter.

He walked over to the bed and peeled off the t-shirt he wore then unfastened and slid off his jeans. Lifting the blanket, he got into the bed, pulled her to his chest, and enveloped her in a tight embrace. Kissing her forehead, he said, "I'm going to be able to sleep better with you here."

"Me too," she agreed. Next to Chance was the safest and calmest she'd felt the entire day. She realized then why she was so relaxed around Chance and why she seemed to crave his presence. She didn't have to be guarded, disciplined or hide her feelings. She wasn't the world's only Priestess. She was a flawed woman with wants and desires, not a fighter of supernatural beings. She could be herself around him. Sutton and her brother were the only other people she was able to do be comfortable around, but those relationships were different. It wasn't as intimate of a connection as she had with Chance.

Nestling her head on the pillow next to his, she absently ran her fingers over his shoulder and arm, tracing circles over his tattoo. "Chance?"

"Hm?" he responded, sounding tired.

"Thank you, for not letting me..." She wanted to say, not letting me run away, but instead chose, "Thank you for being here." Pressing her lips to his she was rewarded with a long sensual kiss that comforted her more than sent her pulse racing.

He ended the kiss, combed a hand through her hair, then cradled her head against his shoulder. Resting his chin on the top of her head, he said, "Thank you for letting me see the worst parts of you." He breathed in and out deeply. "They're very easy to deal with."

She smiled, sighed, and fully relaxed into him. Just as she started to settle into sleep, she had a worrying thought because she wanted more time with him than until the sun came up. "Are you working tomorrow? I mean what are you doing tomorrow? Do you have any free time?" she asked hurriedly.

"I already have plans."

"Oh. I'm sorry I kept you up so late. I didn't mean..."

"I have plans to do whatever you want me to do," he interrupted. "If you don't have to work."

She beamed at him. "Sutton took my phone. I have two whole days free." She kissed his shoulder. "Just so you know, after I get some sleep, doing whatever I want could be very exhausting for you."

He let out a short laugh and kissed her temple. "I genuinely hope so."

19

Chance stood next to Simeon behind Tau and Ren, watching a set of monitors in front of them map out music as they listened to music playback. Jack, their British sound technician, sat next to Tau, smiling. "This is good," he said in accented Japanese before turning to the four of them. "The more you two fight," he pointed to Tau and Chance, "the better the song, and this one is," he paused and seemed to consider his words, "bloody brilliant," he finished in English.

Chance grinned, knowing exactly what Jack had said. Getting such a compliment from Jack was very sought after in their industry and an accomplishment for them. They'd spent the last four days in the studio with Jack, recording their latest EP. Initially, they'd planned for six songs, but Chance had pushed for a seventh. A song had come to him, and despite it being rough and unrefined, he'd worked with Tau and Jack to get it on the EP.

Jack's 'bloody brilliant' almost made constant battles over the song worth it. It was true. Chance and Tau had fought endlessly over the sound of every note and beat until both could agree it was acceptable. That was their habit; the two of them had differing ideas of perfection, and they had to constantly fight for a compromise. Jack wasn't wrong; the song was good. He wasn't wrong about their fighting either. Eternity's End's most popular songs were usually representative of small wars fought between Chance and Tau. This one had been their worst yet, and Chance hoped the trend continued because he felt 'Honest Violet' was genuinely good despite his bias because he wrote the song.

"Well, I think we need to redo some of the vocals because the bleed is too heavy, and there is an echo, but after that, we can lay the backup vocals, and this will be ready for mixing." Jack hit some keys on the keyboard in front of him.

"Bloody brilliant isn't perfect." Tau rolled his eyes then added, "I think we should finish this tonight."

"Agreed. As tired as I am, I have to admit the vibe is good, and you need to finish laying all the vocals." Jack turned to the four of them. "Simeon and Ren, you can go, your tracks are solid. Chance, you can take an hour or so break and come back to record the backup vocals. Tau, I think we can get the corrections done in an hour or two, then you can rest your voice for a couple of days."

Chance wasn't paying attention to anything else Jack had to say. He'd been dismissed for a much-needed break and planned on taking advantage of it. Patting Tau on the shoulder to signal his departure, he headed toward the door. Pulling out his phone, he looked at the time and frowned. He was hoping to get a break earlier so he could meet Keely for a late lunch. Once they started recording, no one wanted to stop, and he hadn't texted her since he'd told her he'd be late. They'd hardly spent any time together over the last week and little before they started recording. The one night he did see her, he'd been physically exhausted and mentally spent, so he'd been unable to do more than show up at her apartment and fall into bed. Although, spending the night with her sleeping curled next to him had energized and revived him like nothing else could. When he woke the next morning, he'd wanted to take full advantage of that energy, but he found himself alone. Still, he'd missed her, so he'd asked her to meet him for a short lunch, and now he'd stood her up. He sincerely doubted she'd be mad, but he still wanted to see her, and he'd lost his opportunity.

He affectionately tapped on the picture of Keely wearing a light blue top and showing a dangerous amount of cleavage. It was the selfie she had taken using his phone and programmed as the avatar for her number. After three rings he heard a short, "Hello." Then there was some quick mumbling in English followed by an "Oh my god, oh my god, I'm going to die."

"Keely, are you alright?" he asked, almost panicked. Knowing her job caused her physical damage had not been easy for him especially since she wasn't forthcoming with answers.

"Yes," she sighed. "I suck at video games. I don't think the controller's working right."

"Did you try reloading?" he asked, feeling relieved.

There was a short pause before she said, "Guns need bullets. Makes sense."

Chance smiled into the phone. "Playing meat shield again?"

"Hey, I make a good meat shield. It doesn't work as well when it's only me playing," Keely huffed. "How did recording go?"

"We're laying down the last of the vocal tracks tonight."

"Yeah, I have no idea what that means other than someone might be singing," she admitted.

"Tau is re-recording the lead vocals now, and I'll be recording back up later tonight," he explained, finding an abandoned hallway and leaning against the wall there. "Vocals are the last tracks to get recorded then the song gets mixed."

"Oh, so you're almost done? Will you have time later?"

"I have a break right now, after that I don't know." He kicked at an invisible rock on the floor in front of him. It would be early hours in the morning before they finished. Tomorrow would start a whirlwind of work. There was cover art to consider, press photos to do, and they'd also have to record the accompanying music videos. Then there would be tons of promoting. He'd only have a very few hours in the middle of the night to himself and some nights, not at all. It would be days, if not weeks, before he could have something other than stolen moments with Keely.

"I'm sorry I missed our lunch."

"Me too. I made you a good one," she informed.

"You made me lunch?" he asked, both pleased and stunned by her gesture, wishing he'd made their lunch date all the more.

"Well, yes, a worldly Americanized version of one."

"I'm sorry," he apologized again. Chance was genuinely sorry he hadn't gotten to eat the food she'd prepared.

"You know you could meet me for dinner."

Disappointment hollowed out his stomach. "I wish I could, but your apartment is too far away for me to meet you."

"Yeah, it would be, but I'm not there. I'm at the Manga-Kissa a block from the restaurant you wanted to meet at."

Chance came up off the wall and started heading back down the hallway to the elevator. "The one with the neon cat outside?"

"Hey, don't judge. It's nice in here."

"Judge?" he asked, confused by her statement.

"It means form negative opinions. In other words, stay open-minded."

"I'm not going to judge you." He smashed the button for the down elevator. "I'm about to catch the elevator. You're not far from

184

me, so I'll be there in less than ten minutes."

"I'll meet you outside," she said. The phone disconnected just as the elevator door opened.

Ten minutes later, he made his way through the still-busy sidewalks, shouldering through crowds of people. The brightly lit neon cat of the manga café came into view, and he almost ran the last few steps to get to it, but then stopped in his tracks when he saw Keely waiting for him beneath it. Even if he hadn't been looking for her, she'd have stood out. She was so captivating; he wasn't the only one staring. Her curves were accentuated by her high-waisted, short, purple skirt and fitted, blue shirt. Toned ivory legs stemmed out from the skirt, drawing attention to them. If the eye wasn't drawn there, then it immediately went to her very ample breasts. Chance took all of her in, but his eyes were drawn to the part of her that he found most enthralling, her eyes. Waving her hand, she offered him a smile and the violet of her eyes sparkled with some deep emotion he was sure was for him alone.

He walked up to her smiling. "You've been here for a long time?" he asked, offering her a slight bow.

A blush spread across her cheeks. "A couple of hours," she confirmed with a shrug. "I didn't know if you'd get a break, and I wanted to see you, but now I feel like a stalker."

He couldn't help but laugh. "You're honest, not a stalker." He stepped closer to her and traced a finger down her arm. "I'm glad you waited."

"That only means you approve of me as a stalker, not that I'm not one." She reached down and took his hand. "I got us a room for two if you want to stay here. If not, we can go somewhere else."

"I'm going to choose the option that allows us to be alone the quickest." He wove his fingers through hers and squeezed them slightly.

"Good choice." Her smiled broadened. She turned and went through the glass door of the café, pulling him behind her. Keely waved at the woman behind the counter while he bowed his head politely as they went past into the recesses of the building. They walked through a maze of doors with brightly lit numbers; some had shoes outside, indicating they were occupied. After she led him down two hallways, she stopped at a door labeled fifty-six. "Emi, the lady who works up front, suggested this room because it was slightly bigger than the others. And I'm tall," Keely whispered as she slid off the heeled boots she wore. "She's very nice." She opened the door, stepped inside and waited.

"She is." Chance slid off his converse and followed her into the small chamber. The room had high light blue walls and muted lighting. A large television, a computer, two controllers and two headsets sat on a long shelf opposite the door along with a food menu.

His need was so distracting, he only spared the room a cursory glance. Carefully, he pushed the door closed then he reached out and lightly dusted his fingers over Keely's cheek and jaw. Her violet eyes seemed to glow as her face softened into an expression that was full of feeling. Neither of them said anything. They didn't have to, because powerful, shared emotion passed between them. Though he understood what they'd quietly shared, he was sure he could never explain. He pulled her to himself, and his lips found hers, meshing into them as their tongues coiled together. It only took seconds before his body throbbed and he hardened with want.

He continued his fervent discovery of her mouth as he trailed his hand down her neck and over her collarbone, dipping his fingers inside her shirt and bra. His hand filled with soft, warm flesh, and he ran his thumb over silken skin and soft nipple. It hardened under his soft caressing. That she so quickly reacted to his touch deeply pleased him. She let out a soft sigh and took his bottom lip between her teeth, gently scraping them across it. A small moan escaped him, and he slightly squeezed the wonderfully soft flesh he held.

Unexpectedly, her mouth left his, and she pulled her breast from his reach. Breathing heavily out of her nose, she put a finger to her smiling lips and whispered, "Shh." She pointed to the open partitions of the rooms. The manga café was like any other, the rooms were semi-private. Unless someone was very tall, they couldn't see what went on inside of them, but sound carried, and he'd forgotten that. Looking into his eyes, she kissed the corner of his mouth. Before he could push for more, she moved and licked at the side of his neck. "Sit down and relax," she whispered invitingly as she tugged on the hand she still held and stepped toward one of the chairs.

He stepped forward, sank into one of the chairs and pulled her onto his lap. She settled her bottom on top of his groin and draped her legs over the arm of the chair. He walked his fingers up her stomach,

186

over her breast, and reasserted his hold underneath her top and bra.

"Your hands are warm," she whispered as she spread her hands across his chest, ran them up over his neck, and cupped his face. "Chance," she said softly, with a quiver in her voice.

He was suddenly unsure. They were in a semi-public place. Though he didn't care, he didn't want to be disrespectful. "I'm sorry," he quietly apologized, pulling his hand away, almost embarrassed by his own aggression. "I should have considered where we were and what you wanted."

"I didn't say to stop. I just want permission," she responded, before bending down and softly tracing her tongue over his bottom lip.

He couldn't keep from trembling. "Permission for what?" he asked, forgetting his trepidations.

"To be as wicked as I want to be." Her lips were on his again, and her tongue ignited his desire then she pulled away, slightly smiling.

He stared at her face, wondering at the slight upturn at the corners of her mouth and the ardent way she stared in return. Any concern he had about what she might have been thinking was immediately forgotten to lustful curiosity. "I have a fetish for tall women now. I might have a fetish for wicked ones too."

She smiled. "I think you will." She loosened her hold on his face and pulled away, trailing her fingers over his cheeks and jaw. Her hands went to her shirt, and she nimbly unbuttoned it then pulled it down her shoulders. She laid it in the chair next to them before she folded her hands behind her back. A quick movement later, her plump breasts were bounding free of the constraints of her bra. She leaned into him, pressing her soft flesh to his chest. He was frustrated at his clothes because he wanted to feel her skin against his. Chance tightly wound his arms around her waist, spanning his hands across the smooth skin of her back. Lowering her head to his lips, she kissed the corner of his mouth then traced the line of his jaw with them before she gently blew into his ear. His earrings rattled against her teeth when she took his earlobe between them, making him shiver. Her tongue swirled around his earlobe then licked over the sensitive spot on the side of his neck. A shock went through every nerve of his body, and he sucked in air through his teeth.

"I think I'm going to like being wicked." Her lips found their way back to his, and her kiss was so provocative he couldn't form a coherent thought. After several minutes of heated exploration of her mouth, she started trailing kisses over his chin and neck. Pulling the buttons of his shirt from their holes, she pushed it open then slid up his t-shirt and started dragging her lips across his chest, teasing his skin into reaction. With a decidedly wicked look on her face, she slid off his lap and kneeled on the floor between his legs.

For a moment, she sat before him smiling, lust and excitement burned in her violet eyes. She reached over, grabbed her bag and pulled out a bottle she quickly stowed somewhere on the floor. "I've considered this sort of wickedness for quite some time," she said huskily, smiling coyly. A pretty blush spread across her cheeks, but she still had an enticingly naughty look on her face. He started to lean forward, seeking her lips. She shook her head, used her hand to push him back against the chair, and resettled herself on the floor. Rubbing her hands up and down his legs, she gently massaged his inner thighs making him burn with anticipation. Slowly, she reached up, unfastened his belt, and the snap on his jeans. His zipper seemed unusually loud when she pulled apart the flaps of his pants. One of her hands pulled back his briefs and cold air dusted over the heated skin of his groin. He quickly inhaled and exhaled when she wrapped her fingers around his shaft, gently caressing it. At first, her cold hands were a surprise, but she rubbed her fingers up and down, stimulating his length, and he forgot about the coolness of her skin.

He shifted, gripping the chair's arms as her hand again slowly went up and down his shaft, causing sensations that spread through his groin, up to his spine, and across his skin. She tugged at his pants and briefs pulling them down so all of him was exposed. The bottle of clear liquid appeared, and she poured some into her hand then rubbed it all over his shaft and head, covering him in warm gel and causing him to tremble. Her firm but soft hands felt so good sliding up and down shaft, especially when she ridged her fingers over the head. She made a salacious vison, sitting topless between his legs, staring up at him with burning violet eyes as she stroked his member.

The arms of the chair suffered his pleasure when he dug his fingernails into them because she steadily sped up her movements. Then she dipped her head down, and he felt her lips press to his swollen tip. His whole body reacted. Every muscle in it flexed as her hot mouth surrounded his head, and he felt her velvety tongue flatten over it. The feeling radiating from between his legs trailed exquisite sensation throughout every one of his nerves, muscles, and vital organs. He reached out and put his hand on her head, subtly encouraging her as her mouth slowly slid down, completely enveloping him in humid lusciousness.

Her movements caused soft hair to spill down her face and over his hip, blocking his view, denying him part of his enjoyment. He liked watching Keely, the beautiful woman she was, pleasure him with her mouth and hands. He brushed his fingers through her hair, pulling it away from her face. A slight, high-pitched sound escaped her, tickling him. Her tight lips glided up, and she abruptly pulled her mouth away.

"Ouch," she said, trying to maneuver away from his hand but was unable to move because a large piece of her hair was tangled around one of the thick chain bracelets he wore. Suddenly, he felt like an awkward schoolboy getting his first blow job as he watched her pull strands of hair away from his wrist. He didn't know what to say or do other than to help her pick the colorful tresses from the chain. When they finished, she patted down her hair, looked up and frowned at him with a finger pressed to her lips.

Folding her arms over his lap, she leaned in, tickled her lips across his stomach. Quietly, she whispered, "This isn't going to work." Before he could protest, she stood, reached underneath her skirt, and slid off her pink, lacy panties. She straddled him then whispered, "Lean forward and put your hands behind your back."

For a fraction of a second, he considered denying her request, but the look on her face promised he'd enjoy whatever she had in mind, so he complied. He moved forward and crossed his wrists behind his back. She leaned over him, pushing her bared breasts to his face. Accepting her invitation, he took one of her nipples into his mouth, massaging it with his tongue as he sucked. A small noise escaped her throat. She huffed heavily in his ear and pressed her breast against his mouth. Maneuvering so she could reach behind him, she tied per panties around his wrist. After his hands were snuggly bound together, she asked in a broken whisper, "Is that okay?"

Lightly scraping his teeth against the nipple, he pulled away and got a soft whimper in response. Looking up at her face, he smiled because he could easily rip apart the panties if he wanted. "Yes," he answered, gently biting at the side of her breast.

She started breathing heavily. Raking her fingers through his hair, she hugged his head to her chest. Adoring the way she clung to him, he circled his tongue around her nipple before taking it into his mouth again.

With a soft moan, she pulled away, only to heatedly explore his mouth again. "I think we need more precautions," she whispered breathlessly in his ear as she reached up and pulled the scarf from her hair. "Normally, I like hearing you moan, but it might be a bad idea here," she said teasingly in his ear, untying the scarf and straightening it. "That's a lie. I don't care if you moan. I just want to...." Her voice trailed off. Smiling, she threaded the scarf through her teeth and pulled it back and forth. His brain was so drunk on desire, it took him a moment to understand what she wanted.

Chance never thought he'd agree to being tied up and gagged, but passion made Keely's skin glow, and she looked at him as if he was something to be devoured. He didn't consider denying her request. Dipping his head down, he licked the rise of her breast. She shivered, and he lifted his face and kissed her through the scarf. "Okay," he whispered in English.

"Okay," she repeated and folded her arms around his head, winding the scarf around it. The fabric tightened around his mouth barely biting into his cheeks. He didn't care because she was biting his earlobe and neck again. It was his turn to shiver.

Pressing him back in the chair she tickled kisses down his neck, and her breasts brushed down his body. Their cool voluptuousness rubbed over his chest and stomach before nestling on either side of his crotch. His only thought was he didn't want her to stop. The bottle of clear fluid again appeared in her hands. She looked up, intently staring at his face as she filled her hands with the liquid and rubbed all over their exposed skin. Then she started moving up and down, using the soft flesh of her glorious cleavage to stroke him. He had to bite at the gag to stifle a groan. Her smooth skin enveloped and glided over his length, thrilling his whole body and making it tremble.

Chance let his head fall back, closed his eyes, and gave himself over to sensation. The soft flesh of her breasts that kept rubbing

190

up and down him was joined by the heat of her mouth. He thought he'd lose his mind to the exquisiteness of it as her lips and tongue caressing his head, and her breasts enfolded his shaft. Up and down she went, and with each stroke, he breathed out heavily through his nose. Then she was taking his length into her mouth as one of her hands came up, fondling then cupping the softer parts of his groin and gently squeezing. Over and over her mouth moved up and down him with her tongue carefully running around the tip of his girth. Titillation torrents exhilarated his body and heightening his arousal. Tension started to build, and every muscle in his body trembled with the anticipation. Abruptly, she pulled away, and he felt a sharp pinch in his thigh from her teeth. He barely managed to suppress his lament of protest, but then he felt her tongue flicker over one the soft flesh she'd previously held before she gave it her full attention. Shocks went up his spine and radiated out his limbs. Lost in mind-altering sensation, he forgot all about his pain. As she continued exploring him with her mouth, her hand started moving over his length, and he was almost undone by ecstasy.

He pulled against his bonds and shook his head, unable to express his immense pleasure any other way. Her mouth returned to his shaft and slid down over it, taking in all of its length. Unable to control himself any longer, he started thrusting into her mouth. She met each thrust with her own movements as she brought a hand back up to hold what her mouth had abandoned. The pressure of his oncoming orgasm started to build again as every nerve seemed to migrate south, electrifying his groin. Her mouth continued to slide up and down, steadily increasing speed, deepening the heady pressure. In the next instant, he climaxed, releasing marvelous intensity. His muscles tightened then spasmed as wave after wave of exquisite sensation made his body seize and shudder with pleasure. The orgasm was so potent and astoundingly long that he lost his breath to it then found himself trying to gulp in air through the gag.

When he could distinguish minute sensations again, he felt the back of her throat tighten, and his seed was carried away with the slight tingling. After the last sensational pulses subsided and his breath steadied, Keely sucked hard on him, pulled her mouth up his shaft, and came away, leaving him spent and heaving for air. Opening his eyes seemed like effort, so he remained as he was, delighting the aftermath of his enjoyment.

Soft rustling echoed in the silence. Something cold and wet covered him. He jumped in his chair, opened his eyes, and sat up. "Sorry," Keely mouthed as she wiped a small towelette over him. He softened under the cold cloth as she cleaned away the lubricant and other fluids. Then she was tugging up on his pants and briefs. "Lift up," she commanded. He moved so she could slide his clothes into place. After she settled everything and fastened his pants and belt, she pulled down his t-shirt and re-buttoned his outer shirt. He wasn't sure what he was supposed to do, so he sat quietly, watching her. With a heavy sigh, she stood up, sat on his lap, and produced another towelette. If he hadn't been so drained from her previous wickedness, watching her wipe clean her breasts would have made him hard.

"Keely," he mumbled quietly through the gag.

"Just a sec," she said, picking up a cup sitting on the computer table and taking a long drink from it. Twisting in his lap, she adjusted his collar as she finished the drink in her hand. With a smile, she set the cup down, then put her bra and shirt back on. "I was planning on doing that later when we were alone," she explained as she reached for her bag. "I just," she stopped and stared at him, and a pretty blush spread across her cheeks. "I wanted to please you."

"Keely," he repeated, shifting in the chair so he could break the bonds of her panties.

"One sec." She put a hand out to stop him. Then she rummaged through her bag and pulled a small package of candy. Opening the package, she put a piece in her mouth and said, "I never thought I'd be this kind of woman, but I kind of like you tied up." She reached her arms around his head, undid the scarf, brushing the silk down over his lips, and dropping it into his lap. All the while her eyes sparkled with obvious lust and her slightly heavy breath dusted the scent of mint and citrus across his face.

Chance lost the patience for being tied up. The panties at his wrists gave way with one hard, quick tug. Then he was wrapping his arms around her, crushing her against his chest, and seeking her lips. Their kiss was slow, gentle, and sensual in a way that he felt deep emotion pass between them.

After several enjoyable minutes, she ended the kiss and wound her arms around his neck. "I like being wicked," she whispered against his lips.

"You can be as wicked as you want with me." He licked at her lips, tasting the sweetness of the juice she'd been drinking. "Keep in mind, it gives me ideas."

She giggled and kissed him again. "I can't wait to benefit from your wickedness." She raked her fingers through his hair, making his head tingle. "Are you hungry?"

"Mm," he answered, suddenly feeling exhausted. He was hungry, but he was not inclined to eat because he didn't want to move.

"You can eat whenever or take it with you. Just relax." She moved to get off him, and he tightened his hold.

"Only if you stay where you are." He reached up and caressed the side of her face. "You know, making food is a big deal in my culture."

"One of my neighbors told me that it was. Especially men like it when a woman makes him lunch."

"It means you like me," he explained.

"I do," she said, resting her head on his shoulder. "I think I liked you the first time you smiled at me and even more now."

Her confession exhilarated him, and his heart started pounding in his chest. "I like you a lot too."

"Would you like me more if I told you I bought you a present?"

"No." He shook his head. "I'd like you more even without the present."

"Oh," she laughed against his shirt to keep quiet. "You're very charming today. You deserve a present." She reached down and grabbed the bag that seemed to be a carry-all for everything. "It's just something small though." She reached into the bag and withdrew a small box and pulled out something metallic. Grabbing his hand, opening it, and spreading out his fingers, she carefully set the cool metal in his palm. It was a tiny mechanical bird, maybe four centimeters high, and made of minuscule cogs, wheels, and wires. The bird sat in his hand with its wings spread, staring at him with bronze eyes. Keely tapped one of its wings with her finger, and both of them fluttered. "Sutton and I found this really cool shop with art and collectibles. This guy made animals out of old watch parts. This one was the only hawk, and it kind of reminded me of you."

"It's..." he faltered, staring at the gift. "It's as rare as the woman who gave it to me."

She smiled, cupped his face in her hands, and kissed him until they were both breathless. "I really like being charmed by you. I'll have to be wicked more oft—" A loud shrill tone interrupted her and disturbed the quiet of the café.

He watched trying to hide his displeasure as she scrambled to grab the phone from her bag and quickly answer it. After a brief conversation in English, she turned to him. "I have to go," she said, looking down at the phone clutched in her hands.

"Am I allowed to know anything else?" he asked, picking up the box and carefully placing the bird back in it.

She cleared her throat and brushed a thick strand of hair behind her ear. "I want to tell you, I do. It's part of the reason I waited for you today. But I can't now."

"Why?" He was angry, despite wanting to give her the time and patience she needed to tell him the truth.

"Chance, you have to believe I want to tell you. I can't today, especially not today. I know when I tell you, you'll look at me differently and I can't..." Her voice trailed off.

"You've said that before."

"It's still true," she asserted.

"So, are you're going to tell me ever?"

"Next time we meet." She nodded certainly.

He frowned for half a second then said "Okay. I can be patient a little longer."

Her grip on the phone tightened. "I'm going to be gone a couple of days, maybe a week or more."

"Is it going to be dangerous for you?" he asked, remembering the time she showed up at his apartment looking devastated and bleeding.

"No." She shook her head, but he somehow knew she was lying.

His frustration finally got the better of him. "If you can't be honest then don't tell me anything."

She lifted her eyes to his, and the pretty violet had dulled somehow. "Chance, I will be as good as my word. I promise to tell you everything, but for today can we go on as we are?"

194

He wanted to ask her if she really thought so little of him that her secret would change his mind and how he felt so drastically. Instead, he bit back his frustration and anxiety and forced a soft smile. He knew she was leaving; he knew she'd lied about the fact she was about to be in danger, and he didn't want to send her away upset. He didn't want to be the distraction that put her in more danger.

"Keely. I...I" he stuttered. He wasn't sure how to reassure her and get reassurance from her. "I'll wait until you get done with whatever you have to do." He reached up and smoothed his thumb over her frowning bottom lip.

Suddenly, she was hugging him tightly and nuzzling her face into his neck. "I don't want to go; I have to."

He hugged her tightly in return, concerned by her slight trembling, feeling inadequate because he couldn't do anything to soothe her. "I don't want you to go either. And you should know, there is very little you could say that would make me change my opinion of you."

Several long moments passed before she let go of him. "Thank you," she said before kissing him again. Sliding off his lap, she quickly gathered her things before picking up a large, pastel blue lunch bag. "I did make you a lot of food," she said, offering it to him.

"I'll eat every bit of it." He took the bag from her before reaching out and taking her hand in his. "You'll be safe?"

She bent down and kissed him slowly, allowing him to savor the feel and taste of her. "Yes," she answered, and he wasn't sure whether to believe her or not, considering he wasn't sure if she was lying to him or herself. She stood, turned toward the door and let go of his fingers.

He shared her perceived reluctance and wound his fingers through hers, holding her in place. "Wait, we'll walk out together." He stood and quickly grabbed her gift and the lunch she'd made.

When he turned back to her, her smile was so stunning it nearly stole his breath even though her eyes were glistening. "Thank you," she said softly.

"I'm not sure why you're thanking me, but I like it when you smile at me like that." Stepping closer to her, he lifted the hand he held and kissed the inside of her wrist. She shivered, and he smiled, liking that such a small gesture could elicit a response from her. "Let's go."

They walked out through the café holding hands. Keely only let go long enough to pay the cashier. When she was done, she wove her fingers tightly through his. It was then he realized he was her comfort. While part of him worried over what she was about to endure, he was relieved to find his presence gave her reassurance. They walked outside and found Sutton standing on the edge of the sidewalk, leaning against a large, black SUV. She looked from Keely to him and gave them both an approving nod.

Suddenly, someone grabbed him from behind. At the same time, something hard hit against his legs. In the next instant, he was on the ground, his face scraping against the pavement because a foot pinned his head to the concrete. He didn't have to ask who. His debt collectors had come to persuade him to give them more than the money he owed. They'd come for his music.

20

Keely was caught off guard. She never expected to be attacked by a human, but years of training and instinct prevailed. There were three men. One on top of Chance, and two around him. She lifted her foot and kicked out, hitting the man standing on Chance. Her heel struck his stomach with such force, he was momentarily airborne. Clutching his stomach, he collapsed to the ground. He rolled down the sidewalk, choking and gagging for air. Turning her attention to the second man, she wasn't surprised to find Sutton driving her knee into his groin before slamming it into his head. That left a slightly older man with an intense stare and a knife. He stepped toward her, stopping long enough to drive a foot into Chance's middle. It was a vicious tactic meant to intimidate both her and Chance, but it did the exact opposite for Keely.

"You're going to regret that," Keely said with all the loathing she felt. Before she could think to stop herself, she wrapped the man in an illusion, a torment for him alone.

The man took another step forward, smiling as if he thought her funny, but the illusion took form. He stopped, and a bewildered expression crossed his features. He opened his mouth, and a small noise escaped him as he grabbed his elbow, probably trying to make a tourniquet to stop the spreading of pain. His lower arm twitched, his fingers wriggled back and forth. He lifted his hand and stared at it with wide eyes and opened mouth. His fingers thinned then folded in on themselves as the skin covering his hand stretched then peeled off.

The dried skin fell off in large flakes, leaving behind bloody pieces of muscle and dark gray bone. "I'm sure it hurts," Keely hissed and took a step forward. "Much like violence, it will spread." The man let go of his wrist and slapped at his arm, shoulder, then face. The smooth skin of his cheek started to wrinkle, his eye socket cracked apart, and his eyeball rolled out of his head, swinging from sinew and ligaments. Keely's illusion was so complete, she even gifted the man with the smell of rotten meat and the sight of a shifting street as the eyeball swayed back and forth.

"Keely." Sutton's sharp voice interrupted Keely's thoughts. "What are you doing?"

Hands grabbed ahold of Keely's arms, shaking her hard. It took a moment for her to understand why Sutton was standing in front of her with an irritated expression. Anger made it seem reasonable that the man should suffer living rot. Then she realized what she was doing and immediately dissolved the illusion. The gangster backed away from her, rubbing his hands over his cheek and eye repeatedly.

"Chance." Keely turned her attention to the figure that sat on the ground a few feet away from her. She went to him and got down on her knees. "Are you okay?" she asked, reaching out a hand to touch the scrapes on the side of his face.

He flinched away from her and rolled to his feet. "I'm fine." She'd never seen his features so tight and severe looking. It wasn't anger, or sadness, but a very forced indifference. Turning his back to her, he stepped over to one of the men on the ground and helped him up. "I apologize." He dusted the man's clothes off.

Keely was confused. "You know these men?" she asked.

He didn't acknowledge her question or even look at her, instead went to the second man and helped him off the ground. The second man looked from Chance to Keely then to Sutton. Chance leaned in close and whispered something in the man's ear then bowed.

Keely suddenly felt uncomfortable, more than awkward, she felt out of place. It was a familiar emotion. She'd spent her life continually moving from one country to another. There was never a permanent place for her, she didn't make friends, and she rarely dated. Though she was the revered Priestess, she was an outcast. That was the reason she'd been careful with whom she'd formed attachments. She'd forgotten that precious few people saw her differently. She looked around the street where they stood, watching people walk by and pretend not to notice them or the man still huddled on the ground crying. Then she turned to Chance for reassurance and found herself staring at his back since he refused to face her.

"I'd say they were bill collectors," Sutton said from beside her, sounding like she was under water.

"Makes sense," Keely said, not really understanding because her emotions were so tumultuous, they clouded her mind.

After she took several deep breaths, she looked at each man

individually, making sure they didn't suffer too much damage. The tallest of the three men stood over Chance's now bowed head with a severe frown and a small line of blood trickling from a crack in his lip. The man whom she'd kicked, a young man with blond streaked hair, was leaning on one arm against a wall, trying to catch his breath. The one on whom she'd cast the illusion was now standing but scrubbed at his face as if to make sure his skin was still there.

"What are you going to do about him?" she asked in a cracked voice.

"The ministry will take care of it."

"Did Chance…" Her voice trailed off.

"He didn't see," Sutton confirmed.

The two of them watched Chance bow deeply. The man ignored his bow. He nodded to his companion and the third man went to the one, whom Keely had cast the illusion. The first, the leader, marched up to Keely and Sutton, stomping his feet loudly on the side-walk. "You, foreigners, you have no right to interfere in affairs that are none of your business." He stepped closer to them bowing up his chest. "Maybe, you need to learn Japanese manners."

"Maybe…" Keely started in retort, but Sutton nudged her with her elbow.

"Wait for it," she said in English with a broad smile.

This seemed to increase the man's ire. "How dare you?" The man stepped closer, putting his face mere inches from Sutton's, trying to make himself seem larger and more intimidating. "In Japan, we don't value ugly foreign women, especially those who are nuisances." A loud buzzing could be heard coming from the inside of the man's pocket, interrupting anything else he had to say.

"You may want to answer your phone." Sutton folded her arms across her chest and smiled again. The man jerked away from them, turned his back, and answered his phone.

"What did you do?" Keely asked absently, staring at Chance who still stood in the middle of the street with his head bowed.

"Like I said, they are debt collectors. Chance probably owes them money, and they're here to collect. That is their right. However, they won't be doing it in front of you. After our last encounter with a syndicated family, I made it my business to know who they were and take the time to make introductions. Strangely enough, they are well

informed on the occult and knew exactly who we are, who you are."
She huffed and smirked. "So, once we got these three under control, I
made a phone call to one of my new friends."

The man on the phone half turned and looked at them. A second later his mouth fell open, and he turned ghostly white. He slowly
pulled the phone away from his ear. For a long moment, he simply
stared at them. Sutton smiled, lifted her fingers, and casually waved
them at his shocked expression.

He turned to Chance. "You should have told me you knew the
Priestess, then all of this unpleasantness could have been avoided. The
debt you owe has been absolved."

"No," Chance spoke out as he lifted his head to the man. "The
debt is owed, it is mine, and I will take responsibility for it."

"That is your choice." The leader of the men turned back to
Keely and lowered himself down to his knees. Placing his hands in
front of him he bowed his head so low it nearly touched the ground. "I
apologize for any offense I have caused. Please forgive my ignorant
self, Priestess."

"There'll be no more violence between you and my... companion," Keely ordered.

"No, we've been ordered not to interfere with him or his
friends, but if he wants to repay his debt, his payment is due in two
days."

Keely was livid all over again. "If the debt was not overdue
then there was no need for such heavy-handed violence."

Before she could act Chance stepped forward and stood
between her and the man. "This is none of your business," he admonished briskly.

His anger felt like a sharp stab in the gut with a smoldering
knife. Hurt opened up inside her chest, threatening to stop her heart,
and take away her breath. She looked into his hardened face and
found his unrelenting brown eyes so clouded by his anger she couldn't
even see herself reflected in them. She felt crushed.

"You're right." She looked at the ground.

With as much dignity as she could muster, she marched across
the sidewalk, retrieving the lunch she'd made. The tiny cogwheel bird
lay on the ground beside its white box. Picking it up, she held it in the
palm of her hand, staring at it, feeling like a fool. For a fraction of a

moment, she'd dared to hope Chance might accept and care for her as she was, Priestess and all. Clearing her throat, she blinked back tears and turned around to face Chance. He stood staring at her with a disapproving frown sharpening his features. She walked toward Sutton, who stood waiting with the door of the SUV open. Keely had never been more thankful for her best friend, especially when she needed a strategic exit.

"I'm sorry," she said softly as she passed Chance without looking at him.

Climbing into the SUV, she felt broken. Old feelings she'd refused to confront roared up in her chest, and she felt more alone than ever, more disconnected than ever, more hurt than ever. She settled into the seat next to the window and stared out it. Tears filled her eyes and started to spill down her cheeks. She was sure whatever she had with Chance was over. She was equally as certain her feelings for him had gone way past liking him. Even if she wasn't willing to admit how deep those feelings ran, she could admit her heart was breaking.

A couple of minutes later, the car shifted, and she heard the leather of the seat next to her squeak as the door on the other side closed. She didn't turn around, wanting to keep her tears private. Sutton would try and fix the situation, maybe even try and fix Keely, but there was no fixing any of it.

The seat moved, and she could feel eyes on her back. She couldn't look at Sutton because she would be able to see all Keely was feeling. She'd know Keely's heart was shattered. She'd see all the self-doubt and sadness that came with a lifetime of limited human connection. She'd know the truth about how Keely felt, always a life of combat, never truly winning because there was no way to win with the neverborn. Just then, for Keely, it felt like too much, and her tears turned into streams that dripped off her chin and fell onto her shirt. In a day, she'd be fighting for her life and the souls of a thousand others in the suicide forest. She wasn't sure she had it in her to fight anymore.

"I actually wanted to eat the lunch you made for me," Chance said from beside her. She stiffened at the sound of his voice and quickly wiped at her tears but didn't look at him. "I told Sutton to tell you to call me when you could. She told me she'd break my fingers if I didn't talk to you now. She scares me a little." Keely wanted to say she was sorry, but she wasn't sure her voice would work. There was a long stretch of silence. "You make my life very interesting," he finally said.

"No," she whispered, shaking her head. "I think your life was interesting without me."

"I want to ask you why people call you Priestess, and how come they treat you like you're a queen, but I'm pretty sure you wouldn't tell me. Definitely not right now anyway, maybe not even when you get back," he mused aloud. She didn't say anything, and the car got quiet again, except for the sounds of the street outside.

He sucked in a deep breath. "A long time ago, before Eternity's End was really formed or had the support of a good record label, I borrowed money from the only people who would lend it. With interest, I still owe a lot."

"You don't have to tell me any of this," she said, staring out the window of the SUV. "Like you said, it's not my business. I'm sorry if I interfered and made things awkward between us."

"I was caught off guard. I'm sorry. I shouldn't have been so rude to you," he confessed quietly. "I owe the debt. I'm not disputing it. When we formed Eternity's End, we wanted to do things differently. We wanted to work hard and achieve success our own way. I borrowed some money so Eternity's End could get noticed and have a solid start with a fair label and make the music we wanted to make. To do that without the backing of a label, it takes a lot of money. It takes money for good instruments, places to rehearse, clothes, promoting to get attention, even voice lessons for Tau."

"I know you've worked hard to where you are," she said softly. "You're an artist, and a good one. And anyone who sees Eternity's End on stage can tell you genuinely love what you do. I'm not condemning you for anything you've done to get where you are."

"If I had thought about it, I would have realized you'd feel that way. But there's more to it than paying back the money. My debt to them comes with… harassment. When it came time to sign a contract, we didn't sign with their family label. Like I said, we wanted a good label supporting us. My lenders felt insulted, and there have been consequences. Lots of consequences. And now that our contract with our current label is up for renewal, the harassment is getting worse."

"So, they want you to sign with them," Keely said, feeling

202

angry and suddenly thinking of her brother. If someone truly tried to force Keely to do something she didn't want to do, the streets would be littered with mind-wiped zombies. He was the Sunderer after all. She had a whole new appreciation for his short-tempered over protectiveness because she was feeling short-tempered and overprotective about Chance. She still wasn't sorry she made one of the men think he was rotting.

"Yes, but the contract would be bad. We wouldn't get to keep the rights to our songs; we wouldn't have any control or any revenue coming from our work. The contract would be equivalent to stealing from us."

"I'll admit, I know nothing about the music industry, but I do understand your choices and that those choices came with hard work and sacrifice. I don't think any less of you. I wouldn't have signed their contract either." She got quiet for a moment "Although, I should tell you now that Sutton's gotten involved, their harassment will stop."

"Yeah, because you're a Priestess," he said with a strange tone to his voice. "By their reaction, you're very esteemed." He paused, and Keely could feel his eyes boring into her. "You live such a lavish lifestyle. I was embarrassed. I didn't want you to know how far in debt and how poor..." His voice trailed off.

"My lavish lifestyle comes with a price," she admitted then took a deep breath. "I'm not the kind of person who values money. I guess from your point of view it seems easy for me to say, but it's the truth. Even without money, I'd value someone genuine over anything material. I don't want money or things from you. I want..." she stopped. She had no right to ask him for anything. "I understand if you want to end things; you don't have to explain."

"It's strange you say that." Chance reached out and took her arm so he could take her hand. "I was about to say the same thing to you." He wove his cool fingers through hers, and her pulse quickened, warming her insides. "You have every right, considering my circumstance." He sucked in a soft breath. "I've never talked to anyone the way I talk to you. I've never been this open and honest about myself or my feelings," he admitted. "It's strange. Talking to you feels natural even if it's difficult at times." He stopped again, tracing a finger back and forth over hers, tickling her skin. "I'm explaining, so you'll know exactly who I am. I don't want to end things between us. I... I don't want you to stop looking at me the way you do."

Keely was so unsure about their relationship and what the future held that it terrified her because it was very precious and very fragile. She was certain about one thing, her feelings for Chance. Even though they'd known each other for a short time, even though he was poor and in debt, even though she was a Priestess, her feelings for him flowed from deep inside her. They were strong, genuine, and for him alone.

Neither of them said anything until she found the courage to look at him. His face was tight with worry, but when she looked at him, he seemed to get pensive.

"And when you look at me like that," he whispered. His thoughtful expression softened, and he smiled at her. "I feel like I'm drowning." He reached up and wiped away the few stray tears trailing down her cheek. He leaned in and brushed his lips against hers, calming, reassuring, and exciting her all at once.

"I don't know what to say," she admitted, moving away from him.

He pulled her back into him, nestling her head against his shoulder as he wrapped an arm around her. "Say you'll call me when you get done working." He brushed his lips against hers again. "Sutton seems to be under the impression you won't talk to me again after today."

"I don't think… I don't know." She stared at his throat. "There are still things I haven't told you."

"You said you would tell me when you got back. I trust you." Chance put a finger under her chin and lifted her face. "I can't leave things between us like this. I know you have your own secrets to tell. I promise I will listen with an open mind." He kissed her again, his soft lips carefully caressing hers as he slowly tasted her and sent her pulse racing. Gradually, he ended the kiss. "I'm still hungry." He moved the lunch she made him from between them and drew her closer. "And," he grabbed the hand hugged to her chest and pried her fingers apart, "you gave that to me."

Keely hadn't realized until then she was still holding the tiny bird in her hand. She held it out for him. "I thought it was pretty in an odd way."

"It's pretty in a remarkable way." He took the bird from her

204

hand. "Just like you." He leaned in and pressed his mouth to hers again.

The door behind him opened and Sutton stuck her head into the vehicle. "Sorry, but we have to go," she informed them with a stern look on her face.

"Alright," Keely said, and they were left alone. "I have to go."

"I know." He unwrapped his arm from around her waist, reached up, and unfastened the necklace he was wearing. "Here," he said softly, brushing aside her hair as he pulled the necklace around her neck and fastened it.

The metal was still warm from his body heat, and it made her skin react. Lifting her hand, she fingered the pendant, examining the midnight blue stone and the pretty galaxy reflected within it.

"It's pretty," she said softly.

"My mom gave it to me when I first decided to pursue music." He wrapped his arms back around her and kissed the side of her neck. "She told me, 'you might be a speck in the universe, but you can still influence its motion'."

"I'll give it back to you when I get back." She looked at him, feeling more confident than she'd ever felt in her life. "Thank you," she added, pressing her lips to his.

"No, I want you to keep it. I like thinking of you wearing it." Chance ran a finger over her collarbone then kissed her. "Be careful." He cradled her cheek in his warm hand. "Stay safe." He tightened his hold on her. "And call me when you're done with your work."

"Okay," she agreed, running her fingers through his hair then kissing him in return. He smiled and got out of the SUV, taking the lunch and her present with him. Stopping in the doorway, he gave her a look that softened his features, and his eyes sparkled with intense, deep emotion. With one last reassuring smile, he wrapped his knuckles on the roof and stepped away from the car.

Sutton got into the car behind him, looking Keely up and down. Keely gave her a nod of reassurance. "Let's go," Sutton said to the driver, closing her car door. As they drove away, Keely watched Chance, watching her, through the back window, feeling more prepared for the small war she was about to wage in the suicide forest.

21

Sutton lifted a flap of a tent, ducked into it, and held it for Keely to follow. The tent was one of many that made up a small city built by the Japanese ministry at the bottom of Mt. Fuji near Aokigahara. The city had been created to help facilitate Keely when she went into the forest. By way of assisting and preparing for her, every clergyman in Japan had been called to action. Outside the tent, there were monks, priests, and even Rabi's preparing for the upcoming battle.

"Okay." Keely looked around at the large tent, empty except for an altar, which housed candles, and a basin that held a large jug of water and a changing screen. "What now?"

"You prepare and get dressed in decent clothes." Sutton pulled the large duffle bag from her shoulder and dropped it to the tarp-covered ground. "You stink," she said, wrinkling her nose.

She was more than mildly concerned about her best friend. If Keely and Chance hadn't recovered from their argument, her damaged feelings wouldn't just be a distraction. They would be devastating and life-threatening. There wasn't an undercurrent of tension or sadness in the tent, but Sutton wasn't sure if the situation had resolved itself or not because Keely hadn't said anything on the car ride from Tokyo.

"You smell like sex. You need to clean up and change." Sutton dug into the bag, looking for the toiletries and robe she'd brought for Keely.

Keely leaned over the bag and peered inside. "Hopefully you brought panties. I may have left mine at the manga café."

"Again. Dude, how do you keep doing this?" Sutton admonished playfully while mentally exhaling.

"Well," Keely hummed. "When you're using them as makeshift bondage—"

"Okay, that's enough, mistress." Sutton raised a hand to stop her. "Yes, I grabbed a pair of panties." She found the soft, bunny-patterned, pink robe and handed it to Keely.

"So, I thought this was happening tomorrow night?" Keely asked, taking the robe.

"It was supposed to, but well… we discovered an anomaly in the lunar calendar. Tonight is a lunar eclipse, which means other spells can be cast to help you. And I had to force an issue."

"What issue?" Keely asked in a low voice as she folded the robe over her arm. "If you called Jasper…"

"No," Sutton interrupted, glaring at her before she resumed rifling through the bag. "You do realize when I piss you off, I automatically piss him off, even when I'm right." She snatched a small pouch from the bag and stood up. "Since you forbade me from going with you, I had to think outside the box to keep you safe." She offered Keely the bag.

Keely carefully took the bag, acting as if it might bite her. "Okay?" She cocked her head sideways and narrowed her eyes. "Tell me what's on the outside of the box."

"The Japanese ministry has agreed to perform an allocation spell."

Keel shook her head. "No."

Sutton didn't have the energy for a lengthy argument, so she immediately used the only tool in her arsenal that would effectively silence Keely's stubbornness. "I'll call Jasper whether the two of you get pissed off or not." Sutton pulled her phone from her back pocket and waved it at Keely. "An allocation spell is the only way I'm willing to let you walk into Aokigahara."

"But the inheritor will suffer all the wounds I take. They could die."

"Yeah, kind of like some dumb-ass Priestess who plans on going into the suicide forest alone to face umpteen neverborn, but that doesn't seem to matter to you." Sutton raised an eyebrow at her friend. "Anyway, I knew you'd object, so I put a lot of preparation into this spell. Your inheritor will be well taken care of. Also, remember an inheritor sleeps for you, eats for you, and even eliminates the need for bodily function."

"So you found someone willing shit for me while they take all my wounds? How noble of you."

"Don't do that." Sutton was suddenly genuinely angry. "When I suggested the idea to the ministry, they had several people volunteer." Keely's opened her mouth to say something, but Sutton cut her off. "And before you start lecturing me, you should know when I told you I prepared, I did. I put a lot of thought into it. I've had a coven flown in from Italy. There's five of them, so wounds can be healed almost instantly, besides anything else that might need to be handled."

"What about…"

"No. No what abouts. When will you trust me, trust the people around you? Even though there are only a few people who know you exist, the world needs you. And yes, I know how that sounds, and I know you're tired of fighting. Maybe that's why you agreed to do this. I'm not going to let the suicide forest be a suicide mission for you."

Keely's face turned pink with embarrassment. Sutton hated that she'd confessed some of her best friend's worst thoughts for her, but she felt like she was being forced. "I'm sorry," Sutton apologized. "I wasn't trying to embarrass you. I know I wasn't supposed to say anything about it, but Keely I'm not just your monk. I'm your friend, your best friend. A real best friend looks out for you, even when you don't look out for yourself."

"I know." Keely looked down at the robe laid across her arm. "It's hard to face inner demons and all." She looked at Sutton with certainty and assurance in her expression. "For the record, I'm not suicidal, nor do I plan on this being a suicide mission. And I don't hate my life. I've just been tired lately that's all."

"Okay," Sutton said softly. "Then we don't need to talk about it anymore."

Keely cleared her throat. "So, you flew in a coven from Italy?" she asked.

"They're not my coven, but they're decent." It was Sutton's turn to look away. She missed her family, especially her parents, but she didn't let herself dwell on past pain because she couldn't afford the distraction.

"I'm sorry," Keely said quietly.

Sutton looked up to find her staring at her with a soft, comforting expression. It was a rare magic Keely didn't know she possessed. When her emotions were heightened, she could project those feelings. At that moment, Sutton could tangibly feel Keely's desire to comfort her.

"I'm sorry. You can't find your coven, your family," Keely sighed. "Sometimes I forget I'm not the only one who has sacrificed a life for this war." There was a short silence then she nodded. "So, chicken and waffles when we're done?"

"That and another trip to a host club." Sutton smiled. "I love being able to pay hot men to fawn all over me. I don't care what the connotation is."

Keely smiled in return, half turned, then stopped. "Correct me if I'm wrong. Aren't allocation spells performed with both participants naked?"

"Well, there is that," Sutton raked her fingernails through her bangs and watched them fall back into place.

"And?" Keely asked, raising an eyebrow.

"Well, a coven has to be there."

"And..." Keely prompted impatiently.

Sutton breathed out heavily. "For the spell to work, it has to be heartbeat to heartbeat, with no barriers." Keely's mouth fell open with instant understanding about what 'heartbeat to heartbeat' meant. Before she could object, Sutton started sputtering. "And I took that into account when I chose an inheritor. He's a younger clergyman, healthy, kind... and totally hot. And you know him, a little."

Keely rolled her eyes, tilted her head back, and inhaled and exhaled several times. "I suppose that is a tiny bit better than an older or aged clergyman."

"You'll approve. I promise."

"Sure, yeah. I can't wait to get naked and cuddle with a stranger I sort of know, so we can be 'heartbeat to heartbeat'. That's exactly what I was looking forward to in this whole scenario," Keely said sarcastically. "Him being hot should make it less awkward, thanks." She stepped behind the changing screen. "Still, no panties?" she asked, peeking around its edge.

"I told you I have them, but remember, allocation spell, no barriers between participants." Sutton raised an eyebrow at her.

"This is going to be lots and lots of fun," she said derisively as she disappeared behind the screen. "I'm thinking, taking my chances with death might be better."

"It's only going to be a tiny bit more awkward than you think, but you'll get over it quickly," Sutton said, walking over to the screen and set the bag next to it. "There's a plastic bag in there for dirty clothes."

"I know, I know. I smell like sex." There was some slight

rustling, and a few minutes later, Keely emerged, wearing the robe and smelling like citrus bath spray. "Better?'

"Much." Sutton walked over to the flap of the tent, opened it, and nodded to the short, stout clergyman on the other side.

A moment later, Shoma entered followed by his slightly younger assistant. Sutton knew something was wrong before he spoke. His wrinkles were more inset than they had been earlier that day and a deep frown marred his features.

"Priestess." He bowed. "I hope this day finds you well."

"I am well," Keely responded and bowed in return. "Japan has been very hospitable."

After a short silence in which Shoma stared at the ground, Sutton asked, "Cassock, if something bothering you, please share, as it could prove risky for the Priestess."

"Well, it seems our activities have drawn a crowd, and they've drawn the attention of the media." Shoma's frown deepened. "I apologize. The responsibility for this sudden notice is mine. I ordered several clergy to patrol the forest and keep people out of it and harm's way."

Keely visibly tensed before she asked, "Are people going into the forest?"

"No," the Cassock's assistant spoke out. "We've had a solid perimeter around the forest for five days. Any hapless souls who attempted to enter the forest were met with clergymen blocking their way and offering assistance."

"Yeah, that would definitely get attention," Sutton mused aloud. "You'll have to tell them something. Offer a statement."

"We cannot," the assistant objected. "Aokigahara is, well, it is an unspoken shame."

"Then ruin its stigma and take away its shame." Keely stepped to the Cassock and took his hand. "Tell them the forest is being blessed so it's sorrow will not attract the desperate any longer."

Shoma smiled. "An acceptable truth."

Keely smiled in return. "An acceptable promise of hope."

"Just the same, let's keep Keely away from the crowds and reporters and keep a close watch on the perimeter," Sutton ordered. "Be extremely vigilant. Reporters get curious." The assistant bowed and left the tent hurriedly.

210

Shoma was the next to speak. "I assume you are prepared for the allocation ceremony, Priestess."

"Keely," Keely corrected him, "and define ready. Accepting, yes. Ready, no."

Shoma smiled at her. "I understand, but I agree with your monk. It is necessary to protect you." He bowed his head. "I do, however, apologize for the sudden notice of change in arrangements. Even though the moon is the smallest speck on the horizon, there is a lunar eclipse tonight. One of our clergy has found an ancient spell. It is said that it will make it easier to release the stolen souls. If true, we hope you will not have to spend as much time engaging the neverborn in order to free those who seek heaven."

"That would be very helpful," Keely agreed. "You were right to take advantage of the opportunity. If the spell works, how long will it last?"

"For those affected, until the moon appears again," he said. "So, current circumstances are fortuitous since we can still cast the reveal-unseen spell once the lunar eclipse is over because no moonlight will touch the ground."

"Well, then I suppose we should get started and not waste the opportunity presenting itself."

"Very well." Shoma nodded to a clergyman standing next to the tent's entrance. He pulled back the flap and motioned to someone outside, then held it open for them to enter. An older woman with long, white-gray hair came in followed by two men and two women. Sutton nodded to them in greeting. A tall man with dark brown hair, wearing a robe, came in behind them. Keely looked to Sutton with raised eyebrow, indicating she recognized him. Eli bowed deeply to Keely then Sutton before he took a stance next to the members of the coven.

"Eli?" Keely whispered to Sutton between tight lips. "Really? No, this isn't going to be awkward at all."

Sutton smiled and replied. "I think I chose well, considering the Cassock was one of the volunteers."

22

Keely stood on a wide path that narrowed into a forest laden with trees, staring at the deep shadows created by the thick growing of trees that seemed to block out all light. She suppressed a small shiver of fear and turned her attention back to the crowd of clergymen and monks surrounding her. They could not go into the Aokigahara, not that she'd ask them to, but they gave her courage because she knew they would if asked, without hesitation.

"Okay." Sutton appeared beside her. "You won't feel hungry or thirsty, but that won't mean you won't get the urge, so I packed you a thermos. There are some other supplies and a bit of magic just in case." She handed Keely a backpack. "Let me see your arm."

"Why?" Keely asked, eyeing her suspiciously.

"Just let me see it." Keely gave in and held out her arm. Sutton pushed back her sleeve and used a pen to quickly draw a scrolling symbol on Keely's inner forearm as she spoke in an archaic language Keely didn't recognize. "There," she said and blew on the patterned swirls. "That will keep your soul hidden to any neverborn trying to track you."

Shoma was suddenly on the other side of her. "We've cast a barrier around the forest. Only those who bare the weight of their own soul can leave." He paused and looked from her to the trees. "When you're done, one of our monks has found a blessing that will deter the neverborn from coming here. It will not stop them, but it will make this forest distasteful."

"Good." Keely nodded then turned to Sutton. "And you're going high?"

"Yep." Sutton combed her fingers through her hair in a nervous gesture. "They've got me a crane." She pointed to a large metal crane several feet away from them. "I hate heights."

"I know, but I need you a safe distance away." Keely frowned. "It would be too hard—"

"I get it." Sutton took her hand and squeezed it. "I've got your back." She smiled then let go. "Now, you've got your radio and a GPS tracker." Sutton unnecessarily adjusted Keely's earpiece. "But if something goes wrong there's a flare gun in the backpack. You keep firing the flairs until we find you, understand?"

"Understood." Keely saluted. "I will be safe…safe as I can be."

"Priestess." Shoma stepped in front of her. "If you will allow, we would like to offer a final prayer of protection." He didn't wait for her to answer before he took her hands in his warm withered ones. Everyone around her except for Sutton bowed their heads or sank to their knees. The Cassock lifted his voice in prayer, asking for her to save the souls of the trapped and pass safely through Aokigahara.

"Thank you." She bowed and offered her appreciation to those around her. Keely looked to Sutton, gave her a nod of reassurance, and then turned and walked into Aokigahara—the Suicide Forrest.

Pulling one of three flashlights from her bag, she turned it on and looked around. Moss-covered, twisting trees stood out from the ground with their winding roots clawing at the earth to hold them upright. The ground was covered with weeds, leaves, fallen trees, and broken roots. Sutton had warned her once she left the paths, there would be large cracks, crevices and underground caverns Keely could easily trip over or fall into. Keely heeded the warning due to her inability to see the dangerous cracks, even when she scanned the terrain with her flashlight.

She still couldn't tell how many neverborn were in the area because there was so much misery trapped in the forest. She could feel it stronger in some directions and assumed those were a cluster of souls trapped by a neverborn. Looking at the compass pinned to her jacket, she decided to follow the trail of sadness left behind by the closest cluster. "Heading northwest. For now, I have a path to follow," she said into the earpiece.

"GPS confirmed. I've got you, mistress Keely." Sutton's voice came back through the earpiece.

"Funny," Keely smirked.

"Remember, be careful once you get off the path."

"I know, obscured, unsteady footing," Keely said, walking forward as she slowly pivoted the light back and forth. "Warning heeded."

"If you see any tents or campsites, call out the mark. Unless you see actual signs of life, we will handle those," Sutton instructed. Keely didn't detect any signs of human life, but then, she couldn't be sure, considering her sense for souls didn't feel as reliable, maybe it was overwhelmed. She sincerely hoped there weren't any other living humans in the forest, because she wasn't sure she'd be able to get them out safely.

"Moving to head east," Keely said as she turned east with the direction of the winding path. It was solid, compacted dirt that offered secure footing, so she wasn't in a hurry to veer from it. She walked at a moderate pace, continuously scanned the fir and cypress trees for movement. The light of her flashlight reflected off the moss growing on the trees, making ghost-like outlines. It was almost as if the densely growing trees were tombstones marking the sorrow of the deceased. Keely felt those trees knew what she knew. There were no ghosts in Aokigahara, only trapped souls.

Without warning, the air around her started to tremble, and she felt the cluster of souls move in her direction. Slowly at first, but then more quickly. "Damn," Keely cursed out loud. "They'll be able to see the flashlight."

"Shit." Sutton's voice hissed. "Douse the light."

"I can't fight blind," Keely said, suddenly panicking as she aimed the light at the misery she felt coming towards her.

"You'll be able to see it in thirty seconds. Turn off the damn light," Sutton ordered over a whining machine sound into Keely's ear.

Keely clicked the switch on the light the same time the noise in her ear stopped, and she was left standing alone in pitch-dark. There was no sound except for the steady rush of her breathing and the heavy beating of her heart.

"Sutton," she whispered, fear making her hands cold. She felt powerless and helpless as memories of real childhood nightmares stirred.

"It's because you can't see," Sutton reassured, and she could hear soft panicked whispering, which in turn, made Keely panic.

"I can't fight it." Keely's breath started coming out in pants as the menacing cluster got closer. The forest was still, except for the distant crunching of leaves and the snapping of branches. "I need to see." Keely moved her finger over the springy plastic button of the flashlight.

214

"Don't turn your light on. Give three, two, one." Something warm tingled in her forehead, and her eyes started to water. "Cat's eye. You'll be able to see now." Sutton's voice soothed over the earpiece as the tears in Keely's eyes washed away the dark and the world brightened. "I'm sorry. I should have thought of it sooner."

"It's alright." Keely wiped at her tears. Panic subsiding, she looked around at the now greyscale but seeable forest. "This is good." She breathed a sigh of relief.

"I told you I had your back." Sutton's voice reassured. "And in three minutes the lunar eclipse will start. Hopefully, the Cassocks ancient spell will work."

"I guess we'll find out."

"Keely don't engage; I can't see it."

Keely turned her head toward the movement in her peripheral vision. A tall neverborn with overly broad shoulders and a large belly was pacing back and forth in the trees to her left. It wasn't wearing a human skin, so that meant it would be desperate for a soul. Now that it had a sense of her, it wasn't going to give up on its prey. Keely carefully lowered herself to the ground and removed the backpack. It was cumbersome, and she needed to be able to move quickly to combat the neverborn's speed and strength.

"It's not wearing human skin; you wouldn't be able to see it until the dark night spell has been cast."

"Then run. In a couple of minutes, they will all be lit up like Christmas trees, but that spell can't be cast until the lunar eclipse is over."

"It's not going to wait a couple of minutes," Keely whispered softly as she watched the neverborn pace close and closer.

"Keely…"

"Shh." Keely shushed Sutton, afraid the neverborn would hear the sound coming from her earpiece. They had heightened vision and hearing. The slightest noise or movement might draw its attention, and Keely wanted the element of surprise when she attacked. Stepping several feet away from her bag, she watched and waited until the neverborn's pacing placed it within her vicinity. When it was about twenty feet away, she clicked on the flashlight and threw it near her backpack.

The neverborn wretched its neck and twisted its head in the

direction of the light. Then it ran at her, using its long arms to swipe forest brush and tree limbs out of its way. Branches popped and cracked, and the ground shook underneath Keely's feet. The neverborn advanced on her backpack, waiving its hands in the air, looking for the soul it was thirsty for. It groped around in the near darkness, and when it came up empty handed it slammed its massive fist down on the flashlight, extinguishing its light. That was when she made her move.

The tromp of Keely's hiking boots got the neverborn's attention when she ran toward it, and it started flailing its long arms in an effort to capture her. She ducked underneath its long reach and found herself standing in front of it. The neverborn were truly terrifying up close with their white eyes staring out of their nose-less and mouth-less faces. She'd seen them many times, been near them many times, but she still shuddered when she was in such close proximity. Syncing her movements to the neverborn's, she managed to stay directly in front of it. Owing to Sutton's spell, it couldn't see or sense her, and could not land any of its attacks.

The souls it carried called out to her as if they knew she was there, and their suffering was about to end. A long chant wouldn't be needed because she was confident they'd respond to her voice. However, as soon as she spoke, she'd give away her presence, and the neverborn would know precisely where to strike. It was the same height as her, but she was sure if she got caught in the grip of its arms, it would crush her to death.

Raising her hand, she let it hover over its throat and summoned both her mental and metaphysical power. "I, Keely Sheppard, Priestess," she said in heaven's beautiful, powerful language, "call you from your prison and set you free."

She felt, more than saw, the neverborn's arms close in around her, but they came to a jerky stop. Then it let out a high-pitched hiss, that made her involuntarily shiver. The skin on its face tore into the shape of a mouth, and a thread of black blood oozed out of its jagged corner. The inside of the ripped hole that was its mouth started to glow before a tiny, flickering light trickled out and hovered between them. Another speck of sparkling color dripped out behind it. Its black, oozing mouth started to radiate light so brightly, its face began to glow. Souls spilled out of the creature in a stream of watery bril-

216

liance. Soon they were surrounded by hundreds of flickering souls, and their prismatic glimmering was slowly getting brighter. The grey trees reflected a kaleidoscope of colors as the souls got more luminous. Keely could feel the resonance of their pain and misery. Some of them had been trapped so long in their despair, they'd given into insanity, forgetting what goodness was.

With tears of sorrow spilling from her eyes, she whispered, "Heaven waits."

The sky withdrew, and boundaries of heaven opened inside the sea of trees. There was no brilliant light or heavenly trumpet signaling the opening of heaven's gate, but the atmosphere around them changed. Absolute love filled the air; filling it was pure joy and happiness. The souls grew more brilliant with heaven's adoration healing and welcoming them. One by one they started to ascend into the gloriousness awaiting them. The tiny souls floated upward like a beautiful reverse rain. Keely couldn't help but smile through her tears as their hope turned into happiness, and that happiness transformed into love.

She watched the last light ascend, but she couldn't relish her small victory. The neverborn had started to move again, and its giant fist was aiming for her head. She ducked back beneath its dangerous hand. Rolling between its legs and underneath it, she managed to get out of the way of its wrath and get to her feet.

"Time to light these bitches up." Sutton's voice blared in her ear and a wind carrying the whispers of chants rustled through her hair. The neverborn started to glow a dull grey.

Keely wasn't really paying attention to the implication of those words because the neverborn had turned and was coming at her. She sidestepped out of the way of one of its blows and raised her hands to block another, but it was inhumanly fast and powerful. A rocklike fist slammed her arm into her ribs, and she was knocked off her feet. Again, she rolled, but she was no longer on the path and the ground split underneath her. One of her legs got wedged in the crevice, and there was a loud pop. She didn't have to look to know her leg was bent where it should have been straight. Keely braced for pain that didn't come, and when it didn't, she yanked her broken leg from the crevice, most likely taking off the outer layer of skin, and crab crawled away from the neverborn.

"My God," Sutton whispered, sounding terrifying. Two arrows

pierced the neverborn's face. One hitting his eye and the other lancing through its cheek. "These guys fell off the fugly tree into a toxic vat of horrifying," she joked, but her voice still cracked. This was the first-time Sutton had seen the neverborn entirely without human skin. "I hate heights, you sack of nasty." Another arrow seemed to pop out of its shoulder. "Move your ass, Keely."

Keely scrambled to her feet prepared to limp away, only to find her leg was completely healed. She walked a couple of steps when a strange, warm pull got her attention. She turned in the direction of the warmth, so did the neverborn. The slight sounds of music blew on the wind as the serenity in the air got more inviting. With what she could only describe as a sickening smile, the neverborn pulled its foot from a crevice and started walking toward the warmth.

"What just happened?" Keely asked, watching the neverborn move away from her. After it was a safe distance away, she rested her hands on her knees and took several deep breaths.

"Oh, that?" Sutton asked. "The Cassock is projecting a chant of joy. It will draw the neverborn out of the forest so you wouldn't have to fight them more than once."

"Impressive." Keely closed her eyes, trying to settle her racing heart and breathing.

"There's only one catch, only an empty neverborn will be tempted by it." Sutton was quiet for a moment. "Keely, the neverborn? Do they all look like that?"

"More or less," Keely replied. She pulled up her pant-leg and assessed the damage. There was some blood, but the bone was whole, and her skin was unbroken. "In general, they're scary as fuck," she said flippantly, ignoring the knot of fear still residing at the pit of her stomach.

"And I let you go alone into a creepy-ass forest full of them."

"Right, because you have the power to control me."

"I can't no, but—"

Keely cut her off. "You do realize if you say my brother's name, you're going to start a fight?"

"I wasn't going to say it," Sutton huffed in her ear. "Truth. I would have followed you into the scary-ass forest and proceeded to piss myself every time we encountered a neverborn. You're kind of my hero right now. Although, I can't decide if you're stupid or brave, but you're still my hero."

"I'd like to point out, I'm not alone, badass witch with a cross-bow."

Sutton laughed. "You better believe it. I'll shoot eyes, hearts, dicks. Hell, by the time I'm done they will look like porcupines."

It was Keely's turn to laugh. "Works for me." She stood back up and slowly walked over to the discarded backpack. "Please tell me its coffee in the thermos."

"You better believe it. It took me three days, but I magicked you a thermos that would never run out," Sutton replied. "But don't take long. You got one at your three o'clock and one at your six. They probably sensed the release."

"Awesome." Keely picked up the backpack and slid it on. "I guess coffee will have to wait."

"It'll have too. You have more scary-monster ass to kick."

23

Keely sat on a fallen rotted tree trunk, staring up at the pre-dawn sky through a small clearing of branches. The stars always seemed brightest at three in the morning, but then, the sky always seemed darkest. It was both peaceful and foreboding. Reaching into the backpack next to her, she pulled out a black thermos, with cat eyes, ears, and a tail that doubled as a handle. "Thank you for magicking me a coffee thermos," Keely said quietly.

"You're welcome," Sutton replied. "It wasn't an easy thing to accomplish. The never-ending flow part, yes, but finding the right latte flavor was damn near impossible. I had to go to, like, seven different cafés."

"Wow, you put a lot of thought into it. I really do take you for granted."

"Yeah, you do," Sutton agreed.

Keely smiled to herself and unscrewed the cat head lid/cup. "I really appreciate it. Where'd you get the cat thermos?" she asked, twisting off the inner cap and filling the cup with coffee. Steam streamed up from it, and the aroma of coffee mixed with vanilla and hazelnut filled the air.

"Please. Japan is the land of cute. You can get cat, bear, insert cute animal, anything—including condoms."

Keely took a long sip of the coffee, savoring the heated, creamy, bittersweet fluid. Despite having an inheritor to take on her physical ailments, she was tired. That probably meant something potentially dangerous, and it was very likely to have consequences, but Keely didn't want to dwell on the implications of magical imbalance. She'd been fighting neverborn for almost thirty hours, and it was all she could do to keep her focus. Though only a day had passed since she walked into Aokigahara, it felt like a lifetime. She'd nearly lost count of the neverborn she'd fought until she could count down the ones remaining. After her last fight, there was only one, although that fight had probably cost her her inheritor. Because she'd grown impatient to be done with fighting, she'd taken on three neverborn at once. It was a bad decision and probably would have killed her any other day. Still, she'd managed to free their captive souls and send the neverborn away from the forest.

"How's my inheritor?" she asked, looking down at the splotches of dried blood that covered her clothes. There was no doubt in her mind Eli had been severely injured on her behalf.

"Well, he hasn't had the best day."

"Ya think?" Keely took another sip of her coffee.

"He's resting comfortably," Sutton assured Keely.

"Right. I'm sure," Keely huffed. "How many times did I come close to dying tonight?"

"I'm not going to answer because you want to feel guilty."

"Sutton, let's pretend for a second I'm not stupid. By my count, I've had a broken leg, ribs, and back, fractured jaw, and the left side of my face, from my head to my chest, is covered in dried blood from a head wound."

"Keely," Sutton said with a sigh. "I don't want to discuss this with you now, so don't make me lie to you."

"So, he's alive?"

"Yes."

"Any permanent damage?"

"Maybe." Sutton was quiet for a moment. "You're right; the head wound was bad. Eli was promptly healed, but he may be permanently blind. Only time will tell."

"I don't know what to say," Keely said softly. "I feel both terrible and grateful."

"Well, you can tell him when this is over." There was another long pause. "I've scanned the forest four times. I'm getting nothing. You sure there's one left?"

"Yes. There is," Keely confirmed. "I can sense it coming and going, but there's something weird about it."

"Is it hunting you?" Sutton asked, sounding concerned.

"I'm not sure, maybe stalking me. It feels like it is trying to find me and not be found."

"That is the definition of a stalker," Sutton pointed out. "And it may actually have a problem stalking you because your soul is obscured. That doesn't mean it won't be able to find you. It can use its other senses. Maybe it's looking the old-fashioned way, on foot." She was quiet for a moment. "I got nothing on scope."

"I can't see it either. I can only sense it," Keely explained. She took another sip of her coffee and strained her senses. She could feel the misery and longing of the souls, but it didn't feel the same as other neverborn. It felt like those souls were weak, sick.

"I guess that means tracking it on foot."

"I know. Hence the extended coffee break." Keely said, finishing the cup of coffee and reassembled her thermos. "Time to go back to work." She re-packed her bag, stood, and stretched. "Heading north."

"Copy that. Remember, stay—"

"On a path. Yeah, I know, that was the plan," Keely interrupted.

"You don't have to be rude about it," Sutton huffed in her ear.

"I'm only rude when you're annoying."

Keely consulted her compass and took a path leading in the direction she wanted to go. It was nearly overgrown. Dead leaves and twigs crunched under her boots even as she stepped over fallen branches or waded through brush. An hour and a half later, she passed underneath the shadow of the mountain and past their base of operations. She felt the air was getting colder because her breath came out in larger mists, but she couldn't feel the cold. Still, she hugged her jacket closer to her as she made her way up the path, as the wind had started to pick up.

She was about to change direction when the smell of something noxious and fetid caught her attention. She didn't have to question what the smell was; she already knew. Once encountered, the scent of a dead and rotting body was hard to forget. "Sutton, I think someone was here," she said, turning toward the smell and suddenly feeling uneasy. She'd seen a dead body before, but her instinct told her this would be different. As much as she wanted to turn away, that same instinct told her she needed to investigate. "I'm going to check it out."

"Be careful," Sutton advised needlessly.

In order to follow the scent, she eventually had to deviate from the path, so she found a reasonably straight piece of long wood to use as a walking stick. The stick and her cat-like vision allowed her to avoid the cracks and fissures she could fall into and made it easier to navigate through or around the open crevices. Some of those crevices were large enough to be considered small caves and dangerously hidden by overgrown trees and foliage. As she followed the scent, it got stronger. It got so nauseatingly toxic she had to hold a stretched-out shirt sleeve to her nose and mouth with one of her hands. The trees and brush got denser, and she found herself pushing through large branches. They scraped at her skin and pulled at her hair until she came bursting through a thicket of branches. A swarm of bugs greeted her. She cut off a startled scream as she waved them off her face and away from her eyes. After the swarm of insects cleared away, she found herself standing in a throng of body parts.

"My God," Keely said, looking around, eyes watering against the smell.

"Keely, are you okay?"

"Yes," she replied softly as her brain processed what she was seeing.

Black blood covered the ground, the trees around the clearing, and even the leaves that hung above. Keely took a step forward, and the edge of her boot got caught on something. She looked down to find a filleted arm. It was oozing with rot and covered with insects. Despite the arm's decomposed state, she could see it had been cut into pieces. There were deep gashes that tore at muscle and broke bone. Carefully, she stepped over the arm and found another like it. She found half of a torso next, it's stomach, spine, and legs resembling the same evisceration the arms went through.

"I've never seen anything…" Her voice trailed off when she found not one, but two heads piled together. They would have been unidentifiable even if the maggots and flies hadn't eaten more than half of them, because they looked like someone took a mallet to them, splitting them apart in several places. "There's two…what's left of two bodies here." She stared at one of the heads' eyeless sockets, trying not to think on what had happened to those people or wonder whether or not they suffered. Something glimmered from the bushes behind the heads, and she was thankfully distracted. Giving them a wide birth, she stepped around the low bushes then wished she hadn't.

There was not one, but two wheelchairs. One fallen over, covered in blood, the other, still held half the torso that belonged to its previous occupant.

"Sutton," she managed to croak out as she registered the uniform on the body. "They were still in middle school."

"Who? Keely, I can't see through the trees." Sutton said, sounding panicked. "Who was in middle school?"

"The bodies, they belonged to..." She forced herself to take slow, shallow breaths. "Someone slaughtered children and threw their body parts..." She couldn't finish. "I can't." She turned to leave, to walk away from the horror, but she stopped dead in her tracks.

In front of her were three symmetrical gashes across one of the tree trunks. She knew those gashes, had encountered them a hundred times in her lifetime. "Sutton," she said, finally giving in to panic and breathing hard. "A neverborn did this."

The implications of all she saw immediately overwhelmed her. "A neverborn did this," Keely repeated.

"Keely what are you seeing?" Sutton's voice came through the earpiece but didn't break the haze of Keely's horror.

"We can't win, not even small victories if the neverborn kill their victims. All we could ever do is release souls. They'd hunt and kill, and we'd fight, and they'd hunt and kill." Keely was momentarily stunned into silence when she realized the full repercussions of what she was seeing. "Oh my God." She choked out. "They watched their bodies being torn apart."

Her stomach lurched, and bile and coffee rose up. She managed to take three steps away from the unholy slaughter she'd stood in before she stopped and emptied her stomach's entirety onto the ground. The sounds of her retching echoed around the forest for more than five minutes, before she finally managed to regain control of her body. Her next thought was that she needed to get away from the awful smell of heinous murder. She started walking blindly away, pushing her way through the thick branches that cut at her face and exposed skin. Overgrown brush and winding roots tripped her more than once, but she got up, and he kept going because all she could do was run away. A long time passed by as she fought against Aokigahara to get out of it. She eventually came upon a grouping of trees canopied together, trapping the wind between them. Mercifully, the wind swept away the smell of dissected, decaying bodies.

She slowed her step, breathing in the fresh air. At that same moment, an unseen crevice caught her foot, and she tripped and fell hard onto the ground. All the air was forced from her lungs in one singular, high-pitched hiss. Breathing a mouth full of rain-soaked soil and leaves, she started coughing and gagging. Still, she was not inclined to get up. She lay on the packed dirt and hard roots, gulping in air, trying to truly comprehend what had just happened. She found it inconceivable, and thus, found it impossible to pick herself up.

"Keely," a soft voice whispered from beside her.

A moment passed before Keely realized it was Sutton's voice. "Sutton?" She lifted her head, expecting to see an empty forest and found Sutton was kneeling over her. "How did you..." She stopped, unsure what was happening because her mind was so overwhelmed it couldn't process the smallest of thoughts.

"Astral projection," Sutton said with a smile. "It's Kindergarten witch stuff, but it comes in useful. Now, you need to get it together and tell me what's happened."

Keely took a deep breath, held it for ten seconds, and let it out slowly. Tears filled her eyes. "Two...children. It killed them..." She told Sutton what she'd seen between fits of tears and long silences of shock.

"Okay, so what do we do?" Sutton asked, folding her arms over her knees. "Because, well, at the present moment, you're not really accomplishing anything other than scaring the shit out of me. I'd pull the plug on this right now, but I think this is something we...you need to deal with. So, what do you want to do here?"

"I don't know," Keely cried, covering her face with her hands. "I don't know," she repeated. "I wish I was back at Chance's apartment. I felt safe there." She confessed through more tears.

"I know." Sutton reached out a hand and covered Keely's. Though she wasn't actually touching her, Keely could feel a slight, vibrating warmth.

She knew she needed to pull herself together, get up, and go hunt down the neverborn who had murdered two children. Unfortunately, it was easier realized than done. It took ten minutes of breathing heavy through tears before she was calm enough to actually think logically. It took another fifteen for her mind to truly process what had happened and what needed to be done.

"I want to stop it. I want to set those souls...those children's souls, free."

"I think we need to," Sutton agreed, standing.

Keely looked up at her friend, blinking away the remainder of her tears. "You're naked."

"What about Astral projection says clothes?" Sutton huffed, putting her hands on her hips. She bent down and looked Keely in the eye. "Are you over it?"

Keely pulled her feet underneath and pushed herself up out of the dirt, then stood. "Yeah." She nodded, dusting dirt off her hands, jacket, and pants.

"You pissed yet?"

Keely looked over her shoulder toward the place where the two teenagers had died tortuous and needless deaths. "Yes."

"What are you going to do about it?"

Keely looked at Sutton, a strategy forming. "I'm going to lure a neverborn." She pulled up her sleeve.

"Keely." Sutton put out a hand to stop her, but it passed right through Keely's arm. "Don't..."

Keely spat on her fingers and scrubbed at the ink marks on her arm, ruining the symbol Sutton had put there. She looked at Sutton, feeling her lips peel back into a hard smile. "I think it's time to show this fucker exactly what a Priestess is."

"Keely," Sutton stared at her with an exasperated look. "That talisman wasn't just to obscure your soul, it was to protect it. There is no way of knowing how long that neverborn has been here or how many souls it's carrying or how that will affect you."

"I don't care," Keely said through tight lips, walked past Sutton, and headed toward something desperate. "I know where it is." She hurdled over a fallen trunk and walked through a large grouping of trees. She looked around at the terrain, analyzing its tactical maneuverability. There wouldn't be enough space, for any real defense and the cracks in the earth would prove dangerous. "Sutton?"

"You got your badass witch right here," her earpiece echoed.

"Can you find me a clearing that looks like it has level ground?"

"Sixty-five maybe seventy meters west, looks solid. In this terrain, you could get there in about seven minutes."

"Good." Keely turned west. The desperate feeling got closer and stronger. She could also feel sorrow, regret, and deep-seated anger in the cluster of emotions. "It's angry."

226

"I kind of figured, considering what you told me."
In the distance, there was a loud crack. "Sutton, it's coming."

∞ ∞ ∞ ∞ ∞

Keely stood in the clearing, atop an overgrown mound of lava rock, watching and waiting. An audience of winding trees surrounded her and stretched their waving arms to the sky in anticipation of the oncoming battle. The neverborn approached her slowly from the north. She wondered if it was trying to catch her unaware but then discarded the idea. Neverborn didn't think tactically unless the soul they'd stolen did. The neverborn would function off the memory of the most recently stolen souls, and teenagers weren't likely to have a tactical mindset. They might be sneaky, but sneaky wasn't enough to catch her flat-footed. When some trees rustled then separated, she was ready and facing the neverborn. However, she was not prepared for the neverborn that had arrived.

A small human foot attached to a spindly, long leg stepped through the opening. Two frail, white hands of differing sizes pushed the bushes apart, allowing the neverborn to step through. A pair of disproportionate, mud-clumped, human feet stepped into the clearing. They supported a pair of spindly, uneven legs that were nothing more than gaunt bone and skin. She couldn't see the details of the anatomy of its torso because the neverborn had dressed in the tattered fabric of an old tent, but it was elongated and skeletally thin. Its face was young, not quite childlike, but lacking in adult features. Even though it had fully formed eyes, nose, and mouth, it was disproportionate from one another in such a way, as to look as if the face had been built with mismatched puzzle pieces. Long and short hair sprouted from its head and would have blown around in the wind, except it was full of twigs and leaves and caked with dirt.

As it stepped to her, Keely found herself at a loss for words. The monk's spell should have forced the neverborn to appear in its pure form, not its stolen skin. As it stared at her with curious, brown eyes, she wondered why this neverborn was immune to such powerful magic. It took a shaky step forward, and that was when she realized why it had taken so long to get to her. Despite wearing a complete human skin, it was still wasn't acclimated to moving like a human.

"You are the human who is hunting us?" it said in both soft, female tones and a low, scratchy, male voice, further baffling Keely.

"I am," she answered. "But then, you've been hunting humans for a long time."

"You mean our body?" it asked in reply, taking another step forward, crooning its stretched neck so it could look at her more closely.

"Your body?" Keely questioned, trying to understand what it was trying to tell her.

"The body was given to us when we chose to die." Its face curved into a smug smile.

Keely stared at the neverborn. She could not only see the pride on its face but feel it, along with a myriad of emotions. Desperation, loneliness, longing, regret, and shame were all emanating from the souls it carried. Its anger is what she questioned. The souls she spoke with normally weren't angry at her, or even the neverborn that had stolen them, but they were angry.

"You didn't die, not completely," Keely explained, choosing her words carefully. "You're trapped here on earth, away from heaven, because something was desperate to have your soul, and now you can never return to your body."

"We don't want those bodies," it screamed, stepping forward as if to attack. It stumbled and caught itself before it fell, then stood up at its full height, trying to be more intimidating. "Those bodies were sickly and useless." It took another step toward her. "We hated those broken bodies."

Keely's agile mind analyzed their anger and their words and came to an unbelievable conclusion. "You destroyed your own bodies… You did that to yourselves." She tried to fathom what the souls she was talking to had done but couldn't really embrace the idea of beheading and tearing one's body apart. "What did you do?" she asked. It didn't respond except to smile and bubble with laughter.

Keely had enough. She didn't want any other answers about what had happened or how the neverborn had become what it was. Her job was to simply release the stolen souls it carried and send it on its way. The why's and how's of it could be investigated and answered

228

by the clergymen waiting outside Aokigahara, the forest of death.

She took a step closer so she was less than five feet separated them and summoned her strength. "It's time to go where you belong and leave all of the shame, anger, and sadness of this world behind," she said in heaven's language, asserting her will over the neverborn and all the souls it carried. The neverborn started to convulse, its arms shaking and its chest heaving. A translucent glow rolled over its skin. "I promise you don't have to be afraid, and there will be no more sickness, no more pain."

The neverborn stood in front of her immobile, its eyes affixed on her. Its mouth opened and the tiny ember of a solitary soul slipped out. A look of abject horror crossed its feature before it slapped the soul between its hands and it sucked it back into its mouth, swallowing loudly and licking its fingers.

"Our body loves those. You can't have them," it hissed in defiance.

Keely called upon all of her strength and determination. This wasn't a battle she could lose, and she could do something a neverborn couldn't. She could force her will to take the shape of an illusion, and that's precisely what she did. Her clothes started to roll and twist, then fingers punched their way through the leather of her jacket. Four sets of five fingers grew into winding arms that waved and snaked out from her torso. She took another step toward the neverborn and was so close she could smell the filth caked on its body.

"Those souls never belonged to you or your body."

One of her many hands struck out, clawing at the neverborn's neck and chest. She imagined the sharp pinch of a scratch and the hard burning of tearing skin and implemented it into her illusion. She pulled her hand away, taking some of its flesh along with a fist full of souls. "They belong to heaven." She held out her illusionary hand, slowly opening its fingers. The real souls had been trapped by the neverborn hovered in her palm then streamed upward.

The neverborn opened its mouth, but before it could say anything, she struck again. It lifted its hand to defend itself, and though it was able to block her strike, it couldn't prevent the blows of her five other arms. Again, and again, she clawed at the neverborn's chest with her illusionary hands, and it clumsily tried to defend itself from her painful, flesh-shredding strikes. She wanted to put the neverborn in pain, as much as she wanted to retrieve the souls trapped within it. After numerous attacks, the neverborn dropped to the ground, hugging its knees and letting out long, shrieking moans. Keely pulled in her illusion and stepped back. Winning the battle of wills, she'd broken the mental hold the neverborn had over its prisoners. The neverborn couldn't hold its captives and started heaving out tiny, glittering lights.

The minuscule illuminations continued to pour out of the neverborn, filling the forest with a prismatic mist. Keely couldn't tell how old the souls were, but judging by the amount that still flowed out of the neverborn's mouth with each violent wretch, they'd been there a while. As the souls continued to spill out so did the sense of hopelessness and shame. Whispers of desperation and sorrow echoed up into the tree branches, around the forest, and carried on the wind. Keely was not prepared for the weight of the feelings, especially from the souls still begged to be released from the misery of their earthly life. They were confused and tormented by regret, so much regret for what was lost, what could have been, and what they couldn't change. They longed for acceptance, love, and absolution. Keely felt so over-whelmed by all the souls calling out to her, to heaven, that she sank to the ground next to the neverborn, clutching at her own heart.

She turned her face skyward just as heaven opened up above her. The forest was filled with pure, beguiling love, a love so powerful it was a tangible force. She basked in its love, feeling warm, safe, and replenished.

"It's alright, you don't have to suffer anymore," she spoke soft-ly, reassuring everyone around her. "Heaven waits to envelop you, all of you, in nothing but love." The souls started to glow like thousands of tiny suns, singing with heaven's adoration. For a moment, they were frozen in place all around her, and then they seemed to swirl together as if they danced. Their joy filled Keely, and she watched as the lights flurried upward, like warm snow, and disappeared beyond the trees, beyond the sky, alighting into love.

The forest dimmed, and she turned her attention back to the neverborn. It was laying on the ground, clutching at its throat and chest with its feet tucked underneath it. Something wasn't right. Human essence still resided in the neverborn. She had a clear sense of two souls, a girl and a boy. They were the last to be taken, the last to die, and the only souls to reject heaven. Keely was confused, not

230

because the souls hadn't ascended, but because she'd never seen souls cling to the body of a neverborn. Did they not understand what heaven was? Or were they too afraid? Involuntarily, she reached out her hand and placed it on the matted head of the pitiful neverborn to offer reassurance.

Her compassion was her mistake.

The emotions of the newly released souls were nothing compared to the anger and jealousy now filling her. She caught images of a life of sickness and pain. One hopeless doctor visit after another, followed by multiple painful surgeries. She watched children painfully struggle to learn to walk, only to lose the ability and be confined to a wheelchair. She watched as the two, a boy and a girl, twins, sat together, longing to be like the people they watched walking by their window. When they jointly made the decision to go into the suicide forest, she watched them wrestle with their wheelchairs, struggling to travel down rocky paths then over rough terrain.

The two of them split a bottle of pills, and neither looked afraid or uncertain. As they started to fall into a drugged coma, the neverborn came for their souls. Instead of being afraid when their souls were lifted from their bodies, they were grateful. A body free of sickness and pain was presented and offered escape from their debilitated lives. It promised them they didn't have to die young; they didn't have to die at all, and they gladly allowed it to take their souls. When they settled into the neverborn and found themselves staring down at their sleeping mortal bodies, they viscously tore apart the things they hated most.

They still hated their bodies. They hated them for a wasted life full of longing. They wanted what was never given to them.

Keely nearly wept for their suffering. She wanted them to be free. It was her duty to invite them to heaven. It's why she was a Priestess, but even as divine words formed inside her, they got caught in her throat. She hadn't sent souls so young to heaven before, and she felt the remorse and regret for the life they never had as if it was her own.

She pitied the twin souls.

There was a shift in the neverborn's mind. Its will got stronger and turned into a force made up of solid iron. Her sympathy was their strength and their triumph.

231

The neverborn jerked away from her and crawled backward across dirt and roots, staring at her with intense hazel eyes, human eyes. "Priestess," it whispered. "We do not want what you have to offer." Slowly it unwound itself and stood. "We want what the world has to give."

Keely watched its eyes darken with hatred because she dared try and take away the life it wanted. It took a step forward, standing over her with murder marring its already disfigured features. She tried to stand, to get ready to defend herself, but her legs were numb, and her arms felt as if they were moving under water.

The neverborn raised a hand, readying it to levy a heavy blow. There was a hiss, a dull thud, and the neverborn started screaming in its combined male and female voices. A bolt arrow had impaled it its wrist, and black blood spilled out of the hole. It turned its attention back to her, exuding murderous anger.

"What the fuck is happening to you Keely," Sutton's voice shouted in her earpiece. There was another hiss and dull thud and a second arrow pierced into its rib cage. It crooned its head back, opened its mouth, and screamed again. This scream wasn't a scream of pain, but a scream of frustration. Another arrow hissed through the air and stabbed into its throat, silencing it.

It reached up and yanked the arrow from its throat, splattering blood all over itself and Keely. "Pointless," it hissed. Its face seemed to relax then smile as if it had decided it didn't want to waste the effort it took to kill Keely. The neverborn turned its back, pushed through an opening in the trees, and sprinted away.

Keely watched, immobilized not just by her weakened body, but by her chaotic and confused feelings, as the neverborn disappeared into the forest. There was one clear thought, she'd lost the battle. Although, she didn't get to consider what that meant for her, or that a soul had chosen to remain captive inside a neverborn, because her body seemed to be quitting altogether. Sharp pain speared through her chest and shoulders. Her spine turned to string, and she rolled off her knees. She tried to keep herself from falling, but her arms collapsed, and she fell onto the dirty, rooted ground. Head spinning, she grabbed handfuls of dirt, trying to stop the pain in her chest. It only subsided when she managed to focus on how the cold wind cooled her face.

"Keely. Keely, fucking answer me," Sutton yelled, her voice breaking through a noiseless haze.

"Sutton," Keely croaked out, struggling to take in her next breath. Calm settled over her, and she managed to breath in the crisp night air. "Something's wrong," she warned with the last of her energy. Even breathing had become so hard it wasn't worth the effort. For a fraction of a moment, she lay in the dirt, listening to her slowing heart as all of her senses were gradually swallowed by the shadows of unconsciousness. She could feel her mind being consumed by the darkness, a darkness that would probably end in death. Though she wasn't afraid, she did regret. She wanted to live to see Chance again. She wanted to see his smile, hear his voice, and feel his touch. Her last thought was that she wasn't unlike the neverborn. She, too, was greedy to live because she wanted to love—love Chance.

24

Chance sat in a cluttered green room at the back of a club with his elbows resting on his knees and his hands folded together, trying to keep his left knee from bouncing. He'd never been more anxious in his life, and it had nothing to do with the crowd outside in the club, waiting on Eternity's End to play the debut of their new album, The Sky at Night. The couch underneath him bounced as someone sat down, and he was pulled from his disquiet. He looked over to find Simeon staring at him with a bland but tight expression.

"I don't think any of us have never seen you nervous before. Or at least, I've never seen you show visible signs of being nervous," Simeon said quietly so Chance alone could hear. "Not even at our very first live." He was quiet for a moment. "I'm not the only one who's concerned."

Chance looked over to a corner of the room, where Tao, Ren, and Itsuki, sat around a small table. Each of them took turns looking at Chance over their shoulders with worried looks. It aggravated him that he was affecting his friend's moods, making them worry. Usually, backstage before a show was playful and somewhat boisterous because it gave the band good energy to perform.

"I'm sorry," he apologized. Wiping his sweaty hands on his pants, he forced the muscles of his neck and shoulders to relax.

"We all agreed on the set list, despite it being before the release. It's okay, and if you're worried about taking lead vocals on Honest Violet, don't be. You have a solid voice. If we didn't have Tao, you'd be our lead singer." Simeon reached into his jacket and pulled out a pack of cigarettes, offering them to Chance.

"I'm fine." He waved them off, bowing his head.

He couldn't tell his friends he wasn't suffering from perform-ance anxiety or that he was suffering from severe disappointment. He hadn't seen Keely in five weeks and barely talked to her. Her texts, though they came daily, had been short and seemed aloof. The times they'd spoken, she sounded tired and distant. Despite her assurances she was fine and there was nothing wrong, he doubted her. He'd tried to see her, to make sure she was 'fine'. However, the day he went to her apartment the doorman had informed him that she hadn't been in residence for more than a month. It crossed his mind she might want to break up with him, especially when she'd taken more than a week to text him after she'd first left. He'd worried that after what had happened the last time they'd seen each other, maybe Keely had changed her mind about being with him. It was a major relief and reassurance when she did text. Since then, he'd dismissed the idea, despite his insecurities. He knew Keely well enough to know if she didn't want to be with him, she'd tell him outright.

So, he had to assume work was what was keeping her away from him and making her sound tired. He'd resolved to give her time and be patient, after all, he was busy with promotions and rehearsals himself, but he was forced to admit his patience wasn't limitless. He was worried and still had a thousand unanswered questions. Most of all, he wanted to see her, more than that, he wanted to touch and feel her, and he needed the comfort of her sleeping next to him at night. After weeks of only hearing her voice on the phone, he'd hoped she would come to the debut show that night. It was important to him, but he hadn't received any responses from his invitation.

He checked his phone for what felt like the thousandth time. For reasons he couldn't explain, he wanted Keely there, and her lack of presence was souring his mood. Chance's sour mood was affecting everyone else. When he glanced up at his friends again, they all looked away.

He stood and bowed. "I'm sorry," he apologized loud enough for everyone to hear. No one said anything, but he could see concern on their faces even as they nodded their acceptance of his apology.

The door in the front of the room opened, and a stage manager wearing a headset held five fingers up at them before disappearing. They all got up and walked toward the door with Chance being the last in line, dragging his feet and trying to muster the spirited energy he usually had when playing a live. Suddenly, Tau was in front of him, closing the door to the green room and shutting everyone else out of it.

"I've known you since before my salaryman days. You don't get stage fright," Tau said with a frown.

"No. I don't," Chance agreed, looking down at the floor to hide his shame.

Tau paused as if deciding what he was going to say. "I would have never thought you'd..." he paused and blew out a deep breath. "I hope she comes." He turned, snatched the door open, and walked out of it, leaving Chance stunned at how observant his friend was.

Chance stepped into the short hallway that led to the stage. The club they played was large and simply decorated, but the acoustics generated from live music was one of the best. Overall, the stage and lighting were well maintained even if it wasn't an overly extravagant visually.

He pulled out his phone and checked it for messages. There were none. With an audible sigh, he stowed his cellphone. By the time he reached the backstage entrance and was ushered onto the darkened stage by one of the stagehands, he'd resolved to give the chanting audience his best performance.

The prelude of their album started playing, and the loud music helped to drown his anxiety. He ducked into the strap of his bass and set it into position. Running his fingers up and down the neck of the guitar, he calmed at the feel of strings vibrating under his fingertips. The prelude was coming to the crescendo, and as he played a succession of notes to stretch his fingers, he turned to Simeon and gave him a reassuring nod. The last notes of the intro nearly drown out the still-chanting audience. It was for Eternity's End to give them what they'd paid their hard-earned money for, an excellent live showing. He twisted up the volume on his bass, and together, with the rest of Eternity's End, struck the chord that exploded into loud music and flashing stage lights. He performed the first song with as much exuberance as he could muster, but he could tell it wasn't enough. The audience wasn't as responsive to him, and Tao, Simeon, and Ren kept eyeing him, as if worrying about his mood more than their performance. As hard as he tried, despite always being able to play and perform above par, he was still distracted and frustrated by Keely's absence, not at the show, but in his life.

After their first song, Tao took the lead of the show, introducing them to the audience, telling jokes, and engaging them in a group conversation. Chance stood, listening to Tao and staring blindly at the black space between the stage lights above the audience. Chance loved his music, loved playing for a live audience, but he wanted the

236

show over so he could be alone with his misery.

Abruptly, something changed. He would have said it was a warm breeze, but no wind stirred. The air in the club filled with citrus and vanilla, or maybe it was just his senses. He breathed in deeply, wondering if it was his imagination, but the sensation only got stronger. His heart felt like it stopped then started pounding hard against his ribs, and his stomach filled with butterflies. His body seemed to relax, and all of his anxiety flowed upward and evaporated out of shoulders, leaving him a strange mix of tranquil, elated, and excited. Chance didn't know how he could sense the presence of the person he'd been longing for, but he knew with absolute certainty Keely was there.

∞ ∞ ∞ ∞ ∞

Keely smiled and offered a slight bow to the bouncer of the club as he marked her name off a list and nodded her in. She was running late for a myriad of reasons, and that frustrated her, especially when she could hear the music of Eternity's End already playing. Walking down a short, nondescript hallway, she entered the nightclub and joined the large crowd. Her eyes immediately went to the stage, or rather, to one of the people who stood on it, Chance.

Though she stood in the back of the room behind everyone, Keely was so captivated by the sight of Chance she was unaware anything else existed. He stood, holding his bass, and smiling charmingly. Besides his sultry brown eyes, which she couldn't see clearly, Chance's smile was her favored feature. Even at a distance, it had the extraordinary power to confuse and enchant her. It made her whole being tingle with a mixture of excitement, lust, and adoration. He flashed his perfect white teeth, and the slight dimples at the corners of his mouth appeared, sending her heart racing at a frantic pace. His lips seemed fuller, softer, and invitingly kissable. Even though Keely hadn't been able to tell him she was coming to his show because she'd forgotten her phone, she believed there was some magic between them and his smile was for her alone.

"Hey, Tau," Chance said, smiling into the mic in front of him.

His voice broke the spell of his smile and somewhat soothed the deep longing she'd had for the past weeks. Talking to him on the phone was not the same as hearing and seeing him in person. He was striking to look at, especially with his stage makeup highlighting his sharp features and defining his eyes. The pseudo-military styled jacket made his shoulders look broader than she remembered. His white pants caressed his thick thighs in such a way they drew the eye of any hot-blooded woman to one place, his accentuated bulge. A familiar deep-seated yearning overtook Keely, and her mind took her to places that heated her skin all over.

"I feel like this is a special crowd tonight, don't you?" Chance continued, side-eyeing his bandmate. The audience conveyed their excitement at his comment with a soft yell.

"Really," Tau answered, looking at Chance. "How can you know?"

Chance nodded at his friend. "I know." He gazed out into the audience with a soft, knowing smile. Keely was sure that somehow, he knew she was there. "I think tonight is going to be a lot of fun."

Tau stared at Chance for a moment then smiled in return before saying, "I think it will be too." He turned and nodded to Simeon and Ren. The others grinned and nodded at Chance, then Tau wrapped his fingers around the mic stand in front of him and gave the audience a sultry, bewitching stare that only someone with massive stage presence could. "I think maybe we should escalate things a little and see how exciting they get."

A soft undivided agreement echoed from the audience. Tau smiled and raised his hand. He sliced his knifed fingers downward, and music erupted from Eternity's End. The song was fast paced with a heavy beat, hard guitar, and intricate bass. Almost all of the audience jumped up and down in unison with the three front members of Eternity's End. The exhilarating music filled every corner and crevice of the club, making it pulse with the lively beat.

Tau started singing, and his voice was beautifully melodic with its low pitch. Keely was reminded why he was the front man for the band; he had undeniable charisma and a haunting voice. Still, her focus returned to Chance. He swayed and thrashed his head in time with the beat, mouthing the words along with Tau. Occasionally he'd smile, stick out his tongue, bob his head, in turn making Keely smile.

238

One of his hands slapped and strummed at the strings of his bass while the fingers, on the other hand, moved up and down the neck of the guitar with quick expertise. Keely had ghost sensations of those fingers running over her skin, making her shiver.

The song ended, seemingly too soon, leaving both Keely and the audience energized and wanting for more. Everyone waved their hands and softly yelled their approval. Their controlled exuberance was still unusual to Keely, but she could sense their enjoyment regardless. The stage went dark, there was a slight metallic scraping sound, and Keely could see the shadows of curtains falling over the stage.

A lone spotlight was ignited, and Tau and Chance slipped through a split in the curtains onto the stage. "Hey, Chance," Tau said into the mic he held. "How do you feel about breaking the rules and singing a new song tonight?"

The audience responded their approval by chanting Chance's name and more hand waving. Chance laughed into his mic. It was a melodious sound mixed with bass and pitch, and Keely found herself giggling at his laughter. His exuberance and excitement were infectious. After weeks of painful mental and physical restoration, his laughter was better than any remedy given to her by the doctors and monks of the ministry.

"Well, I suppose we could play a song before it's officially released," Chance answered, pushing up the sleeves of his jacket and exposing his chorded forearms. He looked thoughtful. "Should I sing?"

Keely replied, "Yes," along with the rest of the audience.

Chance laughed again. "Should I play something new?"

Again, the unanimous answer was, "Yes."

More laughter erupted from Chance. "Okay, it's decided then." Both he and Tau disappeared through the slit in the black curtains.

Keely had never heard Chance sing before. She'd seen him on stage and had been lulled to sleep by soft strumming as he practiced, but it never occurred to her that he could or would sing. She took it for granted Tau was the only singer in the band, and she felt foolish for limiting Chance's talent. Of course, he'd be able to sing he could play the guitar, the bass, the harp and a myriad of other instruments.

A violet spotlight illuminated a perfect circle in the middle of the stage, and its reflection coated the room in soft ambiance. The curtains slowly pulled apart, revealing Chance sitting at a pretty harp. Keely inhaled her surprise and brought her fingers to her mouth, lest she shout out encouragement that would embarrass them both. He glowed underneath the violet halo, looking ethereal and beautiful.

Chance turned to the audience and grinned as he adjusted the mic hovering above him. "I don't think the song needs a lengthy introduction. I hope you will all like it." He turned to the harp, lifted his hands, moved them up and down over the strings, not quite touching them. By outward appearances, it would seem he was nervous, but Keely knew differently. She knew when objects carried the resonance of a soul, and Chance's harp held some of his. He hesitated, dancing his fingers just next to the strings. It was as if he was asking the strings to join him in the creation of music. He didn't just play the harp, he used it to create beauty.

Chance ended the silence when he plucked a quick succession of soft chards on his harp. His fingers danced over the strings, and the rhythm of the music repeated as the chords changed in tone. Chance's music settled into Keely. It wasn't sad or even slow, but the song he played was evocative and pretty. The tempo got slightly faster, and Chance swayed with the harp while rocking his head back and forth. He paused, his fingers hovering above the strings, and when he plucked the next chords the rest of Eternity's End joined him, enriching his harp with guitar, bass, and drums. The rhythm of the music repeated, and then Chance opened his mouth, and his marvelous tenor voice filled the air, making Keely shiver.

> In the profoundness of night
> Past a quiet still
> I hid an impassioned dream
> Inside what I longed to feel
> I believed this vulgar world would destroy my treasures
> All its black and white pretense would devour my desires
>
> I had disregarded part of me
> I underestimated what someone genuine could see
>
> I didn't seek the sincerity of color
> But I lost my trepidation to something brilliant

My truth was revealed by its allure
My bland world was restored by honest violet

In the discord of the day
Past dismal pretense
Conformity doesn't have appeal
I will not be ruled by despondence
Despite the world and the obsceneness that smothers
The day and night are beautifully painted in vibrant colors

I had disregarded part of me
I underestimated what someone genuine could see

I didn't seek the sincerity of color
But I lost my trepidation to something brilliant
My truth was revealed by its allure
My bland world was restored by honest violet

I hear honest words
I feel honest passion
I see honest violet

I had disregarded part of me
I underestimated what someone genuine could see

I didn't seek the sincerity of color
But I lost my trepidation to something brilliant
My truth was revealed by its allure
My bland world was restored by honest violet

Keely stood, staring at Chance, overcome by a multitude of intense emotions. There was no doubt what his beautiful song was about. She'd never been given, or expected to receive, such a precious gift. The more she thought about it, the more she was overwhelmed by what he'd given her.

To her, it seemed everything went silent, despite the noises coming from both the audience and the people on stage. Tau was talking, but she was unsure what he was saying because she was drowning in all she was feeling. Something wet slid down her cheek. She reached up and touched her fingers to her moistened skin. She was both bewildered yet unsurprised to find she was crying.

At that moment, she knew for certain she loved Chance.

She loved his sultry eyes and contagious smile. She loved the way he looked annoyed when he was feeling embarrassed. She loved how the sound of his laughter could brighten her day. She loved it when he teased and bantered with her. She loved how patient he was, even when she exasperated him. Most of all, she loved that he accepted the parts of her that were weak, afraid, and awkward.

She wasn't sure when she'd fallen so deeply in love with him; she just knew she was. She was equally sure she needed to tell him how she felt. More importantly, she needed to tell him she was a Priestess, how, and why it happened. She felt selfish and untruthful for not telling him. It hurt to know that, despite his song proclaiming her honesty, she had hidden a good portion of her life, maybe even a good part of who she was.

Eternity's End played several more songs before they ended their show. Though Keely stood watching, she felt as if she watched from a distance, as if she didn't belong. However, she'd come to a decision. That night would be the night she told Chance despite the negative reactions she would get from him. Part of her fully expected him to reject her, but part of her hoped he'd return her feelings. He accepted the more fragile portions of who she was, so she hoped he'd accept the warrior as well.

An announcer came to the stage and instructed the audience that Eternity's End's merchandise table would be open for a short time for anyone who had not already visited the table. The room quickly started to empty. People made their way to the exit, lining up in an orderly fashion, except for the group waited around the merchandise table. They stood, patiently waiting for their turn.

Keely stood with a few stragglers in the middle of the floor unsure what to do and feeling anxious. She didn't know if, or where, she was supposed to meet Chance because she didn't have her phone. She figured he'd want to meet after the show, but that was an assumption on her part. There was always the possibility he'd be busy.

For half a second, she considered getting in the line to buy some Eternity's End's merchandise but thought better of it. Self-doubt suddenly overwhelmed her, and she was assailed with all of her old familiar fears. Her resolve to tell Chance everything, including how she felt, started to crumble. She was a Priestess. It was a choice she'd made and one she continued to make. How could she explain to him, explain the importance of it, and explain her feelings for him, that he was as important to her? Her heart needed him in her life, despite how complicated that life was, but she was sure it would shatter if he rejected her, any part of her. She'd never been more terrified.

She again pondered buying a CD, towel, or a bracelet but changed her mind because her anxiety was starting to make her stomach knot. Hiking her bag up on her shoulder, she turned, and almost ran into a broad-shouldered, lanky man. He was wearing a knit beanie, red hoodie, and a face-splitting smile that softened his dark brown eyes. "Are you Miss Keely?" he asked in heavily accented English.

"Yes," she answered in Japanese.

He stood staring at her a few seconds longer, then seemed to startle into a small bow. "I'm Itsuki Hara. It's nice to meet you." He bowed again, stepped in closer to her, and said softly. "I'm to escort you."

"Do we know each other?" Keely asked bluntly, wondering who Itsuki was.

"We were to meet for coffee, remember?" he asked with a subtle wink.

For half a dreadful second, Keely thought the ministry had sent Itsuki to collect her. Before she realized it was an irrational fear, because there was no way for them to find her without her phone, the man offered her his cell phone. She looked down at its face and nearly burst out laughing. On the screen, there was a picture of Chance with a mischievous smirk, winking, and pointing with the instruction 'that way' written underneath it.

Giggling, she said, "I'm sorry. Yes, coffee." She bowed. "I had forgotten in all the excitement of the show." She understood why Itsuki was being discreet. Very early on, she'd done her research and learned the rules for Japanese V-Kei subculture. Band members didn't openly show favoritism to one woman or fan. They were always to appear single and never available, and if they chose to date or bed anyone, they needed to be very discreet. Of course, there was gossip, but gossip was considered to be a half-truth and not taken seriously. However, if a band member got caught in any sort of intimate relationship, it could prove costly to the band and dangerous for the woman because of overzealous fans. Not that Keely couldn't handle herself, but she didn't want to damage any reputation Chance had established. If his fans found him more appealing and relatable because they thought he was single, then she wasn't going shatter that illusion.

"I know a place close by open late. They have good coffee and service." He motioned for the door.

"Alright, lead the way," she agreed, still smiling.

He led her out of the club and onto a brightly lit alleyway. The late winter, crisp, night air cooled her cheeks and calmed her apprehension. She walked under flashing signs, colorful light displays, and pretty lanterns, thinking how Japan had a strange sort of foreign familiarity. She was starting to grow attached to Japan and Tokyo. She wondered how much of that attachment was a byproduct of her affection for Chance.

Itsuki didn't lead her far. They walked down a slight hill and into a narrow entryway that had a set of stairs directly inside of it. "This way," he said, bowing and pointing up a set of stairs ascending into darkness.

She was about to ascend the stairs, when a hand slipped inside hers, and warm fingers wove together with her own. "Thank you, Itsuki," an achingly familiar voice said from beside her.

All of Keely's emotions knotted at the pit of her rib cage, and she felt breathless. She turned to look at Chance, only to find her lungs had honestly forgotten how to work. His slightly smiling face was such a gorgeous sight, especially when he looked at her with a softened sultry expression full of emotion. It took a moment for her to inhale, and for her heart to start beating again.

"Hello, Chance," she said in English, forgetting herself.

He bowed his head slightly. "Hello, Keely," he replied in the same language. His face softened, he lifted a hand and used the soft tip of his finger to trace a line across her cheek before carefully tucking her hair behind her ear. He smiled brilliantly, squeezed her hand, then ran up the stairs, pulling her behind himself.

244

25

Keely was so enraptured by Chance's warm hand holding hers she didn't really pay attention to where they were going or how they were getting there. She had vague awareness of winding hallways and fluorescent lights. When they finally burst back out onto the street, she only noticed the crisp night air, not her surroundings. Her cheeks stung for the briefest of moments because in the next instant, she was sitting in the back seat of a taxi.

Chance recited her address to the driver before turning to her with an unsure look. "Your apartment is closer."

"Yes, it is. I don't care where we go. I just want…" Keely couldn't finish her sentence because she lost herself in the dark amber of his eyes and overwhelming emotion sparkling within their depths. His gaze felt like a reflection of her own feelings, and her heart swelled.

He smiled, bent close to her ear, and whispered, "When you look at me like that, I get more impatient to get you alone." She squeezed his hand and smiled at him.

The cab seemed like it was moving backward, it took so long to get to Keely's apartment. When they got there, she couldn't clearly say how they got upstairs into her living room, but she did know that before her apartment door banged closed, they were kissing. His lips barely touched hers before she was exploring his marvelously silky and heated mouth with heady fierceness. His lips were supple, and she savored the familiar taste of coffee and sweet spice. It felt like it had been a lifetime since she'd seen, much less touched him. She deepened the kiss, and he pulled her into himself, nearly crushing the air out of her with his embrace. After all, she'd been through Keely was finally exactly where she wanted to be, doing exactly what she wanted to do, touching, holding, and kissing Chance.

Breathing became a necessity, and she pulled away, panting heavily. She stared into Chance's half-smiling expression and almost lost herself in the storm of overwhelming emotion that burned within the depths of Chance's sultry brown eyes. Her own emotions welled up, and she was out of breath again, for an entirely different reason.

"Keely?" Chance questioned. His expression tightened into concern. "What's the matter?" He let go of her so he could reach up and wipe moisture from her cheek with the back of his hand. For the second time that night, Keely was surprised to find herself crying because her feelings for him were so overwhelming.

"It's not anything wrong," she said softly. "Would you believe me if I told you..." she stopped faltering for words. "It's..." she paused again, suddenly feeling awkward. She wanted to say she loved him, that a piece of her soul would forever be his, but there didn't seem to be any words that could express how she felt. Instead, she wrapped her arms around his neck and settled her face against his neck. "I've missed you."

He tightened the arm around her waist and dug his fingers into her hair, cradling her head against him. Soft lips pressed to her temple then he whispered. "I know. I hadn't seen you in so long that I couldn't stand myself."

"I'm sorry," she apologized into his shoulder. Suddenly, she felt week in her knees because for the briefest of moments in the suicide forest she thought she'd never see him again. She couldn't stop the few tears that slipped down her cheeks or her quivering.

He brushed his fingers through her hair and again kissed her temple. "You're here. You're here with me." He held her, enveloped in a tight embrace, giving her the comfort of his warmth until her emotions settled and her trembling stopped.

Slowly, the hand at her waist slid underneath the lace shirt she wore. Hot fingers traced circles over her skin, making it react. Desire reignited within her, and she looked to him, wondering if he felt the same. There was hesitation in his eyes, though his lips were slightly pursed in invitation. She barely moved and their mouths intertwined so provocatively that her body immediately tensed with desire.

The hand underneath Keely's shirt made its way up, spreading warmth across the skin of her stomach before it pushed underneath her bra and cupped her breast in a firm grasp. The pad of his callused thumb rubbed over her nipple. The tough skin tickled against its softness, causing it to harden. Her want got the better of her, and she needed to be free of the obstacle that was her clothes. She lifted her hands and pulled at the buttons of her top, yanking the shirt apart and

246

tearing off the offending buttons. They ticked across the floor to the pulse of their hard breathing. Knowing her shirt was probably ruined didn't deter her in the slightest. There was a flurry of frantic kissing along with a frenzy of hands, both hers and his, stripping off her clothes. In the next instant, she found herself laying on her couch with Chance on top of her, and she had no idea how they'd gotten there. She didn't care. All she cared about was her desperation to have the fulfillment only Chance could give.

Reaching down between them, she unbuckled his belt and unfastened his pants without ever losing contact with his mouth. Their kiss had gone beyond fierce to uninhibited passion. His mouth was a hot, spicy drug she couldn't get enough of, and she wouldn't suffer the loss of it, not even for the seconds it would take to undress him. Pulling back his pants and pushing his underwear out of her way, she caressed and stroked his freed shaft, pleased to find it thick and hard.

"Keely," Chance breathed into her lips. Shudders passed between them, and she couldn't tell if it was from her anticipation or his.

Chance lifted himself up on his hands slightly, panting between parted lips. There was a tight look on his face she couldn't interpret. "Chance?" she questioned.

"I had every intention of being patient and tormenting you every wicked way I could imagine." He bent down and licked at her lips. "But..." he stopped, tilting his body so the head of his shaft rest at her entrance. "I jus can't." He pushed forward and slowly slid inside of her.

Keely let out a moan, vocalizing her enjoyment as he filled her and joined their bodies together. Their position on the couch was awkward, but it did allow for her to wrap one leg around him and use the other as leverage for movement. She took advantage of the leverage and moved so he glided in and out of her. He followed her movements with small strokes that caused exquisite tremors as he slid in and out of her. She wound her arms around his neck and pulled at him, wanting his mouth back on hers. He smiled devilishly, thrusted harder, then allowed her to draw him to herself. Between his velvety, spicy mouth and wonderful penetration, Keely's senses were overwhelmed, and an oncoming torrent of bliss tightened her body and made her scream out her pleasure.

247

Again, he pulled away from her and cradled her chin with one hand, forcing her to look at his impassioned features. He slowed his pace and pushed harder and deeper. Her climax stalled, but the enjoyable pressure of want for that climax intensified. He stared down at her with dark clouds filling his ardent eyes. Keely felt like Chance was trying to devour her body and soul, and she was more than willing to let him. He continued to pull in and out of her at a slow pace. She could feel how hard and thick he was, and how perfectly he fit her. Every one of his gloriously slow strokes made her muscles contract, and her nerves vibrate with arousal that eventually culminated into a storm of pleasure that wreaked incredible havoc on her body.

His mouth was on hers, stealing away her screams and her breath, and replenishing them with his own. Then his body hardened, and she felt the muscles of his back flex against her hands. His movements stilled, he let out a low moan, and she felt him pulse with climax before he collapsed on top of her.

"Keely," he whispered in her ear between huffs, wrapping his arms around her and holding her close to him.

"Chance," she replied breathlessly, kissing his cheek and temple.

After several steadying breaths, he lifted his head and looked at her with a gentle expression. "My real name is Misato, Misato Takeda."

"Misato Takeda," she said softly. "Misato," she repeated, liking the feel of his real name in her mouth. Then she realized what a precious gift he'd given her. He was giving her his true self. It made her love him all the more. At that moment, she was convinced she needed to tell the whole truth about who she was no matter the consequence. More importantly, she needed to tell him she loved him. "Misato," she said, caressing his cheek with her hand. "There's something you should know."

She felt his body stiffen and he seemed to stop breathing for a moment. He reached up caressed the side of her face then ran his fingers through her hair cradling her head. "Keely," he said closing his eyes and resting his forehead against hers. "I know you have truths to tell. Truly I'm happy you finally trust me enough to want to tell me." He breathed out hard. His essence coffee and spice dusted over her face. She felt reassured and hopeful he'd accept her truths. "Right

248

now, I just want to be with you." He was silent for a moment then lifted his face away from hers. She looked up to find him grinning down at her. "I want to spend the night exploring your wickedness and taking advantage of your fetish."

She smiled up at him in return. "What fetish?"

"If I told you, I couldn't take advantage of it." He bent his neck and brought his mouth to hers for a soft kiss.

"Okay, Misato," she agreed with a giggle. "But you don't have to limit your discovery to tonight. I'm more than happy to explore my wickedness with you whenever and however you want." She stopped, kissed the corner of his jaw then nibbled at his ear, appreciating the shiver she got in response. "I have nothing better to do than to devote my entire being for your exploration."

He let out a long breath then his lips found hers. "That may prove to be very exhausting for you."

Keely laughed. "I genuinely hope so."

26

Chance sat in the corner of a large studio next Simeon, fingering his bass and joking lightheartedly about nothing and everything. They were waiting for their turn for make-up touch-ups so they could finish the b-roll shots for the music video for Honest Violet. Their label felt the song could be a major success with the right marketing, especially after they'd debuted the song and gotten such a positive reaction from the audience. The production of the video was larger scale than other videos they'd done. That meant a professional director of a higher standard and a more sophisticated video shoot.

Usually, they'd shoot the standard band playing on a box frame or against a green screen. Those videos could be shot in less than twelve hours, depending on the special effects. The video for Honest Violet had a storyboard, planned locations, as well as the standard box frame band feature. This video would probably take thirty hours to shoot.

Chance knew he should be tired. He'd spent the previous night with Keely, and they'd only gotten a couple hours of sleep, but instead, he was exhilarated. He was excited about the support and prospects for Honest Violet, his song. He was excited to know Keely would be waiting for him at his apartment when the video shoot was finished.

Simeon started beating out a cadence with his drumsticks, using the chair back as a drum. Smiling, chance joined in and started plucking out a rhythm on his bass. The impromptu playful song flowed with the sounds of retro American jazz and resonated with Chance's good mood. They were making up nonsensical lyrics when Ren came over and interrupted them.

"Your turn in the hot seat." He pointed with his thumb towards the back of the room where two chairs were set up for hair and make-up. There was a slight frown on his face, but Chance ignored it, attributing it to being tired.

Getting up, he set his bass on a nearby stand and walked over to the empty chair, whistling the tune he was previously playing. He sat down, grinning at Tau. Tau's mouth was twisted in a deep frown, and his eyes were cut with sharp anger. It was unusual for him to get angry, much less express it.

"I'm sure we are almost done," he tried to reassure his unhappy best friend.

"Chance," Elisa, their make-up artist greeted with a small bow before turning her attention back to Tau. "It was even on the news, the night they went into the forest. I swear it's all true," she said, continuing a conversation she and Tau were having.

She was a pretty gothic girl who had just come onto the V-kei scene when Eternity's End did. They both seemed to gain popularity together. Although, Elisa's popularity was as much due to her looks as it was to her ability with make-up. She had startling, ivy colored eyes and prominent bone structure reminiscent of her Italian grandmother. The only reason Chance knew of her lineage was because Elisa liked to talk about her family, especially their heritage. She claimed she was descended from witches. Chance listened to her stories, smiling politely but internally rolling his eyes. He thought it all too incongruous to be believed.

"It seems too strange," Tau said. "I want to see it for myself. Can you send me the videos?"

"Sure," she replied excitedly. "As soon as I'm done with you and Chance."

Chance looked at Tau with an unspoken question on his face. Tau lightly shook his head and circled his finger, indicating they'd talk later. Shrugging, Chance went back to his whistling and ignored Tau's glaring grimaces, attributing them to tiredness and another failed attempt to bed Elisa.

For Chance, the retakes were a lot of fun and took no time at all. His excitement didn't wane even as the small hand on the clock ticked toward predawn hours. He really loved his job, despite all the hard work. After the director called it a wrap, and they clapped and congratulated one another, he sped over to Elisa because he wanted to be first in line to get his make-up removed. He couldn't wait to see Keely. He texted her saying as much, smiling happily as he hit send.

"Chance," Tau called out from behind him, forcing Chance to slow his step so his friend could catch up. Tau's mood hadn't gotten any better. Deep lines appeared between his eyebrows, indicating his attitude had gotten worse. "Why don't you and I share a cab home?"

"We're going in opposite directions," Chance pointed out.

"I'll ride with you to your house, then go home. There's something I want to talk to you about."

"Sure," Chance shrugged, not really caring how he got home, or that Tau wanted to talk to him. He only cared about getting to Keely.

Fifteen minutes later, the two of them stood on the street, waiting for a cab to pass by so they could hail it.

"I've known you for a long time," Tau said, staring at the ground with a hard expression.

"Yeah, I've known you since before you were a salary-man." Chance grinned, thinking of their chance encounter at a record store. "And look what we've done together."

"I know." Tau kicked at the ground. "There's something I have to show you because you won't believe me when I tell you... What I've already told you."

"What are you talking about?"

Tau was quiet for a moment. "Keely. We need to talk about Keely."

Chance rolled his eyes. "Tau, she's not a prostitute."

"No. Prostitutes get paid for getting passed around."

Chance's anger roared up in his chest so suddenly and so powerfully he had to take a step back from his best friend. "We're not having this conversation."

Tau didn't say anything, just held up his cellphone for Chance to see. Chance was already raising his hand to smack it away, when the video playing got his attention, or rather, the nude woman with long brown hair in it got his attention. Though he couldn't see her face, he immediately recognized the curvy body, perfect, ivory skin, and long, multicolored hair. There was no doubt in his mind the woman was Keely. He knew it even before her head fell back, giving the camera the perfect view of her face. Even if he wanted to deny it was Keely, he couldn't, because of the perfect view of the necklace he'd given her.

Her face was tight, and her eyes were unfocused, staring at nothing. She was held up by a tall man with sinewy muscles and dark hair. Keely and the man were entangled in a tight embrace, and both

252

of them were naked.

Chance went cold, then hot, then his stomach turned and fell to his feet. The video played on, zooming on the upper half of the couple. They seemed to be convulsing together in unison, obviously sharing a moment of intimacy. He didn't want to look, but he couldn't look away even as pain tore through his chest. Then the camera zoomed out, showing, then focusing on, a circle of people holding hands around the pair. At least, they were fully dressed, or Chance was sure he would have gotten nauseous. There was no sound on the video, but the people in the circle appeared to all be speaking, maybe chanting, he couldn't really tell. Before he could try and process what he was seeing, a flash of light blurred the screen of Tau's phone, and it went dark, ending the video.

He wanted to believe what he'd seen was somehow a trick, or there was some other reasonable explanation, but he knew Keely had her own secrets, secrets she'd refused to share because she believed his opinion of her would change. Was Tau's video the truth Keely didn't want to tell? Was that what she did for a living and why she was so well off? Was she some kind of high-priced whore? One that took part in things like he'd just seen?

His mind replayed all the tiny moments they'd shared that could have been clues. The time the man in the café payed her two million yen for her services and the time he'd seen her wearing an expensive Kimono, walking with suited escorts. Then he thought of the time she'd shown up at his apartment, bleeding, and telling him a family had been irrevocably torn apart. His mind went through it over and over again, and he couldn't fathom any other reasonable explanation for what he'd watched.

Chance stood, staring at the replay button in the middle of the screen of Tau's phone. The world felt like it had stopped spinning before it caught up to itself in a rush of dizzying lights and color. For a moment, his mind went blank and he couldn't move, couldn't think, or couldn't breathe. His chest started to burn from the breath he held, and he let it out in one harsh exhale. He could have sworn his high-pitched pant of pain was the only sound in the universe. Momentarily, he couldn't understand why the sight of her with another man was so painful to see.

It was then he knew...he loved her.

Laughter bubbled up in his chest, and he found himself laughing bitterly at the sad irony of his life. The same moment Chance realized he was in love for the first time, was the same moment he saw a video of someone sharing in something he thought was his alone to have. He laughed so hard he had to hunch over and rest his hands on his knees so he could catch his breath. It was only then he saw the tears falling from his eyes and dotting the sidewalk with dark spots.

"We promised," he whispered, thinking of the night they'd agreed to be exclusive. The night he decided to be hers and she his alone. "She promised."

"Misato," Tau said softly, and put a hand on Chance's shoulder.

Chance looked at his best friend, disliking the worried, sad expression ruining his normally attractive features. "Tell me all of it."

Tau pursed his lips together, and the nodule in his throat moved up and down as he swallowed. "The only truth I can say for certain is what you and I saw on the video. The rest sounds like a weird science-fiction. But I will tell you what Elisa told me." He took a deep breath and gently directed Chance to a nearby wall. Tau probably could tell Chance needed something to lean on. "I will be honest, I don't give a lot of credence to what Elisa says. I pay attention and humor her, but she caught me by surprise when she started talking about a Priestess. This is the first video she showed me." He tapped on his cell phone screen then turned it so Chance could see a local newscast showing footage of Aokigahara. In the distance, a woman, Chance easily identified as Keely, walked toward the forest surrounded by people. The headline underneath read, 'Monks bless Aokigahara'. Tau frowned. "That was over a month ago, right about the same time you told me Keely left for work."

Chance looked to Tau. "I remember seeing that, but I didn't notice." He shook his head in disbelief.

"I'm sorry," Tau said sadly. "Elisa also told me her family participated in a coven for a Priestess about six weeks ago. She was quite proud since this Priestess is supposed to be the only one in the world. It was a great honor for them."

Chance cut his eyes and stared sideways at Tau. "I'm sure it was," he bit out, trying not to be mad at his best friend because he was telling him a truth Keely should have. He leaned against the nearby wall. His chest and stomach hurt, and his legs were shaking with the jealousy he was trying to control.

"I'm sorry, Misato. I'd give up everything I own not to... You're my best friend. I wouldn't tell you this to hurt you, but I thought not telling you would hurt you more." He squeezed Chance's arm. "According to Elisa, it's a warrior's ritual, used before a chosen warrior goes into battle. It's used to make them invulnerable. And they needed the Priestess to perform it. From what she said, the Priestess is known the world over, recognized as an authority by all the world's most powerful politicians and religious leaders. And they regularly call on her for her services."

Chance put his hands to his head and rubbed his temples. He didn't want to hear anymore and yet, he had to know. "And?"

Mercifully, Tau shook his head. "Yeah, that's all she knew. It seems even though the Priestess is of some importance, they keep her existence a secret. Elisa didn't know much else but couldn't wait to be inducted into her family's coven so she could find out more and take part in such rituals, like the one you saw in the video."

Chance wiped at the moisture pooling at the corner of his eye. "It really does sound like science-fiction or a really bad erotic manga."

"Yeah," Tau agreed. "I know, if it were me, I wouldn't want to share the person I cared for."

"I don't," Chance agreed.

The two of them stood together in silence, Tau resting his hand on Chance's shoulder, and Chance trying to gather his racing thoughts. Minutes ticked by, and all he could do was stand and watch the mist of his warm breath disappear into the night. The silence was interrupted by tones emanating from Chance's pocket. With shaking hands, he pulled out the cell phone and opened the message, then lost his breath all over again. Keely had sent him a picture of herself lying in his bed, wearing a pink, lace-trimmed pajama top with bunnies printed on it. The fabric was thin so he could see every soft curve of her breasts. She was smiling stunningly, and her eyes were bright with passion. Doubt made him wonder if he was the only one she looked at with such passion. He almost smashed his phone against the concrete.

"She's waiting for me at my apartment." Chance slipped his cellphone back into his shirt pocket.

"Well," Tau stopped and bit at his lower lip. "You can always come to stay the night at mine."

"Thanks." Chance considered Tau's offer, but avoidance wouldn't solve anything. He didn't know what to say, or do, or how to handle the stabbing pain in his chest. It felt like he had a heart attack, only he knew he wasn't. Still, there was a tiny fleck of a part of him that hoped the video was a lie, or there was a reasonable explanation, and everything he was feeling was wrong. He needed to hear the truth from her, whatever that was. "Keely and I have somethings to discuss."

∞ ∞ ∞ ∞ ∞

Chance opened the door of his apartment, walked into the savory and spicy smell of seasoned beef and vegetables. As he slipped off his shoes, Keely bounced through his kitchen to him, smiling brilliantly and making his heart ache. She wrapped her arms around his neck and kissed the corner of his mouth. "I thought you might be hungry, and the lady at the store said sukiyaki was good to serve on a cold night and easy to make, like American soup."

It took all his willpower not to crush her to himself. He'd just come in from the cold. She was soft, warm and inviting. "Thank you," he said curtly, extricating himself from her arms. He pulled off his jacket, hung it up, and walked past her into his living/bedroom only to find she'd organized, cleaned, and did his laundry. He looked to her feeling a mixture of emotions he couldn't really define. Part of him was delighted she'd do something so magnanimous, but he was still feeling the sharp pains of hurt, and he didn't like the idea of her going through his things. It felt too personal.

"You cleaned?" he questioned, faltering for words.

"Weird, right? I don't think of myself as the housewife type, but I got bored." She walked past and motioned to table set for two, decorated with candles, and purple flowers. "Then when I was done, I was still bored, so I went to the market and got food to cook." She took his hand and smiled up at him. "Are you hungry?"

He probably did need to eat, but he wasn't hungry. "Keely," he started then stopped, distracted by the warmth of her hand and the sensations it caused. He pulled his hand from hers and the smile on her face faded. She finally sensed his sour mood.

"Misato, if you're too tired…"

"Keely," he interrupted her. "I want to talk, not eat."

She frowned, pursed her lips together then said, "Okay." She folded her arms around her stomach and looked at the floor. "What do you want to talk about?"

"I think you know," he replied. Keely's response and pensiveness did nothing to settle his fears or anxiety. The small part of him hoping for a reasonable explanation from her had become a large part of him.

"I do." She looked at him. "Please, listen to all of it, and try and keep an open mind."

His heart raced, and his stomach flip-flopped, and all at once he lost his courage to hear what she had to say. He turned on his heel, went into the kitchen, and opened a topmost cabinet. Pulling out a bottle of saké, he grabbed two small porcelain tumblers, then walked to the living room. He moved one of the plates aside and set the bottle and glasses in its place.

"Sit," he said, motioning to the couch as he took a seat on the floor. He wanted to reassure her, but he couldn't manage it because he needed reassurance himself.

She cautiously stepped around the table and sat down, taking the cup he offered. He didn't follow tradition. Instead, he simply filled both their cups, then picked his up and drank it in one gulp. Though the liquid was smooth and the sweetness perfect, it still burned his throat and made his eyes water slightly.

Keely picked up her cup and sipped it. "Okay, here goes." She took in a shaking breath. "One thing you have to understand is Priestesses, or Priests from a long-time past, aren't chosen or trained to be what they are, it isn't something they inherit. Being a priest, or in my case Priestess, is a choice. I made a choice and accepted the task. There are some politics I have to deal with, but when I get called to do my duty, it's my choice."

Chance managed to keep from grimacing, but his inward thoughts were burned with the vision of Keely in another man's arms, and he wondered if it was typical for what she did. "How old were you when you first chose?"

"Thirteen," she said softly, again staring at the cup of sake she held between her hands. "I...that was a hard time in my life. The choice wasn't a hard one, dealing with the aftermath was. A lot of people, including my parents, didn't understand. Luckily, the ministry found my brother and me before anything too terrible could happen."

"Is your brother a priest?"

"No." Keely shook her head. "He's the Sunderer. And I have to tell you about me before I can tell you about him, but we both work with the ministry."

"Ministry?" he asked, not really sure he wanted to know what the ministry was because his mind was focused on a thirteen-year-old child, choosing to do the things like he saw in the video.

"Basically, every religious organization, actually cooperating together. They can't agree on theology, but they agree on my existence and the need for my...services."

"Keely." Chance stared at his own cup. He swallowed, wondering at the services she provided, that she chose to provide. The part of him that prayed she wasn't some sort of ritual concubine still hoped she had a reasonable explanation. "What does a Priestess do? What do you do?"

She cleared her throat and lifted her eyes to him. "This is the part you have to keep an open mind about. There's always been a need for a Priest or Priestess because there's always been..." She stopped, pursed her lips, and took a deep breath. "We call them neverborn, and they hunt humans. They hunt humans to steal their souls. I hunt the neverborn, and I take those souls back. That's why I am called Priestess. I'm the only one who can fight them and win." She looked up at him a strange sort of tight look on her face. It was an expression he'd never seen her make before. "It's that simple and that complicated."

Chance looked at her, feeling incredulous. She was telling him she hunted monsters, monsters who stole human souls. "I don't believe in monsters," he said truthfully. If he was completely honest, he did believe in monsters. He thought humans were monsters. They could steal, kill, and they could lie. They could lie, keep secrets, and rip your heart from your chest. "I don't believe in monsters," he repeated softly as he stood up. He was suddenly anxious and couldn't

258

sit still. Her excuse for everything she hadn't told him was monsters. She said she fought monsters, but he had proof it was something different altogether. He didn't believe her. Still, he wanted an explanation he could understand. "You're telling me the secret you've been keeping is that you fight monsters, and you're the only one who can?"

"Yes," she said simply. "There is more to it, but that's the truth. There are others who can fight them, but I'm the only one who can rescue human souls. I'm the only one who can restore a soul to a body. Or if I can't, I'm the only one who can free a soul so it can ascend to heaven." Her face was still hard, but she was frowning, and her beautiful eyes had dulled.

"You don't expect me to believe you?" he asked, finally able to read her expression. "You don't expect me to believe this lie about monsters?"

"No." She shook her head. "Not without proof, and I won't... I can't give you proof." She stopped and looked at her hands, and he wasn't sure what to say.

The loud shrill tone of her phone pierced the silence and echoed around his apartment. Her face tightened, she got up and went to where her bag and the phone sat by his apartment door. "Hello," she said crisply when she answered. There a short pause, then she lowered her voice and turned her back on him. He caught small details about a meeting she was to attend.

Something inside of Chance, maybe his calm and ability to reason, snapped and broke. His thoughts raced out of control. He hated her phone, he hated that every time it rang, she was taken away from him. Most of all he hated that the one thing he wanted from her, she didn't give, an explanation he could believe.

The images from the video kept replaying in his head and were so vivid there was a ghost imprint of them wavering in his vision. He couldn't stop thinking of the times she'd left his bed, went to work, then came back to it, to him, and this 'ministry' was calling her again. He thought he'd be sick, thinking of her sharing her body with someone else then coming to him. After that, his mind twisted with jealousy, and he couldn't stop wondering at what she did with other men? Other women? He wondered if she talked, laughed, and bantered with them the way she did him? He wondered if she touched them the way she touched him? He wondered if they sated their lust with her body? He wondered if she looked at them the way she looked at him? He wondered if they lost themselves to her impassioned looks the way he did? He wondered what he was to her, or if she cared for him at all? His heart and mind couldn't wholly comprehend both his love of Keely and the feeling of betrayal. Unfortunately, neither could it handle the full weight of his jealousy, and it evolved to uncontrollable rage. When she finally turned to him, he was seething with it.

Before she could say anything, he pulled out his phone, clicked on the video Tau had sent him, and held it up for her. "This doesn't look like fighting monsters."

She looked at the video for only half a second before her eyebrows knotted together. "Misato, it's not what you think."

"Chance, you can call me Chance. It appears we don't know each other as well as I thought we did. Or, at least, I don't know you."

She looked down at her clenched hands then back to him. "Okay, Chance. That was an allocation spell."

"Something warriors use before a fight?" Chance dropped the phone on the table, uncaring that it clattered against, and probably broke the dishes there. "So, one of your duties as a Priestess is to share yourself intimately with warriors, so they can go fight? What? Monsters?"

"Define intimately, because there was no sex, just awkward nakedness. And, yes. I fight monsters," Keely said, staring at him with a calm on her face that further infuriated him. She stood in his apartment, looking as if the video wasn't betrayal, as if she hadn't betrayed him. The spike of hurt and anger drove itself deeper into his soul.

He ground his teeth together, trying to calm his rage, but failed. Chance couldn't stop himself from saying the next thought that came into his head. "I don't believe you, but it doesn't matter anymore." A small voice, his reason, begged for him to be quiet, be still, and listen to what else Keely had to say, but the voice was drowned out by the burning fury of jealousy. "I wanted to fuck an American. It was never going to be anything more. I'd already decided to end things between us," he lied. He could have stopped there; he could've kept his mouth shut, but his anger demanded he hurt her as much as she'd hurt him. "I can't have this circulated amongst people I know or my fans. As low as my status is, a whore, even a high priced one, would ruin it."

She looked at him with wide eyes and mouth agog, seemingly stunned. There was a long stretch of silence, and he thought she'd rage at him. Instead, her face fell, and he could see disappointment and hurt in her severe frown. She shook her head, and her face hardened.

"You don't mean that," she said in a soft voice.

She walked past him and into his bathroom, leaving him alone to seethe. He paced back and forth again, trying to will away the sharp ache in his chest and the need to destroy something. No more than a minute passed, and she emerged from his bathroom, pulling a frilly shirt down over torso.

"What you saw was an allocation spell. It's a warrior's ritual performed so an inheritor's body will take the wounds of a fighter during a heated battle. That spell was performed for me, not to me. Just so you know, my inheritor almost succumbed to his wounds, nearly killing us both," Keely explained, putting on her shoes, and grabbing her jacket. "I was the one doing the fighting." She pulled on her jacket grabbed her purse and phone, then turned toward the door and stopped. "I've wanted to tell you the truth for a long time now. I was too afraid," she said to the door. "I knew you wouldn't believe me. So, your disbelief isn't a surprise. Yes, I'm a coward for not telling you sooner. I didn't tell you at first because the truth would put you in the middle of a supernatural war with the monsters you don't believe in. But my reasons for keeping my secret changed over time. You'd see me differently. And if you didn't believe the truth about what a Priestess is, then you wouldn't believe anything else I needed to tell you. Even now, I know you won't believe the most important thing I have to say. I'm still going to say it." She turned and looked over her shoulder at him, her eyes shimmering with deep emotion. "I'm very in love with you, Chance…Misato. You can stand there staring at me accusingly or lash out at me in jealousy, but that doesn't change how I feel. I do love you. And when you realize that…" she stopped and blinked back the pools of tears forming in her eyes, "I mean, really realize that I do love you, I'll accept your apology."

For a moment, she stared at him with the softest expression, her eyes conveying both her love and her pain in their violet depths. All of his jealousy and anger were instantly quieted. Before he could say or do anything, she turned and walked out of his apartment.

Chance was rooted to the floor. Once again, he couldn't think or move, and he was certain Keely had stolen his breath away. A long time passed as he tried to sort through everything she'd said, everything he said, and everything between them. The tiny bit of reason he'd ignored was now screaming inside his head, and it was calling him a fool. Urgency filled him. He needed to apologize. He needed to tell her he loved her too. "Keely," he shouted at his closed door, knowing she was too far away to hear. For the second time that night, he didn't know what to do. Luckily, his feet started moving on their own, propelling him forward and out of his apartment. Then he was running.

27

Keely was halfway down the breezeway and heading toward the stairs of Chance's apartment building when she heard the distant click of his door closing behind her. She didn't stop, look back, or turn around. If she did, she'd be imploring him to listen and pleading with him to believe her. She'd be down on her knees, begging him to return her love.

Keely would have been down on her knees, begging, but in her heart, she knew Chance would have to make the decision to come to her. He needed to determine if he was willing to fight for them, even if they had to fight through his doubts and jealousy. If he didn't come to her, then he'd never be open-minded enough to listen to or believe the truth.

Wiping at the tears that had started to roll down her cheeks, she descended the stairs and walked to the street. She was frustrated, disappointed, and angry at herself. She was to blame for most of their misunderstandings, especially the damming video. She understood why Chance believed she'd betrayed him. In a way, she had, since she hadn't trusted him with the truth. She hadn't trusted either of their feelings. It would have been so easy to cast an illusion to show proof, but then even with evidence, she doubted he'd believe.

Once upon a time, she was convinced there were no such things as monsters either. She was a skeptic until the fateful day when she encountered one, accepted heaven's task, and chosen to be a Priestess. Now she was a woman, walking away from the man she loved, and all of her hope and happiness were held together by the slim possibility he'd come to her. Still, she was barely resisting the urge to turn around and beg.

The more she resisted, the faster she walked and kept walking until she found herself on the corner of a deserted street. The cold wind whispered down the empty alleyways and pricked at her exposed skin. Keely looked around at the darkened buildings and the stagnant flashing lights, searching for signs life. Finding none, she turned her eyes upward, seeking hope and solace in the stars. The city skyline had dimmed them so much there was nothing but blackness. Suddenly, she felt absolutely alone and hopeless.

"Chance is never going to come to me, is he?" she asked heaven through her tears, not expecting an answer.

A lifetime of moving from one city to another and leaving behind people she cared for overwhelmed her aching heart. She was a soldier in a never-ending war who couldn't gain any ground against their enemy, that was all. She gave in to her hopelessness, and her thoughts fell into the trap of wishing she'd never met Chance and fallen in love.

"I'm so stupid." She covered her face with her hands and sank down to her knees, indifferent of where she was. Unable to control her tears, she wept.

She wept for all she'd traded away to be heaven's Priestess and all she would continue to give away. She cried pitifully for her broken heart, afraid she'd spend the rest of her life in love with a man she'd never see again. Her hands filled with the tears of her unrequited love. For a long time, she sat in the middle of a deserted street, lost in Tokyo, crying because she didn't know what else to do.

Eventually, the flow of tears subsided, and her eyes dried out. She used the back of her sleeve to wipe away their remnants and the hopeless they carried. Taking a deep breath, she looked around, feeling as if she could see things more clearly. Even in the middle of the night, Tokyo was a marvelous wonder that blended old-world culture with technology. She could sense all the lives around her now that she'd cried out her misery. Again, she turned her eyes skyward and caught glimpses of twinkling stars. They were there. She couldn't see them before because she couldn't see through her own despair. It wasn't the stars she couldn't perceive, but it was her own heart. Though it was aching with pain, and though she may never see Chance again, she knew despite all the mistakes she'd made where he was concerned, it wasn't a mistake to love him.

"I'm sorry," she apologized to heaven, and got up off the ground, drying her hands on her pants, then dusting them off. It was then she felt the malevolence floating on the air. Her fit of misery and hysterics had attracted a neverborn.

It was close, closer than she would have liked. In fact, it was probably less than a kilometer away. "Crap," Keely said out loud, feeling unprepared. She hadn't fought with a neverborn since the battle in Aokigahara and had only recently gotten back into a training regimen.

She pulled out her cellphone and pressed the icon to call Sutton. While Keely waited for an answer, she turned toward the direction of the neverborn, trying to get a better sense where it was. Only she didn't just get a sense of where it was, she got a sense of familiarity. The anger, loss, and happiness, of two people, were combined with a ravenous hunger for souls.

"I thought you were spending the night with Chance," Sutton answered with the slight slur of someone who had just awakened.

"Sutton," Keely whispered as chills ran up and down her spine. "It's the neverborn from Aokigahara."

"Fuck, fuck, fuck, fuck, fuck. Run."

"I want to I really do, but…" Keely stopped looking in the direction of the oncoming torrent of fierce emotion. The intense feelings she felt belonged to multiple souls, probably more than ten. "It's been a month. It's not just the two souls anymore." Keely stared down the empty street, straining her eyes, trying to see the neverborn.

"Then fucking hide until I get there," Sutton ordered.

"Okay, I wi—"

"Keely," Chance's voice called to her like a song, and the essence of coffee and musk floated on the night air. He'd surprised her, taking away both her words and her breath. For a split second, she was elated to hear Chance's soft voice, but then unrelenting fear paralyzed her, turning her flesh to stone and keeping her from doing so much as taking the smallest of breaths. She was standing in the middle of an empty street, with no monk, the worst neverborn she'd ever encountered heading right for her, and Chance had unwittingly put himself in the middle of her war.

28

"Keely," Chance repeated. Panting out puffs of mist and staring at the back of her head as he tried to catch his breath. He'd left his apartment without grabbing his jacket and ran nearly two kilometers looking for her so he could apologize. Judging by her straight back and stiff shoulders, he wondered if he'd get the opportunity, or if she'd reject him and his apology. His stomach twisted when she slowly turned around. Preparing for an angry tirade, he took a deep breath. When she finally looked at him, the last thing he expected to see was her pretty features distorted with fear.

"Chance," she said in a cracked voice. The cellphone she held slipped from her hand and fell to the ground with a solid crack. Shaking her head, she said, "You can't be here." She looked over her shoulder then turned wide, violet eyes back to him.

"I..." he started to reply, but she slapped a cold hand over his mouth.

"Don't move, don't speak." She stopped, again look around her. "And calm all of your emotions." She said in a bare whisper. A shaking hand wrapped around his, and she pulled him down a nearby street, frantically looking around her. "There's nowhere to hide it won't find you." She stopped and looked at him then past him down the street.

"Keely, what's wrong?" he whispered. Her fear was so potent he could sense it in the air. It was starting to make him afraid.

"It's coming." She pulled him to a nearby wall, placed herself in front of him, and pressed her body against his, pushing it into the wall behind them. "Don't move," she repeated, lifting her still shaking hand. Beneath it, streams of fog started to snake up from the ground, thickening and spiraling around them. "It will know we're here, but it shouldn't be able to see us," she whispered more calmly, but there was still strain in her voice.

"What is happening?" Chance questioned. Involuntarily, he wrapped a protective arm around her waist and held her against him.

"One of the monsters you don't believe in is coming." She

pushed at the arm around her waist, but when he resisted her efforts to disentangle herself, she stilled.

Before either of them could say anything else, the street filled with something ominous, silencing them. The lights seemed dimmer, and the dark of the sky felt like it was closing in. Keely's body was so stiff she slightly trembled with the strain of her tension, and her gaze was affixed at the end of the street. Shadows shifted and moved. Then someone appeared from the shadows, walking down the middle of the road.

Chance couldn't see the details of their features, but it quickly walked toward them moving strangely, as if they were trying to do a swaying, jerking dance. It wasn't until they got closer that he could see why. One of the legs connected to its lanky body was longer than the other. The leg wasn't just longer, but it was much thicker. As they continued to limp in their direction, Chance started to make out other abnormal features. Their arms were also overly extended and bone thin. At the end of each arm were massive hands. The fists matched the person's giant-sized head.

A shiver crept up Chance's spine. The word monster whispered in his mind. The person, whoever they were, got closer, and he could see even more of their features. At first, he thought the person was wearing a patchwork romper. They weren't actually wearing anything. Instead, they looked like they were painted a stone-grey color with patches of skin showing through. Although, he couldn't really tell for sure. As the person continued down the street toward them, he wondered if they noticed the nearly freezing temperature. Then their face became discernable, and Chance lost any concern for its wellbeing. Patches of hair sprouted out in places all over their head, falling onto their crooked face. One eye was unusually large and stark white. While the other eye was normal, it was set below the eye socket. He couldn't discern a nose, but it could see a clearly formed mouth with gaping lips and a plethora of uneven teeth.

His brain took the person in and came to the only conclusion it could. "Monster," he hissed under his breath, finally realizing the thing coming toward them wasn't human.

"Neverborn," Keely whispered over her shoulder.

It, the neverborn, walked to the end of the block and stopped. It scanned from left to right then back again, almost twisting its head completely backward before its gaze settled on the building they were standing against. Its odd-eyed gaze settled on them. A broad, toothy smile split its face as it took a step forward. Then it was running at them.

The cold hand of fear wrapped its fingers around Chance's spine and dug its sharp nails into his flesh. Instinct told him it had come to devour them, devour Keely. He couldn't move. He couldn't breathe.

"Chance...Misato," Keely said softly, thawing the icy grip of his fear. "You have to let me go."

It was only then he realized he had both arms wrapped tightly around her middle, crushing her to himself. Before the word 'no' could form on his lips, she'd pried his arms apart and stepped away from him.

"Keely," he croaked out, reaching for and grabbing her arm, but she pulled away from him. Her cold fingers slipped through his.

Without looking at him, she extended her arm and shoved him back into the wall. "Don't move," she ordered in a voice sharp enough to cut through his fear, and he remembered what she'd said. 'We call them neverborn, and they hunt humans. They hunt humans to steal their souls. I hunt the neverborn, and I take those souls back. That's why I am called Priestess. I'm the only one who can truly fight them.' Confusion and fear muddled his brain for a moment, but then his mind cleared. Chance knew everything Keely had said was true. He knew there was so much more she hadn't told him, much more he needed to know. There was so much he needed to say.

Chance focused on Keely's sturdy and solid form. She was the most beautiful, intelligent, alluring woman he'd ever met, would ever meet. He knew without a doubt, Keely was the love of his life, and she was about to fight something that looked like it came straight from hell, ready to take the life of anything it came across. He'd never been more terrified.

Keely stepped into the middle of the street just as the neverborn reached her. There was no hesitation, posturing, or taking one another's measure. The two of them were immediately locked into combat as the neverborn lifted its hammer-like hand and swung it down on her. She sidestepped and ducked out of its attack, kicking a heel into the side of its knee. The neverborn was knocked off balance, but its fist still made hard contact with the street, cracking the pavement beneath its feet. The resounding thud vibrated the ground Chance stood on.

The neverborn looked up and stared in Chance's direction, giving him an up-close view of its face. It was more terrifying with mere meters between them. The white eye rolled around, looking all directions, while the human-looking, brown eye pivoted back and forth. The obscuring fog Keely had created must have kept him hidden because the neverborn's eyes never focused on Chance even though he was sure it knew he was there. He had no idea what he'd do if it came at him. He felt like a useless coward.

The neverborn stretched out its other arm and crawled a step toward Chance. At that moment, Keely took advantage of the neverborn's kneeling position and kicked out a second time. Her foot connected with its neck, and it jerked sideways from the impact. It sputtered and grabbed at its throat, rolling away from her and increasing its distance from both Keely and Chance. That was when he realized she was drawing the thing, the neverborn, away from him. He was thankful while ashamed of his inability to do much more than cower in the shadows.

The neverborn rolled back onto its feet and immediately retaliated, swinging both of its arms at her head with a speed that surprised Chance. Such a huge deformed creature didn't seem like it should have the agility or ability to move so quickly. Keely easily ducked underneath the strikes, and they missed by a wide margin. She wasn't able to avoid the long leg that kicked out and swept her feet from underneath her. Chance thought his heart would stop as he watched her fall to the street in slow motion. At the last possible moment, she caught herself with her hands, twisting her body and rolling back onto her feet. The foot stomp aimed at her head missed, leaving behind a cracked pothole in the middle of the street.

Chance was both awed and terrified by her skill. He'd never imagined when she said she fought monsters she was telling the truth. Nor could he have fathomed that she could stand her ground against something so terrifying, and she did it with a beautiful grace even though she was in a violent confrontation.

The neverborn tried to land several more blows, and Keely nimbly avoided each one. Chance watched with his heart in his throat, afraid of the moment when one of the neverborn's fists would make contact. Keely continued to step around its kicks and dodge its strikes. After a blow aimed at Keely's midsection missed, the neverborn drove its fists into the pavement, pummeling it into scraps of asphalt. Its wide mouth opened, and it let out a loud shriek. The screams of several people from some otherworldly hell pierced the night air, making him shiver. He covered his ears and pushed himself back against the wall, seeking its protection.

"You are the most wretched of all souls. We sensed your fear and anguish from far away. Why are you fighting us when we can offer you release?" the neverborn asked as it stomped a foot into the ground, scattering debris.

"My fear and anguish are mine alone. So is every other emotion I have." Keely stepped away from the neverborn. "You can't have any portion of my soul."

"We are not sickly humans anymore. We can and will have you." The neverborn attacked again. One kick or punch after another was aimed at Keely's face and torso. She simply stepped, ducked, or pivoted out of its reach, proving how skilled she was. Still, she had to work harder and move faster to keep from being hit.

As he watched, Chance had several critical realizations. He'd been the cause of the neverborn's appearance. If he'd had actually listened, instead of insulting and trying to hurt Keely, they'd be safe in his apartment. She'd be safe in his arms. He was the one that weakened Keely and put her in danger. The neverborn was relentless in its attacks. It threw punch after kick after punch. Keely, on the other hand, never really retaliated. She simply maintained a defensive position that allowed her to dodge its attacks. The neverborn had otherworldly strength. If even one of its punches made contact with Keely, whether she blocked it or not, it would probably be decimating. It didn't appear to be getting tired, and it wasn't going to give up. Keely didn't have the same supernatural abilities. She didn't have unmeasurable strength and endless energy. Eventually, she'd get too tired to fight or dodge its blows. Ultimately, if something wasn't done, she'd lose to the neverborn. She'd lose her life.

He couldn't lose the love of his life to something so wretched. His fear and anger culminated, changed shape, and grew into courage. Chance had to do something.

270

He looked down at his clenched fists, frustrated at his own ineptness and lack of ability. Learning to fight wasn't something he'd ever considered a necessity. Just then, Chance wished not only that he could fight, he wished he had a weapon powerful enough to hurt the neverborn. He looked back to Keely as she dodged another fist aimed at her head. Her face was glistening, and her hair was stuck to her forehead and neck. Obviously, Keely had been trained well, but all humans had limits, and even the Priestess was reaching hers.

Chance didn't have a plan, a weapon, or the aptitude for fighting. He needed to help Keely. Chance waited until the neverborn was facing away from him before acting. Gathering up his courage, he swallowed and took a step forward on shaking legs. Immediately, the haze he was looking through fell away, and Keely's gaze turned to him.

Her eyes went wide, she reached out a hand, and her mouth opened as if to say something, but it was cut off when a heavy, grey hand drilled into her chest. To Chance's horror, she flew through the air, landing on the sidewalk on the other side of the street and rolling across it. She lay motionless in the middle of the street, her arms, and legs bent around her unnaturally. Hair obscured her face so he couldn't see it, nor could he tell if she was breathing. Before he could do or say anything, the neverborn ran over to Keely and drove its foot into her head.

Chance opened his mouth to scream, but it was caught in the warmth of a hand slapped over his lips. "Shh," Keely whispered in his ear as the familiar essence of vanilla and oranges scented the air. "It's just an illusion. Look away," she ordered softly, and an arm snaked around his stomach, and he was pulled backward. His mind was so lost in the horror and confusion of the situation, he didn't consider closing his eyes. He wished he had because he got to witness the neverborn stomping repeatedly on Keely's body. Its foot crushed her neck, stomach, leg and then the head. Keely's illusionary arms and legs flailed with each kick as blood splattered all over the neverborn and the street. Chance managed to close his eyes when it reached down and picked up a blood smattered Keely. Despite having the softness of Keely's body wrapped around his, he still questioned reality. His soul was devastated by what he'd witnessed. A small noise escaped Chance's throat, and he felt tears sting at his eyes.

"It's not me," Keely's soft voice reassured, and her warm breath dusted over the side of his neck and face. The scent of citrus and vanilla filled his nostrils as she pulled him back against her warm body and repeated, "It isn't me." New tears, tears of relief, pooled in his eyes and escaped underneath his eyelids.

"Chance, listen to me," she whispered. "We don't have much time. I've created several illusions, one to protect the people around us, one to hide you and me, and the other is keeping the neverborn distracted. But that illusion won't keep the neverborn occupied forever. Eventually, it will realize it's been tricked. After that, it will be madder and more desperate for a soul. Our souls are easy targets right now, and it will sense us. It can't take mine...but... It can take yours."

"What do we do?"

"I need you to leave. Run as far and as fast as you can." Keely started to tremble slightly.

Chance turned into her embrace, wrapped his arms around her waist, and pulled her to him. "I just watched my worst nightmare." He too was trembling. "I can't... I won't leave you. I have to..."

"Now is not the time," Keely said seriously, despite the firmness of her embrace. "You need to go."

Chance could hear the steady thumps from the neverborn stomping on the fake Keely behind him. The smell of copper and rust was on the air, and he could even hear the slight pop of bones cracking. He wanted to run away. He wanted to take Keely's hand and drag her somewhere safe, but he realized there was nowhere safe. There was no hiding from that monster, it would eventually find her. If not that one, then another one like it. He wanted to hurt them. He wanted to punish them for every time they hurt or made Keely afraid. He wanted them to feel pain and fear. More than anything, he wanted it to stop the monsters.

"Chance, you have to—" Keely's words were cut off by a loud bellowing roar that sounded like the war cry of an army, and it came from right behind him.

Chance let go of Keely and forced himself to turn around. He wished he hadn't. Parts of Keely's doppelganger were scattered across the gore-covered street. The neverborn stood amongst the carnage, holding a clump of hair in one hand. Brown tresses dripped red chunks of scalp onto the ground as it slung it across the street before kicking the mutilated body in front of it. It let out a second roar and pounded both hands into the street. All around it, the body parts of Keely's illusion liquefied into pools of red then melted into black shadows.

The neverborn bellowed out its frustration and went on a rampage. It kicked a nearby vending machine, knocking it over. The sound of breaking glass was accompanied by popping soda cans as the machine's light flickered out. A hard kick from the neverborn sent the machine flying into a nearby concrete and steel fence. Blocks and iron bars scattered across the street, clanging and thumping loudly. The neverborn tramped through debris, pacing back and forth in front of them. Chance shivered; it knew they were there.

"I will kill you," it bellowed before using its fists to pummel a nearby delivery van to half its size. Then it picked up the van and threw it ten meters, into a powerline post. With a loud crack, the pole broke in half. Power lines sizzled, sparked, and stretched to their limit as the top half of it toppled down to the street. Bright blue lightning stretched upward from the box at the top of the pole then everything went dark and quiet.

The rush of Chance's heavy breathing echoed really loudly, but then he realized it wasn't him panting. Nor was it him shaking with terror. It was Keely.

Chance squeezed Keely's now cold hand as he scanned the darkness for movement and strained his ears to hear the smallest noise. City lights glowed far off in the distance, but the light wasn't substantial enough to break the shadows around them. He had no idea where the monster was. Hopefully it worked to their advantage too, because maybe it would have no idea where they were.

"Chance," Keely said in a soft shaking voice. "Sutton is on her way. I just have to buy some time…" her voice faded. He heard her take a long breath through her nose as if to calm herself. "You need to—"

"I'm not leaving you," he hissed and placed himself in front of her, pressing against her shaking body.

"I can't protect you," she said in a broken voice tinged with fear. Chance already knew she was afraid, they both were, but there was something more happening. She was shaking so severely her tremors were causing him to shake.

There was a scrape of stone against stone nearby, maybe ten feet away. Chance turned toward the noise, staring into the darkness. A slight rhythmic, hollow, rushing sound that could have easily blended into the wind revealed the neverborn was getting closer to them. Anyone else wouldn't have heard it. Keely probably didn't hear, but Chance had had years of listening to music to find the undertones within it. Moving slowly, he pressed a hand on Keely's hip, forcing them both to take a step away from the soft noise.

The noise faded and the street got quiet and still again. "It's close, but I can't see where it is," Keely said in a bare whisper. Her shaking got worse. Chance couldn't fathom why she would suddenly be that terrified of the neverborn especially after going toe to toe with it for several minutes. "You have to run," she said. His fear was compelling him to run as far and as fast as he could, like Keely had said, but his gut disagreed. If he left Keely alone on the darkened street, he was certain the neverborn would kill her more torturously than he'd already witnessed. "Please go," she pleaded. He could hear tears, desperation, and bleakness in her voice. That only confirmed what his instinct told him.

He wasn't going to run away, not when she was too afraid to fight, or she couldn't fight. Chance finally understood what had Keely so scared. She was scared of the dark.

Chance couldn't really understand the entirety of what it meant for Keely to be a Priestess, not really. He knew there were horrific things that hunted humans, and they were something more than immortal. He understood Keely fought them and had a supernatural ability that included making very powerful replicas of herself, but that was all. Despite that, and despite the fact he was as scared as she was, he'd meant what he'd said. No matter what happened, he wasn't going to leave her.

He could offer a solution to the current problem, the blinding darkness. Reaching into his pocket, he pulled out his cellphone. He quickly unlocked its screen and tapped the flashlight button

"No…" Keely tried to stop him, but he'd already flicked his wrist, and the phone was floating through the air. It landed with a loud clack and the small led light aiming toward the sky.

The light broke the darkness, and the shadows pulled back, revealing both the street and the neverborn, making Chance regret not heeding Keely's warning. Less than two meters in front of them, the neverborn stood with its back to them, looking even more terrifying in the eerie shadows because he could see it more clearly than he ever wanted too. The bony prominences of its shoulders, spine, and hips were more skeletal than he initially thought. He couldn't tell if the bones were growing out of its skin, or if the skin was trying to grow over the bones. The grayness that could be seen between the torn parts of its hide looked less gray and more like a space devoid of any color. It seemed like the skin it wore was just there to keep the bones and the emptiness in human form.

Chance pushed against Keely and the wall, trying to put more space between the neverborn and them. The wall was immovable, trapping them in place. When the neverborn turned around, he had to bite down on his lip to keep from yelling out. Its face had changed, become more deformed, and looked more and less human all at once. Its mouth got bigger, so big its jaw curled out and its teeth pointed straight at him. While its eyes and nose had gotten smaller. Its other features were more disproportionate. One of its eyes stared at him from its cheek and the other from just above his nose. Both were now brown now, but no less terrifying as the iris's scanned back and forth.

Chance was able to take in a breath when he realized it couldn't actually see where they were. However, his relief didn't last long. In the next instant, the neverborn stomped down on Chance's cell phone. There was a small crack, the light went out, and they were once again plunged into darkness.

"Misato," Keely whispered. She slid from behind him, taking her softness and warmth away. "I need you safe." She tried to step away from him, but he squeezed her hand tightly, unwilling to let go. "Get ready to run." Keely's cold fingers wrapped around his wrist and she pried her hand out of his grasp. "Keeping you safe is how I win today." There was sad courage in her voice that had a finality to it. Before Chance could say or do anything, she disappeared into the darkness.

"Keely," he whispered loudly, afraid he'd give away their positions. "Keely," he repeated more loudly, moving toward where he knew she last stood, reaching out into the darkness and searching for her.

A loud yell that was almost a growl resounded from somewhere in the darkness. There was a hollow thwump followed by the deep clatter of shattering rock, and the ground shook. He was sure the monster had found Keely. He also knew he was supposed to run, but he still wasn't going to leave her.

He reached over his head, grabbed the neck of his shirt and slid out of it to the trickling sound of rocks falling together. The night and then the street went quiet. Pulling his lighter from his pocket, he flicked it to life. The single flame cast a small orb of light that didn't really illuminate anything more than his hand until he offered his shirt as fuel. The flame grew, and he dropped the burning shirt to the ground. The fire lit the destroyed, empty street, coating it in a deceptively warm yellow.

"Keely," Chance nearly yelled, scanning the wrecked street in front of him. More of the wall had been wrecked, and there were new holes in the street. He wondered what the neverborn had done to Keely. Before he had time to truly contemplate what that could mean he spotted a small patch of pale skin, probably a hand, some ten meters away. Not much more was visible, because the rest of her body was in a heap, wedged between the ruined delivery van and a partially destroyed pylon. "No," he said breathlessly, his mind bracing his soul's worst fear.

He stepped over the curb and maneuvered around jagged piles of stone and deep potholes, trying to get to Keely. He rounded the end of the crushed van and slammed into something solid hiding in the shadows there. A misshapen face, full of protruding teeth and misplaced brown eyes, suddenly filled his vision, leaving him unable to move. "You were what she was protecting," a soft female voice hissed out between the jagged teeth. The statement was followed by deep laughter that sounded distinctly male. "Delightfully sad," the deeper voice said loudly.

Chance found his ability to move and took a step backward, but it was too late. A spindly arm shot out and a large hand wrapped around his throat. The iron grip compacted his airway and breathing became difficult. Air wheezed out of him before he barely managed to gulp in more. "He is so pretty. Can we have him?" the female voice said. A second hand appeared and opened up, splitting down to the wrist. Ten spindly fingers wriggled apart, revealing two hands. That was when he realized the neverborn didn't have hammer-like fists as he'd thought, but instead, had two full hands attached to each arm.

The neverborn spread its hands and fingers apart, cupping his face and running its bony fingers over his lips and cheeks. Fear and revulsion twisted his stomach, making him want to vomit. "She was willing to die to protect him, so he must be special." The female voice whispered. Chance wheezed in air trying to catch his breath and control his shudders.

"If you want him, sister," a male voice replied. The hand around his throat tightened, completely cutting off his air.

He was pulled closer to the twisted face and found himself staring into the neverborn's brown eyes. Their pupils seemed to open up and expand as its eyes, irises and pupils, faded entirely to white. Deep inside them, he could see the reflection of an endless infinity. Instinctively, he knew something awful would happen if he kept staring into the emptiness, but he couldn't move. He couldn't fight back, scream, or look away from the wretchedness buried within the monster's white eyes.

Suddenly, he was impaled through the center of his chest by a sharp pain. It pulsed over his ribs and sternum and radiated into his heart and lungs. He was sure his chest was being pulled apart. Then the pain spread outward like lightning, burning through his body. His fingers, toes, arms, and legs felt like someone was using a sharp knife to hollow them out. He would have screamed if he was able to take a breath, especially when the pain reached his head. He couldn't tell if it was going to implode or explode from the intense pressure. All the while, the empty abysses of the neverborn's eyes pulled at him.

The pain turned into sharp agony that tore at his limbs, crushed his chest, and clawed at his mind. He couldn't fight it any longer, the pain and the pull of the void. He was sure he was dying, and his mind played out his life in a rapid succession of images, sounds, and feelings. He thought of everything he'd wanted to do, and everything he hadn't yet done. He thought of how he could have changed the circumstances of that night. Mostly, Chance thought of Keely, how much he loved her and how he'd essentially betrayed her, how he'd betrayed them. The infinite desolation that held his death rose up and took his memories and feelings. All that made him who he was, was stolen away. That was when Chance realized, he wasn't dying. What was happening to him was much, much worse.

29

Keely fought against her body's need to fall into unconsciousness. Bass throbbed in her ears, and the sounds of the night went up and down in volume. The blow to the side of her chest could have been much worse. If she hadn't managed to deflect it at the last moment, it would have probably broken her in half. As it was, it had sent her flying. Luckily, the crushed van had offered her a little protection, even if the cold metal and glass hurt when it acted as a velocity stopper.

The throbbing bass returned along with the rushing sound of her pulse. The darkness of the street gave way to a sort of emptiness despite her best efforts to hold onto her consciousness. At that moment, she lost the battle and felt her illusions fall apart. She hoped Chance had listened and ran away, but she knew he hadn't.

Emptiness dissolved into cold night air and warm flickering shadows. For a fraction of a second, Keely wondered where she was and what had happened, but the pain in her head and side were a harsh reminder. If that wasn't enough, she could sense the near delight of the wretched neverborn nearby.

"Chance." Keely's heart started racing, and her skin tingled as a new dose of adrenaline was released. The pain of her injuries was forgotten, and she pushed herself up off the ground and rolled up onto her feet. The flame of a dying fire gave light to her worst nightmare. Not far away, the neverborn stood, holding Chance suspended in midair, his shirtless form dangling lifelessly, as it examined him with a leering smile.

Keely started running.

Everything moved in slow motion, even her legs. Sound was muffled; the wind stilled, and the contrast of the light and dark of the street was more vivid. The neverborn's deformed face seemed to curve into a smile as it brought Chance's face closer to its mouth. A voracious foulness polluted the street. Everything within the neverborn's vicinity seemed to shrink away from its unnaturalness, and the theft about to take place.

Jumping over debris and dodging potholes, Keely pressed her body to move faster. She'd never felt so lacking in physical power. Her feet and legs felt clumsy and cumbersome. Desperation drove her to push harder. Keely needed to get to Chance.

Twenty steps separated them.

The neverborn bent its head as if to press its lips to Chance's.

Fifteen steps.

Chance's mouth fell open, and he let out a gurgled breath.

Ten steps.

Chance's body spasmed, and the inside of his mouth started to glow.

Five steps.

A glittering light, Chance's brilliant, shining soul, fell from between his parted lips.

Three steps.

Chance's dazzlingly pure soul hovered between him and the neverborn. The street echoed with the music of his soul, filled with the essence of coffee and musk, and saturated with all of his emotions, love, and fear. For what seemed like an eternity, Chance's light hung between him and the neverborn. Keely lifted her fist and flexed her muscles, preparing to drive her it through the neverborn.

One step.

The neverborn's lips gaped open as its teeth split apart. There was a strange, rushing sound. Chance's soul was sucked into the neverborn's mouth, swallowing all that made him who he was.

Keely let out a gut-wrenching scream that reverberated through the street as she let loose her fist. Her knuckles hit against what felt like solid stone. Several of the bones in her wrists and fingers popped. If there was pain, it was too infantile to register, because getting Chance's body away from the neverborn was all that mattered. An ominous intent emanated from it, and her fighting instinct sent out warning bells, but she was too focused on getting Chance free to heed the warning. She didn't see the sidekick aimed at her stomach until the last second. Though she partially dodged, the wide foot contacted her soft abdomen.

Air heaved out of her lungs as her stomach muscles spasmed. For a split second, she couldn't move as she tried to catch her breath.

Before she could retaliate, the neverborn lifted Chance higher into the air, grinning at his shell of a body. With one violent shake, there was horrifying crack, followed by shrill laughter echoing of both the feminine and masculine. At that same moment, the fire burned itself, and the street went dark again.

Keely was horrorstruck. If Chance died, part of her would die too. The tiny hope that his body was still alive kept her grief and sorrow away. She sunk her teeth into her lip, to keep from crying out her pain and anger. The salty metal taste of blood made her remember a neverborn could bleed too. Despite the terrible darkness and all the tragedies it hid, she focused her mind and forced her body to move.

Reflexes that had been honed over years of training took over, and she moved, relying on her instinct. When she lifted her leg and threw out a hard kick, her foot connected with a hard surface. There was a satisfying hard thump. The neverborn let out a low groan then inhaled, making a hissing noise.

Sensing the neverborn releasing its hold on Chance, she, pivoting slightly, reached out. Her hand connected with cold skin and sinewy muscle. Circling her arms around Chance's cold flesh, she grabbed him from midair before he could crumple into the ground. He was heavier, or she was weaker, than she expected so she couldn't lift or carry him. Instead, she used their combined momentum and rolled the two of out of the path of the neverborn. Carefully, she cradled his torso and head so he wouldn't suffer more injury.

The remains of a stone wall stopped their motion, Keely's shoulder hitting hard against one of its jagged edges. Moist warmth spread across her back, but she ignored it and the pain of the new wound. She didn't move, except to wrap her arms around Chance's cold body and carefully cradle him against her. The neverborn's steps echoed a partial retreat away, indicating it was still as blind as she was without light.

Swallowing back panic, she carefully ran her fingers over Chance's face, jaw, and neck. Her fingertips encountered a bony point on the back of his neck where it shouldn't have been. "Chance," she whispered softly, knowing he couldn't hear her. Tears filled the back of her eyes, and her throat constricted. Again, she pulled him close, cradling his head against her neck as she continued to gently feel for his jugular in search of a pulse. The same moment she felt the faint pulse beneath his skin, was the same moment his soft breath dusted across her neck. Hugging his head to her, she buried her face in his silky hair and wept. He was alive, barely, but alive.

There wasn't time to savor the small blessing, as time was running out. Chance was still dying. Moving him as little as possible, she pulled off her jacket. After she wrapped the warm leather around him, she carefully held his head and neck and laid him on the ground. She smoothed a hand through over his hair before bending over and pressing her lips to his cold cheek.

"I'm sorry," she said, fighting back a new round of tears. "I promise, I will fix this."

She rose, hating to leave Chance mortally injured and laying in the middle of the street, but she didn't have a choice. The neverborn still had Chance's stolen soul. Cautiously, she used her toes to navigate through the destroyed street, until she found flat ground that would allow her the advantage. Pulling herself to her full height, she forced her muscles to relax as she took up a wide-legged battle stance. Wind whispered through her hair and over her skin, warning of the menacing monster hiding in the darkness.

The souls trapped inside the neverborn had suffered more than any other souls she'd freed. Overwhelming pain and confusion assailed her senses. Unfortunately, that sense wasn't strong enough to discern where it was. Keely just knew it was nearby.

Even though the ministry had tried to train her how to fight blind, it was something she'd never managed to master. Still, she had to try. Purposefully, she let out a heavy sigh. As expected, feet slapped against the pavement as the neverborn ran at her, goaded into action. Keely relied on her intuition and got a sense of an impending strike. Without being able to see, all she could do was take a defensive stance and use her arms to try to protect her head and vital organs. A slight burst of air preceded a hard strike to the side of her hip. The blow knocked her off balance, and she tumbled sideways. Rolling back onto her feet, she prepared to strike back should the opportunity arise.

A second blow to the back of her legs dropped her to her knees. Again, she rolled back up, only this time she stayed in a crouching position, trying to make herself a smaller target. Fervently, she searched her mind, thinking back to the training that would have allowed her to fight in the darkness. High emotions kept her from remembering anything helpful.

"Poor Priestess," the neverborn hissed from nearby in a soft female voice. "We know who you are now." It laughed. "Our new soul is so fascinating." The street went silent Keely strained all of her senses to try and get a feel for where the neverborn was. "It doesn't want us to hurt you, and that makes us want to kill you even more than we already did."

A loud whump was followed by the sound of a stone falling to the ground. Then there was a whisper of noise and a rock tinkered across the street next to her. The neverborn was still as blind as she was. The two strikes it had landed were pure luck, or those strikes would have been deadly.

There was another sold thump somewhere behind her. "Aw, the new soul is sad and forlorn because it can't protect you or be with you." It laughed again. "When we get done tearing you apart, we will finish destroying its wretched body, it will be ours forever."

Anger burned through Keely and allowed her mind to overcome her more tumultuous feelings. Rage-filled adrenaline made her hands shake with the need to do physical damage to the neverborn. The neverborn was trying to draw her out by enraging her. Its plan was working. She was tempted to try and land her own strike. Her intelligence prevailed, and she remained quiet and still. If she could get an accurate fix on where the neverborn was, she'd have an opportunity to disable it and release its stolen souls.

Another rock skidded against the asphalt next to her. "We will find you," a male voice stated. "We will kill you, despicable Priestess."

Something in the air changed. Keely couldn't say what, but she could sense unheard music carried the scent of coffee and spice on the slight breeze. "Chance," she whispered softly, almost smiling. She may not know where the neverborn was, but she knew she could find Chance's soul.

Reaching beside her, she felt for and found a piece of broken concrete. Its edges were jagged and sharp, and when she lifted it, she was satisfied with its weight. It wasn't too heavy to throw, but bulky enough to do damage. Cocking her arm back, she heaved the stone with trained accuracy.

A screech pierced through the night and deep into her ears. She would have covered them, but the deep thumps shook the ground under her feet. She'd given away her position. Every fiber of her being wanted to run because she knew fighting it blind would be a losing battle. Sensing where the neverborn was didn't allow her to fight blind. Blinding darkness kept her from fighting at her fullest capability. She'd be able to strike, but she wouldn't be able to dodge. Standing, she prepared herself for the fight, hoping her skill would allow her to prevail. The night got quiet, and her tension grew as the neverborn crept closer.

"Surya!" a loud familiar voice echoed through the street.

Something above her head ignited and started to burn. A tiny sun had been brought to life. Its light filled the street, and its warmth radiated down on Keely, cutting through the cold and her fear. Scanning the street, she found her best friend, standing on top of a car, crossbow readied. She'd never been more thankful to see Sutton.

Keely didn't have time to thank Sutton since the neverborn was bearing down on her. Its eyes blazed, and its face was drawn into an angry sneer. Landing a blow had infuriated it, probably due to the deep gash on the side its face that oozed black blood. She imagined having two souls fighting for dominance made it hard for the neverborn to take on a human form. Skin would be precious and worth killing over if damaged. Keely was glad she'd pissed it off.

The neverborn stomped the last few strides to her, leaving more holes in the street. "You are one, Priestess. We are legion. Our body is stronger and better than yours, and it cannot die!" it shouted in both its male and female voice. "We will kill you!"

"You will try." Keely's mouth curved into a sneer. With Sutton at her back and light over her head, she was able to combat her fear. Her sharp mind started to strategize. The power to release souls wasn't her only ability, and her illusions were captivating. When she was touching her target, they were inescapable, and that was how she planned to defeat the neverborn.

Ducking beneath two wide swings, she stepped in closer, making it harder for the neverborn to make contact because of its long reach. The neverborn raised its fist as if it meant to pummel her down into the ground. Lifting her hands, she blocked the attack and wrapped her fingers around its spindly wrist.

It wasn't until that moment she considered the folly of her decision. Tormented souls trapped inside the neverborn screamed their pain. Flashes of bloody and beaten and crushed corpses played inside her mind, telling horrible truths about what the neverborn had done. Gruesome images of limbs being torn from bodies and torsos being crushed assailed her. Keely's pity and empathy for the neverborn, and the children who were fighting to control it, dissolved into hatred. It was an emotion she hadn't felt before, not even when she'd almost been taken by a neverborn herself. As the feelings of the tortured souls poured into her, her new hatred burned out of control.

For the first time in her life, she wanted to inflict real pain on something. She could, and she knew what the neverborn and the two predominate souls inside it feared most. Priestess might be her title, but at that moment, she was heaven's punishment force.

An idea formed, and she lent it a portion of her physical energy. The idea manifested into reality, winding itself around the neverborn. Plumes of mist emanated from where her hand held the neverborn's wrist. They swirled and crawled up the neverborn's arm, leaving behind an itching sensation wherever there was human-looking flesh. The neverborn tried to jerk its arm away from her, but only managed to yank her closer. Staring up into its white eyes, she hoped it saw all the loathing she felt. Streams of mists started to lengthen, coil around the neverborn's arm, and wind upward. The streams tethered around its neck then split off and vined around its head and torso.

Everywhere the illusionary mist touched skin, itching followed. Further manipulating the neverborn's perception, she amplified the itching and made its skin start to prickle. With its free hand, the neverborn slapped at the mist.

"I'd threaten you with death," Keely said in an echoing voice enhanced by her ability, "but I'm not so merciful."

The itching and prickling turned into a severe burning. Iridescent color flooded into the vapor as it condensed and formed small nodules. Inaudible whispers started to float around them. Tiny spindles sprouted from the nodules and grew larger. The whispers got louder, and occasionally, the word 'body' or 'need' could be heard. Keely enhanced the intense burning and added the sensation of crawling skin just before the nodules took on the form of tiny, faceless humans. The hushed voices got louder and demanded, "I need my body." Other voices joined in and asked, "Where's my body?"

Where Keely's fingers were wrapped around the neverborn's wrist, she made the cold burn so penetrating that the skin under her fingers started to blister. "I'd say you're the most wretched creature in existence, but that would be a lie. You're the most malicious. The souls you carry are the most wretched creatures in existence, and they want you to know it."

The quiet voices turned to soft cries of, "Please, our body. We want to live. We need a body." The small, misty humans evolved in detail and fully formed, their tiny mouths opening and closing with their cries for life, and their large, sullen eyes glowed slightly. They crawled over the neverborn's skin, weeping loudly and begging to be returned to their lives.

"Those souls don't belong to you," Keely said. "They hate you."

The neverborn again tried to pull away from Keely. Her fingers dug into its flesh. She wasn't letting go. She augmented the illusion with more power so she could affect what the neverborn felt. Pain was a good lesson, and the neverborn needed to feel it.

One of the wisps raised its voice above the others. "I will take this body," it said, scuttling up the neverborn's chest and onto its neck.

"This is our body," the neverborn roared in the combined male and female voice. It clawed at its throat, trying to catch the illusion, but only managed to tear at the human skin it had grown.

Black blood started to ooze from the fresh wound, and the aggressive, little human crawled through it then grabbed one of the pieces of torn skin and started to pull. "My body," the illusion screeched with desperation and tugged, tearing more of the skin away.

The neverborn let out a loud roar and again tried to swat at the little human. Even as the human was smashed into a cloud of slightly glowing dust, it reformed and started pulling a piece of torn flesh again. "I want to be human," it shrieked. A chorus of voices joined in, and they all started chanting, "Human. I'm human. I'm alive. My body, this is my body." The other souls followed suit of the first and started pulling at the parts of the neverborn that looked human.

"This body is ours." The neverborn slapped at its chest a second time, then stopped suddenly and looked to Keely. "Make them stop." Swinging its free fist at her, it aimed for the hand that held it captive.

Using the neverborn, Keely lifted herself off the ground, swung her foot up, and kicked the hand away. "It's less than you deserve," she spat.

The wispy human illusions continued their sad demands for a body as their efforts to take the neverborn's got more aggressive. They were using their hands, feet, and teeth to pull at human skin and hair. As that flesh disappeared, they started attacking the grey skin underneath, pulling it off in chunks. The stench of putrid meat and rotting flesh began to permeate the air. It was the same smell of the bodies Keely had encountered when she first found the mangled twin souls who now resided in the neverborn. She felt it appropriate to add the scent to the illusion so those two souls could know what death looked, felt, and smelled like.

"Stop." It opened its mouth to scream, but one of the illusions climbed into it and started pulling on one of its teeth, while another attached itself to a lip. Several of the fake humans made their way up to its face. While two pulled and scratched at its nose, several others reached into one of its eye sockets and dug at its eye.

Keely amplified the burning sensation again, making it sharply painful. The tiny, imaginary humans started to burn a dark purple. The neverborn's real skin started to crack, and the illusions gathered the pieces, sticking them to their bodies. Purple, burning wisps began to solidify with each part of stolen body. Slowly, the neverborn was clawed and bitten into tiny pieces and started to whittle away. First, the human outer layer, then the grey stone looking inner layer was whittled away by Keely's illusion.

The neverborn repeatedly tried to jerk away from her hold as it slapped at the imaginary humans destroying its body, but its efforts were feeble. The illusion had done its damage and weakened it. Keely felt heaven waiting for her to call, and she opened her mouth, speaking in its language. "You who've suffered," she spoke to the trapped souls. "Know that your suffering as its end. I've come to free you. And though, it is time for you to leave this world, you don't have to be afraid. You're going to a place you will forever be at peace. You will not remember or ever know fear. You will never be alone. Most importantly, you will forever be deeply loved. I call forth all the souls imprisoned inside this empty vessel."

Several small, radiant souls exploded from the neverborn, filling the street with their pure light. For a moment, they were suspended in the air, permeating the atmosphere with fear and grief. Their lives had been ended too soon, their deaths were too violent, and their souls were tormented when they were devoured by the neverborn. "You will never suffer again," Keely promised as more souls seeped from the neverborn's body and gathered around her. Carefully, she reached out and gently cradled one in her hand. "I give you the strength to ascend," she said with authority. The sky seemed to fall down, and heaven opened up, spreading its welcoming affection.

The essence of each soul filled with heaven's love, and they were healed. Their pain and misery were forgotten. Inside them, their life's song and the light grew, and so did their splendor. The destroyed street was coated in beautiful color and echoed of happiness from the humans who had been freed. Tenderly, Keely lifted her hand and gently pushed the soul she held upward. Peace and tranquility emanated from it as it rose into heaven. Gleefully, the rest of the souls followed and soared into heaven's waiting grace…all except three souls.

Turning her gaze to the neverborn, she found its face hard set, its eyes staring at nothing, and a hand covering its throat in a protective gesture. It was concentrating, trying to hold on to the one soul Keely would die to retrieve—Chance. "That human essence you're frantically trying to keep is the soul that hates you most. You can't keep it." Keely whispered with venom in her voice.

Tears stung her eyes as she thought of Chance's beautiful smile and soft, alluring eyes. The memory of his voice echoed in her head, and she felt ghost sensation from the thought of him combing his fingers through her hair. Love empowered her, and all her intense passion came out in her voice. "I call you forth, Misato Takeda." The neverborn jerked backward, hunching over slightly as if someone had punched it in the gut. Light began to pulse from its chest. Keely sensed Chance trying to break free.

Because the neverborn had dared to hurt someone she loved so much, had dared to try and destroy him, she sought justice for that injury. She wanted the neverborn to be hurt and afraid like every life it had ever taken, like Chance. She didn't just want it to suffer, she wanted it to remember that suffering for all its immortal life, for all eternity.

"Set him free." Keely imagined, and the souls cried in unison as they all crawled over the neverborn's body to its throat. Gathering around its neck and chest, they started digging and biting at its body with their needle-like claws and teeth. Once again, the neverborn tried to get free of Keely's grip. She allowed it to break her hold, but only after she made it believe its wrist had cracked apart with soft snaps and more sharp pain. It let out a loud cry, which she immediately silenced with her illusion. A creature getting its throat torn out couldn't scream. To her, it didn't have the right. The tiny humans kept pulling apart skin and stone sinew until malformed pieces of bone were exposed.

Chance's soul glowed even brighter, and she could feel him calling out. Keely stepped forward, holding out her hands. The light inside the neverborn converged into one point and emerged from the hole the tiny souls had dug into the neverborn's neck. Music filled the night as the scent of coffee and spice scented the air. Chance's soul glowed more brilliantly than she'd ever seen of any other soul. When it floated down into her hands, she was filled with a familiar warmth that quickly spread. In return, she cradled him inside her hands, inside her love. She would be the vessel that carried such a precious person back to his body.

Mercy broke through her anger, and she looked to heaven, then the neverborn. "You two, brother, sister, you have suffered and regretted and known the loss of never having. But heaven awaits with nothing but freedom from pain and suffering. I call heaven to you and you to it, so now and forever more you will be whole. And you will be loved."

The neverborn clutched at its heaving chest, looking down at the hole left behind by the now disappearing souls. It ran its hands over its sternum, then looked to her. Besides its fear, there was a darker, scarier emotion present. The neverborn and the two souls inside it hated her and every living human everywhere. Keely was confused. Heaven wasn't pulling at the souls, and they were not longing to ascend. She'd never encountered a soul that did not want to be joined with heaven.

"Please," she begged the two souls inside the neverborn as she softly cradled Chance's essence to her chest. "There is nothing to ha—"

288

"We are Legion," it cried, interrupting her. "You cannot kill us, and you will not destroy us." It took several steps backward, seeping hatred. Then it turned, jumped over the wrecked van and ran away from her, disappearing into the darkness.

30

Sutton ran after the neverborn, continuously firing at its retreating form. As much as she wanted to go to Keely, she couldn't, not until she was sure the damn thing wouldn't come back and attack them again. After firing most of her arrows into its hide, she stopped, satisfied when it ran out of her line of sight.

"Keely." She turned and found Keely kneeling beside Chance's unmoving body. A slight glow radiated from her hands as she clutched them to her chest. Sutton didn't have to ask to know it was Chance's soul. "Keely," she said again, running towards her. Blood stained her clothes, and tears ran down her cheeks. It was the blood that was most concerning.

Sutton skidded to a stop and fell to her knees next to Keely, dropping her crossbow. Before she could say anything, Keely looked at her with a pleading expression that nearly broke her heart. "Chance. You have to heal him," she begged in the barest of whispers.

Sutton looked to Chance, noticing his head was resting in an awkward twisted angle that a human spine wouldn't allow. All the blood drained from Sutton. There was no way she could tell her best friend the man she loved was dead, and there was no witch on the planet that could undo it. "I don't thi—"

"He's not dead," Keely nearly shouted. After a moment, she repeated more calmly. "He's not dead."

Holding her breath, Sutton reached out with shaking fingers and rested them on Chance's cold neck right beneath his ear. Before there was the slight jump of his pulse, her witches healing sense told her there was a tiny bit of life left in the body. "I can't heal him until his soul is returned and repairing that much damage would mean I can't heal you, Priestess. Not for twenty-four, maybe even forty-eight hours."

"I don't care," Keely replied vehemently. "If this world doesn't have Misato in it, I don't want to fight for it anymore."

Sutton was stunned. "Keely? You don't mean that."

"I do," she cried. "Oh, God." She stopped, fear contorting her face before she turned it toward the sky. "NO!" she shouted.

A soothing humidity filled the night. Sutton was suddenly calmed and reassured, and she wanted to bask in whatever was saturating the night. Looking to Keely with a question on her lips, she stopped, silenced by awe. A pretty light rolled over Keely's hair and skin, transforming her into something beautiful and ethereal. It wasn't that she was beautiful, she felt beautiful like she was made up of pure love. Sutton felt tears of joy pool in her eyes and fall down her cheeks because she got to behold such a thing. For the first time, she truly understood why Keely was called Priestess.

Keely's hands suddenly jerked upward, and Keely cried out in pain. Sutton was confused by the sound. She didn't understand how someone encompassed in so much love, and beauty could be in any pain. Before she could try and comprehend what was happening, Keely was lifted off the ground and pulled upward. Sutton didn't even think to try and stop her from drifting away.

Keely's voice suddenly filled the air, chanting in that beautiful language only she knew. Except this time, the chant was unlike any Sutton had ever heard before. It was both forceful and haunting. Sutton could listen to Keely's divine language and forever be lost in it. Her tone changed, and her voice got louder as if she was pleading, demanding something from the sky above them. Keely's voice got so loud, she nearly yelled. Abruptly, everything went quiet, and it felt like the whole world went silent.

Keely spoke again. Though Sutton couldn't understand the words, she felt the meaning in them as if it was her own. They were words of love. A flash of color lit the sky, and then Keely was falling. She landed in a near heap next to Chance, still clutching his soul. It glowed so brilliantly Sutton couldn't look at its light. The alluring sensations thinned and seemed to dissolve into the night, or maybe they floated upward. Sutton couldn't tell. She looked skyward, longing for the feeling to return.

"Sutton," Keely said softly. "I need you to heal Chance's body."

"I… I…" Sutton stammered.

"Heal Chance's body, or you won't have a Priestess to protect because I will follow him into heaven."

Sutton looked to Keely and found herself trapped inside the

most sorrowful emotion she'd ever felt. "You have to put his soul back." Sutton took a deep breath and found herself wiping at tears. "And Chance is... It's going to be agonizing."

Keely sniffed and hubbed, trying to keep from outright sobbing. "I know."

Sutton put one hand on Chance's heart and the other on his forehead. "Okay," she said softly.

Keely held her cupped hands over Chance's mouth and spoke softly in her beautiful language as she carefully opened her fingers. Her words ended like a soft song, and the two of them watched the brilliant light of Chance's soul fall into his mouth. Half a second later a light pulsed from his chest. Sutton was already starting the healing incantation when Keely whispered, "Now."

Sutton's magic flowed into Chance, and for one horrifying moment, she thought he'd died until she heard the echo of his barely beating heart in her ears. All her strength was drained. She felt like she was fighting against something trying to drown her, but her words didn't falter. She managed to continue to recite the incantation despite the nearly painful weakening of her body.

Soon, Chance started to spasm, then shake violently. Soft moans came from his parted lips. His head twisted back into place with a soft snap, and his moans turned into yells. Arching his back, he started flailing his arms, pounding his fists on the ground. Keely sat next to Sutton, hands over her mouth, stifling her soft cries as tears soaked her face. The cast had to be continued despite the pain inflicted on Chance, and the heartache it caused Keely. After one the longest minutes of Sutton's life, she uttered the final words of the spell. Chance got quiet and went limp.

Sutton pulled her hands back, reeling at the sudden drain of her magic. "He's healed," she said breathlessly, turning her attention to Keely. She was in desperate need herself. Her wrist looked like it had been twisted, and it seemed impossible she could still use her fingers. Blood trickled down from a deep gash at her temple, and the right side of her back from her shoulder down was crimson. That was just the injuries Sutton could see. Keely was so overcome with adrenaline and heartbreak she probably didn't know the extent of them herself.

"Keely," Sutton said softly, but Keely wasn't paying any attention to her.

With a shaking hand, she reached out to Chance. Just as her fingers touched his cheek, he sat straight up. He opened his mouth as if to scream, then closed it and turned his gaze toward Keely. Fear and panic contorted his features, and he let out a low groan. His soul had only just been restored. He probably didn't know who they were, what had happened, or why he was in so much pain. Keely scooted closer to him, offering her hand. He flinched away from her touch. The movement caused him to lose muscle control and sway sideways. Keely caught him before he could fall to the ground. Something between a yell of anger and a cry of pain came from Chance.

"I'm sorry," Keely said softly as she carefully pulled him into her embrace.

At first, he tried to fight, pushing at her arms. Keely held him even tighter, whispering softly in his ear. After several weak attempts to break her hold, he stopped. "Keely," Chance croaked. He managed to wind stiff and shaking arms around her, grabbing fistfuls of her shirt. He buried his face in her neck. "Keely," he repeated and started crying loudly. Keely pulled him closer and combed her fingers through his hair, trying to soothe him, as she gently kissed his temple.

Sutton knew from years of watching souls be restored that nothing could truly take away the pain, not even a Priestess with the ability to make emotions tangible. Out of compassion, Sutton made several hard decisions. Pulling out her phone, she entered a code and sent a text to a number she'd never used before. It was an emergency call that would be received by the ministry in Japan, and Shoma, its Cassock. Following the beacon of her cell phone, every monk, every clergy, everyone in the Japanese ministry would come. It probably was overkill, but it would mean Keely would be healed.

Unfortunately, it also meant every Cassock in the world would know the emergency sequence had been activated. Jasper would know. Sutton shook her head against her deep-seated fear of the Sunderer and reached into her bag. Pulling out her medical kit, she quickly opened it and grabbed a syringe and vial of narcotic.

Minutes later Chance's cries had quieted, and he rested peacefully in Keely's arms. When the Cassock showed up with the Japanese ministry in tow, Keely had passed out from either blood loss or pain, but still managed to be holding onto Chance.

∞ ∞ ∞ ∞ ∞

Keely sat staring down at Chance, holding his hand and gently combing her fingers through his hair. He was laid out on a futon covered in heavy blankets in an ornately painted room with a wall to ceiling window that faced a beautifully manicured garden. The room was one of many in the private mansion they'd been brought to to heal and recover by the Japanese ministry. Keely had come to hate the room and its beauty. For more than a day, the bedroom and its garden had played host to Chance's torment.

His soul had suffered the trauma of being torn from his body. Though she rebound his soul, the soul had to readapt. It wasn't a painless or easy process. Despite the narcotics, he was given his body still seized and spasmed violently. Sometimes the seizures were mild, but other times his overly flexed muscles would lock his joints in place. In those times he let out pain-filled moans. All she could do for him was whisper softly in his ear as she lay across his body to keep his flailing to a minimum. It wasn't until the late day rays of the sun had coated the room that he finally started to settle and rest comfortably.

Chance still had a long recovery ahead of him. He wouldn't be able to talk or walk, not at first. All of his systems would be out of sync, so much so that even breathing would be difficult. It would take him weeks maybe months to readapt, and it could be even longer before he'd be able to play any instrument.

Keely wiped away a stray tear. She'd selfishly thought Chance rejecting her was the worst heartbreak she could feel. Nearly losing him to the neverborn was heart-shattering, and all of it was her fault. She loved him with every fiber of her being, but her love was and would be torment. Whether she was a Priestess or not, she was a coward, and that caused Chance's suffering.

Despite knowing all the damage she'd wrought, she couldn't leave his side. She wouldn't abandon him at the worst moment of his life. Eventually, she would have to go, for his sake. So, she sat next to him, massaging his stiff muscles when they needed it, and smoothing the wrinkles of pain on his forehead when he started to get restless. She spent that time memorizing his face and going over every word they'd ever said to one another. She wanted to be able to have those things with her always. When she did leave, she wouldn't be able to come back.

The sky was still purple when she heard the door behind her slide open then close. She didn't have to look too know it was Sutton. Not even the Cassock would dare to walk into the room when she'd ordered them all out.

"Keely," Sutton said softly, squatting down and taking a seat next to her on the floor. Keely didn't have anything to say. After a short moment, Sutton must have realized she wouldn't speak because she softly said, "I'm sorry."

Keely wanted to scream at Sutton. It wasn't Sutton's fault. Keely was the one to blame.

"Keely, I know there is nothing I can do to change or fix the current situation, but my first and only duty is to you." She was quiet for a moment. "You've had a hard fight. The monk's healing charms are powerful, but they didn't completely heal you. And you've been in here for forty hours." She reached out a hand and pulled back Keely's hair. "Your face and neck are still black with bruises. I know you want to stay with Chance, but you need to recover, yourself. You need to eat, and you need to rest."

Keely thought the minor pains and soreness of her body were nothing compared to that of her heart. Even then, that pain was minimal compared to what Chance was experiencing. She was helpless to undo the damage wrought on his body and soul. What happened to hers didn't matter.

"Keely, everyone is worried, and I'm sure Jasper tried to call a million times because he would have known when I activated the crisis protocol." There was movement from beside her. "Oh look, your cellphone, and Jasper has called…twenty-eight times," she said, trying to sound flippant. "I really wish I had known he was calling you since he wasn't answering me. Oh, shit." Her voice trembled slightly. "He texted he'll be here in twelve hours, and that was fourteen hours ago."

Keely didn't have anything to say. Chance was her only concern. Of course, Jasper would come. The Japanese ministry would be in turmoil when he got there. She didn't care.

As if he'd been summoned, the door to the room opened again, and a sure male voice ordered, "Out."

Sutton scrambled to her feet and disappeared. Her spot was soon filled by a tall, strong, familiar presence—Jasper.

Keely bit back a sob as fresh tears dripped down her cheeks. Jasper would know something was wrong, and ultimately, he'd know what she'd done. Minutes ticked by, neither of them spoke or moved. Eventually, she turned her face to the one person on earth she hoped would understand. He looked the same as always, short, curly, red hair, a face that seemed to want to naturally smile, and violet eyes matching her own.

"Jasper," she said between blubs and sniffs. "I can't... I tried..." She couldn't explain through her loud sobs. Finally, she managed, "I don't know what to do."

"It's okay," Jasper reassured softly. "I do." He lifted a hand and put three of his fingers on her temple and cheek. "Sleep, big sister."

Jasper's will stabbed into her mind like a sharp needle. Usually, he would never be able to invade her mind, but she welcomed his thoughts of warmth, comfort, peace, and sleep. It flooded into her body like a powerful drug. Her arms and legs got heavy before her spine turned to liquid. She found herself leaning into him just as her eyes closed.

"Goodbye, Misato," she whispered before dreamless sleep welcomed her.

296

31

Chance leaned on a pile of pillows, watching the rays of the morning sun stretch across the sky. Another rough day was beginning. He'd never realized it before, but the world was too bright, too loud, and too harsh. Existence was cold and depressing. He knew this for sure because he knew something better. A strong memory, a promise of happiness that existed beyond his imagining kept him longing to escape the brutal cruelty of reality. Chance didn't want to live in the world anymore.

Wood sliding against wood sounded from the door, and he strained his eyes, trying to make them look to see who'd entered his room. He wasn't sure why, but his body didn't work, not like he commanded. The smallest movements took monumental effort and severe discomfort. Even when he wasn't moving, everything hurt. Another reason why life was cruel.

His eyes finally fixated on the door, and he was surprised to find a very large man standing in his room. The man was so big he made the room look small. Not only was he bulky, he was intimidating. There was an air of power about him that made Chance wonder if maybe he was some sort of spirit.

"No," the man shook his head. "I'm not a spirit." The man took a step into the room. "And before you ask, your thoughts are loud, unprotected, and easy to hear." His legs folded, and he settled his large frame on the floor next to Chance's futon. "That should make things easier for you and me both. Mind reading can be difficult and painful when people resist."

Chance didn't know what to think. He did believe the man wasn't a spirit, and he didn't believe he had any ill intent, or he wouldn't bother with the effort of explaining. He didn't doubt his mind was being read. In fact, it gave him ease. At least he could communicate with someone.

"Oh, good, you're smart," the man said, smiling as he ducked underneath a shoulder strap and slid his bag off. "Of course, you'd be smart. Keely likes smart people."

Keely. Just the mention of her name made Chance anxious. Though his thoughts were constantly of her, he hadn't heard from her, and no one was forthcoming with any information. His heart started pounding, and sweat formed on his forehead. A jumble of memories from the last night he saw her made his head swim. They were muddled and chaotic, and he couldn't really piece together all of what had happened. He remembered his broken heart and their fight. He knew he'd insulted and driven her away. He also knew he followed. After that, it was a blur of fear for himself, for her, shock, loss, and finally pain. It wasn't just pain; it was agony. That was where his memory ended.

Adding to his unbearable happiness was his longing for Keely. He missed her with every fiber of his being, in a way that was physically painful. When he slept, he could hear her voice and almost feel her touch. He always woke up to the nightmare of the cold and lonely world. So, he tried his hardest to avoid sleep since his dreams of her had become torture. That didn't stop his thoughts from always drifting to her. He had so many unanswered questions. Did she still love him? Because he knew he was desperately in love with her. Why didn't she call? Was she hurt? Did the same thing happen to her that had happened to him? As he remembered the agony, he wondered if Keely had suffered the same. A small noise escaped his throat.

"Yes and no," the man said as he unzipped the bag, bringing Chance's focus back to the present and alleviating some of his anxiety. "For the most part, Keely is fine. For the rest of it, I'm thinking you're going to help, but let's not get ahead of ourselves." He stopped his movements and crooned his neck, so his face was closer to Chance's. "Mind readers are extremely annoying, aren't they?" Chance was caught off guard by the question, and the man's intense stare. His eyes were the exact same colors as Keely's, violet. How did this man know her? Did he do what she did?

"No. No one can do what Keely does." The man smiled, then went back to his bag. "And, I apologize for not introducing myself sooner. I assume everyone knows me because I feel like I know everyone. It's another one of those annoying mind reader things." He pulled out jug from his bag. "I'm Jasper Sheppard. Keely's much bigger, younger brother. I thought you and I should talk. I was told you wouldn't eat or drink; I figured we could both use some chocolate milk." He held the jug up for Chance to see. He shook it and smiled again.

Jasper reached into his bag and pulled out two cups, then two straws. "I prefer it when it's nearly freezing. Like a chocolate milk slushy, but it's still good when its ice cold." Carefully, he filled the two cups, added the straws, then offered one to Chance.

The gesture annoyed Chance. Obviously, it took a great deal of effort to make the tiniest movement, and there was no way he could hold a glass. Not that it mattered, he didn't want the chocolate milk anyway. He just couldn't express it verbally.

"You'll want it in a minute." Jasper set the cup down and took a swig of his chocolate milk. "Ah, that's good." He took another long drink, all the while eyeing Chance. "Hm, I can help you with that whole mind/body disconnect thing if you want," he said. "It will hurt, but I can help."

Chance simply thought, yes.

"Okay, then." He set his cup down and scooted closer to Chance. "Try not to resist too much because when you do, it hurts me, making me hurt you more." He leaned in close, and his face got hard. "Don't make me hurt you more."

That was when Chance realized Jasper wasn't moving his lips, or actually talking. Everything said between them had been said inside of his head. Startled, Chance jerked, and his body responded with pain. He started breathing hard, trying to calm his protesting muscles.

Jasper lightly patted his shoulder and waited for him to settle again. "Yeah, I forgot to explain that part. I don't speak Japanese, and you don't speak English. Yet." He smiled. "Right now, you and I are speaking… Brain." He waved his hands, wriggled his fingers, and smiled. "You've gotten into some really scary shit."

Chance felt like he should be scared. He wasn't. Somehow speaking brain made sense. "Speaking brain isn't that hard."

"No, for you, it's not," Jasper said, with a pondering look. "Let's deal with the immediate problem." He lifted a hand and pressed two fingers to the center of Chance's throat. Nothing happened. "Well, shit. I tried the easy way." Without warning, Jasper balled up his fist and hammered it into the center of Chance's chest.

Chance's body was slammed into the bed. All the air rushed out of his lungs, and he felt like every one of his ribs had been snapped. As he tried to suck in air, his fingers and toes started to tingle, cool, then burn. The burning spread up his hands and feet. He was consumed by cold, and that coldness was full of needles. It extended up his legs and arms, deep into his bones. The frozen needles reached his groin, and he was sure his dick going to break off. The pain merged in his stomach. Retching, he fought for breath, feeling like he was suffocating. He felt like he was going to die.

A chaotic whirl of thoughts passed through his mind before it settled on one thought. He didn't want to die. As much as he disliked the world, its harshness, he realized he wanted to live. With his realization, an intense heat emanated from the back of his head. The sensation was almost euphoric with its warm pulses. Quickly, the feeling spread over his face, neck, then chest and webbed out over his body. The freezing needles were washed away in one tidal wave of exhilaration. A second later, he found himself sitting up, groaning loudly.

He breathed in deeply, and pain free, feeling like it was the first time he'd actually taken a real breath. Momentary dizziness kept him from moving until it cleared. Lifting his hands, he watched as he made fists, then flexed each finger individually. Without thinking, he grabbed at the sheet, feeling for his groin. Happily, it was still intact.

Laughter reverberated from beside him. "I did the same exact thing."

Heat flooded into Chance's face. Still, he was relieved. Especially when he could move all his fingers and toes, turn his head, and his spine and legs moved as they should. He wanted to try and stand but thought better of it. He didn't want to fall in front of Jasper. After a second check to make sure everything moved, Chance turned to find Jasper offering him the previously rejected chocolate milk. His mouth dried out, and he was suddenly unbearably thirsty. Reaching for the cup, he took it, thankful his hands obeyed and gripped the cool glass firmly. He gulped down the thick, cold, sweet, chocolatey concoction. Nothing had ever tasted so good.

"Thank you," he thought and bowed his head.

"No problem."

The two sat in silence drinking. When the tale-tell, slurping echo came from Chance's cup, Jasper refilled it. Chance started to feel better, and when he emptied the glass for the second time. He stared into its bottom, wondering if chocolate milk had some strange power he didn't know of.

"It's delicious and comforting, but not magical." Jasper finished his glass, took Chance's, and set both of them down on the floor. He turned back to Chance with a severe scowl in place. "So, you have decisions to make, and you'll only have a couple of seconds to decide." Chance was confused, but before he could ask for clarification, Jasper went on. "Do you want to know the truth about Keely? About you? You can take a moment to think about it, but remember if you answer 'yes,' you won't be able to unknow what I tell you, and it will forever change you."

Chance looked out at the bright garden. The sun had started to melt the dew on the leaves, and the water from a small fountain cast rainbow waves into his room. Newly formed spring buds started to grow in their color, and the grass was turning bright green. His thoughts wondered and fell the one place they always did, on Keely. She had already affected and changed him, and that couldn't be undone.

"You're right," Jasper agreed. "You've both affected and changed each other, but you can still walk away from her, from a much larger and very dangerous world. Maybe one day you will remember everything that happened, and it will change you anyway. Most likely you won't ever remember if you go on with your life as if nothing happened. You will forget it all, and probably her."

"No. I will never forget Keely."

Jasper went quiet for a moment. "If you want to know the whole truth, I will tell it. This is my last warning. After you learn everything, your life will never be the same." Jasper paused, and Chance turned to find himself caught in a scrutinizing stare. "Do you want to know the whole truth?"

Chance didn't stop to consider or hesitate. He felt like his entire life depended on knowing the whole truth about Keely, and what had happened the last night he'd seen her. He needed to know everything. Maybe in that truth, he'd discover why she hadn't talked to him since. Hopefully, he'd find the answers so he could repair the damage done between them. "Yes." He nodded his certainty.

Jasper wiped a hand over his face. "I thought you might say that." He lifted his hand and offered it to Chance. "This will probably hurt you and be really awkward for me."

Chance lifted his hand and set it into Jaspers. Immediately the room started to fade and melt away. His vision darkened. "Before I can, I show you anything, I have to teach you English. While you and I can speak brain, my memories are in English, and you won't understand if I don't give you a crash course in it."

Dull pressure pushed at his temples and started spreading across the top of his head. It wasn't painful, just uncomfortable. He had the passing thought he didn't like it and wanted it to stop. Jasper's voice sounded in his ears, "Don't resist; it makes it harder." Chance took a deep breath and forced himself to relax. The pressure got more intense. "Better. It makes it easier if you accept that you're going to be uncomfortable."

A multitude of sounds started echoing in his ears. They were like noises a child would make, but then they began to form more solid tones as characters flashed in front of his eyes. Soon, he recognized those characters as letters and started to associate those sounds with each letter. After that, the letters joined together to form words. Words began to pour into his brain, thousands of them, along with their meanings. Sister, food, and sunshine flashed in his mind. He knew what they meant and how to pronounce them. Then those words strung together and formed sentences, and those sentences opened his knowledge of speech and understanding. Chance knew for sure he could speak English with ease.

"Well, my English, anyway. And it comes with very colorful expletives," Jasper joked. The words stopped, and a grey mist formed and surrounded Chance. It reminded him of early morning fog on a rainy day.

"I never thought about it that way, but I guess my mind is kind of murky."

The fog started to roll away, and clear, and Chance found himself standing in an expansive half-empty parking lot. The sun had set, and the night sky above the streetlights was speckled with sparkling stars. It must have been summer, as it still felt hot. Sweet bread and fried food wafted on the air. Off in the distance, there was a clicking and roaring sound, followed by screaming. Chance looked up to find the skyline of an amusement park. He immediately recognized trademark ears known the world over.

Laughter got his attention. He searched for its source and

302

found a young girl with dark brown hair, and gangly legs and arms, tossing a stuffed bear into the air. Next to her was a short, plump boy with red curly hair and a bright smile. He caught the bear and hugged it to himself. A much older couple followed behind them, arm in arm, smiling fondly at the children.

"I've altered most of the memory so you can see it from a third person point of view, but there will be times when you'll see things as I saw them," Jasper said from beside him. "Keely was thirteen, and I was ten." He started walking behind the group as they passed through rows of parking spaces interspersed with parked cars. Chance followed. "Scary things happen in the places you think are safest, surrounded by people you love, and often when you are happiest. Especially where the neverborn are involved." As they strolled behind the four people, the lights dimmed. "The neverborn are attracted to happiness. You do remember what neverborn are?" Ghost images of obscured gray, lanky monsters without faces flashed around them.

"Yes," Chance answered, his voice shaking with both anger and fear, mostly anger. He walked behind the four people, his focus solely on Keely. She was all spindly legs and arms, and happy smiles.

A loud belch echoed around them, and young Jasper lifted his hand to his forehead, making an 'L' shape with his fingers. "You ate it, Loser."

Keely turned toward her brother, and another loud belch was heard. "Right back at you, bro." She held up her hand, making the same gesture.

"That is not how a lady should behave." The elderly woman tried to admonish, but there was a grin on her face.

Another belch sounded, this one much louder and longer. The older man lifted his hand to his head and made the 'L' with his fingers. "Ha, I win."

"Gross, Pawpaw." Keely turned around, walking backward. "Awesome." She held up her hand, and he slapped it.

"I swear." The older woman shook her head. "No more soda for any of you."

"As if that will stop it," Keely said. "Can we get tacos for dinner?"

"Yeah, so we can burp out our butts?" Jasper added, turning around to walk backward with Keely.

"No," both the older man and woman answered in unison, smiling at one another.

All at once, Keely looked up, her pretty brown eyes focusing on something, and she suddenly stopped. Chance was caught off guard for two reasons. He thought she might be seeing him, but he remembered that everything he was seeing was Jasper's memory. Secondly, her eyes weren't the violet he'd come to know. Still, they were familiar, full of passion and life, and it gave him a sense of familiarity.

He looked to Jasper for an explanation. Jasper frowned. "When someone returns from heaven, they are marked." Chance was about to ask what that meant, but Jasper pointed to Keely, and his attention returned to the memory.

"Did you see that?" Keely asked her grandfather, who'd stopped beside her and turned to look where she was looking.

"See what, sunshine?" He stared for a minute then turned to Keely, smiling and patting her head.

Keely's pretty, brown eyes scanned the parking lot. "I don't know. A dark raincloud. A weird shadow, it's like the lights are dimming."

"Probably a trick of the humidity." The man took her hand, and a moment later, the lights around them went out.

"Pawpaw?" Keely's voice shook.

"I'm sure it's just a power surge." Keely's grandfather reassured as he wrapped an arm around Keely, prompting her to move forward. "Come on, love," he said, taking his wife's hand. "I promise, I won't give into the grandkids demands for tacos." Another light went out, and the four of them were plunged into near darkness.

Chance could see their outlines well enough to identify which one was Keely, but not much else. She twisted, seemingly looking over her shoulder, then started yelling, "Pawpaw, something's... Grandma…." For a moment, Chance lost sight of Keely, but then her shape appeared between the couple and an ominous shadow.

"It's a neverborn." Chance stated, feeling the air thicken with something he could only describe as hunger. "Could she see it?"

"I think we were both sensitive to the neverborn, which is why you can sense it now. This is my memory," Jasper said quietly. "For Keely, yes, I think she saw it."

304

"Grandma," Keely shrieked, and the shape of the old woman crumpled to the ground. Everything shifted and bounced, and when the night came back into focus, Chance was staring down at Keely's shadowed, unconscious grandparents.

"Keely," the younger Jasper cried, reaching for his sister, but seemed to be alone in the dark. "Keely, what's happening?" Young Jasper cried. Chance felt confused and afraid, and he had the urge to stretch out his hands and search the darkness. Instinctively, he knew those weren't his emotions, they were Jasper's.

There was a strange sucking sound, then Keely screamed, "Run, Jasper. Run." The ground shook, and Chance felt as if he was running, with his heart pounding in his ears. A car's headlights shone on them from a distance, and there was a flash of something grey and skeletal, with white eyes. Jasper's terror permeated into Chance, and he found it hard to breathe.

"Keely, where are..." Jasper's words were cut off by fear. Traces of pain tingled across Chance's arm and chest. Screams echoed around in the darkness, and another car's headlights flashed on a grey face with empty, white eyes, and mouth of torn, grey skin. Chance let out a startled yell in time with young Jasper's screams. His lungs burned as if he held his breath; aching soreness radiated through his body, just before everything went dark and silent.

"I'm sorry," adult Jasper whispered from beside him. "This memory is still hard for me. You'll still feel traces of what I felt." Chance didn't say anything. There was nothing to say.

A loud pounding filled the blackness. It beat strong and fast for a short time, echoing all around. It sped up, skipped several times, stopped altogether, then started again at much slower, weaker pace that faded. There was a brief, dizzying silence, then Chance's ears were suddenly filled with the screams of hundreds, if not thousands, of tormented voices. They cried out so much pain he could feel their suffering as if it was his own. He recognized those voices within himself. He hated the familiar sense of terror, and he covered his ears against the screams. Jasper said nothing, even as the shrieks got louder. Chance didn't have to ask to know they were inside of the never-born.

Chance recognized the agony. He knew the chorus of anguish filled madness. He remembered how it felt to have his soul stolen.

"Let me go," his own cries joined the cries around him. "I want out." For a horrifying moment, he forgot he was inside of a memory and truly believed he was trapped.

Suddenly, a warmth radiated down from above. The sky opened, and Chance looked up into the stars then beyond them. Happiness and love so pure it was tangible, surrounded him. He calmed because he was reminded he wasn't actually trapped in a neverborn. Still, he knew the sensation and nearly wept at being able to feel it again, even if inside Jasper's mind.

Amid love and happiness, the screams had gone quiet. All around him, tiny lights started to flicker to life and glow. They floated on the air, basking in the same feeling he basked in. Chance watched as they got brighter and brighter. From a distance, he heard a familiar voice, talking, maybe singing, in a beautiful language he'd never heard before. He looked all around him, searching for Keely. When he couldn't see her, he started running in one direction, then another, careful not to touch any of the glittering orbs. Why he looked for her, he couldn't say. He only knew the chanting, singing voice was his salvation.

The pull from above got stronger, and he could feel happiness coming from the glowing orbs. That was when he realized they were souls. He stopped running, stopped moving, and watched as they alighted.

"This is a memory?" Chance questioned, not just Jasper's memory, but the familiarity of it. The souls ascended and disappeared into the night sky. "Is this the truth?"

"As truthful as memories can be. Yes. This is what I remember when my soul got torn from my body. But keep in mind, I was ten and traumatized." Jasper lifted a hand and snapped his fingers. The memory blurred. Its colors bled together then washed away to black. "The rest of that night... Well, suffice to say we were both tasked by heaven, and that is private. But it was the first Keely ever saved and set souls free, including mine. After that, everything changed. We changed."

"Our grandparents died seven days later, minutes apart."

A dimly lit room appeared with two coffins. People sat around them with bowed heads. In their epicenter were Jasper and Keely. Chance walked through the memory and stood next to her, wishing he could offer her comfort. Someone said, "Amen," and she looked up. Her eye color had changed, they were now the familiar violet. Her countenance had changed, as well. The carefree, smiling girl was gone. In her place was an angry and determined young woman.

The memory pulled away and disappeared, leaving Chance back in the murkiness of Jasper's mind and feeling dizzy.

"At first the change was hard," Jasper explained. Flashes of Jasper's past played out in front of him all at once. In one scene, Jasper and Keely hid in a closet, behind a rack of clothes holding hands. In another, they looked like they were being pursued by a shadow as they ran down a sunlit street. The next scene was of their parents telling them monsters didn't exist. The memory faded to a crying Keely sitting on her bed as her mother packed her things. Keely's mother told her the doctors could help her with the monsters. Afterward, Keely and Jasper sat on a couch across from a stern looking woman in a white lab coat, furiously writing onto a clipboard. They held hands as the room filled with people wearing drab green scrubs. One of them grabbed Jasper and tried to pull him away from Keely. There was mass chaos, and the scene blurred. The next memory was of Jasper and Keely walking out of a hospital hand in hand. Jasper wiped blood from his nose, and Keely had a severe look on her face. Behind them, staff fought with one another, sat on the floor crying and screaming, or stared with vacant expressions. The stern-looking woman stood near a wall, beating her head on it as blood poured down her face.

Chance wasn't shocked because he was angry for the two of them, especially Keely. He hoped after that, they were left alone.

"We were," Jasper said softly. "But then, no one wanted to try and control or challenge two children who left disaster in their wake." There was laughter in Jaspers voice. "For the record, the doctor was her doing not mine."

Chance couldn't help but smile. He was proud of Keely.

"I was too," Jasper agreed. "Luckily, the ministry found us."

A neat looking man with light hair appeared. Jasper's view changed, and a different memory played out, from a higher vantage point. He watched as the man walked down a pebbled driveway from behind full leafy branches of a tall tree. The memory was so vivid, Chance could hear the crunch of his shoes, smell the heat of summer on the air, and hear a soft whistle carried on the wind as it rustled the leaves. Though the man looked young, his face had the thoughtfulness of someone wise. He casually walked up to a small house and stopped. Instead of knocking on the door, he turned away from the house, shielding his eyes with his hand. He looked up at the tree, waved, and smiled. "Permission to climb up."

Keely appeared next to Chance, standing on a wood platform. "Denied, for your own protection. Didn't the doctors tell you? There be monstrous children up here. You're much safer where you are."

"I happen to know you children are not monsters." The man walked closer to the tree, looking up at them from the bottom of its trunk. "I know that as fact. I've encountered and know what the real monsters are."

"No. You don't," Keely said confidently.

"Go away," Jasper added.

The man looked away from them, scanning the yard and the house before he turned back with a severe look on his face. "They're called neverborn, the monsters that killed your grandparents, the ones that almost killed you."

"How do you—" Jasper started to ask, but Keely slapped a hand over his mouth.

"Mister, I don't know who you are or what you want, but you should be very careful. We are monstrous children. That is the truth."

"You're not monstrous. You're very special." The man's face was soft and serious all at once. "You're fighters, tasked by heaven, and you shouldn't be scared of the neverborn. They should be scared of you, because the two of you are the only ones in the world capable of fighting them."

Several minutes passed. Jasper and Keely stood staring down at the man. He didn't move or look away until someone from the house opened the front door. A blonde girl with dark grey eyes and a lot of freckles yelled, "Mom says, come eat." She turned around and bounded back into the house, slamming the door behind her. The girl didn't seem to notice the man.

The man looked at the door then back to them. "I tell you what, why don't we go inside and discuss how I can help you."

Keely and Jasper looked at one another. Keely's face had an annoyed look, and she rolled her eyes. Walking to a low, wooden rail-

308

ing, she sat down on the edge of a wood plank and let her feet dangle off its side. "Mister—"

"Frits," the man interrupted her. "My name is Frits."

"Cut the crap." She leaned onto the railing and folded her arms over it. "We aren't your friends, and even if you get my parent's permission—"

"I'm not asking your parents for permission. I'm asking yours." The man interrupted her. "I'm asking you, Jasper and Keely Sheppard. Would you like to save countless souls from the same monsters that killed your grandparents?"

Frits started to blur and fade, and so did the tree Chance stood on. Jasper's mind turned gray again. "After that, we were taken in by the ministry and trained." Adult Jasper said from beside him. "We were taught to fight and how to use our abilities."

"What ability does Keely have?" Chance asked.
"A lot like mine." Jasper shrugged. "She can't read thoughts, but her ability to enter into and influence people's minds far surpasses mine. I have yet to meet someone who can see through her illusions." He turned to Chance, and pain started to radiate around his skull. "And, now you know about the choices we've made. I want to know about your choices."

The murkiness faded to black, and Chance found himself standing in the center of a darkened street in the middle of a suburb of Tokyo. A shirtless doppelganger of himself lay motionless on the asphalt nearby. In front of him stood Keely, covered in dirt and blood. Around him, voices echoed, ordering him to wrap his fingers around her neck and strangle the life out of her, and that was precisely what he wanted to do.

32

Chance backed away from his memory, from his past self, fighting the urge to strangle the woman he loved. His deformed hands struck out at her, trying to tear her heart out. "No," he shouted, trying to run away. His stomach turned, and he was sure he was going to be sick. How had he gotten here? What had happened to him and Keely that had made him want to hurt her? "This is not me," he said, trying to step away from the awfulness of wanting to murder the person he loved.

"No, It's not." A firm hand grasped his shoulder and held him in place. "It's just a memory, and it's not even your memory," Jasper explained.

Everything froze in place. Chance closed his eyes. He was afraid to know anymore and couldn't look. Had he killed Keely? Was that what Jasper wanted to show him. He remembered seeing her blood and feeling elated thinking of ripping her body apart. A voice that wasn't his, relentlessly screamed for him to destroy what he loved most in the world. His stomach turned, and he started retching.

He opened his eyes to find himself back in the sunlit room. His stomach revolted against all that he was feeling. He turned side-ways and vomited up its contents onto the wood floor. "I didn't kill her," he said between heaves. "I didn't." When the contents of his stomach had emptied, and he managed to catch his breath, a pair of firm hands maneuvered him back onto the futon. He was sure his very soul had been torn apart. Jasper sat over him with a stern look on his face, his violet eyes so like Keely's.

"Keely," he whispered before his heart completely and painful-ly shattered. Chance threw an arm up over his eyes and wept.

"I'm going to let you have your moment since you're not going to believe me when I tell you what you saw is a partial truth. Plus, regurgitated chocolate milk is disgusting." Jasper's actual voice reverberated around the room. "You didn't kill, or even try to hurt Keely. That memory wasn't really yours."

Chance didn't believe Jasper. What he'd seen was too real, his emotions too palpable, and he was convinced he'd given in to them. At least he knew why Keely hadn't talked to him. Tears soaked his face, and he couldn't stop the small noises of pain that escaped between breaths.

A long, immeasurable time later, Chance had cried himself out. Probably because his heartbreak went deeper than tears could quench. He heard a noise next to him and realized that Jasper was still there. Anger erupted, burning through his veins. Without thinking, he found himself standing over, Jasper fisting his shirt and shaking him. "You should have just said she was dead." He shook him again. "You didn't have too…"

Pain exploded in his head, starting at his temples and radiating all throughout. He released his hold on Jasper and pressed his hands to his head, trying to subdue the discomfort. He was aware of falling to his knees before he curled into the fetal position. The pain was relentless.

"You and I are not friends, yet. You come at me again before that happens, and I will leave you crippled for the rest of your life." The pain suddenly stopped. "Now, get up," Jasper ordered angrily.

Chance rolled onto his side and slowly pushed himself up. The pain had left him dizzy, and he wasn't sure he could sit unassisted. After he managed to hold himself upright, he looked to Jasper, feeling ashamed on top of his despair. "I apologize," he said hoarsely.

Jasper looked thoughtful for a moment. "Keely isn't dead." He reached out and placed a hand on his shoulder.

Chance's vision blurred, waivered, and he was unable to focus on any of the details around him. When his eyes came back into focus, he was staring at Keely. The sight of her startled him because she was covered in blood and bruises. Her clothes were just as tattered as her skin, but she sat next to a past image of himself. He lay motionless on the futon while Keely held his hand and gently combed her fingers through his hair. Tears dripped down her cheeks and fell to the floor.

"Keely. I'm okay." He reached out to comfort her. His fingers encountered nothing but air.

"Memory. Remember?" Jasper said. The image fell apart. He blinked and returned to himself.

"She's alive," he said, feeling such a flood of relief he could have cried again.

"Yes, but she's not unhurt," Jasper confirmed. "It's complicated." He let out a deep breath. "Neither of us can help her until we know the truth, and everything about that night seems effectual. I need to know the cause." He lowered his hand. "I'm sorry for pulling out the thing you wanted to forget first, but I needed to unblock your mind so we could both know the rest."

"I... I...thought you knew." Chance was confused.

"No. That is why I want you to show me." He again held out his hand. "I can sense it's important to you, so it's even more important to my sister."

Chance scowled at him, then slapped his hand into his palm. Immediately, he fell into murkiness and found himself standing next to Jasper. "First, you're going to have to teach me Japanese."

Again, Chance felt uncomfortable pressure at his temples. Images strobed around him and Jasper. They flashed too quickly for him to see them all, but occasionally he did catch kanji, hiragana, or sounds of letters or words. It seemed like less than a second passed before Jasper said, "Well, that should make talking to the Cassock of Japan a lot easier." He stopped and looked at Chance. "I imagine this is going to be difficult, and I can't promise I won't judge you. Tell the truth anyway." He shoved him forward.

Chance lost his balance, stumbled, and found himself in his apartment facing Keely, his face twisted with jealousy, pain, and anger. He'd never been so ashamed or remorseful. "I already know what happened here," he said in a small voice.

"I don't," Jasper replied, walking into Chance's apartment. "But in your mind, this is where everything begins. It's where everything went wrong."

Time unfroze, and Chance watched with fresh eyes as Keely tried to explain who she was and what she did. She was unsure and afraid, fearful of his reaction. She was afraid of his rejection, and reject her is exactly what he'd done. He turned into the worst person Chance had ever known, and there was nothing he could do to change it.

"You should have listened to what she had to say," Jasper admonished sharply.

Chance's apartment darkened and the lines and colors of

everything bled together, split apart, and reformed. Chance found himself inside a white room, surrounded by people. Keely stood on front of him naked, wrapped in another man's arms, as the people around them chanted. "I took these memories from several people because I needed to know what happened. I think you need to know as well." Jasper shoved him closer to Keely. "Take a closer look, lover-boy. This wasn't cheating. This was a ritual done to protect her from this."

The scene pulled away from Chance, and he had the sensation of being yanked before he found himself standing in a path in front of a darkened forest. Cool wind blowing around him as he watched Keely stare into the trees. She had a determined look on her face, but he could see her lips quiver. She was also afraid. Wordlessly, she stepped onto a dirt path and disappeared into the trees.

The forest faded away as images of monsters appeared, monsters and Keely. She fought them, all of them. There were so many he lost count. He could count how many times they hit, kicked, tried to crush her in massive arms, or threw her into hard ground or rigid tree trunks. Then came the horrifying moment when she collapsed into the ground and lay there covered in blood and dirt, fighting for each breath she took.

"There was a neverborn," Chance said, frantically looking around.

"Sutton drove it away. Her arrows tend to hurt. Just because a neverborn can't die, doesn't mean they can't feel pain. Sometimes that gives us the advantage." Jasper walked over to Keely, squatted down next to her and reached out a hand. Chance had the inclination to do the same but stopped himself when Jaspers hand passed through Keely's image. "The spell meant to protect her rebounded because her inheritor was dying. It took them nearly an hour to find her." His voice cracked. "She's afraid of the dark." Chance already knew but chose not to comment. "Keely lay alone in the forest, scared and knowing she was dying, trying to cling to life." He stood up and the forest flickered back to his apartment. "That's why you didn't see her for a month."

He walked over to Chance and stood over him with an angry sneer pulling at his mouth and a clear 'give me a reason to hurt you,' written in his eyes. "You should have listened to her," he repeated.

"I truly wish I had." Chance blinked back tears of guilt and self-loathing. "I wish…" he stopped, there was nothing he could do or say.

"You and me both," Jasper stepped aside and the scene in his apartment started to play out again.

Chance watched Keely leave his apartment, leaving him standing alone with a shocked look on his face. "Stop her," he said. His past self didn't move. "Idiot. Go after her," he yelled, but nothing happened. "I'm so stupid," he said, watching himself finally find the courage to run after Keely. "If I'd listened, then everything after…it wouldn't have happened."

"It's possible." Jasper agreed, sounding less angry. "But it's pointless to dwell on what ifs. Neither of us can change the past."

There was a blur of light and cold as he ran through the empty streets of Tokyo, frantically searching. When Chance found Keely standing in the middle of the street, he could feel his own anxiety all over again. Only this time, his chest hurt with it because he knew what was coming. The neverborn appeared, and the fight between it and Keely ensued. Keely was so beautiful, powerful, and confident. He saw both grace and calculation in her movements. "She's magnificent," he said, turning his gaze back on himself.

His past self cowered against a wall, feeling powerless to do anything and hating himself for it. Chance wanted to say something to justify his actions but could think of nothing. Even when he stepped out of the shadows to try to help, he was useless. As the fight continued, he was reminded he wasn't just pathetic, he was in her way. The street went dark for a moment before he saw himself emerge from the shadows again. His skin crawled with traces of pain when the neverborn grabbed his neck and lifted him off the ground. The street disappeared, and his vision filled with the grotesque face of the neverborn as he slowly sank into the empty depths of its white eyes.

Chance grabbed at his chest, feeling as though he couldn't breathe. He knew what he was seeing wasn't real, but he couldn't fight against everything the memory evoked. His throat felt constricted, and he felt as if the air had thickened. Something deep inside his torso started to ache and throb then hurt. He would have screamed if he could have managed it. Panic set in, and he dug his fingers into the flesh of his throat and chest, trying to rip out whatever was causing him so much torment.

Suddenly, everything went quiet. There was no light, no sound, no sensation. Nothing.

Chance thought there wouldn't be any more pain. Then everything shifted, and he was pulled backward with such force; he lost his balance and fell. He tried to find his footing, flailing his arms and legs, trying to catch himself, but the darkness started to get heavy, then solidified, and he could no longer move.

Something in the black moved against him, over his body, invading his personal space and touching him seemingly intimately. A force tore open and violated his very essence, reading his feelings, and taking his memories. He let out a scream. It was taken from him, swallowed away before it could really form. His cries, like the rest of him, were shredded into fragments and scattered then devoured.

For an eternity, he fought to pull the pieces of himself back together. When he finally managed it, he found his soul damaged. It was damaged and missing its natural container, his body. Before he could mourn its loss, a light formed above him, maybe in front of him. He could not tell for sure. The light spread into the night, and the colors within it focused, and he found himself staring at Keely. She was so beautiful, his heart swelled with love. Something awful ate away at that love, and he found himself wanting to kill her.

"NO!" he screamed. The urge to strike her, to wrap his hands around her neck and choke the life out of her was overpowering. "No!" His hand struck out, trying to punch through her chest. He knew he had the strength to kill her, and the punch landed, he would have succeeded. "Stop!" His heart started pounded painfully against his ribs as he started coughing and gagging.

"Breathe," Jasper commanded.

Everything froze. The monster's deformed hand was mere centimeters from Keely's temple. Chance fell out of himself, out of the neverborn and stumbled backward, clutching his chest. Hunching over, he placed his hands on his knees, hoping that what he was feeling would pass and the pain in his heart would subside. He truly had wanted to murder Keely. More than that he'd wanted to relish in painting the street with her blood. Visions of doing just that hid in the patches of darkness around him.

Jasper placed a hand on his shoulder. "Deep breath. It's only a memory. All of it."

"I tried to kill her." Chance confessed between coughs. He was shaking with fear. He was afraid of his own impulses. Finally, he managed to fill his lungs with air.

"No. You didn't. The inclination wasn't yours. The inclination belonged to the neverborn that stole your soul." Jasper stepped in front of him, studying the malformed monster, and the horrifying happenings hiding in the dark. "More, the inclination belonged to one of the souls inside it." He sounded confused as he examined what Chance's memory more thoroughly. "I wish I could skip this part, but your mind is telling me it's important. Not just to you, but for Keely." He turned to Chance. "I'm inclined to agree with your instincts." With a look of concern on his face, he stepped back to Chance and blew out a breath through puffed cheeks. "I'm not sure this is the truth. It is the truth for you, but your being manipulated by your worst fear. Something's off."

Chance could point out an infinite number of things that weren't right with what had happened. Instead, he chose to remain silent. Jasper had confused him; if his memory wasn't the truth, than what was. He was trusting himself less and less with each passing second.

Jasper frowned. "I'm sorry to have to push this, but remember, this isn't real."

"I know." Chance put his fingers to his temples and rubbed them, breathing in deeply several times. "It's a memory." He whispered to himself. "And it may or may not be the truth."

"The manipulated truth. There is a distinction." Jasper said next to him. "And no matter what we discover, you weren't alone that night."

"I know," he repeated. "Keely was there."

"She was. She wasn't just a Priestess fighting a neverborn, she was fighting for your life."

"And I was fighting for hers," Chance said absently, then stopped short. Taking in a sharp breath, he looked at Jasper, feeling surprised at his own admission. "I fought it," he said positively, knowing without a doubt he spoke fact. He felt elated with relief, and that gave him courage. "Both of us fought it."

"I believe you. Now show me."

316

Able to think more clearly because he was less afraid, he allowed his mind to open so he could really explore his memories. He walked back to the monster and stepped back inside it. The neverborn started moving again, and immediately, he was inundated by a cacophony of screams. They didn't affect him, nor did persistent thought, attempting to convince him to kill Keely. Chance knew it was a lie.

This time he recognized it for what it was. A pair of souls were trying to pollute his with vileness and murder. He saw the things they had done, the things they were willing to do, and how much they enjoyed blood and gore. They thought to entice him with murmurs of love and promises of eternal life, using his feelings and memories as a lure. Chance would never let them trap him inside the monster with them, even with the offer of eternity. The memory and the feeling of being in close contact with those souls made him shudder. He wasn't scared. He was disgusted.

His thoughts and will were still his own, and he resisted. By resisting them, he fought for control of the neverborn. As weak as he was, he did little more than misdirect its attacks, but it was enough to give Keely the advantage.

She took it, striking back, then unleashing her illusions on it. Keely manifested the souls worst fear. When its body was being torn apart, the two foul souls started to scream with fear and anger, joining the other souls they'd trapped with them. He did feel the pain of the illusion, not as his own, but there was definitely pain. To him, it was justice for everything the neverborn and the horrible souls had done.

A soft but powerful voice reverberated inside the neverborn, offering peace and comfort. This voice belonged to Keely, and it so was full of goodness and love that it was to be believed. He followed the path of the voice, seeking escape, but he was weak. It hurt trying to pull himself out of the neverborn. The pain went deeper than any he'd ever felt, and he couldn't fight it. For a moment, he thought he'd forever be trapped.

"I call you forth, Misato Takeda." Keely's voice turned into a physical force. Wrapping him in warmth and strength, he was filled with the essence of oranges and vanilla. In the next instant, he was freed from the neverborn.

Chance stood inside his memory, hyper-aware of everything,

sights, sounds, tastes, colors, sensations. Each had an effect on all of his sense, overwhelming them, making them useless. He did know Keely was there, next to him, holding him close.

Something from above shifted, and the sky opened up. Chance would have said there was a light, but there wasn't. It was just a beautiful feeling that got stronger and stronger until he was enveloped in it. Unconditional love and happiness surrounded then filled him with pure joy. He'd never been so happy or so at peace. Love had become tangible. He could do more than just feel it; he could touch it. Heaven had told him that he could, and he started to alight. Heaven's love was everlasting, and he would spend eternity basking in it.

"Don't go." A soft song floated around him in a language he didn't know but still understood. It was beautiful and haunting all at once. For a moment, he didn't recognize the voice.

"Not this soul," the voice said. "Not this beautiful precious soul," it commanded and begged all at once. "Please," it went on somewhat more forcefully. "I have done all I agreed to do. I have fulfilled my duties as tasked. I have suffered and fought alone in this never-ending war   for reasons I will never understand. Please. Not this soul."

If he'd been given pause, it was very short lived. What did he care what the voice had to say? Heaven called to him, and he wanted to answer.

"I'm begging you, Misato, Chance, love of my life. Please… let heaven wait." Upon hearing his name, Chance gave the voice consideration and sought its origin. A figure formed and appeared in front of him. He was astonished to find the voice belonging to Keely, even more surprised that he'd momentarily forgotten her. As his pure soul beheld her pure soul, he wondered how he could ever forget such an exquisite woman.

Under heaven's light, he could see her as she truly was, without any barriers, physical or mental. She was so beautiful, especially with the glow of the divine coating her lovely body in iridescence. All of what she was, was bared for him to see. He saw it all. Her strengths, her weaknesses, her insecurities, her courage, and her compassion. Everything she meant to say, every truth she meant to tell, he knew it. No words passed between them, yet somehow, he knew her more intimately than he knew himself.

318

"I know it's selfish. I know you belong in heaven. Please, don't go. Something inside me will break if you go, and I won't be able to fix it. I need your courage, patience, laughter, and music. Please, don't go and take a part of my soul out of this world." She stretched out a hand, and he reached out. When the tips of his fingers touched hers, he was filled with a different love, Keely's love. It was powerful, strong, and pure. Though different from heaven's, her love promised all that she was and would be. Keely's love promised eternity, her eternity.

He didn't want to say no to her love. Somehow, he knew he didn't have too. Heaven would always be there. He was mortal, and one day he would return. Keely needed him. She needed him to protect her, not just her body; she needed him to safeguard her soul. Only his love could do that.

She pulled at his hand, and he started to descend, falling back to Earth, back to Tokyo. He knew what he was leaving behind, what he was about to face, but was determined. Chance would find a way to stop the neverborn because that was the only way to stop the monsters from hurting Keely. Loving her meant protecting her; it meant loving that much more, and he absolutely knew he could. As he fell, a soft command, that wasn't a voice, took shape as an inclination that wasn't his own and yet still was.

"That is now your task."

∞ ∞ ∞ ∞ ∞

Chance was staring at the walls of the room he'd occupied, but he didn't see them for some time. His vision still held Keely, and his senses were still filled with her essence. After a time, the vision faded along with the scent of oranges and vanilla. What remained was his resolve to protect Keely, and he was determined to love her. Before heaven, he'd chosen a purpose.

"That's what you wanted me to remember?" he asked Jasper in English, standing, walking to the window, and looking out of it.

Everything looked different. Outside, the water of the pond rippled with tiny waves as coy happily played in the sunlight. The grass, flowers, and stones of the garden had shed the night's dew in exchange for vibrant greens and light browns. Spring scented the air. The world wasn't as sharp and as awful as he'd thought. He couldn't really say what it was. One thing he did know, everything was fleeting, goodness, and cruelty. Everything was fragile.

Jasper came to stand next to him. "I needed to know about the neverborn that Keely fought. I'd already suspected it wasn't like any other we've ever seen. It's going to be a problem." He was quiet for a moment. "And, yes. I needed you to remember because I needed to know what Keely wouldn't tell me, and I'm fairly certain her point of view on what happened greatly differs from yours. You needed to know so you could understand it's a choice. We all choose to be part of this fight. Now, so have you." He pulled out his cellphone, turned on the camera, and handed it to Chance. "Now that you've remembered your choice, you can't renege on your decision. It's already changed you."

Chance looked at the image of himself. Instantly, he was caught off guard. His eye color had changed from brown to striking, light, golden yellow. As shocking as it was, he didn't regret anything he'd done or learned. Everything would be different. He already knew, but he was ready to face whatever was in store for him.

"I'm not going to change my mind," he said, pushing the cellphone away. "I want to see Keely."

Jasper folded his arms over his chest, and he frowned. "You can't. Someone who calls my sister a whore doesn't have the right. Maybe you can earn it, maybe not. That all depends on you."

33

Keely strolled through a pair of sliding, glass doors, hugging her jacket closer to fight off the cold. She looked out at the rain and frowned. Rain didn't bother her, nor did the cold, separately. Together it wasn't her favorite, especially since she was on the sunny shores of Tahiti less than twenty-four hours earlier.

"Here." Sutton shoved a thick, red wool coat at her. "I bet you forgot Scotland would be cold this time of year."

She smirked. "I did. But in my defense, I was on a beach in a bathing suit yesterday." She took the jacket and slid it on more grateful than ever for her best friend. One day, she hoped she could return the many kindnesses Sutton had bestowed over the last months.

After she'd left Tokyo with Jasper, she'd been debilitated by her heartbreak. Jasper and her sister-in-law, Addison, had done their best to comfort her, but she was inconsolable. Eventually, Jasper had called Sutton. Not because he didn't want to help, he couldn't. When Jasper realized that, he also realized Keely would have to learn to live with her shattered heart. The only way to do that was to carry on with her life and learn to live it as she was, broken. Telling her that he needed to go help train a new monk, he'd packed her clothes and picked up the end of her mattress and dumped her out of bed. Sutton was waiting to pick her up. She had a four-month itinerary of traveling to the world's most elegant spas.

At first, Keely found herself going from one sleeping spot to another and not much else. After a couple of months passed, and with Sutton's constant pestering, Keely got up and did little things like going out to eat. Those little things turned into bigger things, like lounging on a beach. One day she spent the entire day out of bed, and that led to more days of the same.

Nights were still hard. Keely couldn't stop thinking of Chance, or how much she missed him. She hated herself for it, as she didn't have the right to miss him, not after all the pain she'd caused. There was nothing that could be done, nothing could fill the hole inside her, but she was learning to cope.

Their four-month sojourn had ended, and it was time for her to go back to work. Part of her needed to so she had something else to focus on, and she knew she was needed. Still, she was worried. She wasn't as physically strong as she'd been, and she hadn't done any training.

Scotland was probably a good choice for her to return as a Priestess. Its population was relatively small, even if they had a major influx of tourists. The Scottish ministry didn't report as many attacks as other countries; therefore, they weren't a high priority. They probably would have remained a low priority if Sutton and Jasper hadn't both demanded Keely be sent somewhere with a smaller concentration of neverborn. That Keely had always wanted to see the city of Edinburgh, also had factor in the decision. However she got there, she considered it a bonus her wishes were considered.

"Believe it or not, even though its booked years in advance, the Scottish ministry got us rooms at that luxurious, gothic hotel you wanted to stay at. We've got our rooms for an entire month," Sutton announced with a smile. "After that, it'll be your standard apartment, but hey, at least we get the posh hotel and delicious food for a month." She maneuvered their bags into one pile and looked around. "Although, there was supposed to be a car here for us." She looked at her watch. "Our flight was delayed, but I seriously doubt they'd forget or leave us."

Keely shrugged, unperturbed by their lack of a ride. "Well, there's always the tram." She pointed to a nearby platform.

"In the rain?" Sutton pouted. "I want to be warm and dry inside a car."

As if summoned, a black car roared up and screeched to a halt in front of them. A door opened, and a middle-aged man got out. He tipped his grey cap and slightly bowed his head. "My apologies for bein' late, lasses. There was a touch of confusion about when you'd be needin' transport. Somethen' about yer monk cominae a few days hence, delaying yae."

Sutton looked at Keely and shrugged. "I'm Sutton, the Priestess's monk. Present and accounted for," she said to the man then smiled and waved.

"That yae are." He smiled to the both of them. "I'm Finlay, official hack of the Edinburgh ministry. End it's a right pleasure to be meetinae the Priestess."

"It's Keely," Keely corrected and shook his hand.

"A kind, bonnie lass yae are." He smiled broadly at them before opening the back door of the cab. "Let's get you tae lasses out o' the rain."

∞ ∞ ∞ ∞ ∞

Keely and Sutton walked together in silence down one of many nearly empty streets somewhere in Edinburgh. They weren't lost. However, they didn't have a destination, and though it was almost three o'clock in the morning, the city was inviting. A nearly full moon glowed in the sky above as the city lights beckoned from below. They walked on cobble-stone streets past stone and brick buildings that looked as if they'd been transported from a fairy-tale. Keely could only marvel at their cupola, turrets, buttresses, and columns as they passed quietly through street after strcet. Occasionally, they'd find themselves facing a gothic-looking monument or an open park with a magnanimous view, and they'd have to stop and stare out at the lights and hills of the sleepy city.

It was Keely's fault they were out in the middle of the night. Sleep was impossible, and she didn't want to stay in her bed, mired in tears, wondering if they'd ever stop. Her natural inclination for urban discovery offered her some serenity, so she'd spent every night since they'd arrived in Scotland walking. Still, she couldn't walk away from her own mind, and she couldn't stop thinking. She was plagued by what if's, or wondering what Chance was doing? At least the walking kept her tears at bay, and by four or five, she was tired enough to sleep, fitfully, but sleep all the same.

Sutton walked with her because she didn't want Keely walking by herself. After their encounter with the neverborn calling itself Legion, the ministry had ordered that Keely never be left alone. If they should encounter Legion, they weren't to engage without back up. Considering neverborn traveled the world with ease, Legion could be anywhere. Although, after learning so much about it, Keely suspected it would be drawn by densely populated first-world cities.

Edinburgh, though a tourist hotspot, would hold no appeal.

Of course, those were the official reasons Sutton walked with her. The unofficial, unspoken reason was that she was worried about Keely. Keely could see it on her face. Though Sutton would freely admit Keely had recovered some of herself since her devastating heartbreak, she also had to recognize Keely wasn't the same person. So, Keely walked, and Sutton walked with her.

Their shoes clicked a rhythmic tattoo on the stone sidewalk as they passed underneath an ornate streetlamp, casting its light through the branches of a silver birch tree and creating intricately woven shadows. Stopping, Keely looked up into its branches almost expecting to see fairies adoring the yellow and orange leaves.

A cold blast ruffled the branches overhead and prickled against her cheeks. "I wish there was a café open," she said. A hot cup of bittersweet, creamy fluid would go well with her wonderings.

"I have some coffee," Sutton offered.

Keely turned wide eyes to her friend. "Really?" she asked excitedly.

"I do." Sutton cleared her throat. "I never waste a good spell." She reached into her backpack and pulled out a black thermos with a cat head and tail. "It's just, anything from Japan seems to hurt your heart. So, I didn't know..." Her voice trailed off.

Keely smiled and blinked back tears that suddenly formed. Yes, anything that reminded her of Japan made her heartache. Nevertheless, it's not like she wasn't always thinking about Japan, specifically Chance, anyway.

"You know what? Coffee and friends are the best magic." She motioned toward a bench.

"I was hoping you'd see it that way."

The two of them walked over to an iron bench and sat. Luckily, both were wearing long coats, or the metal would have made them colder. Sutton opened her bag and produced two plastic cups then filled them with decadent-smelling, hazelnut coffee. She handed Keely a cup before taking a sip of her own. "Oh my god, that's good."

"Mm," Keely agreed as the hot, creamy concoction filled her mouth. "Damn, your magic is..." she stopped when another gust of wind blew around them. Desperation and sorrow were carried within its prickling coldness. "Sutton," Keely warned, standing.

324

"Neverborn. Of course, there was bound to be at least one." Sutton stood. "How far?"

"Three, maybe five kilometers."

"Is it…"

"No. The souls trapped inside… feel old, very old." Keely stared in the direction of the sensation she felt. "You may as well report it. I know you have, too, so my feelings won't be hurt."

Sutton blew out the breath she'd been holding. "Oh, thank God. I have strict orders from your brother to report everything." She set her coffee on the bench next to her, pulled out a cellphone, and started tapping on its screen.

Keely took a large gulp of her coffee. "It's heading north."

"Of course, towards the castle, because it would be completely appropriate to fight an immortal monster at a historic war monument."

After they quickly finished the contents in their cups, Sutton repacked everything. She held out her hand, and the air warmed slightly. "Bellearmos," she summoned, and the crossbow appeared in her hand. "Okay, I'm…" the beeping of her cellphone interrupted her. "So help me. How am I supposed to protect you if I have to stop and text mom and dad every five seconds?" She pulled out her cell phone. "'Wait.' What does that even mean? Wait."

Keely smirked. She didn't know why, but she was itching for a fight. Hopefully afterword, exhaustion would make her sleep for three days straight. She wasn't going to wait. "Do we tell them no or ignore them."

"I prefer the whole ignore it, and it will go away approach."

"Me too," Keely agreed and started heading north. "Shall we go visit the castle?"

∞ ∞ ∞ ∞ ∞

"Keely. Get your shit together," Sutton shouted from the other side of a large courtyard. They'd tracked the neverborn to an upper level of the castle. When it started to feel trapped, it attacked.

"I'm trying," Keely said under her breath, using the cannon she'd been thrown into to hoist herself off the ground. Sutton was right, she didn't have her shit together. She wasn't focused, and her maneuverers were clumsy and lacked her usual grace. She was barely holding onto the illusion that kept the people around them from being aware of their presence. The neverborn had the upper hand, and by the twisted smile on its face, it knew it.

Taking in a deep breath, she ran at the neverborn, ducking underneath an open palm slap meant to knock her head off her shoulders. This neverborn was wearing the shell of a burly, middle-aged man with a neat beard and large beefy limbs, but the shell was fading. The man's skin had a grey hue, his teeth were falling out, and his irises were tiny dots in the center of his white eyes. If she had to guess, the neverborn had probably been wearing the shell of the man's soul for more than a month, and it was most likely hunting for a new one.

Keely tried to sidestep away from an elbow aimed at her stomach but tripped over her own feet. She pitched forward, falling into the neverborn. It simply grabbed her underneath her arms and threw her across the courtyard. She slid across the stone ground, tearing the clothes and the skin on her left side before she flipped over some benches and hit a wall. Without stopping to consider how hurt she was, she quickly rolled to her feet and ran at it again.

"Get your useless ass out of there," Sutton shouted from behind her. "We'll track it…"

"No." Keely objected as she dodged a foot meant to sweep her legs from under her. "I'm setting those souls free."

"Fine. Then do it, and quit fucking off."

The neverborn stepped into her, extending its arms, meaning to embrace her in a grip that would probably crush the life out of her. She dropped to her knees and rolled away from it, landing in a kneeling position. As it came at her again, it offered her the perfect opening that would allow her to release the souls inside of it, she suddenly realized she wasn't just out of focus. She was weak. Her connection to heaven had faded, and so had her ability to call upon its power. The words and language that usually flowed from her freely wouldn't come. How she didn't comprehend her own weakness before that moment, she didn't know. She did know, for the first time in her life, she couldn't concentrate enough to speak in the language that had been freely given to her by heaven. It was her own fault. The consequence of being unable to mend her heart. She'd never felt more alone.

"Sutton," Keely said, feeling panicked. She wouldn't leave the souls inside the neverborn, but she couldn't help them, not on her own.

The echo of fast approaching boot stomps came from behind Keely just before a black-clad, hooded figure appeared. "I told you to wait," an accented, male voice said sharply.

He maneuvered around her, whipping something metallic around him before he launched into the air. It caught the neverborn's arm and wrapped around it. With a firm yank, the man pulled at the neverborn, and it stumbled away from Keely. Turning its attention to its new attacker, the neverborn swung on him. The man, clearly a well-trained monk, ducked underneath its fist before dexterously coiling another length of chain around the arm meant to strike him. The monk leaped into the air; using the string tied to the neverborn, he swung around it. His weight and momentum forced it onto one knee, and he tethered a leg in the chain then tied it to its bound hands. Using the ground as leverage, the man again yanked, and the neverborn fell onto the stone pavers with a loud thwump. Then he quickly tied the remaining free leg to the rest of its limbs, leaving it hogtied on the ground in front of Keely.

The neverborn yelled, thrashed, and managed to roll onto its side. The hooded man jerked the chain again, pulling the neverborn onto its back, then planted a foot on its collarbone. Keely was astounded at how fast the man had subdued the neverborn and rendered it virtually harmless. Turning his attention to her, the man removed his hood and lowered the scarf covering his face.

Chance.

A multitude of tumultuous emotions, some of which she couldn't identify, overwhelmed her thought processes. She opened her mouth to say something, but only managed a small squeak of surprise. She had absolutely no idea how to feel, much less what to say or do.

"You should have waited," Chance said harshly, staring down at her with a severe frown.

"Holy fuck," Sutton said from beside her, echoing Keely's thoughts.

The neverborn on the ground let out a loud roar, bringing her attention back to it and her purpose. Her chaotic mind managed to find focus because the souls inside the neverborn were something she could deal with. Slowly, she unwound herself, stood, and walked over to the neverborn.

Though she was overwhelmed by her own feelings by Chance's sudden appearance, she felt stronger than she had mere seconds ago. Her heart filled, and the language of heaven flowed from her lips. "You don't have to suffer anymore. You don't have to feel pain anymore. You don't have to be afraid anymore. I've come to show you all of you, the path to heaven." She carefully knelt down and gently placed a hand in the center of the neverborn's chest. The pain and torment she experienced coming from the souls inside felt like a physical blow. Tears formed in her eyes even as her strength grew. "I am Keely, Priestess, beacon to those who are stolen and lost." Heaven opened up, radiating its inviting love. "Those of you who have been deprived of peace, love, and happiness, I call you forth."

Beneath her hand, light exploded from the neverborn's chest. Hundreds of souls filled the night, fluttering and sparkling with hope. Standing, Keely lifted her hand and gently caressed one of the souls. She got the sense of a woman, one that longed for the love of heaven. "I'm sorry I didn't get here sooner." The pure soul warmed and tickled her fingers. "I set you free and send you home." She lifted her hand, pushing the soul skyward. Like a shooting star, it streaked up into heaven and disappeared. It wasn't even a second later before the other souls followed, leaving trails of joy in their wake.

Keely had forgotten how glorious it felt to return souls to heaven. She was so awed by its splendor she'd also forgotten a very dangerous immortal creature was nearby. Without the constraints of its human shell, it was stronger, and it was ravenous to replace what it had lost.

"Keely," Sutton yelled.

She startled and looked back to the neverborn. It had somehow freed itself, and a deformed hand was heading for her face. Her reflexes failed her, and she couldn't do anything but watch the dangerously sharp claws come at her. An arm snaked around her waist, and she was jerked so hard she lost her breath, and her feet came up off the ground. She was snatched out of the neverborn's reach a second before its hand would have done some significant damage.

"Sutton," Chance shouted from next to her ear. Powerful arms

328

wound tightly around her, hugging her to a toned chest, as she was carried across the courtyard. She didn't remember Chance being so muscular, and it left her mystified.

The familiar sound of wood cracking against stone indicated Sutton had unleashed her own attack. She found her footing and lifted her head in time to see the neverborn try and deflect Sutton's arrows. It was a futile effort. The bolts dug into its stone hide, leaving holes bleeding black. With a low growl, it smashed its hands into the stone ground, cracking it apart, before it turned and jumped over the castle wall, disappearing.

"You should have waited," Chance repeated low in her ear.

So many feelings and emotions surged up inside her, and she was once again dumbfounded. Her self-preservation instinct made her do the only thing she could think of to protect her heart from any more loss, guilt, and pain. Escape. Quietly, she pushed Chance's arms from around her waist and walked away from his warm embrace, despite her painful desire to stay.

Sutton gave her a worried, questioning look as she walked past. Keely simply shook her head no, hoping her friend would understand she needed to be alone. As she took the stairs that lead down the and out of the castle, she focused all her thoughts on making her heavy legs move. Left foot, right foot, left foot, and on Keely went, ignoring the swirling thoughts in her head and the aching of her heart. Two hours later she found herself at her hotel, her body so exhausted it hurt to move. She fell into the poster bed, not bothering to remove her clothes or wash away the blood from the earlier fight.

34

Something startled Keely awake, and she found herself sitting up in her large, poster bed. Still drowsy, it took her senses a couple of extra seconds to wake. Her hotel room looked undisturbed; the intricately carved and ornate furniture was as it had been. The only difference her still blurred vision could make out was that it was now day. Behind the thick, velvet curtains and the diamond-etched windows, rain patted against the glass. She was about to lay down and go back to sleep when a soft noise caught her attention, and she jerked her head toward its direction.

In a darkened corner across from the corner of her bed, there was a chair. That chair was occupied by a black-clad figure. Chance.

Pulses started pounding in her ears from her suddenly heavily beating heart. He sat, eyes closed, head leaning on his hand, and his now blond-tipped hair falling over his forehead. Even though he was relaxed and sleeping, his face looked worn and tired. Still, he had an overwhelming allure that made her head swim. Too many nights, she'd dreamt of waking up to find him next to her. She couldn't think clearly or stop her body from physically reacting.

Panicked and unsure, she slid out of bed and tiptoed to the bathroom. Before she closed the door behind herself, tears were stinging at the back of her eyes. She'd thought when she'd left Tokyo, he'd be free of all the pain she'd caused. She'd prayed he would eventually get over everything she'd done and be happy. Instead, he was in Scotland fighting monsters as a monk in the predawn hours of the night.

Crossing the spacious floor to the sink, she turned on the water, rinsed out her mouth, and splashed some on her face. The brisk water stopped her tears but did nothing to soothe her turmoil. After washing her hands and drying them, she decided a quiet corner in the ornately decorated bathroom was as good a place as any to hide and have a meltdown. So, that is where she sat, not even trying to sort through all her overwhelming thoughts and feelings.

Soft fabric was pressed to the side of her face. She jumped a second time and jerked away from the cloth, from Chance. "Why are you here?" Keely asked in a voice tinged with tears. Being near him was so painful, it felt like the heart inside her chest was being torn apart. She didn't know how much more she could take.

"Because you're here," Chance answered, crouching in front of her.

Coffee and spice, his natural essence, filled her senses. She had to get away from him or get him away from her. "Right." She slapped his hand away. "The last meaningful conversation you and I had, you called me a whore."

He slowly dropped his hands then looked down at the floor. "Words can't express how sorry I am that I didn't listen to you. I should have never said or done what I did. I should have never let you walk out of my apartment. I'm sorry." He wiped a hand over the back of his neck. "I didn't mean it, but you already know that."

Keely sniffed back tears. An apology from him was not what she wanted. He was right. She'd always known he didn't mean what said. She knew it the moment he'd said it. That didn't change how things were or absolve the horrible things she'd done to him. Shame kept her from looking at him. If she did, she'd lose her mind entirely and breakdown. So, she stared the blooming flowers painted on the floor tile. "It doesn't matter anymore."

"Yes, it does, or you wouldn't have brought it up." He paused. "Or are you pushing me away?"

"I want you to go away," she answered honestly.

"You don't mean that."

"How do you know what I mean? Go back to Japan, Chance."

Chance slowly shook his head. "I have a question." He took a deep breath. "Why did you leave Japan? Me?"

"You ended it."

"I did," he agreed. "But that was before…" he faltered. "Before you said you loved me."

If she answered his question, she'd enter into a conversation that would tear apart the remainder of her fragile heart. "Why are we rehashing this?"

"Did you mean what you said? Did you love me?" Keely didn't answer, and after a few seconds, he continued. "Do you still love me?"

"No," she lied.

"Priestesses are supposed to be truthful."

"Not all of them," Keely countered, then realized what she'd admitted when a slight smile turned his lips up for a moment.

Soft knuckles brushed over her cheek, weakening her further. "Would your answer change if I told you I loved you?" His fingers caressed her jaw, then lifted and turned her chin so she was forced to face him. "Because I did."

She couldn't stop herself from looking into his handsome face. That was when she noticed his eye color had changed. They were no longer the soft, comforting brown she'd known. Now, they were a fiery gold. He wasn't just a monk, he was a Cassock. Chance had been tasked by heaven and would always be mired in the fight against the neverborn.

The pad of his thumb ran over her lip. "Would your answer change if I said I still love you?"

Keely was undone.

All the hurt and guilt burst out of her in a pained sob before the ocean of tears she'd been holding back broke free. She jerked away from his touch and covered her face with her hands. "You shouldn't. Not after… Oh, God. Not after everything I've done to you."

Firm hands circled around her, and she was pulled into Chance's lap. His arms wound tightly around her, cradling her against his chest. He kissed her temple. "Keely…"

"No," she said, rejected his comfort even as she fisted his shirt and cried into it. "I can't." She sobbed, taking in several short breaths. "I can't love you. It will only hurt you."

"Nothing could hurt me worse than when you left." His voice was tinged with remorse.

The tirade of guilt and pain was relentless. The truth was about to come out, and she couldn't stop it. All she could do was hope Chance would forgive her once he knew all of what she'd done. "I do love you…so much. I can't stop. I've tried. For your sake, I wish I could. I know you don't understand, but I had to leave… I had to let you go, so you'd be free. Free from all the pain I've caused. Everything that's happened to you is my fault. I've hidden things from you, and I've lied by omission. I've put you in mortal danger. I've self-

332

ishly disregarded your happiness because I was so happy being in love with you. I let a neverborn steal your soul—and worse." She let out a strangled cry. "I took you from the one place you'd never feel pain or sorrow. The one place you would always be happy. You'd have been eternally loved in heaven. I was so selfish when I pulled you away. Why? Because I didn't want to be in this world if you weren't in it. I didn't want to feel so alone. I wanted to love you even if it was from afar. And now, now I've turned you into a Cassock. I accepted a life of fighting. You didn't. And despite that, I went ahead and made a choice that wasn't mine to make. Yes, I do love you, but I don't have the right to."

By the time she was done, she was sobbing so hard she was shaking. "You should go back to Japan," she said weakly, between blubs. His only response was to settle her more firmly against him and tighten his hold. All she could do was weep.

A long time passed before Keely's sobs stopped, and her tears dried out. When she finally quieted, she thought he'd push her away, especially since he knew the truth, but he didn't. His hold on her remained firm as if he had no intention of ever letting her go.

Eventually, he shifted, and for one brief, terrifying moment, she thought he'd release her, but he didn't. Instead, he combed a hand through her hair and kissed the top of her head. "I think a hot bath, some food, and then definitely sleep for both of us. I'm still jet-lagged."

She was about to object when something odd struck her. "When did you learn English?"

A soft snort escaped him. "When I had to."

"That's not an answer."

Putting fingers under her chin, he lifted her face. His eyes went from hers to her lips before he bent down and pressed his to them. They were so supple and warm she didn't even consider moving away. The feel of his lips on hers was so wonderous she forgot about anything else she was thinking for feeling.

"Bath," he whispered softly in her ear when he ended the kiss.

"Okay," she agreed, incapable of arguing.

A stunning smile parted his lips and brightened his face. "Okay." He kissed her again before pushing Keely off him and up onto her feet. Standing, he stepped over to the claw-footed tub in the middle of the room, plugged it, and turned on the water then pulled her to him. He reached around her and peeled off her ruined jacket. After he dropped it to the floor, he tugged at the hem of her t-shirt. She lifted her arms. He pulled it up over head and threw it on top of the jacket. His eyes held her captive as he reached around her and unfastened her bra. Chance undressed her as if they hadn't spent six months apart, as if she hadn't hurt him, as if they were still lovers. It felt so natural she let him.

All of her clothes ended up in a pile on top of her jacket, and by that time, the bathtub was full and steaming. "Let's get the blood off of you." His fingers wove through hers, and he directed her to the bathtub.

She stepped into the nearly scalding water and slowly sunk down into it. The hot water made the cuts and abrasions on her skin burn, but it was still soothing to her sore and tired muscles. As she settled into the tub, Chance sat on the floor next to it with soap and washcloth in hand.

"I know how to bathe," she said softly, suddenly feeling his presence too acutely. The truth had changed nothing.

"Can you?" he asked. Before Keely could answer, he reached out, grabbed her wrist, and carefully lifted her arm. She could only lift it as high as her chest before she was hissing in pain. She'd had enough experience with bone breaks to know it wasn't broken, but it was definitely injured. Slowly, he let her arm fall back into the water. "I've been told Sutton has one of the most powerful healing incantations known. You should have let her use it."

"I was busy." Keely cradled her arm against her chest and held it there.

"Running from me. I know," he observed. She loved and hated that he knew her so well. He reached into the water, pulled her arm back to him, and began to wipe it with the soapy washcloth.

Chance spent the next ten minutes carefully washing and gently scrubbing the dried blood from her skin. After which he emptied the bathtub, then used the spray nozzle to shampoo and condition her hair. Any time she tried to take over her own care, he'd grab her hand, pull her fingers to his lips, and gently kiss them. By the time he wrapped her in a warm towel, ushered her back to the bed, and sat down behind her, toweling dry hair, she was burning with desire.

334

"Chance," she said softly, reaching behind her head to still his movements.

"Misato," he corrected, bringing her fingers to his velvety lips and kissing their tips.

"Misato," she repeated softly. She turned to look at him, silently pleading for him to sate her body's need or stop touching her. "You should probably leave."

He looked at her with burning golden eyes. A wicked smile touched his lips as he dropped the towel he held, cradled her face in his hands, and kissed her. "I'll be gentle," he whispered against her lips.

Keely couldn't deny him or herself. She pressed her mouth to his, enjoying the way his warm, silken lips caressed hers. Heat and need pulsed through her body, making her want of him painful. She parted her lips, and he took her up on the invitation. His tongue delved into her mouth, twisted and teased hers. Their kiss deepened, and she explored his mouth with the same fervor. Minutes went by, and she spent them savoring his supple lips and velvety tongue. Even as it got harder to breathe, neither of them wanted to stop. They kissed until her lips felt raw, and still she had no desire to stop.

He released his hold on her and pulled away long enough to strip off his shirt, revealing chorded arms, muscular chest, and well-defined abs. Training had transformed him into a paragon of masculinity. Chance wound his arms around her waist, pulling her onto him and she found herself straddled across his legs. Desperate to feel more of him, she yanked her towel away and pressed her chest to his. His smooth skin heated hers, causing her to shiver. He trailed his lips over her neck and jaw, and she let out a groan of disappointment. Winding her arm around his neck, she raked her fingernails against his scalp, grabbing a handful of his hair and forcing his lips back to hers. Their kiss changed and became frenzied.

His mouth left hers a second time. Before she could complain, he bent his head down and took her one of her nipples into his mouth. Electricity radiated out from her chest, thrilling every nerve of her body, and was compounded when Chance turned his attention to her other breast. Even as she was losing herself to the sensation he was causing, she knew she wanted to offer him pleasure in return.

Sliding her hand between them, she unfastened his pants and

reached inside them. Hardened flesh welcomed her touch. When she wrapped her fingers around it and carefully stroked, Chance moaned. His deep voice vibrated across her skin, exciting it all over again. How she loved making him moan, and how she'd missed being able to. Slowly she moved her hand up and down his shaft, ridging her fingers over its tip.

Chance's lips were on hers again. "I've missed the feel and taste of you." He traced his tongue over her jaw and collarbone. "I've missed the sounds of your moans." Rocking her back onto the bed, he pulled her hand from his pants. "But, if you keep doing that, I'm going to lose my mind and forget that I meant to be gentle."

Keely lifter her mouth to his. "I want to touch you. I need..."

He silenced her with an intense kiss. "It's not just about you. There are things I need too. And I need to take my time and savor you," he said with sensual promise, licking his lips. His mouth descended, and he stole away any protests she had along with her breath. One of his hands massaged up her thigh, cupped her intimately before his fingers parted her folds, and slid inside of her. She shuddered and moaned, not minding that he'd pulled his mouth away and was licking and kissing a hot path over her jaw and collarbone. As his fingers slowly manipulated her, his mouth and tongue elicited electrical currents from her skin. He spent long, tantalizing moments on each of her breasts then his heated mouth made its way further down and replaced his fingers. His tongue massaged and manipulated her to climax within seconds and left her screaming.

As good as it felt, she wanted more. Keely wanted to climax with him inside her and his mouth taking everything from hers. Reaching down with her uninjured arm, she combed her fingers through his hair. "Chance," she breathed out between pants of pleasure.

Abruptly, he pulled away, sat back on his haunches, and looked down at her. "Keely..." he started and stopped. He leaned forward, falling on top of her and catching himself with his arms. He stared at her intently before he said, "If you weren't injured, I'd make you pay for forgetting my name with my teeth."

"Misato," she whispered, leaning up to lick the side of his neck. "You're already making me suffer because you won't give me what I want." She ran her hand over the taught planes of his chest and

336

stomach in search of what she wanted. Her fingers met soft hair, then hardened flesh. "Please," she begged as she cradled his length in her hand.

Chance sucked her lip between his teeth and lightly bit at it before he pulled away. "Keely," he said between pants. "I...dammit, I can't say no..." He was kissing her again before he finished his sentence.

His hand slid between them, and again, he pulled her hand away. A sharp zipper sounded, and a second later, she felt his swollen member at her entrance. Both of them stilled. She stared at his bewildered face, lost in the fire in his eyes and the suggestion on his lips. Exquisitely slowly, he slid inside of her, joining them. Winding her arms around his neck, she let out a gasp of wonder, nearly climaxing for the sheer joy of being intimately connected.

"You feel so good," Chance quietly moaned before he brought his lips back to hers.

For a singular moment, Keely was the happiest she'd ever been in her life, joined to the man she loved and held in his arms. The part of her that deeply loved him remembered their reality and protested, drying out her lust. They couldn't stay together. She wouldn't ask him to leave his life or give up his happiness for her, and she couldn't change who she was for him. It confounded her that she could be so happy and so sad all at once.

Suddenly, Chance pulled away. "Keely. Did I hurt you?" he asked in Japanese.

"No." She shook her head.

"Then why are you crying?" He cradled the side of her face and wiped away trails of tears she didn't know were there. She shook her head again, unable to tell him what she was feeling. He let out a long breath. "We should talk."

She didn't disagree. "I know." A sad sigh came out of her because she didn't want to lose their intimacy or leave the warmth his embrace. She unwound her arms and moved to get off him. He tightened his hold and rocked her back onto the bed so his weight and his grasp kept her in place.

"Be still." He kissed her. For a moment, they stayed as they were, joined with one another, lips locked in a slow kiss. Eventually, he pulled away and looked down at her.

"Are you sure you want to talk... like this?"

"I can't think of a better time, place, or way to talk." He resettled himself, pushing deeper inside of her. Involuntarily, she arched her back against him, wanting more.

She honestly couldn't think of a better way to have a conversation with Chance. She pulled his mouth back to hers, savoring the taste and feel of him. He was right, she didn't want to let him go, not yet.

He ended their kiss by licking her lips. "Keely, I can't help you, or us, unless you tell me the whole truth."

"I did tell you the truth, but that doesn't change how things are. We shouldn't...can't be together. You should go back to Japan," she repeated.

"Listen carefully." He brought a hand up and brushed strands of wet hair away from her forehead and out of her eyes. "I'm not going anywhere, not now, not in five minutes, not ever. I won't be going back to Japan unless you're going with me."

"It's too dangerous for you to stay with me."

He frowned. "I don't agree."

"Didn't they tell you how this all works. You're a Cassock. That is uncommonly rare. Even with the ministry's protection, they die all the time."

"I know. I also know you're the first Priestess in over a century. They die young. And despite the belief Priests and Priestesses were extinct until you were discovered, the expectation is that you fight on the front line—practically alone."

"That's how it is for me." She stopped and took a deep breath. "You should know when I told you what I did was more important than me, it was true. It's more than that. I know I will die fighting, and despite that, I won't change who I am. I won't stop, even if sometimes I hate the life I chose. Do you understand? I don't love you enough to choose you over the task I accepted from heaven."

"I would not ask you too..."

"And I wouldn't ask you either. You deserve a life full of happiness and music—your life—not a life of constant fighting. I do more damage to the neverborn than anybody, and it's still not a victory. The neverborn can't be killed, they can't be captured, and very few can even hurt them. All I do is rescue souls, and that's considered a victory. Even after I free those souls, the neverborn go off stealing other souls and destroying other lives…and I go hunt them again. The war between the mortal and them will never end."

"God, I know. I know more about it than I ever wanted." The arm around her waist tightened. "You put this beautiful body and precious soul of yours in danger over and over and over again. You've rescued and will rescue countless souls, souls like mine. And I'm not talking about the last night we were together. That first night, when we met. After our show…"

"Ayano," she remembered. The pretty girl was obsessed with Eternity's End.

"If I hadn't run into a Priestess that night, my soul would have been taken."

She shuddered, wrapped him in a tight embrace, nuzzled her face into the crook of his neck. "Your soul was taken… It was my fault."

He scooped a hand behind her head and brought her mouth to his. "It wasn't your fault." He let his forehead fall to hers. "I've relived that night in my apartment over and over again. I wish I had listened. I wish I hadn't said what I'd said. I wish I hadn't let you leave. I wish I hadn't hurt you."

Tears stung at her eyes. "I was so stupid. I thought your rejection was the worst thing that had happened to me. It wasn't. Watching the neverborn steal your soul and break…" She couldn't finish. "I was petty, but I can't say I wish I had told you sooner. I wish I had not done the things I've done to you. I wish I had not turned you into a Cassock."

"You didn't." He breathed out heavily, and his breath dusted her face. "Keely, you know how it works. You can't force a soul to leave heaven once it's decided to stay. I knew what heaven offered, and I chose to return to my mortal body. I wasn't the exception to that rule. I accepted heaven's task. Me—not you. I accepted because I wanted to protect you. I accepted because I wanted to love you. And I needed to be loved by you."

Keely stopped and stared deep into his eyes, combing her fingers through his soft hair. "I'm… I'm your task?" she asked, overwhelmed.

He kissed her. "You are my task." He breathed out, staring into her eyes. The golden yellow burned with sparks of intense assurance. "No. I have no intention of giving up my music. And I'm not asking you to change for me. But you should know, you're part of my soul and I need you. So, I'm asking that you let me love you like I promised heaven I would."

Keely searched her heart, knowing above anything, she wanted Chance happy. What he wanted was to love and be loved by her. So much so, he'd refused the absolute love and joy of heaven. New tears formed in her eyes, tears of happiness. There was nothing left for her to object to. All she had to do was give in to what her heart truly wanted. Keely just had to love Chance in return.

Caressing the side of his face and running a finger over his lips, she smiled. He caught his breath. "You know that could prove very exhausting for you."

His face split and joyous laughter shook the both of them. Then he was kissing her as he slowly slid out and back inside of her. Her breath hitched, and pleasure started to reawaken and spread through her body. "I truly hope so."

∞ ∞ ∞ ∞ ∞ Epilogue ∞ ∞ ∞ ∞ ∞

Chance opened the door to his apartment and was greeted by bright lights, soft music, and the smell of spiced beef and vegetables. It surprised him as it was after one in the morning. He'd been late getting home since rehearsal went late. Rehearsal went late because their promotional interviews got behind schedule. An internet celebrity Eternity's End agreed to meet had invited fifty of their fans, so the interview turned into an impromptu meet-and-greet. It was good publicity for their upcoming show, but they had gotten behind schedule. The day had been hectic, and he was glad to be home.

Setting his bag down on a nearby table, he walked into the apartment. "Keely?"

"Kitchen," she replied.

He picked his way through a myriad of boxes in different stages of being emptied and walked into an open kitchen. Sitting at a wooden table next to a moonlit window, was the treasure he sought, Keely. She was dressed in a light pink camisole, fuzzy pajama shorts, and bunny slippers. Her hair cascaded over her ivory skin, and he could see the outline of her breasts and the pink peak of her nipple through her shirt. Despite being exhausted, he made plans to rediscover her with his mouth, later.

Impatient to feel her lips, he walked across the room and kissed her. It only took seconds for their kiss to become impassioned, setting his blood ablaze with desire. Before he stripped and took her in the kitchen, he ended the kiss.

"Welcome home," she said softly, combing her fingers in his hair.

"I'm glad you're awake." He stood, and his attention was drawn to an aromatic steaming pot. "You made sukiyaki?" he asked, going to the stove and eyeing a boiling pot of beef, vegetables, and spices.

"I thought you'd be hungry," she answered.

"I am." He smiled, hoping to convey his gratefulness. "But I want to sit down for a moment, before I eat."

"Okay," she patted the seat of the chair caddy-corner to hers. It

341

was then Chance noticed the icepack wrapped around her knee. That explained why she didn't get up to greet him.

"Training?" he asked, taking the chair she offered and scooting it closer so he could examine the injury. Cautiously, he pulled back the icepack and gently brushed his fingers over her dark red skin.

She huffed. "I'm not as fast as I used to be."

"You'll get there." He replaced the pack and took her hand in his. While he hated the harshness of training, it was necessary, for both of them. Although his training was less intensive than hers, only because he had a strict regimen over the last six months. "What are you doing?" He looked at the computer. One of Eternity End's videos was playing.

"Well, I've turned into an obsessed fangirl," she tried to joke, cleared her throat, and stared at something outside the window. "I couldn't know anything about you when we were apart. I couldn't listen to your music, or watch your videos, just seeing your face was too hard… But now I wanted to see all I missed, you know the music videos, the interviews…the fan-cam videos. I just…" Her voice trailed off.

Part of him was disappointed. While they were apart, every word of every song he'd written was a message of love for her only. "Tau wrote that song." He scooted closer, took control of the mouse, pulled up a video. "I wrote this one."

Kissing his cheek, she turned toward the video and watched it with undivided attention. When the song had played out, she turned to him with a soulful expression that conveyed both her love and regret in her luminous violet eyes.

"I'm sorry, Misato. I… I was…"

He wasn't about to let her torment herself. He'd witnessed how broken she'd been without him, and how much it had hurt. If he could help it, Keely would never suffer that much pain ever again. "You don't have to explain." He rested his forehead against hers. "I had the luxury of knowing that we'd be together, and you didn't."

She smiled, cradled his face in her hands, and kissed him. "It's very beautiful. I wish I had seen it sooner. I'm sorry." Pulling away, she kissed his forehead. "How did promoting go? Any problems at rehearsal?"

"We ended up having an impromptu fan meet, it set our schedule back, but our Scottish fans are a lot of fun. We sold out tomorrow's show. Which is pretty amazing given that they only started advertising a week ago. Tau, Ren, and Simeon are ecstatic."

She giggled. "You are too. I can see it."

"I am," he admitted.

"I'm sorry I missed the meet and greet, but Sutton and I will be at the concert."

"I'd have been mad if you skipped training."

"But I missed all the fun," she huffed and pouted.

"We have an in-store event in Glasgow in two weeks. You can go then." Honestly, he wanted Keely with him everywhere he went, and he knew she felt guilty about missing his events. Especially since they'd spent six months apart. However, her safety was more of a concern. She'd lost a lot of weight and muscle mass. If she was going to continue to hunt and fight neverborn, she needed to be able to hunt and fight neverborn. Training was more important. She was frowning, so he changed the subject. "I would have never guessed the ministry wasn't in the industry. They are surprisingly efficient and as driven as our old record label. They've scheduled two concerts in Glasgow. I'm told they're close to selling out as well."

"The ministry is extraordinarily efficient in whatever they endeavor to do, but I think they see what your record label saw. Profit. Which is why they said yes to your demands and bought out Eternity End's contract."

"They didn't have a choice either way. I'm greedy. I wanted you and Eternity's End."

She squeezed his hand. "Misato… I really want you to be happy."

"I know. I want you to be just as happy. I'm pretty sure that means we are."

"I hope we always will be." Her face fell. "With the war against the neverborn, it won't be easy."

"Nothing worth having ever is." He carefully pulled her out of her chair and onto his lap. Sitting across his legs, she settled her bottom against his groin and draped her arms around his neck. He couldn't stop himself from pressing his lips to the rise of one of her breasts. Keely quivered then bent down and kissed, then suckled the sensitive spot on the side of his neck. It was his turn to shiver. "Keep doing that and dinner will have to wait until after I get you naked underneath me."

She stopped and looked down and him, and he lost his breath to the love and passion burning in her violet eyes. "So, naked dinner?"

He licked her lips. "I'm never going to say no to naked anything with you."

∞ ∞ ∞ ∞ ∞

Special thanks to:
My cover artist, Phatpuppy Art
My graphic designer, Deric Pearce
They made my book pretty.

And, a very special thank you to you dear reader. Thank you for taking this adventure with me. I hope I fulfilled my promise of chocolaty romance and butt-kicking action. I think we both deserve a piece of cheesecake and some deliciously fruity tea.

Don't forget there is extra content, deleted scenes, and a ton of cool stuff at: www.evilbunnyempire.com

Special thanks to MK Editing Services, LLC. Editing is a painful process for a writer. You got me through it and helped me take a story that I love and make it into a book I'm proud of.

Made in the USA
Columbia, SC
11 August 2019